"I HAVEN'T ASKED YOU TO CONCERN YOURSELF IN MY AFFAIRS," SHE FLUNG AT HIM HOTLY.

His jaw hardened and anger flared in his eyes. "What I'd give to put you over my knee," he gritted. "You're spoiled, reckless and as as stubborn as any mule."

Suddenly, all the anger drained out of Chloris. Why had she let her tongue run so wild? She must have been more tired than she thought, for the tears pricked her eyelids and she bit her lip to keep from crying.

Quentin's arms encircled her, turning her into his shoulder. There was such comfort in the feel of his beating heart beneath her cheek that she clung to him weakly.

"Dear, foolish, Chloris," he murmured into her hair. "What am I to do with you?"

"Leave me to my fate," she said in a muffled voice. "It's all I deserve."

He laughed softly. "Don't tempt me."

She raised her face to his and was strangely moved by the tender expression. "Why do you bother with me, Quentin? I'm an ungrateful, hot-tempered idiot. You'd far better stop trying to reform me."

"I don't want to reform you, only to save you from your own actions."

Also by Marjorie Shoebridge:

RELUCTANT RAPTURE

MARJORIE SHOEBRIDGE

Destiny's Desire

LEISURE BOOKS   NEW YORK CITY

A LEISURE BOOK

Published by

Dorchester Publishing Co., Inc.
6 East 39th Street
New York, NY 10016

Printed in the United States of America

Destiny's Desire

1

The wind, rising a little, fretted the dark clouds that masked the faint glow of the waning moon. Pale light filtered down, gilding the motionless figures on the headland. To one of the three people stretched out on the damp grass, eyes strained to catch the early movement at sea, it was a first introduction to excitement. It was, in fact, for Chloris Blair, the first time she had ever been out of her bed at midnight, and to be here in such company was little short of a miracle. Her heart gave a flutter of mingled excitement and awe as she slid her gaze sideways to rest on Matt's strong face, and the intent brown eyes under wind-ruffled dark hair. It was as well that his eyes were fixed on the narrow inlet below or he could not have avoided meeting that adoring glance from eyes as green as shoalwater.

But it was not missed by the third person, a middle-aged, strongly-built man whose small eyes overlooked nothing. He raised a calloused hand to scratch his beard and Chloris, catching the movement and the direction of his gaze, lowered her head, thankful for the sudden darkening of the moon that hid her swift blush. She was not sure that she liked Mr. Sefton. He had not seemed very pleased with Matt for bringing her along but after all, she reasoned, she had not asked to take part in the actual operation. Perhaps, being an old seaman, Mr. Sefton held to the view that women brought bad luck to seafarers and were better engaged on kitchen tasks, net-mending or some such occupation. Not that she had experience in either art. The occasion had never arisen at Miss Sinclair's Academy in Dorchester. Deportment and etiquette were more in Miss Sinclair's line with petit point and water color painting running a close second. Chloris fought down a giggle as she visualized Miss Sinclair's expressive eyebrows rising to extinction beneath her curly fringe could she but see her recent pupil's present lack of deportment. To tell the truth, she was a little shocked herself. Only the desire for Matt's approval had persuaded her to don the outgrown breeches and reefer jacket of Matt's young brother, thankfully away at school where he would not miss them. Under the shapeless cap, Chloris had bundled her long black hair, pulling down the peak until it rested just above her thick dark brows. She practiced a villianous scowl and her brows almost met with the concentration of it. No-one, with the exception of Matt and Mr. Sefton, must know that she was a girl.

Matt Trevelyan stirred, speaking in an irritated undertone. "What the devil's keeping them, Sefton?"

"I know no more than you," Sefton replied in a calm voice. "Maybe they've hove to somewhere out of sight of the revenue cutter that's patrolling these waters, or maybe those Frenchies have kept them waiting. There's no accounting for foreigners."

"They're late—at least half-an-hour."

"The waiting's always harder than the going. Perhaps next time they'll take you along—seeing that you're paying the reckoning."

His tone held amusement and Matt shot him an angry look. "Don't you ever get tired of waiting, now?"

"Of course, but I've learned patience which is not to be expected of a young fellow like you. If it hadn't been for that run-in we had in Weymouth with the dragoons last year, I'd still be out there with them." He stretched his stiff leg, turning into a more comfortable position. "Have patience, Mr. Matt. They'll be along well before dawn."

"I think," said Chloris slowly, blinking a little, "that I see a sail."

There was a moment of silence as eyes strained seaward, then Sefton operated the steel and flint, thrusting the spark into the waiting tinder of the open-doored lantern. The light blossomed, illuminating their faces as Sefton swung the lantern three times. An answering flash and he doused the light.

Now that the moment for action had arrived, Chloris felt herself trembling.

"Come on," said Matt. "Down to the beach."

"But I hadn't intended—," she protested but he grinned and took her hand.

"All hands needed. Yours too."

He led her down the rough path into the sandy bay. What on earth am I doing here? she thought in rising panic. They'll think I'm a spy or more likely a bubble-headed youth who'll give them away. How could I let Matt persuade me into anything so shocking? And my father a Justice of the Peace at that!

"Matt—," she began.

"Don't worry," he said, as if reading her thoughts. "No-one will bother you if you're with me, and you shall have the finest silk and lace handkerchief in the consignment."

Silk handkerchief indeed! I'd rather be in my bed, she said to herself, but to Matt she answered, "Well, for heaven's sake don't present it to me down there or your friends will think I'm a peculiar kind of boy to be wanting a French silk and lace handkerchief."

Behind them, Mr. Sefton chuckled. He knew her identity but as a faithful friend of Matt's, he would not betray her, she knew. It was a strange partnership, the rough ex-seaman turned freetrader and the twenty-year-old Matthew Trevelyan of a respected Dorset family. Matt's father had been the connecting link, a shipowner in comfortable circumstances until the night he had boarded his ship on its last journey to London. From Spain and the Canaries the ship had sailed, bringing a cargo of the finest Toledo steel rapiers and embroidered Spanish shawls. At Weymouth Mr. Trevelyan had boarded with the intention of accompanying his ship on the final leg of its journey, but a sudden fog bank well out to sea had muffled the approach of a revenue cutter and subdued the screech of splintering timbers. The Trevelyan ship had foundered within minutes while the cutter had limped painfully and blindly into the nearest harbor, bringing with it only one survivor and that one being Sefton.

Mrs. Trevelyan, while suffering the loss of her husband, had nursed Sefton back to health, afterwards installing him in a small cottage in the grounds. Matt at seventeen had spent a great deal of his time there, listening to Sefton's stories of the sea and of the years when he and Mr. Trevelyan had served in the Royal Navy, albeit of different rank.

What had inspired Matt to throw in his lot

with the freetraders, Chloris thought with more insight than she realized, could well have been an unacknowledged wish to make someone pay for the loss of his father, and the only way of doing that was by cheating the Government whose servants had manned the cutter that foggy night three years ago. Mr. Sefton, on the other hand, needed to earn a living and with his career at sea behind him, he had found a profitable sideline.

By the time they reached the sandy bay, the rowing boat had been dragged clear of the water and men were bent over its sides transferring wooden tubs and tarpaulin-wrapped bundles to eager hands. Half-a-dozen ponies were being loaded, tubs roped on either side. Sefton and Matt joined in, leaving Chloris staring about her with interest. She caught the eye of a bearded individual who had stopped to mop his brow and at his growl of, "Lend a hand, lad," she came to herself with a start and moved to help him lift a heavy cask from the boat. It was taken from them and the man clapped her on the back, almost pushing her face down in the sand.

"You're a scrawny youth," he said on a laugh. "Haven't seen you on this run before, have I?"

"No-no," she stammered, drawing her eyebrows together in what she hoped was a forbidding scowl. "I'm—I'm Matt's cousin and I'm very strong really."

"Hey, Mr. Matt," he called. "Your cousin'll have to broaden out a bit before he can handle a cask on his own."

Matt turned, staring. "My cousin?" He caught Chloris's agonized gaze. "Oh, yes, young—er—Clem there. He wanted to come. Saw no harm in it."

"As long as you'll vouch for him," growled the bearded one.

Chloris swallowed hard and bent to the boat. The men worked silently and as Chloris saw them pass and repass the lantern, she recognized each one. Farm workers, grooms from surrounding estates and even the clerk from ladies' haberdasher in the village. Only with the big, black-bearded man was she unacquainted. He seemed to be in charge of the operation, deferring only to Matt who, if Sefton's remark had any substance, was paying the cost of this night's work.

Matt appeared at her side, renewing her strength and dissolving her qualms under his laughing gaze. "Haul away, Clem," he said and the occasion took on the glow of a gay adventure. They worked shoulder to shoulder until the boat was empty and every pony loaded. The boat was relaunched and swiftly pulled away while the pony train, hooves muffled by scraps of sacking for a silent journey through the village, faded into the night, taking Sefton with them.

Chloris sank onto a rock, feeling the unaccustomed ache in her shoulders. Matt watched her and she saw his smile in the faint glow of the moon. He held something out towards her. "A reward for cousin Clem."

It was a handkerchief of delicate silk with soft lace edging. Chloris wiped her hands down the sides of her breeches and pulled off the cap, letting her hair fall to her shoulders and shaking it free in the cool breeze before taking the gift.

"I had the packet specially marked so that I knew which one held the handkerchiefs."

"It's beautiful," said Chloris, holding the softness against her cheek. "But did you have to call me Clem?" she asked reproachfully.

Matt laughed. "It was the first name that

12

came into my head. You'll have to be Clem from now on."

"It makes no difference now. What time is it?"

"Probably after one o'clock. I'd better take you home."

They climbed the track, passing the solid round walls of the Martello Tower built under the threat of Napoleon's invasion, and turned towards the village. In the grounds of her home, Chloris looked up at Matt.

"Thank you for the adventure. I—I think I enjoyed it."

"Only think?" His voice held a teasing note and she smiled.

"Well, it was an experience to be sure but a strenuous one. I shall be as stiff as buckram tomorrow."

"As to that, a few more runs and you'll go with the best of them. You're a freetrader now, cousin Clem, and as guilty of defying the law as the rest of us."

She gasped. "I hadn't considered that. What would Father say?"

"Don't worry. No-one will ever know. It will be our secret."

His expression reassured her. It had been exciting posing as a boy and no-one would ever know, as he had said.

She slipped into the house through a ground floor window and tiptoed up to her bedroom. Once there she removed and bundled together the clothes she had worn, tucking them into the back of her wardrobe beneath her winter cloak. She climbed into bed thinking warmly of Matt. All her life, it seemed, she had loved him. Hero of her childhood, it had been Matt who had dragged her in and out of innumerable scrapes, but even the punishment she knew would result from discovery was nothing compared with his approval of her pluck and willingness to go along with his schemes. She fell asleep with her mouth curved in a reminiscent smile.

It seemed no time at all before her maid, Molly, was pushing back her curtains and bidding her drink the tea she had brought. Chloris sat up quickly and grimaced, stretching her back and feeling the ache in her muscles. Once was enough, she decided. Matt would understand her reluctance to go to the beach again. As the daughter of Mr. Justice Blair, discovery of her action would be twice as appalling as for any other girl.

"Come along, Miss Chloris. If you hurry sharpish, you may join your father for breakfast. I believe he is dressed to go out and the carriage is called for nine o'clock."

As Chloris entered the dining room, her father laid down the newspaper he was scanning and rose to greet her. Tall and spare, he was immaculately, if somberly dressed. His white hair and side-whiskers were still thick and although his face was lined with age, he was an imposing figure. He smiled and she glanced across at his briefcase and cloak laid ready by the door.

"I have to go to Dorchester this morning, my dear. It seems the authorities have some new preventative schemes in mind concerning this fresh outbreak of smuggling along our coast."

Chloris's hand shook a little as she lifted the coffee pot and she stared at him. "Smuggling? You mean they are trying new ways to catch the—er—freetraders?"

"We would rather call them smugglers. They break the law and defraud the Government irrespective of the name."

"But if taxes on everyday things are so prohibitive, one cannot really blame the men who risk their liberty to obtain those things."

Mr. Justice Blair raised his eyebrows. "You are in favor of their activities I gather, my dear. I grant you it sounds highly romantic and daring to pit oneself against the Government forces but it is not always a case of good-natured deception. Some of these gangs are composed of violent men who do not hesitate to murder any who try to capture them. Certainly our Dorset coast is not as plagued with them as is Kent, Sussex or Cornwall, but it is our duty to support the forces of law in all things."

"I agree, Father, that violence cannot be tolerated."

He smiled and patted her hand. "But you still see these freetraders of yours as modern buccaneers, striking a blow at the oppressors of those who like French brandy or Holland gin?"

Chloris laughed. "Put that way, it does sound rather ridiculous but perhaps it is only the excitement of the venture that intrigues some of the younger men and they would not resort to violence."

Mr. Blair rose, laying down his napkin. "I am sure you are right, my dear, but it is a dangerous road to take. Smugglers don't look kindly on those who enter lightheartedly into their enterprises. In most cases the road leads—at best—to Newgate and the colonies, and at worst to the hangman."

After he had gone, Chloris sat in thought for a few minutes. Of course he was right but Matt and the men last night were not ferocious characters. She could not imagine any of them offering violence. Most of them she had known for years, except for the big, black-bearded man. She must ask Matt who he was. She smiled as she recalled little Mr. Tibbet from the haberdasher shop. A married man with four young children, trying to exist on a minute salary, his reasons were obvious and good luck to him. It was too much to imagine him involved in violence, he was so meek and obsequious behind the counter.

As she left the room to collect her riding hat and whip, she glanced into the drawing room and up at the oil painting over the fireplace. Depicted was a young woman, also in riding habit, against a background of trees. Slender hands held the reins of a white horse and the smiling green eyes might have been her own. She wished for the hundredth time that her mother had not died so suddenly and tragically. In her final year at Miss Sinclair's, Chloris's first intimation had been the summons to the hall, twelve months ago.

There she had found Molly, red-eyed and parchment-cheeked, perched on one of the hard chairs that were, according to Miss Sinclair, the ideal shape to keep a pupil's spine erect. At the sight of Molly's ravaged face, Chloris had grown rigid with fear, unable to utter a word.

"Your poor mother," Molly had said through tight lips. "Such a terrible accident. Thrown by that horse she was so fond of." And then she had broken down.

Two days later, Chloris stood in the village churchyard with her father, holding tightly to his arm. Everyone, while listening to the vicar's words, seemed to be looking at Mr. Blair with compassionate eyes. Chloris looked at him too. His skin was pale, drawn tightly over his cheekbones, and the grey eyes were as dull as the sea under mist but he held himself stiffly, as if one incautious move might shatter the brittle image he presented. He was never quite the same in the weeks that followed and Molly warned Chloris against questioning her father.

"I have never seen a man so stricken," she said. "He adored your poor dear mother and it would be a kindness not to remind him of his loss."

"But he keeps her picture in the drawing room. That must be a constant reminder."

"Yes, but that was painted a year before and when he sees that, he remembers her as she was then. I believe his mind never goes beyond that point."

"How did it happen, Molly? No-one has ever told me exactly."

"A riding accident, it was."

"But what happened?"

"That horse, the one in the picture, killed her."

"But Mother was a superb rider. I remember seeing her riding every morning. She could handle any horse in the stable."

"Even the best of riders can come to grief. The tragedy was that your father himself found her. He saw the white horse first in the gloom, lying near the Martello Tower. Its knees were broken Then he found your mother some distance away."

"Was she—?" Chloris's voice shook.

"Already dead," said Molly. "Her poor neck was broken." She put her arms round Chloris's shoulders. "You shouldn't have asked, my love, for I knew you'd be shocked. Now you understand why you mustn't talk about her to your father. But it was strange all the same," she went on in a musing tone. "That she should have been on the cliffs by the Martello Tower."

"How was that strange?"

"Because she had been dining at Field House

and the way back is nowhere near the Tower."

"But why, if she was dining out, did she not take the carriage?"

"Mr. Justice wanted her to but she said it was just an informal meal to say goodbye to a Field House guest, a Lord Chalmers, who was taking ship from Weymouth early the next day. Your father wasn't able to go with her so she said she preferred the exercise of riding and she needed no groom trotting behind." Molly regarded Chloris severely. "There was a mite too much recklessness in my lady's nature," she said, with the critical outspokenness of long service. "And I pray that you have not inherited that fault, for you're as like to your mother at eighteen as two peas in a pod."

Chloris kept her gaze on her hands. "Poor Father. He loved her very much, I know."

Molly nodded. "For all he was so much older, he doted on her and allowed her more liberty than a younger husband would."

Chloris was disturbed from her long contemplation of her mother's painting by the sound of hooves on the front drive. She adjusted her hat in front of the hall looking glass, admiring the fall of red chiffon from the band, then took up her whip and passed from the house. Her own horse was the dam of the one her mother had ridden, a steady mare and one on which Chloris had learned to ride.

The groom held out his cupped hands and Chloris vaulted lightly into the saddle, thanking him with a smile. Out of the front gate she turned up the rise towards the village, deciding to pay a call at Field House, the home of her father's old friend Sir Lionel Field, who was, in addition, her godfather.

Crossing the common she glimpsed a party of three cantering in the opposite direction and spurred her horse to intercept them. Quentin, son of Sir Lionel, she knew, and Ruth Baxter, a small dark girl of her own age, but the second girl was a stranger to her. As they met and dismounted, she greeted Quentin with a smile and Ruth with a hug.

"May I make you known," said Quentin, "to Miss Georgina Davenport? She is a house guest of ours. Georgina, this is an old family friend, Miss Chloris Blair."

"How do you do, Miss Davenport." Chloris's hand received the lightest of pressures from one of the most elegant creatures she had ever seen. Tall, almost as tall as Quentin, she was slim and fine-boned with gleaming russet hair caught up in a chignon beneath her riding hat.

"How do you do, Miss Blair." Georgina's voice was attractively low. "Quentin has spoken of you as a friend of his childhood. You and also Miss Baxter whom we came upon so felicitously during our ride."

Her voice was polite but lacked warmth, thought Chloris, as if she was remembering all she had been taught in the way of manners by a strict parent.

"By the way, Chloris," said Quentin. "Father said, if we saw you, we must bring you back to take a glass of wine with him. He is laid up with a touch of the gout and will take it badly if you neglect him much longer. He complains that you've been home a week and haven't been near him so you must have grown too grand for your old friends."

Chloris laughed. "Dear Sir Lionel. I wouldn't upset him for the world. I was on my way to call and I'll gladly take wine with him for Father has gone to Dorchester and will not return until dinner time."

"In that case he will expect you to stay to

luncheon, so I will do the honors and invite both of you and Ruth to come and cheer him up. He is as cross as two sticks but I can rely on you to charm him into amiability. That will be splendid, won't it, Georgina?"

"Most delightful," said the girl with a lift of her fine glossy eyebrows.

"You must hold me excused, Quentin," Ruth said. "I appreciate the invitation but I am promised to Mrs. Trevelyan. Do convey my kind regards to Sir Lionel."

Chloris was conscious of a stab of envy at Ruth's words but the unworthy feeling was dispelled as Ruth went on to explain that Mrs. Trevelyan had a heavy cold and Matt, although most solicitous of his mother, might easily forget the medicines that must be given at regular intervals.

"Very true," said Quentin with a smile. "And one cannot imagine Matt producing dainty meals to tempt the appetite of an invalid."

"Are there no servants?" asked Georgina.

"Yes, of course." Ruth looked with surprise at Miss Davenport. "But I had the experience of nursing my own mother until she died last year. I can do no less than nurse her dear friend when she is ailing. Why should I not?"

With a slight heightening of color, Georgina sought to make amends. "Forgive me, Miss Baxter. I did not intend criticism. I am full of admiration for those who can minister to the sick so bravely. My own feelings would be so overwrought by the suffering of the invalid that I should be quite useless in a sick room. Mama says it is an excess of sensibility but one cannot change one's nature." She sighed. "But I do so admire your courage, Miss Baxter."

"Well," returned Ruth briskly. "We cannot all

be affected by such tender emotions for who then would care for the patient? It is, after all, only a heavy cold in Mrs. Trevelyan's case so I am unlikely to fall into a state of uselessness."

Chloris bit her lip in amusement, silently applauding Ruth's matter-of-fact manner. Ruth had always been such a gentle person, unwilling by so much as a word to upset anyone, that it was good to hear her defend her actions in so spirited a way. Unlike Chloris and Matt, she had never indulged in wild pranks but neither had she condemned them, remaining always a loving friend, a friend to whom they could turn for sympathy. There was a serenity about the fresh-faced girl with the neat dark curls that attracted those in need and Ruth never failed to ease their troubles.

As Quentin assisted Ruth in mounting her horse, he promised to instruct the gardener to send over a basket of fruit for the invalid. Chloris added her good wishes for a speedy recovery, promising to ride over herself in the morning. Ruth smiled and cantered away in the direction of the Trevelyan house.

The small party remounted and after a brisk gallop drew rein outside Field House where grooms took their horses. In the drawing room, Sir Lionel was seated in a leather armchair, his gouty foot supported by a cushioned stool.

"You will forgive me not rising," he said heavily, "but the sawbones has just left, after manhandling my foot in a most obnoxious manner. I'm an old man and will not be dictated to by a young squib just out of medical school—if indeed he ever went there!"

"Too much port, Father?" asked Quentin blandly, guessing the import of the squire's last remark.

"Nonsense! The fellow doesn't know what he's talking about." He glowered at the company, then his gaze fixed on Chloris. He was delighted to see her but had no intention of being cheated of a victim for his ill-humor. "I suppose that now you have acquired a touch of Dorchester polish, your old friends will be too rough for you. Is that it, my lady? Too high in the instep to visit a sick old man?"

Chloris tossed aside her gloves and bent to kiss his cheek, undeceived by his scowl. "School in Dorchester is not quite a season in London," she said lightly. "And I hardly think Miss Sinclair at the Academy would acknowledge me her most successful pupil. I never could remember the degrees of nodding and curtseying that were 'de rigueur' for every personage, depending on their rank and how well one knew them."

"Quite right, too," said Sir Lionel. "I shake a man's hand or I don't. I can't be doing with fancy ways. Straightforward dealing is best."

"I know," Chloris replied in a voice of honey. "And I longed to tell Miss Sinclair that those ways may be all right for London society where one might come across a duke or a prince of the blood any day, but in our little corner of Dorset we follow the example of our squire who is a true gentleman."

Sir Lionel stared hard into her solemn face and his lips twitched.

"Little baggage," he growled. "You've learned to turn a man up sweet, if nothing else. Now ring the bell, there's a good girl, and we'll share a glass of wine."

From the ensuing conversation, Chloris learned that Quentin had taken over almost completely from Sir Lionel the management of the estate and was investing in up-to-date farm machinery. It was during one of his periodic visits to London that he had met Georgina at the home of a relative. Chloris gathered there was a distant connection by marriage to the Fields and, as Georgina was a little overtired by a hectic London season, it was thought that a few weeks in Dorset would refresh her. Watching them, Chloris could see that Quentin was very attentive to the girl. Her carriage was graceful and there was an air of innocent helplessness in her bearing, a quality that never failed to arouse the protective instinct of the male. She wondered if Georgina was quite as innocent as she seemed. Quentin was the only son of a wealthy Dorset landowner with a rich inheritance and a centuries-old manor house. Tall, with good shoulders and a confident manner, he was fair where his father was gray but they had in common the Field strength of feature and the same gray eyes with the slightly hooded lids that gave a deceptive air of indolence to each face.

Although she had never considered Quentin in any other light than as an old friend, it was obvious that he was an eligible bachelor and Georgina's manner towards him was an indication of that eligibility.

Chloris left the squire in the greatest of good humor, he declaring that Dorchester had not ruined her character as he had supposed and she was quite forgiven for not visiting sooner, and she promising faithfully to call again bringing as many illustrated magazines as she could carry to relieve his boredom, made her farewell.

Quentin accompanied her to the door. After assisting her to mount he said. "I'm glad you are home for good, Chloris. Perhaps you may be able to bring your father over sometime. He has rather cut himself off since the accident. It is sad to see him so changed."

Chloris was touched by his kindness. "I will do my best," she promised, then, feeling she must make some comment on the house guest, said, "Your Miss Davenport is quite the most beautiful person I have ever met—apart from my own mother, of course."

The gray eyes lifted to hers with a strangely intent look, then he nodded. "Yes, she is—almost of that beauty but hardly my Miss Davenport."

"Not yet," Chloris said, smiling. "But perhaps one day."

"Perhaps."

He stood back, unsmiling, making her feel somehow dismissed, and she turned her horse towards the gates and rode thoughtfully away.

Quentin had always been a very private person, disguising his thoughts behind a mask of polite inscrutability. Perhaps she had been a little forward in her remark. Matt would just have grinned and made some joke but she knew Matt so much better than she could ever know Quentin.

After dinner that evening, Mr. Justice Blair filled his pipe in an abstracted manner while staring into the flames of the fire. Chloris placed his coffee cup on a small table by his elbow, then sat on a footstool regarding him, her chin in her hands. After a few moments of silence Mr. Blair looked up.

"I'm am sorry, my dear, for being such dull company. It has been a tiring day."

"Tell me about it, Father."

"I doubt it would interest you, my dear, for it is just business. It concerns a move afoot to do away with the coast blockade as it now is."

"Do away with it?" Chloris showed her astonishment. "But you told me only this morning of an increase in free—in smuggling on our coast."

"Exactly, and the coastguards have con-

24

sequently become even more unpopular. The men complain of the greatest difficulty in obtaining lodgings hereabouts. They are prevented from doing their duty by the very people they serve, although the villagers don't quite see it in the same light. They consider it no crime to aid these lawbreakers, in fact, they reap profit from turning a blind eye."

"But without the coastguards . . . "

"Oh, we shall not be without them. A new body called the Preventative Water Guard is being formed. Their quarters will be on the old ships no longer used at sea for active duty. These vessels are to be stationed in creeks and bays, affording the best of outlooks upon the sea."

"So instead of being called from their lodgings, the men will already be there watching the coastline."

"That is the idea. They intend to cover the entire coastline from Essex to Cornwall. Sailors from the Royal Navy will man the ships, each station commanded by a naval lieutenant."

"I see," Chloris said slowly. "It will be a great deal more difficult and dangerous for the smugglers when that comes about."

"Indeed it will and then perhaps your romantic young men will decide the risk is too great."

Chloris looked up swiftly. Mr. Blair's eyes were smiling. She thought fleetingy of Matt. "And when does all this take place?"

"Not yet awhile, for it takes time to organize such major changes. J.P.'s like myself are only brought in when we are required to be acquainted with new regulations. At the moment we are committed to silence until the scheme is established. You will not speak of it, I know, my dear."

Committed to silence! How could she warn

Matt without revealing the source of her knowledge? She could not, for he must instantly come to the right conclusion and that would be a betrayal of her father's confidence. Once he told the freetraders it would be all over the village and her father would guess rightly from where the news came. She must remain silent and try to persuade Matt by other means that his adventure was too dangerous to continue. But there was no immediate hurry.

She was still deep in thought when she kissed her father goodnight and went upstairs to Molly. She only half-attended to Molly's gossip, which was centered as usual around the doings at the big house.

"And how did you find Sir Lionel's health, Miss Chloris? I hear he's got the gout, which is awkward for him, seeing that he's always been a man who likes to ride out and visit his people."

"Oh, he was complaining bitterly about the doctor when I arrived."

"Well, perhaps the young lady staying there will take his mind off it. I haven't seen her myself but cook, whose daughter is under-housemaid at Field House, says she's a real London beauty."

"Yes, she's very beautiful and most elegant."

"Do you suppose she and Mr. Quentin will make a match of it?"

Chloris considered the question. "It's hard to say what Mr. Quentin feels. He seems different—more aloof and reserved."

"Poor young man, it's not to be wondered at. They do say, in the village, that he was disappointed in love."

"Really? I didn't know that. Who was the girl?"

"That we don't know but it seems that he and that Lord Chalmers were both keen on the same

26

lady. They had high words on the night before his lordship left but no names were mentioned."

"Or none that the servants could manage to overhear," added Chloris scathingly.

"You're right, Miss Chloris, and I'm ashamed of myself for repeating gossip that's naught to do with me. I'll keep my tongue between my teeth in future."

Chloris chuckled and gave Molly a hug, knowing full well that such a resolution would be forgotten by morning. " 'Twas probably just some lady guest amusing herself by flirting with them both and caring nothing for either."

Chloris woke early. From her bedroom window she could just make out the shape of the distant Martello Tower standing gaunt and gray in the early morning mist. It had always held a fascination for her as a child but now, thinking of her mother's death below the Tower, her fascination was tinged with sadness. Why had her mother taken that route home? And why had no-one from Field House thought fit to escort her? Chloris shook her head. From an early age she had realized that her mother was not of the usual style. Born in London and reared by pleasure-loving parents, she had grown into a beautiful, captivating but entirely capricious creature. No-one could be angry with her for long. Her gaiety stemmed from high spirits and was never malicious. But when she had met, in her nineteenth year, the forty-year old Gerard Blair, a man who declined to pay extravagant compliments, a man who treated her with cool courtesy and seemed not to care when she flirted with other men, her interest had been caught. This was not a man to dance to her tune, and perhaps because he was unlike any she had met before, she fell in love with the serious-minded gentlemen from Dorset.

When Chloris was born, Estelle Blair surprised her friends by proving to be a devoted mother. She was finally accepted and loved by the villagers who, while disapproving in principle of married women doing ungenteel things like riding at breakneck speed along quiet lanes and instigating horse races across the fields, were secretly rather proud of her. An independent spirit was Estelle and one who resented the smallest check on her actions. Yet she was not one to create scandal and her behavior always remained within the bounds of propriety. It was left to Mr. Justice Blair to add the cloak of decorum to his adored young wife but at times even his patience was strained. Chloris knew the look, the compressed lips, the measured words and then the retreat into silence. And because Estelle hated to be at odds with anyone, she would set herself to coax him out of his displeasure.

According to Molly, Mr. Justice Blair had been unable to accompany his wife to Field House that last night. Had she, wondered Chloris, freed from all restraint and declining escort, sought to refresh her spirits by a moonlight gallop along the cliffs? It would have been in keeping with her nature. But death waited by the Tower, swift and sure, a simple stumble by the horse over an unseen obstacle. Both rider and horse had died on those cold cliffs, with no witness but the old gray Tower.

Curiosity drew Chloris to the spot during her morning ride. The sun had broken through, illuminating the lichen-covered walls, and she reined in her horse, then sat motionless and thoughtful. The mare, taking advantage of the slack rein, dropped her head to the wet grass from which the mist still curled upwards.

For several moments Chloris remained still, her green eyes unseeing, and it was only a sudden movement seen out of the corner of her eye that brought her head round sharply. A small boy stood with his back pressed hard against the stone wall, an upturned basket spilling mushrooms at his feet.

His gaze, riveted on Chloris's face, was filled with horror, his eyes wide and shocked.

Chloris frowned and loosened her foot from the stirrup, dropping lightly onto the grass. His reaction to the step she took towards him made her fear for his sanity. He turned paper-white and lifted an arm as though she had threatened to strike him.

She stopped. "What's the matter, child?"

"Don't missus," he croaked. "I didn't tell."

"What are you talking about?"

"You're dead—I know you're dead! I saw you gallop by, laughing, and then you screamed. I won't come here again, not ever. I promise—only don't come near me."

"You're making a mistake," Chloris said gently. "It wasn't I. You must have been . . ."

"Where is he?" the boy interrupted jerkily, his gaze darting behind her.

"Who?"

"The man chasing you—the angry man—is he hiding?"

"What man was that?" asked Chloris through suddenly dry lips.

"You know! As mad as a wet hen he was, calling your name. Stella—Stella—he was shouting!"

Chloris closed her eyes as pain stabbed her temples. Only close friends shortened Estelle to Stella, but why was one of them chasing her mother along the cliffs? She forced herself to speak. "This man—what did he look like?"

The boy was losing his terror as nothing terrible had happened to him but he still eyed her warily. "A tall man. His hair was silver."

"Silver?"

"That's all I saw. I hid in the Tower then."

She gazed unseeingly over his head and the mist curled round the hem of her habit. At last she turned away, moving slowly back to the mare. She leaned her head against the soft shoulder, her mind full of questions. Silver-haired? Was he elderly then, like her father? Or could it have been the moonlight glancing off light-colored hair? The boy had obviously seen something but had kept quiet through fear. Who had the man been? And why had he disappeared instead of raising the alarm? Could her mother have been saved had help come sooner? What kind of heartless man would leave a woman dead or dying on a deserted stretch of cliff and go calmly home to bed?

When Chloris raised her head again, the boy was gone.

2

Chloris remounted and set the horse to a canter, hardly caring in which direction it took her. What could have happened that night? Her mother must have known the man galloping behind. Had he simply been urging caution on the clifftops at night or was there a more sinister motive for his presence? It had been assumed that Estelle Blair was alone, the horse had stumbled and both were thrown to their deaths. After twelve months the truth would be hard to find. No-one had come forward at the time. Why should anyone do so now? Perhaps the boy had been exaggerating and the man had turned back, exasperated by Estelle's willful behavior and fearing to risk his neck with only the moon to guide them on a wild clifftop gallop.

She came to herself with a start as she heard her name being called. Glancing up she realized that the path had taken her beyond the Trevelyan house. Matt was at her stirrup, his eyes crinkled with amusement, mock indignation on his face.

"Straight by without a single glance," he complained. "What have we done to offend you? And

Ruth telling Mother you meant to call this morning."

"Oh, I'm sorry. I was thinking and forgot where I was for a moment. How is your mother?"

"Still a bit wobbly but coming along well. She'll be glad of your company."

They entered the house, passing the solid oak door standing ajar to catch the early sun, and Matt led her into a small bright sitting room. Mrs. Trevelyan, dark-haired and dark-eyed like her son, lay on the couch, a shawl round her shoulders and a woolly blanket across her legs. Ruth straightened from tucking in the blanket and smiled as Chloris crossed to drop a kiss on Mrs. Trevelyan's pale cheek.

"Hello, Chloris. I'm glad you are here. I promised to go to High Grange Farm so I may leave Mrs. Trevelyan in your charge for an hour or so."

Matt sighed deeply. "I know I am only a mere male but I may be trusted to hand round tea and biscuits without turning the house into a beer-garden."

Ruth and Mrs. Trevelyan exchanged smiling glances.

"If there are any biscuits left," said his mother, "after your frequent forays into the kitchen—and if you remember what you did with the teapot when you took away my breakfast tray for Martha swears it's not where it should be—then yes, I trust you, my dearest."

Matt clapped a hand to his forehead. "Teapot? Oh, Lord, I remember now. Martha said tea leaves were good for the herb garden so I offered to empty the pot for her when I suddenly thought I'd have a look at the mare—she was sweating a bit last night—and I put the pot down somewhere."

Three pairs of eyes regarded him questioningly.

"Now where did I leave it?" he asked hopefully.

"Not in the stable, Matt!" his mother said faintly.

Matt's face cleared. "That's it. In the stable. I'll fetch it immediately."

Mrs. Trevelyan gazed after him in bewilderment, then turned to Chloris, smiling.

"Well, sit down, my dear, and tell me all the news while Matt recovers the teapot and Ruth runs off to visit her beau."

Ruth laughed. "No such thing. I'm visiting Neil Kernick's mother. She gets lonely with Neil about the farm so much. I can hardly do less for she was, after all, a second cousin of my mother."

"Oh, I remember Neil," said Chloris. "A good-looking boy with red hair, wasn't he?"

"Yes, but he's not a boy now. He's a very steady young man and devoted to his mother. He was most helpful when my own mother died, sorting all my affairs and making the necessary arrangements."

"I don't like to think of you alone in your cottage, Ruth," said Mrs. Trevelyan. "With no-one to keep you company. I keep asking her," she said to Chloris, "to come and live here but she refuses."

Ruth shook her head, her fresh color deepening a little. "Thank you but I would rather stay in my own house. I could not be idle all day and your Martha would most certainly bar me, or any other female, from the kitchen."

"Yes, indeed, I won't deny that fact," agreed Mrs. Trevelyan. "Martha is most jealous of her domain. I hardly dare set foot in it myself."

Matt entered at that moment carefully bearing a tray of tea and biscuits which he placed on a small table beside his mother while casting her a virtuous glance.

Ruth picked up her gloves declaring that she must be on her way and Matt escorted her from the house to where her horse waited.

"Such a sweet girl, Ruth," said Mrs. Trevelyan. "She would be a perfect wife for any man. There is a gentleness about her that is most pleasing."

Chloris nodded. "Perhaps this young farmer has also noticed her."

"Perhaps, but when I tease her about him she always shakes her head and changes the subject although she blushes a little too."

"Perhaps she is fond of him all the same."

"That may be so. And now, my dear, tell me all about Dorchester. From what I know of you, it wouldn't surprise me in the least to hear that the lady in charge of the school heaved a sigh of relief when you left."

"I protest most strongly," said Chloris, smiling. "You forget that I am a young lady now and don't indulge in mad pranks as I used to do with your son. He must take half of the blame for all the upsets we caused."

"I cannot argue with that but thank goodness you have both learned a little decorum and I may now walk through the village with a clear conscience."

Chloris thought of the night of the run. Both she and Matt were involved in something far more serious than childish pranks should it ever become known. And yet she knew in her heart that if Matt beckoned, she would join him again, in spite of her misgivings.

On Matt's return, the conversation took a

general turn and Chloris learned of local events since her sojourn in Dorechester, Sir Lionel Field's activities being the focal point of the village's interest.

"Is it true," asked Mrs. Trevelyan, "that Quentin Field is about to announce his engagement?"

"There is certainly a young lady staying at the Field House but whether they will become engaged or not, I couldn't say. I had luncheon there yesterday but saw no lingering glances from Quentin although she is exceptionally beautiful."

Matt laughed. "Quentin always was poker-faced when he didn't want to show his feelings. Do you remember, Chloris, when that brewery horse stepped on his foot a few years ago? As white as chalk he went but never moved a muscle while the drayman backed it off. You'd think he was carved from stone the way he pokered up."

"And a bone in his foot was broken too. Yes, I remember. It must have been agony for him but he never made a sound." She recalled the suddenly blank face of Quentin as he bade her goodbye after her remark about Miss Davenport. One never did know what was in Quentin's mind until he chose to reveal it.

As Chloris was leaving, Matt placed a detaining hand on her arm as soon as they were out of earshot of his mother. "A profitable run the other night, Chloris. Recouped the money I laid out and made a tidy profit."

"I'm glad, Matt, but be careful. Those revenue men may have some new tricks up their sleeves."

"What do you mean?"

"N-nothing, but don't take any risks. It would be terrible for your mother if anything went wrong."

"Nothing will go wrong. We're planning

another run soon. Sefton says there's bad weather coming and it will be just right. Cloudy and wet, with hardly any moon, and the best time to trade."

Chloris looked at him anxiously. Perhaps the Royal Navy would not be in position for some time. Perhaps they would have time for another clear run. If only she could warn him. But she must not reveal what she knew. It would be a breaking of her father's confidence.

Chloris rode home deep in thought. If she could find out from her father just when the Royal Navy meant to begin operations, it might be possible to drop some casual and indirect remark to Matt.

Mr. Justice Blair was returning a letter to its envelope as she entered the dining room. He looked up, smiling.

"Sir Lionel has invited us to dinner, my dear."

Mindful of Quentin's request concerning her father, Chloris said quickly, "I do hope you will accept for Sir Lionel is laid up with the gout and would take it kindly if you visited him. You are old friends, after all."

Mr. Blair nodded. "Yes, I believe I must accept. I have some business to talk over with him which should be done face to face. He is the squire and must be acquainted with the facts."

"Facts, Father?"

"Nothing to concern you, my dear. Put on your prettiest gown for I hear there is a very elegant guest at Field House."

Chloris was more than willing to comply. While in Dorchester she had purchased several lengths of patterned silks and spotted muslins that had been made up by the local dressmaker. Tonight she would wear the white and gold spotted muslin over a white satin under dress. It had three gold-edged flounces falling softly from a darted waistline and the neckline was not so low to be thought indecorous, nor yet so high to be considered girlish.

Molly brushed her dark hair until it glowed and Chloris regarded herself in the looking glass, approving the arched brows, wide greenish eyes and high cheekbones over which she had dusted a little Java rice powder. Compared with the interesting pallor of Georgina's complexion, she had no wish to go looking like a well-scrubbed young miss from the country. Georgina's dress was sure to have been made by a high class London modiste—perhaps even a French one. Molly was draping her silk evening cloak about her shoulders when they heard the carriage wheels.

Mr. Blair stood in the hall gazing upwards as Chloris descended the stairs. Only a gleaming white high-collared shirt relieved the somberness of his tailcoat and black waistcoat, but his very somberness gave him an air of magisterial dignity.

She sensed an instant of rigidity in his stance, then he relaxed visibly, forcing a smile.

"I never would have believed you could be so like your mother," he said. "In the lamplight and in that white dress—she was fond of white too—you rather startled me for a moment."

Chloris was touched with pity. To have loved and lost in such tragic circumstances would have broken a lesser man but Gerard Blair's strong will had carried him through the agony physically unchanged, but Chloris knew that his grief was deep and silent. She smiled gently but said nothing. What was there to say? Nothing could alter her likeness. They must both live with the memory of Estelle Blair as best they could.

The lights of Field House were a landmark in the darkness, the large Elizabethan house with its tall chimneys looking as durable as when it was first built. Quentin met them in the hall. His gaze, showing a hint of surprise, rested on her for a moment before he turned to greet Mr. Blair. He had only seen her before in a severe riding habit or as a schoolgirl and she guessed that he too was surprised at her likeness to Estelle.

A maid took their cloaks and Quentin led them into a large sitting room where a log fire blazed in an enormous inglenook fireplace. Numerous oil lamps glowed around the room, Sir Lionel having an aversion to the new form of gas lighting, declaring it to be dangerous and unhealthy. Chloris suspected him of disliking anything that might change the nature of his beloved house. Perhaps, she thought, if he had the job of filling lamps, cleaning wicks and polishing brass, he would willingly turn to an easier method of lighting.

Sir Lionel, while still suffering from gout, greeted them in his loud hearty voice. "Come in, come in, both of you. At last I've persuaded you to visit an old friend, Gerard. Pull up a chair, we have much to talk about. Quentin! Ask Belling to fetch up a bottle of the St. Emilion. You'll find it as smooth as silk, Gerard. One of the finest of its year. Give me a kiss, Chloris, then go and talk frills and furbelows with Georgina."

As this was all said without pause, Chloris laughingly obeyed, catching an amused glance from Quentin as she moved to where Georgina was sitting on the couch, her moss green velvet skirts arranged with elegant simplicity.

Impulsively, Chloris said, "How do you do, Miss Davenport? What a clever choice of colors is your gown. It sets off the shade of your hair most becomingly."

"How kind of you to say so. I pride myself on

having a flair for fashion." Her long eyelashes fluttered in Quentin's direction as he approached to seat himself in a leather chair beside them. "Quentin has been kind enough to compliment me already on my gown. One must keep up standards, even in the country. Mama impressed the fact upon me before I left."

"Yes, indeed! We are most fortunate to have you here to set us all an example," Chloris returned earnestly. "Do not hesitate to call us to account if we fall into countrified ways. We have not your experience of London society, after all." She turned a limpid gaze on Quentin who was regarding her fixedly. "I have known the time when even Quentin has dined wearing top boots. Horrifying, isn't it?"

A reluctant smile twitched the lips of her younger host and he said with an air of resignation, "Silly of me to think you might have changed. You're still the terrible child you were."

"I'll have you know that I am now eighteen years old and quite grown up."

"Really? I would never have guessed it for all your fine feathers."

"How deflating you are! Why don't you pay pretty compliments like the gentlemen I met in Dorchester?"

"Because I had the misfortune to know you in your youth," he replied with candor, but his eyes were amused. "I never knew such a helter-skelter girl as you."

"Did you really sit down to dinner in top boots, Quentin?" asked a gentle voice.

He turned a blank face to Georgina. "I beg your pardon?"

"As Miss Blair said you did."

"Miss Blair," Quentin said slowly, casting Chloris an evil look, "will talk herself into Newgate one day if she doesn't curb her tongue. And yes, I have been known to dine in top boots but only when Father and I were alone. There hardly seemed much point in dressing up after a hard day on the estate."

Miss Davenport sighed and smiled kindly at him. "I knew you would have good reason for falling into such slipshod ways."

In the pause that followed, Chloris avoided Quentin's eye and said hastily, "Do you have brothers, Miss Davenport?"

She could have guessed without confirmation that Miss Davenport was an only child. Brothers would have blunted that air of high-minded delicacy and it was apparent that Miss Davenport, carefully screened from the rough world, had met only such gentlemen as were considered suitable by a doting parent. To be allowed a visit to the home of one such gentleman indicated that hopes were entertained for a happy outcome. Chloris allowed her gaze to rest on Quentin. No doubt he was an eligible man, a good catch for any girl, having riches and an impeccable family tree. She wondered if he would take a London house on his marriage for Georgina was not the sort of girl who would be content to spend her days in the heart of Dorset.

As he bent his head to catch a remark of Miss Davenport's, the lamp glow touched his fair hair with a silver sheen. Silver? She recalled the boy's words. Could it have been Quentin that night on the cliffs with her mother? But would he have called her "Stella"? She had never known him to do so but then, she had been away at school for two years. Her mother had been gay and beautiful enough to turn any man's head, even one ten years younger than herself. But Quentin could not have ridden away after the accident. He was too much the countryman to let any living thing suffer. She had seen his tenderness with sick animals. How much greater his concern would be for a human being. Unless, of course, he had good reason for remaining uninvolved! Was it to be that she would go through life eyeing with suspicion every fair or white-haired man? Asking herself—"Is he the one? Was he on the cliffs that night?"

Sir Lionel's voice broke in on her thoughts. Belling was announcing dinner and Sir Lionel, lifting himself up from his chair with difficulty, called to her that he would lead her into dinner. Glad to put such dark thoughts behind her, Chloris rose and took Sir Lionel's arm. They moved slowly into the dining room, followed by Mr. Blair who had courteously offered his arm to Miss Davenport.

The ladies, seated to the right and left of their host, were entertained by a long account of how improved was Sir Lionel's gout and if he was able by early autumn, and the ground had hardened sufficiently, why then he would take his place with the Gilminster Hunt as had been his custom these forty years.

"And Field House can mount you whenever you wish to join us," he said to Chloris. "For I don't suppose that hack I saw from the window the other day could take a fence without fumbling it."

Chloris laughed. "Poor old Bessie. She's a good, gentle mare and one I've had since I was eleven so it's not to be expected that she'll take to hunting at her time of life. But thank you, Sir Lionel, for your kind offer."

He turned to Georgina. "And if you are still with us, my dear, we'll find you a suitable mount."

"Thank you, sir, but I don't hunt. Mama thinks it too strenuous for my constitution."

For a moment Sir Lionel was taken aback but recovered swiftly. "As you wish, my dear. You're not a country girl, after all," he conceded tolerantly.

"But I ride in Hyde Park most regularly when I am in town," Georgina said earnestly. "Mama is quite in favor of that form of exercise."

"Not the place for a good gallop." Sir Lionel's tone was scathing. "Full of fribbling fellows showing off their new clothes and trying to set the fashions. A speck of mud and they're off home, screaming for their valets to change their clothes."

Seeing that her father was about to launch himself into a condemnation of society, aiming to see and be seen in the confines of Hyde Park at a fashionable hour of the day, Quentin deftly changed the subject by asking Georgina if she was fond of history. Field House, he said, was of Elizabethan origin and he believed that a Field had lived here ever since the time of that Tudor queen.

This served to turn Sir Lionel's thoughts to the subject of his ancestral tree and as he was proud to relate, he was the fourth generation of Field to occupy the manor house. Quentin would duly inherit, not only the mantle of fifth baron, but the fruits of three hundred years of carefully husbanded resources, together with the home farm, numerous cottages, rich pastures, a pheasantry and a park full of deer.

"And the pigeon house, Father," Quentin added. "Never forget that distinctive honor for it shows our worth, let me tell you, Georgina."

Sir Lionel chuckled at Miss Davenport's puzzled look. "Ignore the boy, my dear. He is referring to the times before this century when only the Lord of the Manor was allowed to keep pigeons to supplement the winter diet. Before root crops were introduced, only a few cattle could be kept in hay throughout the winter, so most were killed and salted down. The other obvious source of food was from the air so pigeon houses were built by the Lords at their manor houses. Apart from supplying eggs, the birds provided a welcome change of meat in the winter."

"And as they fed themselves from the land, not excluding the peasants' strips and gardens," added Quentin, a sardonic glint in his gray eyes, "the poor old peasant came off worst in all respects. Not only was he compelled to give a percentage of his crops to the lord, he fed his pigeons too and wasn't allowed to catch one himself."

"It does seem rather unfair," said Georgina solemnly. "But it was the law, after all. One must remember that."

"A great comfort to their starving families, I don't doubt." Quentin's tone was dry.

"Can they keep pigeons now?" asked Georgina and Quentin grinned suddenly.

"Any amount. As long as they don't trap one of Father's pheasants by mistake, there'll be no trouble from our noble lord."

By the time the covers had been removed and the dessert dishes brought forward, Sir Lionel was in a mellow mood, his face glowing with the good humor of a man who had satisfactorily worked his way through several courses of a well-cooked meal. Quentin, Chloris noted, ate little and drank less while Georgina refused several dishes and ate daintily of those she accepted. As the owner of a healthy appetite herself, Chloris wondered if it was fashionable in the Metropolis to display no interest in food as Georgina did.

Her attention was suddenly caught by Sir

Lionel replying to a remark of her father's. "By all means, my dear fellow. We'll go to my study after dinner and discuss the matter."

Did her father intend to acquaint Sir Lionel with the news from Dorchester of the new scheme to outwit the freetraders? If only she could find out what the plans were. A way might suggest itself for her to warn Matt. She watched her father in silence, a slight frown between her eyes. How could she acquire the knowledge she so desperately needed?

"Why the frown, Chloris?"

She started and turned a quick look on Quentin. He glanced at her father, then regarded her keenly. She sought swiftly for something to say. He must have heard Sir Lionel's remark too.

"Oh—I—no reason really. I was just thinking Father looked tired. I hope he will not stay too late talking to Sir Lionel."

"I suppose that depends on the subject under discussion."

She looked at him uncertainly. "Do you—do you know what that subject is?"

"Not specifically but I should guess it concerns your father's visit to Weymouth."

"How can you know that?" she asked, startled.

"It's only a natural surmise. Your father is a Justice of the Peace. My father is the squire. It doesn't take a great deal of intelligence to put these facts together with my own knowledge of something stirring in Weymouth." He smiled. "But there's no magic in it. I happened to see your father in the company of several uniformed gentlemen. I was in Weymouth myself, discussing a cargo I expected shortly."

"And what are they saying in Weymouth? I take it that it concerns the freetraders? My father

44

told me of an increase in their activities." She spoke in what she hoped was a casual manner.

Quentin raised an eyebrow. "Freetraders? Ah, I see! To you they are 'The Gentlemen,' champions of the poor. Your romantic heart declines to call them smugglers."

Chloris flushed and answered hotly but low-voiced. "It seems hard for poor people to be compelled to pay so dear for the enjoyment of a packet of tea when it may be theirs for the asking at three or four shillings a pound. And the same with tobacco. I think it most unjust of the Government to tax so highly such ordinary things to pay for their eternal wars."

Quentin laughed softly. "Your trader, my dear, is not as philanthropic as you imagine. Most likely he bought that tea in Holland for sevenpence a pound, so his own profit is quite considerable. And the brandy he sells at four pounds a tub would cost him no more than one pound in France."

"You seem to know a great deal about the business," Chloris said darkly. "Could it be that you . . ."

"Are financing 'The Gentlemen'? No, really, Chloris, I won't have it!" he interrupted, his eyes dancing. "You are about to suggest that the fifth proud Field is a cove creeper, are you not?"

"Well, your new machinery must be costing a large amount of money. One cannot help wondering . . ."

"Take care before you cast such a slur on my family. Father would hang me himself from the highest nesting box in the pigeon loft if he thought I was involved in that trade."

Chloris laughed. "No, of course, I don't really think it. You are more likely to be in league with the Excise officers was what I meant to say."

"On the side of the angels, yes," he said, smiling wryly. "Not a romantic figure at all; in fact, a most dull and law-abiding creature, unworthy to appear in high drama on the seas. But you, Chloris—why this sudden interest?"

"I have no interest," she said quickly but it was said too quickly, she realized, seeing Quentin's eyes narrow.

"I hope not," he said slowly. "Apart from the normal curiosity of us all. I wonder," he went on in a speculative tone, "if your freetraders really understand the penalties they face on capture. Do they fancy a spell of imprisonment in the hulks, those floating prisons moored in Portsmouth Harbor and other places? I understand they are a most verminous and insanitary accommodation with rats as companions. Then there is the treadmill used in land prisons for those sentenced to hard labor, and we must not forget the colonies where flogging is still very common. But I am sure your heroes are well aware of these consequences and are prepared to take the risk." He glanced sideways at her, his gray eyes glinting sardonically. "I doubt they deal any kindlier with the fair sex. Do I shock you, Chloris?"

She shook her head and looked down at her plate saying nothing but concentrating on the apple she had begun to peel. Those clear gray eyes of his always made her feel that he could read her thoughts.

"As you remarked before," she said with an air of indifference, "my father is a J.P. and I feel only that I should at least show an interest in what his work entails, in spite of your so graphic illustrations."

"Of course," he replied and leaned forward to address a remark to Georgina, leaving Chloris wondering if she had aroused any suspicion in his mind.

A few minutes later, she and Georgina were in the drawing room, having left the three men alone. She had taken the precaution of pausing by the hall table and tucking her lace handkerchief, unnoticed, behind the silver candelabra in order to give herself an excuse for leaving the drawing room later. She doubted that Quentin would be included in the meeting in the study, so when he joined them she would be warned that her father and Sir Lionel were about to discuss the Dorchester news.

Georgina, she found, was a most conventional creature, her interests lying solely in recounting the balls, outings and exhibitions she had attended, what she had worn and what compliments had been paid her, together with quotations from her widowed mama on the behavior of a lady.

Chloris felt an overpowering urge to describe some of the scrapes she had been in as a child, if only for the satisfaction of shocking her companion. She restrained herself with difficulty, saying instead, "How you must miss all that gaiety. I expect you will have had enough of the country by the time the London season starts again."

"I do miss it, of course," replied Georgina. "But Mama thought it best that I leave town, not only for my health but because of . . . of someone who appeared to be attaching himself most particularly to me."

Chloris's interest was caught. "And you didn't care for him?"

"His devotion was most flattering. He was a poet, you know, but Mama said it would never do."

"Why not?" Chloris asked bluntly.

With a hint of sadness in her smile, Georgina said simply, "He was ineligible."

"You mean he was not a gentleman?"

"Oh, his birth was high enough but he had no fortune. Mama says one must not encourage pretensions from one so unsuitable." She paused, a faraway look in her eyes. "He once sent me a bouquet with a sonnet concealed in a rose. He would have used my name in the verse too, except that he was unable to find a rhyme for Georgina. It would have been easier, he said, if I had been called Rosabelle or Maisie."

Recollecting Miss Sinclair's passion for poetry, Chloris said dryly, "Even so, I rather think Sir Walter Scott was there before him."

"Really? It is rather flattering, though, to have a poem dedicated to one," she finished wistfully. "Don't you think?"

"Yes, indeed," Chloris said, trying to control her voice. "That is something I have sorely missed, myself. I wonder if it is too late?"

"So handsome too," Georgina went on, unheeding. "He reminds one of Lord Byron except, of course, that he has never been to Greece or carved his name on a pillar in that temple. I forget its name."

"I'm sure he will make up for that omission in some other way," Chloris said encouragingly. "Perhaps he will win a fortune at the tables or become heir to some long-lost relative."

"Oh, do you think so? But Mama does not approve of gambling and I don't think he ever lost any relatives. None that he has mentioned, anyway."

What a literal-minded girl she is, thought Chloris in amazement, thankful to be spared further complications by the entrance of Quentin.

He accepted a cup of coffee, poured with easy grace into the fine china cup by Georgina, and seated himself on the settee beside her. He had no difficulty in choosing topics of conversation to suit his guest and they were soon deep in a theatrical discussion as to whether or not Mr. Macready's Hamlet was the finest they had ever seen. To Chloris's surprise, Georgina was quite knowledgeable on the more serious plays being performed in London, although she could not imagine her being allowed the same freedom with farces and comedies. Quentin, it seemed, had visited most theatres in the capital and was happy to talk of Shakespeare or Goldsmith.

He hardly attended when Chloris excused herself briefly with the murmur of a dropped handkerchief. She left the room, closing the door quietly behind her. Moving across the hall, she paused outside Sir Lionel's study. There was the muted sound of voices but unless she pressed her ear to the panel—or better still the keyhole—she realized she would gain nothing. Undecided, she stared for a moment at the solid door. A slight movement behind brought her head up sharply. With a drop of the heart she swung round expecting Quentin, but it was Belling, the butler, his eyebrows raised in inquiry. It was a bad moment. Covering her alarm, she said, "Oh, Belling. I rather think I dropped my handkerchief somewhere, perhaps in the dining room."

"You should have rung, miss. I could have sent one of the girls to look."

"I didn't want to disturb anyone. I can quite easily look for it myself."

She hoped he would go away but instead he bowed gravely. "Allow me, miss," and moved to open the dining room doors. She watched in rising frustration his slow progress round the table and his return to the hall. "I'm sorry, miss, but your handerkerchief does not appear to be there."

"Well, never mind, Belling. I must have dropped it somewhere else."

"I will call a girl, miss."

"Please don't bother. It is of no consequence."

His gaze traveled round the hall. She moved across, blocking his view of the table, fighting down the impulse to scream, "For heaven's sake, Belling, go back to your kitchen and leave me alone."

Above the table was a gilt-framed looking glass through which she watched him impatiently, while pretending to tidy her hair. One hand stole towards the candelabra and with a smooth motion she transferred her handkerchief to her sleeve, contriving that it should fall to the ground when she dropped her arm.

"Oh, how silly of me. It was in my sleeve all the time." She smiled brightly at him, willing him to disappear, and this time he obliged her by bowing and stepping towards the door to the kitchen quarters. Re-pinning the brooch on her shoulder to give him time to pass from view, she waited until the door clicked before moving from her position. With her ear pressed against the panelled door, she tired to decipher the words.

"More trouble than it's worth," she heard Sir Lionel say. "Do they hope to recoup the cost of this venture from the sale of confiscated goods? I'll guarantee they'll be lucky to break halfway even."

Mr. Blair's quieter voice answered. "You may be right but that is not for us to question. White-hall, in its wisdom, has decreed that this will be done and we are the ones chosen to implement the ruling."

Chloris recognized the dry note in her father's voice. Whether he considered the change to be good or bad, he accepted the law and administered it. She waited in tense silence, willing them to make some mention of when the naval officers were due to arrive. The silence was broken only by the clink of glasses.

Then a new sound penetrated her consciousness. A weary sigh, followed by a soft murmur as a voice said, "Really, Chloris. Eavesdropping? And you so grownup too!"

Her eyes, shut in concentration, sprang open and she caught her breath as she beheld Quentin leaning against the wall beside her, arms folded, ankles crossed negligently.

Color surged into her cheeks and she drew herself erect, staring wordlessly at him.

"Of course, I am sure you have a perfectly rational explanation," he said, his eyebrows raised, his expression so mocking that Chloris's hand itched to slap the smiling face.

She must have made some betraying movement. He came off the wall in one swift movement, his fingers clamped on her wrist in a painful grip.

"Oh, no, I don't think so," he said and his gray eyes were like marble.

She stood quite still, trying to contain the surging anger that boiled suddenly within her. In that moment she hated Quentin. Hated him for preventing her from gathering the information that might save Matt's life.

"There is nothing I need explain to you," she flung at him, her voice uneven with resentment.

"Then perhaps to your father. Shall we go in?" His hand rested on the doorknob.

"No! Please let me go. It is no concern of yours why I am here."

"Now why," he mused, "should a discussion of that nature be of such paramount importance to you? You are too old, I should have thought, for

it to be of mere schoolgirl interest. Was eavesdropping, by the way, one of your endearing
habits at the school for Young Ladies? But at
eighteen? Rather less than adult, I would have
supposed."

She glared at him in silence.

"Unless, of course, there is some involvement?"

Her laugh was scornful. "Aren't you being a
little imaginative? Can you see me sailing a lugger
around the coast with the revenue cutter in
furious pursuit?"

"With a striped sock on your head, streaming
behind like a pennant in the wind." His lips
twitched at the thought and the grip on her wrist
relaxed. "But why, Chloris?" he persisted.

With a shrug she said, "Call it childish
curiosity. I've been away for two years. I was
interested, that's all. You wouldn't understand or
approve. How could you? You aren't like . . ." She
bit off the words abruptly, pressing her lips
together and gazing fixedly at the carpet. She
must not allow herself to be betrayed into
revealing her reasons.

Quentin dropped her wrist and removed his
hand from the doorknob. "I suggest you rejoin
Miss Davenport."

She raised her eyes to see him regarding her
with cool appraisal. "What—what are you going to
do?" she asked.

"Nothing. As you said, it is no concern of
mine. I am not responsible for your actions or
those of anyone else's. Not, that is, until they
touch Field House. Go back to the drawing room."

It was an order, delivered flatly in a voice that
left no room for argument. She turned and, with
her chin raised, crossed the hall and entered the
drawing room without looking back.

"Did you discover it?" asked Georgina.

Chloris's eyes focused, widening. "Discover—?"

"Your handkerchief, of course. Is that not why you left the room?"

Gazing into the mild blue eyes, Chloris gathered her wits together. "Oh, yes, thank you. I found it in the hall."

"Oh, good. When Quentin realized you had gone he said he would go and help you."

"How kind of him," Chloris remarked dryly, "to be interested in recovering so unimportant a thing as a handkerchief."

"But he is always most considerate concerning the well-being of his guests," Georgina said, looking reproachfully at Chloris. "I have found it so time after time."

A number of replies, all of them caustic, suggested themselves to Chloris but she refrained, with an effort, from voicing any one of them. When Quentin returned to the drawing room he was followed by Sir Lionel and Mr. Blair. He did not glance at Chloris but seated himself beside Georgina, engaging her in conversation concerning the visit he had made on his last trip to London to Wombwell's Menagerie. Georgina had never been to it, her mother considering that the viewing of wild animals was unsuitable to her nature.

"Although," she added, "I know several girls who have visited there and they say it is quite the thing."

"What a paragon your mama must be," said Chloris deliberately. "It seems that everything delightful is frowned upon by older people. I can't help being glad that we have not such strict rules here."

"Neither do we have a menagerie," said Quentin briefly. "So the question of visiting it would not arise."

Chloris was defiantly determined not to be put down. "But if we had, then I should certainly visit it or anything else I chose. I hear the Cremorne Gardens in Chelsea is the place for enjoyment, what with balloon ascents, trapeze artists and firework displays. How I would love to go there."

Quentin cast her a sardonic look. "It was at one time the place to go but the tone has gone down and it is no longer patronized by the same classes. Your information, Chloris, is sadly out-of-date."

"Nevertheless," she informed him, conscious of the fact that her knowledge stemmed only from old magazines and was therefore built on shaky foundations, "I should contrive a visit somehow."

Georgina looked shocked. "It wouldn't do, dear Chloris, to be thought fast, especially in London. Reputations are easily lost and one never recovers one's credit."

Chloris shrugged. "It sounds a very stifling, boring sort of life to me," she said with disdain.

"I must tell you, Georgina," said Quentin blandly, "that Chloris yearns for a life of adventure and danger. We are all far too dull for her here. She should have lived in the eighteenth century. I dare say she would have run away to sea and become a pirate wench like Mary Read who went down in history as Captain Buttons."

Georgina's eyes were round with horror. "A pirate wench! Oh, how could you ever consider that sort of life appealing? Mixing with brutal men and living such a rough, common life." She paused. "If I had any such thought, Mama would never allow it!"

Chloris fell into the giggles at her shocked expression. Even Quentin gave a choke of laughter, saying with a gasp, "I wonder if Mary Read asked her mama's permission to become a pirate."

Gergina giggled too. "Now you are teasing me. It's unfair of you to make such fun of me, it really is."

"That's true," he agreed. "But you respond so delightfully. Unlike Chloris who is full of prickly thorns."

Chloris tried to glare at him haughtily but as his brows were raised expectantly, she wisely decided to ignore the opening he offered. Instead, she grinned. "I will not lose my temper so stop tempting me to rise to your jibes."

He smiled in return and as good relations seemed to have been established again between them, Chloris abandoned her attempts to point out the superiority of life in Gilminster over London. As she had never known life farther away than Dorchester, it was not a subject on which she could argue with any certainty, so she set herself to converse amicably with them both.

It was as they were making their farewells that Chloris said low-voiced to Quentin, "I apologize for my behavior in the hall. I should not have flared up at you. It was not the act of a well-mannered guest."

He smiled. "Don't let such a small thing as that inhibit you. It never did before."

"Perhaps I should pattern myself on Georgina who, I am convinced, never deviated from what is right and proper in her life."

She spoke jokingly and was furious when Quentin, giving her a level stare, said, "A most sensible suggestion. One could trust Georgina to consider the proprieties before leaping into any unwise action."

"Is it likely there would ever have been an unwise action considered?" Chloris spoke calmly but her eyes glinted angrily.

"With Mrs. Davenport to guide her? I doubt it."

"Then it is my misfortune to be without such a guiding hand. That is something I cannot remedy."

For a brief moment his expression was unreadable, then he nodded slowly.

"Forgive me, Chloris. I was not making a comparison. But remember we are your friends. You are always welcome at Field House for any reason. Don't ever forget that, will you?"

Her moment of anger was gone. She nodded. "Thank you. I won't forget."

3

Chloris opened the front door of Blair House and eased herself through it silently. It was eleven o'clock on a very dark night. The clouds were low, the sky unlit as far as she could judge by so much as a single star. She pulled the reefer jacket closer about her neck, tugged down the cap and moved with caution across the driveway towards the trees. It was scarcely any darker here, she thought, as she picked her way between them. Out onto the grass, she moved faster, taking the dimly seen Martello Tower as a landmark. A different cove, Matt had said, just in case some long-nosed revenuers had picked up a mite of gossip after their last run. Further west this time but Chloris knew the coast well for she and Matt had explored the coves often in childhood. He had played the hero then. She smiled at the memory of being rescued from caves and ledges by Sir Lancelot, Robin Hood, and Blackbeard the pirate, all three and more played by Matt in great, swashbuckling style, his rapier and broadsword cutting through besieging enemies to inevitable success.

But that was years ago when the unseen enemies were dispatched in triumphal fashion.

The adventure now was real and so were the enemies, but Matt treated them with the same scorn, convinced of his capability to out-think and out-maneuver them. She felt the old familiar thrill of excitement as she neared the cove. It was very quiet, save for the sea hissing on the pebbly beach and the breeze stirring the salt-sprayed grass beneath her feet. Below, her she saw movement, several shapes converging on a taller one she knew to be Matt. She recognized the turn of his head and the way he stood, hands on hips as if challenging the world. She dropped lightly to the shingle and the men turned.

"It's—it's Clem," she whispered hoarsely and moved to stand beside Matt.

A low rumble erupted to her left. "Gawd, Mister Matt, not that scrawny cousin of yours again! Let's see if he's got more muscle than last time." A large shape loomed closer and Chloris caught the whiff of rum. She retreated a pace.

"Let him be, man," said Matt in a cool voice. "One squeeze from you and he'd have no muscle left. Another pair of hands he is, and there's an end to it."

His voice held such firmness that Chloris was relieved and the big man shrugged massive shoulders.

"All right, no offense, though 'tis a puny lad." He moved away and sat on a rock, gazing out to sea.

They waited in silence and it began to rain. Chloris pushed her hands deep into the pockets of the reefer and murmured to Matt.

"What time do you expect anything?"

"Half-an-hour, maybe. The Frenchie won't come close, not enough water, but our boat will row in with a string of barrels astern."

"Where are the ponies?"

"We're not using them tonight."

"Then how . . ." she began but Matt interrupted irritably.

"We're sinking the damned things for collection later. Have done with your questions and wait for the work to start."

Chloris was silent, used to Matt's impatience if she played her part wrongly. But she was not a child anymore and felt a touch of resentment at his tone. She was only here because of him and could have been—no, should have been sleeping in her own bed, not standing here in the drizzling rain with a group of smugglers. Freetrader was a more romantic name but as her father had said, they were lawbreakers nevertheless. She shivered as the rising wind drove rain into her face.

There was a stir amongst the men. Matt grasped her shoulder.

"Did you see that?"

"What?" she asked, staring up at him.

"A light, idiot, on the sea. Where else?"

"No, I didn't," she said flatly. "I'm just a pair of hands, remember?"

Chloris saw the speck of light then, but it was some time later before the sound of muffled oars reached her. The dim outline of a long rowing boat stood out against the faintly lighter sky. The sea remained leaden in color, the long swells stippled by heavy rain.

The group gathered close on the shingle and Chloris saw the fishing net laid out, weighted with stones. She understood what Matt intended then. The weighted casks of brandy were to be sunk in the shallows under some rocky prominence with a marker to indicate the place. Later, the casks would be pulled ashore and a pony train loaded.

The boat was twenty yards offshore when she heard a deep-threatened growl from the big man.

"What in hell are they doing?"

The boat was veering sharply, now broadside on to them, then the stern swung. A man rose in the stern and Chloris saw a broad-bladed knife hack down at the towing rope. The rowers were dipping their oars in frantic haste and as the towing rope came free, the boat sped out to sea, leaving the line of casks bobbing on the swells.

A hoarse whisper drifted towards them from the upright figure in the stern. "Revenuers!"

"God save us," came a voice in their midst, fear cracking the tone.

They had all been so intent on watching the approach of the boat, that none had looked beyond. There, not more than a mile distance, the bow wave of a long, sleek cutter was seen, mast lantern swinging as she altered course.

The shore group broke into confusion, scattering away from the water's edge.

"Damnation!" Chloris heard Matt's voice. "Another ten minutes and we'd have had them safe."

"Still time if you've a mind to move fast," growled the big man. "Stand here like a bunch of keening women and the casks'll float right up to the cutter and a fortune lost. Do you not fancy a swim in that cold water, Mister Matt. It'll wet your fancy boots for sure!"

"Damn your insolent tongue," Matt growled savagely but the derision spurred him into action. He stripped off his coat. "Come on, those who can swim. Into the water and your night's pay will be doubled." He flung himself forward, heedless of followers, and Chloris saw a wave break over his head, then he was swimming for the drifting tow rope.

"In, lads," the big man growled and there was a threat in his voice. "You coast men can all swim.

Hold back and I'll take my fists to you. Here, lad, it's you I mean," and his hard hand fell heavily on Chloris's shoulder. She jumped and looked up at him, her face a white oval in the gloom. "You'll let your cousin risk his life without lifting a hand? You can swim?"

Chloris nodded though her heart was thumping with fear. Matt was out there alone. A few men had moved hesitatingly into the water under the big man's threat but they were unlikely to reach Matt in time for them to be of any use. Reluctance to follow in a serious attempt to save the haul was apparent on their faces. All eyes were on the approaching cutter. What were a few casks of brandy worth if the penalty for being caught was a sentence of imprisonment?

Chloris kicked off her boots and flung the jacket aside. Matt should not be alone out there. She had swum in these coves as a child and was not afraid of them. The first icy wave took away her breath and she gasped. A hot, sunny day was a far cry from this night-chilled plunge into powerful grasping billows of intense cold. She flung up her head, trying to shake the streaming hair from her eyes. Where was Matt? She saw the bobbing barrels to her left and forced her limbs to respond though her body shook and trembled in the icy water.

With teeth gritted she struck out towards them. Against the incoming tide, she imagined she was making no progress and the wind and spray stung her eyes. Sea water was in her throat and she choked, but the barrels were nearer. She pushen doggedly. Matt must be closer now than the shore. She raised her streaming face again and saw the tow line. Under it, his shoulders taking the strain was Matt, his mouth open as he drew in great breaths of air. His face was contorted with the effort of dragging the full casks and he was still alone. She came up beside him, her throat raw from the salt water, and reached for the rope. There was length enough for her to slide behind his flailing legs and put her own shoulder under the rope. The big man's strength would have been useful here and she looked about for another bobbing head. But the sea between them and the beach was empty. She realized then that in his eagerness to drive others into the water that he either could not swim himself or had no intention of risking his own life.

The sodden rope was moving painfully over her shoulder, chafing the wet shirt she wore, but the pain was nothing compared to the fear that they were losing the race and the revenue cutter must be alongside any minute. Dear God, she prayed, let us reach the shelter of the overhang before the cutter turns its flares on us.

The rain drove down more heavily than before and in the darkness the long swells seemed to mount and break over her head with added fury. She could barely discern Matt's straining movements but tried to match her rhythm to his, knowing that her strength must fail very soon. Pictures floated through her dizzying mind as they are said to do, when one is drowning. But she was not drowning, only very tired with the strength-sapping weakness of cold discomfort, her shoulder on fire from the rasping rope. It was perhaps the nag of this fire that kept her mind from sinking into lethargy and made her limbs reject their numbness.

She had not thought it could grow any darker but overhead an extra darkness loomed. Her thoughts scattered wildly. The cutter, it was here, standing high and vast, dwarfing the two heads in the immensity of endless ocean. Lights and shouts of triumph, where were they?

Then suddenly, the trousered legs in front of her were still, the arms no longer thrashing the sea in a flurry of strokes. Her own legs sank and the towline pulled her forward but her right hand still clutched at it with fingers that had to be pried from it, one by one, as if the hand had been stiffened in death. An arm went round her waist and she hung there in total acceptance, limp but gasping in the clear air. The sea no longer broke over her head and the wind had gone, yet she heard its sound from somewhere distant. Her mind grew calmer and she felt the pounding of her heart being answered in the chest pressed into her.

A gasping mutter, "Made it, by God!" Then the question, "Who's this with me?"

Matt's voice! "It's me, Chloris." Her voice came croakingly, infinitely painful.

"Chloris! Good God alive! Where are the others?"

"A sad lack of volunteers," she answered, coughing from a chest that felt scoured by a yard broom.

"Devil take the lot of them! They'll reap no reward this trip. Can you stand?"

"If there's a bottom, yes. Where are we?"

Matt turned her round. "Get a handhold and move along. You'll find bottom soon. I must tow this lot into the pool and block the entrance. Then we'll fetch the weighted net."

Chloris grasped the rock edges with fingers that smarted. She edged along and found the shelving beach under her feet. Working her way slowly, she reached its flatness above the water level and dragged herself upwards to lie on the wet sand, content for the moment to lie without effort. But as her heart slowed and her breathing levelled, the cold air crept through her cotton blouse and sodden trousers and she began to shake. She would freeze to death if she lay here any longer and she forced herself to her knees, unable to stop her trembling. With the aid of the rocks, she came to her feet, swaying in sick dizziness. We'll fetch the weighted net, Matt had said. Did he expect her to help with that, too? For all she cared at the moment, those kegs of brandy could stay in the pool for ever.

She heard him splashing towards her. Far out, almost as if it had never moved, the revenue cutter sat, only its riding light visible.

Matt was beside her. "Come on, Chloris." He too, looked out to sea and she saw the gleam of his teeth. "They must have lost the boat and decided it was a false alarm. You did well," he added casually and Chloris felt an emptiness at his brief reference to her efforts.

They moved in silence to the cove where it had all begun. Chloris picked up the discarded jacket and huddled into it, sitting on a rock to pull on her boots.

Matt stood tall against the sea. "Come on out," he called softly. "All danger gone, my brave fellows."

Only one figure came forward, the big man. He grinned. "Well done, Mister Matt. Did you get them all?"

"Every one and no thanks to you. Where are the others?"

"Sloped off when the revenuer beat down on us. No guts, none of them." He spat on the sand. "I knew you'd be all right with the lad to help you. Never learnt to swim myself." He shrugged. "Well, there'll be only us to share out tonight."

"Then we'll get them netted and sunk while it's still as dark as Hades." Matt looked down on Chloris. "Feel up to it?"

Chloris rose and shook her head. "No." She looked at the big man. "Let him earn his share. I've had enough."

She turned on her heel, ignoring their grins, and crunched her way back up the slope towards the cliff top. From there she walked unsteadily along the cliff and past the Martello Tower until she sighted the porch light of Blair House. Every bone and sinew seemed to protest and in her weariness she felt the hot tears of anger and disillusionment. Let them play their games. Free-trading was no longer a game she wanted any more part in.

4

As Quentin Field drove his phaeton towards Weymouth, his thoughts on that warm June day dwelled on events of a year ago. Today, at the docks of Weymouth, he would take delivery of the Cyprus McCormick reaping machine he had first seen in London at the Great Exhibition of 1851. It had been declared open by Lord Bredalbane in the presence of Her Majesty Queen Victoria and her husband, Prince Albert, whose concept it was. The task of building that great glass palace had taken only nine months. Sixteen acres of Hyde Park housed this great exhibition acknowledging achievements and innovations of the world. Industry and art were represented, the newest designs in printing presses, coach building, sculpture and steam engines. The magnificent elms of Hyde Park, once thought an obstruction to the plan, were left in place and they too came under the soaring arches of framed glass.

Douglas Jerrold, writing in Punch Magazine, had made the skeptical comment that it was nothing more than a Crystal Palace. The name was apt and touched the fancy of the people and so the structure became proudly known as the Crystal Palace.

But during the entire week Quentin spent in the capital, walking under that magnificent arched roof, he returned again and again to the agricultural machinery section.

Ruth Baxter had told Chloris Blair of Quentin's taking on the task of running the estate after Lady Field's death. Although Sir Lionel had been desolate and withdrawn for many months, unwilling to take more than a cursory interest in estate affairs, Quentin had experienced many difficulties in his attempt to modernize. Sir Lionel's reluctance for change was an obstacle that Quentin negotiated with unhurried tact, a step at a time.

The house he left alone, for it mattered little whether it was lit by oil lamps or the new gas appliances, but the crops were a different matter. He fully understood the laborers' reluctance to welcome new methods of agriculture and in this he proceeded carefully. He was countryman enough to acknowledge their fear that machines could oust them from their jobs, and had read keenly the reports of upheavals in the northern counties of Lancashire and Yorkshire following the introduction of spinning frames. He was determined that no such trouble should attach itself to his own introduction of Mister McCormick's reaper or to the further innovations he planned.

It was at the Great Exhibition he had placed his order, and now, a year later, he was preparing to welcome the reaper in Weymouth. Sir Lionel had regarded him steadily over the breakfast table that morning.

"I hope you know what you are doing, my boy," he had said at length. "The corn has always been scythed hereabouts. I see no reason to change the way of things. And what about the men? A threat to their jobs, I shouldn't wonder?"

"No, Father." Quentin had helped himself to another cup of coffee. "I promise you there'll be no turning off of men. You and I," he had stressed the partnership, "are not absentee landlords, living high in London or Bath and not caring a fig for the countryfolk. We'll make our profits without hardship. It's in our interests too, for we live here, and none shall call our Squire a tyrant and a bully, believe me." He had smiled and Sir Lionel had given a reluctant grin.

"Damn, if you don't talk like your mother, lad. Always could twist me round her finger. But this is different, Quentin; just make sure you know what you're doing and I'll back you all the way."

"Thank you, Father." Quentin had laid down his napkin and risen.

Sir Lionel had eyed the tall, slim figure in the gray tail coat, immaculate linen and stylish cravat.

"You're looking mighty fine today. Is it only a ship you're meeting?"

Quentin had laughed. "I shall be taking lunch with Jim Hunter, our esteemed Customs Officer, and his lady. She would be quite put out if I called in farm clothes. If the ship unloads in good time, I'll have the reaper warehoused and send the wagon down tomorrow. No point in taking them down today. The ship is due but there's no telling with winds and tides if she'll tie up and unload her cargo."

He had collected his grey top hat and driving gloves from Belling and strode from Field House. The phaeton was waiting, the mare's head held by a groom. Quentin had swung himself up and nodded to the groom to stand clear.

The morning was fresh and sunny, the mare and himself in high spirits. With his hat on the seat beside him and the breeze of his passage ruffling his ash-blond hair, he enjoyed the drive over the countryside, his farmer's eye looking and judging crops and cattle on the way. His mind was already busy with the next step he intended, the introduction of South Down sheep to increase the meat level of their own. He grinned to himself. That must wait until the reaper had been installed, along with the threshing machine and the new way of winnowing the corn. A step at a time, he reminded himself. Sir Lionel would not thank him for instigating a riot amongst the farm workers by too precipitous a progress.

He slowed on the outskirts of Weymouth and directed the phaeton to a livery stable. It was still early, the tide would not be full for several hours. He picked up his hat, set it securely on his smoothed down hair and strolled along the seafront. A long stretch of exposed sand told him that he was far too early to entertain any hope of the cargo ship being docked; still it was pleasant to feel the sea breeze on his face.

He crossed into the town, moving between shops and stalls until he was passing the offices of the Customs and Excise. A carriage waiting at the curbside caught his eye. It had a familiar look about it. So too did the coachman. It was the Blair family coach. He glanced up the steps as the office doors opened and saw Mr. Justice Blair issuing from them, flanked by men he knew, one of them being his lunch host, Jim Howard. He passed on without attempting to approach them, for they were deep in conversation.

He moved into the meaner streets running down to the harbor area. Here were ship's chandlers and second-hand shops displaying a variety of used sextants, telescopes, lanterns and all manner of things essential to a seafaring man. Interspersed with shops offering well-worn reefer jackets, oilskins and seaboots were other essentials of life, namely the taverns and lodging houses where well-fleshed madams offered extra facilities.

Quentin swung round a corner and looked upon the sea again. Ferries and fishing boats jostled for space, and the baskets of freshly-caught fish lined the jetty, attracting housewives and dealers from the county.

He saw the cargo ship, Atlantic Star, standing off about a mile distant, the McCormick reaper, hopefully, in her hold. Cyrus McCormick's design was the best he had seen and it had been worth the wait of a year for its delivery. He strolled on, past the fishmongers, threading his way between bargaining women, slinking cats and the hopeful urchin awaiting a moment when the fisherman was looking the other way.

More taverns lined the seafront, some with rough benches and tables before them. Most were occupied and from the noise issuing from within, it was apparent that prodigious thirsts were being quenched to a chorus of ribald conversation.

As Quentin strolled by one such establishment, a burly seaman erupted into the cobbled pathway, either by propulsion from within or unsteadiness of his own gait. He staggered to a halt in front of Quentin, blinking from bloodshot eyes. Quentin side-stepped the man who reeked of sweat and rum, intending to proceed to the end of the quay, but the seaman shot out an arm and grasped Quentin's elbow. Quentin stopped and glanced down at the thick, grimy fingers.

"Release my arm, if you please," he said pleasantly.

The man swayed, grinning. "And what if I don't please, guv'nor? At least, not until you've parted with a shilling or two. What's that to a fancy toff like you, and me a poor sailorman with a thirst on him that could sink a barrel and no mistake."

Quentin sighed. "Will you kindly remove your hand and take yourself off?"

"Or else you'll scream for the law, guv'nor?" the man asked, on a sneer.

"Not at all," said Quentin. "But your hand has rested too long on my arm. I shall remove it—so." And he struck the man's wrist with a sharp upward blow from the edge of his free hand. Then he flicked the cuff of his jacket, smoothing out the crease.

"Now, that wasn't nice, guv'nor," said the man in sorrow. "You could have broke my wrist, honest. The least you can do is to buy me a drink—or else—"

Quentin glanced up from eyes that had grown cold. "Buy your own damned drink, if you think you can hold anymore. And don't 'or else' me!" he snapped.

The seaman blinked in surprise at the hard tone and his encounter with that cold stare gave him a moment of uneasiness.

"What's a toff like you doing here, then?" he blustered. " 'Taint no place for the likes of you—"

"I'm minding my own business," Quentin said crisply. "And I suggest you do the same."

They became aware at the same moment of a group of loiterers outside the tavern door.

"Go on, Tam. Knock his hat off!"

"Dust his coat for him, Tam!"

"Lay him down, nice and easy, Tam!"

The big man called Tam hesitated. He had

been about to shamble off but in view of his mates, it had now become impossible.

"Scared of him, Tam?" jeered a voice. "Oh, my, but he's feared without his rope's end."

There was a guffaw of laughter and the color rose in Tam's face. He swung towards Quentin, his fists bunched.

A new voice spoke, a voice of lazy amusement. "If you want to make a fight of it, Tam, give the gentleman time to take off his fine coat and square up all right and tight. I'll hold your coat, Quentin old friend."

Quentin glanced round to see Matt Travelyan regarding him blandly. "I'll be your second, old boy. Your fancy clothes will be safe with me."

"Good grief, Matt. What are you doing here?"

Matt, dressed in corduroy breeches and a checkered shirt, laughed. His dark hair fell tousled over his forehead and his eyes were bright.

"Minding my own business, the same as you. Do you want to fight this oaf?"

"Now that you mention it—no, but do I have a choice?" He grinned at Matt. "But I'm damned if I'll give this fellow the time of day, let alone a shilling." He handed Matt his top hat and gloves and eased himself out of the pale grey frock coat, then he looked down at his white shirt and sighed. "Best take my shirt off too. I can't take lunch with a respectable lady in a torn shirt." He peeled off his frill-fronted shirt, revealing a hard muscled body, tanned dark by the sun in his own field work.

There was an appreciative silence from the loungers and the burly seaman, who had divested himself of jacket only, looked at the strong, lithe body and regretted that he had even left the tavern in the first place.

"I think I'll lay my blunt on the fine gent," said a voice. "Gawd, don't he strip well."

"Me, too," said another. "He don't look like a rum-soaker, not like Tam."

There was so much disappointment in their voices that Tam came to a momentous decision.

"Is this gent a friend of yours, Mister Matt?" he asked.

"Man and boy," said Matt airily. "But don't let that stop you, Tam, though I'll lay odds you'll go down at the first touch."

"Ah," said Tam with immense gravity. "Seeing that you vouch for him and he's a friend of yours, I can't lay a finger on him, don't you see? It would hardly be fair like and him dressed up proper to meet a lady. Give me my jacket, Bill. I'll do no fighting with a friend of Mister Matt's."

"Hey, Tam," called Matt, and a florin spun through the air. "You're a decent cove, Tam. Send Bess out, will you?"

"Well, I'm damned!" said Quentin, still holding his shirt as the group disappeared into the tavern.

Matt laughed. "Put your shirt on, man, before Bess comes out or you'll find yourself in another fight—only this time to get away. Bess has a fancy for well set-up men."

Quentin donned his shirt and had it tucked into his waistband before Bess arrived. He slid into his coat as the girl asked, looking at Matt. "What you want, love?"

"What will it be, Quentin?" Matt inquired.

"Oh, a cider, ifyou've got it, please."

"And a brandy for me, Bess," added Matt.

The girl swung her hips as she walked away and Matt eyed Quentin with amusement. "Nice, accommodating girl, Bess."

"You've quite a collection of friends, Matt,"

Quentin said dryly. He glanced out to sea. "I'm waiting for that cargo ship to dock. Got a machine on her."

"She'll be in about noon," Matt said. "I've got some business aboard her, too."

At Quentin's raised brows, he grinned. "Well I am joining her owners in the autumn, if you remember." His eyes took on a mocking glint. "We're not all landed gentry, you know, with rich fathers to foot the bill for new machinery. Young Philip's school fees have to be paid and Mother to provide for. Precious little left of Father's money."

"Yes, I'm sorry. It's a good shipping firm you're joining."

"One of the best, if you're at the top, but my job will be pushing a pen about." He glanced across at the Altantic Star. "My God, can you imagine it." His look was so brooding that Quentin gave him a sympathetic smile.

"Frankly, no. I imagine, rather, you'd be better aboard one of their ships than dealing with their bills of lading."

"A ship of my own, that's what I'm like and that's what I intend to have one day." He turned his dark eyes on Quentin. "You see if I don't." Then he grinned his reckless, disarming grin and turned towards the girl bringing out their drinks.

"Took your time, Bess, my beauty," he teased and the girl eyed him boldly, a slow smile curving her full lips.

"Not like some," she murmured. "All of a haste for my attention."

Matt leaned forward and patted the girl's buttocks as she whirled and flounced away. Quentin felt vaguely uncomfortable at the girl's familiarity and Matt noticed his slight withdrawal. He laughed easily.

"Not your kind of company, is it, Quentin? But if I'm to be any use to the company I've got to keep my ear to the ground. The firm has two new ships and when they're ready for sea, they'll be wanting seamen, local lads for the main part, as is only right for a Weymouth shipper. And as a local myself . . ." He spread his hands. "I'm told to keep an eye out for sober, industrious fellows."

Quentin glanced towards the tavern where the noise was flowing in great gusts through the open door. He grinned at Matt. "Sober?" he asked with a lift of the eyebrow. "Will any of them be sober tonight?"

"Maybe not tonight, for they're celebrating shore leave, but I know who'll be sober tomorrow and that's what counts. Take Tam, your pugilistic friend, for instance. He'll be lucky to get another berth anywhere. Too much of a rum paunch, poor devil."

Quentin finished his cider and rose, scooping up hat and gloves. "Thanks for the lesson, Matt, and thanks for being on hand to hold my jacket. Can't say I fancied a street brawl above half. I'll be off for I think the Altantic Star is edging in." He nodded and strolled away.

As he turned the corner, he glanced back. The girl, Bess, had left the tavern again and was standing by the table, Matt's arm encircling her waist, pulling her close. The girl was not resisting and Quentin saw her fingers smooth Matt's cheek. Then Quentin was round the corner, wondering if Matt's duties involved him in close contact with tavern girls as well as seamen.

Thinking of Matt brought him to thinking of Chloris Blair. She had always idolized Matt, even in their younger days. Was she now as grown-up as she thought or was Matt still the hero of those early years? He knew his own love for her, but had never figured overmuch in her life, however he had tried to please. Perhaps it would continue to be Matt and the thought disturbed him.

He recalled her remark about "his" Miss Davenport. Why was everyone taking it for granted that the lovely visitor to Field House was there for the purpose of joining his family? The gossips, he was quite sure, were already linking them in marriage but until Chloris was lost to him, he still hoped.

He brought his mind forward and watched the Atlantic Star edge her way cautiously into the harbor.

5

Cyrus McCormick's American reaper stood in the yard outside the barn. Higher than a man, with huge rotating blades above a rear platform, it was eyed with intense curiosity and awe by the farm laborers. Quentin Field himself stood regarding it, frowning. It was a heavy piece of machinery and needed strong shafts and a robust coupling before he attempted to put it into operation. He examined the coupling and the blacksmith looked over his shoulder.

"You'll have no trouble with that, Mister Quentin. As solid a job as I've ever done."

Quentin flashed him a grin. "Your reputation and mine will be riding on that statement, Jim." He patted the thick wooden shafts. "Two heavy horses in tandem, I would think. The Suffolks, perhaps, for they are cleaner-legged and the grass won't catch them." He stood back and admired the American's invention.

He was impatient to try out the reaper but it was too early to cut the corn. But the lucerne could be reaped and the machine tested. He remembered the warning about stones and made up his mind.

"Joss," he called to his overseer, "get all the men you can and send them to the lower field with buckets, and take along the small, high-sided wain."

"Yes, Mister Quentin. What be they going to do there?"

"Collect every stone from the field and see they trample the lucerne as little as possible. Then fetch the two Suffolks from the paddock. They've a job to do this morning. I'll be back in half-an-hour."

He swung himself into the saddle of his bay gelding and cantered back to Field House where he changed his clothes for the oldest shirt and pair of breeches he had. As he ran down the stairs he was halted by Sir Lionel's voice from the study.

"What's the contraption look like, Quentin? Worth the money, do you think?"

Quentin smiled at his father. "It's rather like a toppled windmill with sails of sharp metal. I'm going to try it out now on the lucerne field. Jim has made a strong coupling so we shouldn't lose the thing."

"Better not, boy, or you'll be having the county laughing in its sleeve. If I hadn't this damned gout, I'd come along myself, but one fool is better than two."

His scowl was answered by a grin. "And who'll be cock-a-hoop in the county when we get the harvest in before anyone else? Don't worry, Father, it's a great advance in farming."

"You tell that to the scythe-men," grumbled Sir Lionel. "It's their living, remember?"

"There'll be no turning off, I promise you and I'll make the men understand that."

Sir Lionel nodded. "See that you do for I want no bricks through my windows." He lowered his eyes to the newspaper he held on his lap and only when he heard the sound of galloping hooves did he raise his head and smile. Damned good son, Quentin, and a countryman to his fingertips. But these newfangled things—he shook his head. More machines, less labor needed, but he trusted his son and Quentin never broke his word.

Back at the small home farm, Quentin talked with his manager, Joss Darling, a widower of some ten years with an only daughter, Meggie. He was a middle-aged, grizzled man, short of stature but immensely strong. Quentin had expected argument on his new acquisition but Joss had listened, his shrewd eyes on Quentin's face. Then he had nodded in agreement.

"Progress, Mister Quentin. It has to come so why shouldn't we be one of the first in the field and the first to market? Another field or two you'll be needing to set down to cultivation and there'll be work enough for everyone. You planning to stay with the men, sir?"

"And lead the Suffolks myself, Joss, until I'm satisfied with the performance."

"Right, sir. I'll have Maggie put an extra meal in the basket." He grinned up at Quentin. "I'll possibly take a wee peek over the fence myself come dinner time."

"You do that, Joss," Quentin said, laughing, as he rested a friendly hand on the man's shoulder. "I only hope there's not some great rock left in the lucerne field to damage a blade."

He strode from the farm house, his long legs taking him swiftly to where the harnessed horses waited. He checked that the blades of the reaper were not set to revolve, then took the bridle from the farmhand at the horses' heads. "Come on, Nell, old girl," he urged and the two heavy horses moved forward with such a steady gait that the weight of the reaper seemed to bother them no more than a loaded cart of turnips.

Quentin guided them past the fields of corn, not yet full blown, but looking like a golden sea rippling in the breeze, and towards the field of lucerne that made winter fodder for the cattle. The path wound between the neatly hedged fields with their lines of trees, acting as wind breaks. He smiled inwardly as he turned the Suffolks into the wide gate, obligingly held open by several farmworkers whose ditching activities were suspiciously concentrated about the lucerne field. He nodded his thanks, moving through the gateway with a confident step, his hopes pinned on the invention of that distant American, Cyrus McCormick. He halted the horses and looked across at the line of stone-pickers. A hovering group of estate children caught his eye and he knew that whatever happened in the next hour or so, the eyewitness accounts would flash over the county with the speed of a heath fire in a drought.

He beckoned the children forward. "Threepence a bucket each if you follow your brothers and fathers and pick up any stone they've left unnoticed. And sixpence to the lad or lass who collects most."

The children jostled each other in their race to secure buckets from the extra ones by the gateway, and they scampered off in the wake of the slow-moving line. Quentin rolled up his sleeves and hitched himself onto the fence, waiting until the men were almost at the end of the field. Then he slid off and walked to the patient horses.

"Come on, Nell, lass. This is our big day. Let's hope we don't bungle it." He glanced at the stableman holding the bridle of Nell's partner. "Stop dead, Seth, if you hear a rock clang. Right?"

"Yes, sir." Seth grinned, his eyes crinkling at the corners. " 'Tis a rare contraption and no

81

mistake, but us'll go steady and the old girls here'll not let you down."

Quentin released the locking device and checked the height of the blades, then they moved slowly forward and the great blades began to revolve. The flash of steel cutting sharp-edged through the grass and tossing it back into great swathes, brought gasps from the ditchers and workers who just happened to have business on that side of the estate. Quentin felt his elation rise. It was working, just as he hoped it might and as Mr. Cyrus McCormick had promised. The children were well ahead, scampering about and shouting as they cleared even the most minute stone deep in the grass. Quentin glanced back, seeing the fresh green piles of lucerne. How much easier and quicker this was, compared with the long hours required by the men with scythes. The stone-pickers had done their work well and there was no hitch as they maneuvered the horses across the end of the field.

Quentin barely noticed the time as the heavy horses plodded on. The sun was high and his shirt was soaked with perspiration. His hair was darkened with moisture and he frequently drew a forearm across his brow to clear the sweat, but he was incredibly happy. He patted Nell's neck and was surprised to see sweat on her mane and shoulders. He looked over at Seth, who was chewing on a blade of grass.

The man removed it and said in a laconic voice. "They need a rest, sir, same as us do."

"Dammit, man, why didn't you stop me before?"

Seth grinned. "Enjoying yourself too much, sir, I hadn't the heart but don' take on, the old girls are fine and I've been keeping an eye on them. They're hot but not blown. Reckon they'd like a drink too."

"Too?" Quentin looked about him, seeing the village girls coming down the lane with baskets and jugs. "Is it that time already?" He glanced up at the sun and grinned at Seth. "That time and more. We'll unhitch and take them to the trees. They deserve a rest and an extra ration."

As Seth led away the horses, Quentin climbed to sit on the fence, surveying the morning's work. He chewed on a blade of grass, watching the men collect the lucerne into piles for binding. A good machine and well worth the money, he decided, and his satisfaction was tinged with relief that all had gone well.

Meggie Darling, the farm manager's daughter, came down the path, a basket over her arm, a sun-bonnet shading her face from the sun. She saw Mister Quentin on the fence and knew her father had been right to suppose that the master's son would not leave the task to others. The cider jar and meat patties in her basket were for Mister Quentin, who would doubtless forget the lunch hour at Field House.

She was crossing the lane before entering the field when she heard footsteps behind. She glanced over her shoulder to see Chloris Blair, dressed in a well-worn pink flower-sprigged muslin, her head bare. She paused smiling, as Chloris drew level.

"Hello, Meggie. Taking dinner to your father?"

"No, miss. This is for Mister Quentin. Father is still at the farm. Mister Quentin is working the new reaper and he's been in the lucerne field for hours. Father thought he might like a bite to eat and some cider."

Chloris nodded. "Yes, I heard about the delivery. Truth is, that's why I walked over myself.

I'm as curious as the rest of the village." She smiled at the young girl.

"Are you going to speak to Mister Quentin, Miss?"

"Yes, indeed, and I want to see this reaper for myself."

Meggie hesitated and blushed a little. "Would you—would you like to take this basket to Mister Quentin, please, miss? He's just sitting there on the fence and I don't like to stop him thinking, for that's what it looks like."

Chloris laughed. "He won't eat you, Meggie. He'll be more interested in your basket."

"Yes, miss, but—"

"All right, Meggie. I'm going anyway. Lend me your bonnet, will you?"

"My bonnet, miss?" Her eyes looked concerned. "You've gone and given yourself a headache, walking all the this way in the sun."

"No such thing, I assure you. I shall pretend to be you, that's all. If he's thinking that hard he'll never notice who puts the cider mug into his hand. He won't expect it to be me so I'll surprise him."

Meggie set down the basket and unfastened the strings of her bonnet. She handed it to Chloris with a smile. "Thank you, miss. I'd best get back for I've a pie in the oven and wouldn't dare speak first to Mister Quentin, so I'd stand there while he noticed me."

"What a goose you are, Meggie. He's not different from other men."

"Oh, yes, he is, miss. He's the Squire's son and he'll be Squire himself one day."

"Yes, you're right, Meggie, and he'll make a good Squire, I think."

She put on the sunbonnet as Meggie hurried back the way she had come. Lifting the basket onto her arm, Chloris walked to Quentin's side as he sat on the fence. She stood for a moment watching the tanned profile, his skin drawn smoothly over the clear-cut lines of his face. She noticed the hard, determined chin, the contrasting dark brows under the thick hair, now darkened by perspiration. He was handsome, she decided, in a cool, sculptured way, with gray eyes that watched the world thoughtfully. He had not the dark, rather rakish air of Matt, who looked on the world as a great adventure.

She bent her head so that the sunbonnet shadowed her face. "Your dinner, Mister Quentin," she said in a meek voice.

"Barley in September," said Quentin as if he had not heard her.

"And holly in December, Master," murmured Chloris.

"What?" Quentin was startled out of his reverie. "Holly?"

"Well—yule logs, if you prefer it," said Chloris, still with downbent head.

She felt fingers tweak the brim of the bonnet, then Quentin was laughing down at her. She saw the gray eyes bright with amusement and her heart warmed to him.

"Will you have your cider in a mug or straight from the jar, Master?"

Quentin slid from the fence and took the basket from her. "Take off that ridiculous sunbonnet and sit down. We'll share whatever is in here. Where did it come from, anyway?"

"Meggie was bringing it from the farm. I expect Mister Darling knew you wouldn't be parted from your new reaper just yet." She glanced across the field at the piles of lucerne grass lying ready for collection. "It does seem to have been successful. Are you pleased with it?"

"Enormously. Couldn't be better. There'll be a

85

run of orders to America when this news gets about."

"I think it's almost already. I passed a few strange faces on my way here. Spies, I don't doubt, from other estates."

Quentin lifted out the cider jug. "Let's drink to the coming prosperity of Mister Cyrus McCormick, the inventor of this machine." He spread out the cloth on the grass between them and unwrapped the napkin of food. "A meat pattie and a mug of cider to your taste, Madam?"

"Indeed, my lord of all you survey, such rare delicacies are most welcome."

They sat in the sun with their backs to the fence, eating and drinking from Meggie's basket, and Quentin described the morning's work with such enthusiasm that Chloris was captured by it.

"Corn in August and barley in September," she said. "And next year the rye and oats, too. Is that what you are thinking"

"Yes," he said, looking at her and there was a teasing light in his eyes. "But I didn't expect a young lady of fashion, recently returned from a Dorchester Academy, to interest herself in crop cultivation. Too tame, I'd have thought for a lady who craves the excitement of adventure."

Chloris thought briefly of the last run with Matt. Adventure was all very well in its place but being wet and uncomfortable, looking over her shoulder at the slightest alien sound, was not quite as thrilling as she had imagined. She smiled back at Quentin unaware of the intentness of his gaze. "It's so peaceful here, and tell me, what are those children waiting for?"

Quentin glanced towards the gateway hedge. Half-a-dozen small boys and girls were sitting in a row, a bucket by each side, and they were all gazing solemnly at him.

"Good Heavens!" he said, rising from the grass and brushing at his breeches. "I'd forgotten my second line of defense." He beckoned to the children, who scrambled up, hauling their buckets across the field towards him. Chloris sat up and clasped her hands round her knees, regarding them curiously.

The buckets were lined up before Quentin and the children stood back, looking up at him. He glanced into their buckets. They were each a quarter filled with pebbles and loose tufts of grass, some still with earth adhering. Every bucket save one seemed to hold an equal amount.

Quentin looked at the tallest boy who, by his seniority, appeared to have been appointed spokesman. He stood a pace closer than the others.

"Excellent, Tom. You've done much better than I expected. Very well done, all of you." He glanced at the fullest bucket, then at the tiny girl standing over it. "And what's this, young Becky? Your bucket is half-full. You must have scampered about like a mother rabbit looking for her little lost baby."

"Becky's bonnet is fullest, Master," said young Tom stoutly. "She be keen for the sixpence you promised."

"And shall have it, Tom." He delved into his pocket and produced a handful of silver. "A threepenny piece for you all and a sixpence for Becky. I'm obliged to you all." He extended a hand to Tom. "I'll be happy to call on you again. And there's my hand on it, Tom," he said gravely.

Tom grinned, his face flushing. "Thank you, Master Quentin." He turned and shepherded the children away with immense importance.

Chloris rose. "Are you telling me that a tiny mite like Becky did better than a big lad like

Tom?"

Quentin laughed. "Of course she didn't. They all shared their stones equally and gave Becky a few extra so that she would win the sixpence. Tom knows only too well that Becky's mother is more in need since she lost her man. We have her to the house a few days a week to mend sheets and things."

Chloris laid a hand impulsively on his bare, tanned arm. "You're a good man, Quentin, and you really will be an excellent Squire one day."

"Thank you, Chloris. Perhaps I'll find myself a good woman to become a good Squire's goodwife."

He stared with mock gravity into Chloris's face. "But where do I look for this excellent lady who is worthy of my goodness?" He laughed suddenly. "You will warn me, won't you, when I show signs of pomposity? But of course you will. I have no doubts on that score."

She laughed too and they walked to the field gate, Chloris carrying the food basket and swinging the sunbonnet by its strings.

Quentin watched her go up the lane towards the farmhouse, her dark hair flying and the pink skirt swaying below the trim waist. His expression was unreadable to the men standing about but had they been able to look into the heart of Quentin Field, they would have seen the love he felt for Chloris Blair, the love and the hopelessness, for he knew that Matthew Trevelyan held first place in her own heart. Matt, the rakish, uncaring man whose business took him into the company of seamen and tavern girls on the dockside of Weymouth. He shook his thoughts away and turned back to the reaper.

6

Several days after the successful cutting of the lucerne grass, Quentin Field drove his phaeton into Weymouth again. Immaculately dressed in frockcoat, dove-gray trousers fitting closely about his long legs, he handled the reins with practiced ease. One well-shod foot rested on the front board, his tophat riding the seat beside him.

His hair lifted brightly in the breeze above a face that glowed with summer tan. He drove almost automatically for his mind was still back on the estate, his thoughts progressing from the lucerne field through the many other tasks that needed to be done before and after the corn harvesting. His buisness this morning was taking him in Sir Lionel's stead to the elegant club patronized exclusively by businessmen in shipping and farming. It was an old building of early Georgian opulence, much favored for its cuisine and the quality of its brandy. Sir Lionel had been a member for years, meeting his contemporaries to exchange news of farm and freight charges, air their views of new taxation and exclaim over the rise or fall of competitors. It was not a favorite place of Quentin's but since the running of Field

House estate had fallen on his shoulders since his mother's death, he needed to keep abreast of things to please his father. Sir Lionel had enjoyed the company of other estate owners and it was Quentin's wish that, as soon as the gout left him, Sir Lionel would once more appear at the club to boast or growl at his fellows while indulging in the splendid food and drink.

Quentin smiled as he turned the phaeton into the yard of the livery table, but his smile was rueful, for his father had ordered him to probe into the intentions of his fellow farmers. Had they heard of the Fields' new reaper? Were they impressed by reports? And did they intend, or had they already followed the example and bought a Cyrus McCormick reaper? Sir Lionel, Quentin knew very well, tested the ground before stepping on it, to do, as he put it, a bit of crowing. The Great Exhibition of the previous year could not have gone unnoticed even in Dorset, and Quentin was in no doubt that more farmers than he had looked upon the new reaper and found it pleasing.

He left the livery stable and strolled down the main street, his hat on his head. Sir Lionel would be disappointed for sure, if every other man he knew had invested secretly in that American invention, without giving Field House a head start.

As Quentin approached the meeting place, his thoughts went back to the successful reaping of the lucerne, but his mind dwelt on the girl who had brought his dinner. Chloris Blair, that dark-haired, green-eyed girl, sitting so companionably beside him, eating meat patties and toasting the reaper in cider. Companions they had always been, in childhood, and he had accepted Matt's influence over the adventurous child she was, but now they were adults. Was Matt's influence still as strong? Matt had not changed, he was still the confident adventurer, mixing in surprising company. On behalf of the shipping company he was due to join in the autumn? A glib enough explanation but Quentin doubted that he consorted with drunken seamen and tavern girls on the orders of a highly respected shipping company. Still, it was no business of his what Matt did, save where it concerned Chloris Blair. And was that his business either? She was eighteen now, supposedly a young lady, but she was still that adventurous child. Would she follow where Matt led, now that she was home for good? For the sake of that sad man, Mister Justice Blair, he hoped that no scheme of Matt's would involve her in trouble.

He grimaced to himself as he ran up the steps of the club and handed his hat and gloves to the attendant. For Mister Blair's sake? Not only that but for his own. Whatever the village gossips proposed for him in relation to Miss Georgina Davenport, he knew that he wanted only one girl to be the future hostess of Field House and her name was not Georgina.

He put all other thoughts behind him as he entered the lounge of the business club and gazed about him. Heavy leather easy chairs were angled into small groups over sound-deadening carpet, tall windows framed by red velvet curtains, and the atmosphere was of cigar smoke and the rich scent of roasting beef. Waiters were hurrying by, trays held aloft and glinting with crystal glasses of port and brandy. In a window alcove, he saw Sir Lionel's closest contemporaries, the owners of estates abutting onto the Field House property. Joseph Randall, fifty and florid, had his head bent towards a thinner-faced man, surprisingly corpulent, gray-haired and beak-nosed. William Cornwell, Quentin knew, was a shrewd man, much given to heading the field and feeling himself affronted if balked.

Quentin nodded to a few acquaintances as he moved slowly across the carpet. He spoke a few casual words here and there, concerning the spell of hot weather and the possibility of a bumper corn harvest, but he kept the two bent heads in view. He had no intention of joining them directly but adhered to the casual approach advocated by his sire. "Play bait, my son," he had said, "and they'll rise, never fear. Eaten up with curiosity, I'll be bound," and he had laughed delightedly.

So Quentin drifted, getting distinctly bored with the game and unaware that his boredom showed. So when the thick-necked bull face of Mister Joseph Randall looked up frowning at the shadow fallen over his cognac, he showed a face of complete disinterest.

"The very man," exclaimed Mister Randall in a booming voice.

Quentin started and looked down into the florid face. "Sir?"

"Sit down, young man. I want to talk to you."

"Really? What about, sir?" Quentin's question came blandly as he recovered his wits.

Mister Randall raised thick brows. "What about?" Then he modulated his tone and smiled. "Ah, what indeed?" He tapped the side of his nose. "Keeping quiet, eh?"

Quentin accepted the seat and nodded to Mister William Cornwell. "Good morning, sir. I trust I find you in good health? And you, too, sir." He looked at Mister Randall. "A fine morning. Let us hope the weather holds, though a little rain would not come amiss for the cider apples. How are your fruit crops coming along, sir?"

Joseph Randall gave Quentin a hard stare. "Well enough, but what I want to know—"

Quentin interrupted smoothly. "Ah, forgive me, gentlemen. I see your glasses are empty." He signalled to a waiter. "Brandy is it, gentlemen? And a small cider for me, waiter, if you please." He sat back, crossing his long legs elegantly. "You were talking of your fruit crops, Mister Randall. Please continue. A new type of pear, wasn't it?"

The two men looked at him and exchanged glances. Mister William Cornwell laughed.

"A cool one, I'd say. Fruit, is it? You've something better to talk about than that, unless I'm mistaken and I'm not, for my own agent saw you reap the lucerne field in record time. Do you deny that, young man?"

"Why no, in a record time, indeed, but I was sure you'd know of it for I was told there were spies about. Did you wish to know anything else?"

Mister Randall said. "I've a McCormick myself and so has William, here, but you were first to try it out."

"Congratulations, gentlemen. I hardly expected such an innovation to go unnoticed at the Exhibition. My father will be interested to hear that the reaper is working successfully for us all. A great saving of hard work, though, of course, the crop must still be bundled and bound. Don't you agree, sir?"

He smiled but noted the sour expression in the face of Mister Cornwell.

"Your farm manager must be better than mine, is all I can say. I've a mind to dismiss the damned fellow for he broke a blade, first time round. I'll confess to disappointment, curse it, yet my man said you had no trouble. Is that right?"

"None at all, sir. And you, Mister Randall? A trouble-free reap, I hope?"

The florid face deepened with color. "Haven't used the damned thing yet. Waiting to see how you two went on. I've a pretty good manager. Likely I'll let him have a try."

Quentin beamed genially, guessing their problem. "I took the reaper out myself on the principle that if I got damaged, it was my own fault. Of course," he added thoughtfully, "you had the ground prepared beforehand?"

"Prepared? In what way? It's only a damned lucerne field."

"But the stones, gentlemen. Surely you had the stones removed first? Do you know of any blade that cuts through rock as if it was lucerne?"

"Good God," said Mister Randall.

"I'll be damned," said Mister Cornwell. "My fellow said nothing of that."

"Perhaps he didn't start spying early enough, sir," Quentin said gravely. "If the fellow had approached me instead of skulking under the hedges, I'd have told him. Just as I would have told you—if you'd have mentioned to my father that you had a McCormick too." He drained his cider and stood up. "Excuse me, gentlemen, I have business to attend to. By the way, are there any other McCormick's about? It would really be a shame if other blades were damaged when a word of advice could prevent it."

"No others," said Mister Cornwell gloomily. "Not hereabouts, anyway."

"Good, good," said Quentin affably. "Good morning to you, gentlemen." He strode from the room, watched by the two men in silence. Then they faced each other again and the florid-faced man broke into a chuckle. "Damned young coxcomb. Craftier than his father if that's possible. He's right, though, should have thought of stones. Break anything, scythes included."

Mister Cornwell nodded. "It'll put me back a bit, that broken blade, unless it'll mend." He shook his head gloomily and signalled to the waiter.

In the rose garden of Field House, the exquisite figure of Georgina Davenport drifted between beds of ruby red and golden yellow roses, pausing by the palest pink of young buds. A wide straw hat, silk-banded and with blue hanging tails, shaded her delicate complexion from the sun. A gown of white muslin, flower-sprigged with matching blue hyacinth design, swayed wide skirts as she moved. She had not heard the phaeton of Quentin returning to Field House. The conjunction of color filled her mind, for she was choosing roses to grace the silver vase that stood on the lace cover of the grand piano in the drawing room. The choice of color was important, for as her mama said, a hostess is judged by her floral arrangements, a task not left to maid or house-keeper. A subtle blending of shades to complement each other and the decor of the room was essential. One did not push stems into a vase and hope for the best. One arranged them with the utmost delicacy, not overpowering the company with a riot of color or perfume.

Georgina snipped the last stem and laid the rose in the wicker trug she carried on her arm. A dozen roses, from delicate pink deepening to rich full pink, lay in the basket. Since the drawing room was of ivory with wine-red curtains and an Aubusson rug that held shades of wine and pink, she felt quite happy at her selection. Mama, she felt, would have given a nod of appraisal.

She drifted over the short-clipped lawns towards the house, remembering another of mama's strictures. Show interest in a gentleman's activity and ask a little question or two, for there is nothing a gentleman enjoys more than talking about himself. Georgina sighed. What did she know of farming and when things were planted and harvested? If you are unfamiliar with a subject, just smile and murmur encouragement, said Mama, and be above all, a good listener.

She floated dreamily towards the open french windows, thanking Providence that Quentin was acquainted with London life, its theatres and art galleries. He had not talked overmuch on farming, save with dear Sir Lionel, for he sensed her ignorance and understood the difficulty, choosing only topics on which she could speak. Quentin was such a kind gentleman, yet she confessed herself a little in awe of him for he could look quite cold at times. And when he spoke to dear Chloris, why, he was positively mocking. But dear Chloris was unafraid and mocked him back. Perhaps it helped that they had known each other so long and Chloris feared nothing.

She sighed again. How suitable they were for each other, yet neither showed the slightest romantic inclinations. Georgina thought of dear Robert, her poor London poet, so charming with his verses and adoring looks. No, she must put him to the back of her mind and remember only Mama's words. They were really most sensible and love in a garret must surely be the height of discomfort, however romantic it sounded.

She reached the french windows, thrown open onto the terrace. The voices of men drifted out and she stood on the threshold hesitantly. Sir Lionel, redfaced, his laugh booming to rattle the porcelain figurines on the mantelpiece, was sunk into a leather armchair facing a grinning Quentin. Each held a glass in his hand.

"I'd have given a guinea a second to see Cornwell's face," spluttered Sir Lionel. "A snapped blade, by God, and he so keen to be first in every field. And that hesitating Randall, ah yes, he was always one to let others go first, then crow over his success, having learnt the pitfalls at their expense." He laughed again and drank deeply. "And you're sure we're the only three with the McCormick?"

"I'd say we could rely on that, Father. They were so shaken when I asked them, I'd give odds they hadn't their wits about them enough to lie."

Sir Lionel said, "They won't be leaving their first runs to their managers now." He gave Quentin a shrewd look. "We're crowing at the moment but a snapped blade won't help us when it comes to corn harvesting. Can't have the fields trampled flat by your stone-pickers."

"As to that, Father, I took the precaution of ordering replacement blades, both for damage and the fact that every blade will need sharpening at times. For the stones, I've a scheme to scythe the middle strip, then send in my team of children to burrow like rabbits on their stomachs."

"Damn me!" Sir Lionel shook his head. "I'll vouch that neither Randall nor Cornwell's lads have the brains of you."

"Oh, come, Father, no flattery if you please," Quentin said smiling. "It's common sense and I learnt it from you."

He began aware of Georgina hovering in the doorway and rose to his feet. "Come in, Georgina. What splendid roses you've chosen. And which piece of furniture are they to grace?"

Georgina smiled up at the tall fair-haired young man gratefully. "Forgive me. I did not mean to interrupt your discussion. I will take the vase from the piano, if you permit, and arrange then in the hall."

"Nonsense, my dear," boomed Sir Lionel. "I like to see a pretty woman arranging flowers. You will take a glass of wine with us and I will have Belling send a maid with fresh water."

Georgina subsided gratefully onto the sofa, removing her cotton gloves and placing them with the basket. Then she untied the silk ribbons of her hat. "So beautifully warm outside and such a delightful rose garden you have, Sir Lionel."

"Thank you, my dear, and you have such a glow on you as to equal my golden roses."

Georgina raised a hand to her warm cheek. "Oh, I do hope I did not stay out too long. Mama particularly warned me about the sun in the country. It would never do to have my skin as brown as a tinker." She glanced into Sir Lionel's weatherbeaten face and then at the smooth tanned face under the thick, ash-blond hair of the man beside her. Her blue eyes widened and her voice faltered. "I did not mean to say that a tanned skin denotes someone of low rank like—like a gypsy or tinker, but—but it is different for a gentleman; in fact, one could say it is excessively becoming—and shows a healthy love of—outdoor pursuits where-as—" she floundered.

Quentin laughed at her confusion. "Pray do not involve yourself in explanation. We understand perfectly what you mean. Alas," he added teasingly, "we are not only gentlemen but working farmers and must submit to the perils attendant on exposing ourselves to the sun. The corn will not play the gallant but demands to be reaped when the sun is high." He patted Georgina's hand. "We will grow paler by winter, never fear, and your esteemed mama will not take us for tinkers."

Georgina giggled. "She could never do that for I understand a tinker's tongue is different and she would recognize straightaway that no tinker goes to Oxford or speaks so genteelly. And how many pegs would he have to sell to afford it, anyway?"

Sir Lionel chuckled and Quentin laughed aloud. "My dear Georgina, you are possessed of such logic that you have my poor brain in a spin." He rose, smiling down at her. "Forgive me if I leave you now. I must change and ride out to the farm. I will observe most closely any tinkers I find on the way and make sure that my skin does not darken to that degree." He strode from the room, a smile still on his face.

7

The late summer days followed each other in golden procession and the fear Chloris had felt concerning the new preventative measures spoken of by her father faded into the back of her mind. Nothing had changed; perhaps their Lords of the Admiralty still debated the best methods to suppress smuggling. She, herself, had resolved to resist Matt's cajolery if he attempted to draw her into another adventure. He was still the reckless hero of her childhood, with the power to touch her heart, but her own recklessness had become tempered by thoughts of her father and what disgrace it would bring on him if his own daughter faced him over the high bench. She could not inflict a double sadness on him, just as he appeared to be recovering from her mother's death.

But now, the summer was high and instead of on dark, wind-swept beaches, she spent her time at Field House with Georgina or watching Quentin's progress as the corn grew high and golden. Soon the harvesting would begin and she found herself drawn into the preparations as Quentin drilled his little group of village children.

Sitting on the fence watching him, she laughed with the children as Quentin stretched full length on his stomach demonstrating the art of drawing stones towards him with the aid of a long, hook-ended stick. In worn breeches and old shirt, his chin almost on the ground, he showed them how to draw out stones without disturbing the corn. He rose, flushed and bright-eyed, his hair as tousled as any child's, and answered their grins with one of his own. How good he is with children, thought Chloris, for the boys and girls were jumping up and down in their eagerness to follow his example. The children adored him, that was obvious, and Quentin responded by treating them as equals, consulting their leader, young Tom, as graciously as he would have discussed matters with his farm manager.

In answer to a question from Tom, Quentin rubbed his chin and deliberated.

"We will agree terms in the farm office, Tom. Shall it be piece work or a standard daily rate?"

"My dad says piece work is best, Master."

"Your dad is a wise man, Tom, but this is a delicate job, not to be rushed at helter-skelter, with thought for full buckets and none for damaged corn."

Tom frowned and surveyed his team. "You be right, Master, for there's some here as'll rake out the stones like beavers at a dam with no thought else. Aye, Master, 'twould be better should all get equal, for there be fast and slow 'uns."

"Good man, Tom." Quentin clapped him on the shoulder. "A few years on and you'll be asking for Joss Darling's place, I shouldn't wonder."

Tom grinned. "Happen I might, Master, at that, for schoolmarm do say I'm quick with figures and the like."

He was suddenly overcome with bashfulness

and gave Chloris a shy smile before turning to his team to deliver a stern injunction on the importance of the task and an equally stern threat on what would befall them if they rushed at it, helter-skelter.

"Farmhouse in an hour, Tom," Quentin called over his shoulder as he joined Chloris, and she climbed down from the fence.

They strode past the broad expanse of cultivated fields and Chloris laughed up into Quentin's flushed face.

"I would never have believed, had I not seen it for myself, that the cool, elegant and usually impeccably dressed Quentin Field, heir to the Squire, could squirm between corn crops like a buck rabbit in a vegetable garden."

Quentin laughed, his teeth very white against the tan of his skin. "And I would not have believed that a Dorchester-finished young lady with a taste of adventuring on the high seas could find such amusement in my antics and even show interest in farming practices." He gave her a sideways glinting look. "Is it not too tame an occupation for one with such splendid ambitions?"

"As to that," Chloris replied, "I have given up the idea of emulating the lady pirates for it is—or I imagine it to be," she corrected herself quickly, "a most precarious and uncomfortable existence." She looked into Quentin's face, wondering if he had noticed her stumble, but his smile was bland.

"You relieve my mind, Chloris. A most sensible decision in view of your father's position, and your own, of course. Who ever heard of a lady pirate living happily ever after?" He was laughing again and Chloris felt able to smile her relief.

"And as dear Georgina points out," she said, "it would be impossible to retrieve one's reputation."

"Quite," said Quentin as he untied old Bessie's reins. "Why don't you go over and keep her company? I shall be too busy in the fields until the corn is in."

"Hasn't she been to see the reaper?"

"I showed it to her one evening when the sun was low." In answer to Chloris's questioning look, he continued, "Georgina goes in mortal fear of the sun. How could she face dear Mama if she returned to London as tanned as a tinker? Unthinkable, for a young lady of fashion!" He ran a critical eye over the honey-gold skin of Chloris's face and arms, and shook his head in sorrow. "Really, Chloris, you should know better at your great age than to venture out uncovered."

"Since I am not returning to London and make no claim to be a lady of fashion, I shall ignore that remark. Would you have me sit on the fence at harvesting time, gloved and swathed in veiling? Good heavens, what a thought!"

Quentin helped her mount, then glanced up. "Will you come to our harvest supper when the corn is in? I hope both you and your father will attend, at least until the laborers get down to the serious business."

"What's that?"

He laughed. "To fill themselves with as much ale and cider as they can hold without over-flowing. Even that, too, when the fiddlers strike up."

"I wouldn't miss it for the world. Is everyone coming?"

"Yes, for the first half anyway, then we remove ourselves to Field House and let the jollification proceed unhampered by our presence. The Kernicks and Trevelyans will be coming and Ruth, too. And naturally the families of the estate workers."

Chloris looked down to the cornfield. A small sturdy figure was striding purposefully towards the farmhouse.

"Your enterprising under-manager is on his way, Quentin. I will leave you to haggle terms with him. Beware, for he'll drive a hard bargain and have you in a corner."

"I wouldn't be surprised for he's half-an-hour early and eager to engage the enemy."

Chloris laughed and turned Bessie's head to the path leading past the farmhouse. Quentin saluted her.

"We who are about to die—" he murmured and stood waiting for young Tom.

Chloris rode home by way of the Martello Tower, the breeze from the sea lifting and teasing her long black hair behind. The sun crested each lazy ripple with gold and the azure sky looked down on its own brilliant reflection. She raised her face to the sun and was glad that her life was here and not in the vast Metropolis of grime and turbulence. Ahead of her, about a half-mile distant, she saw a rider. She noticed the horse first, its black, shining coat and the long rangy step as it cantered towards her. A handsome beast, though a trifle showy, as Sir Lionel would have said. She narrowed her eyes and looked at the rider. A white, frilled shirt above black breeches and elegant leather riding boots. She recognized Matt and had a sudden urge to knee Bessie into a headlong gallop but she restrained the impulse and reined in, watching Matt's easy approach with a heart full of happiness.

His grin of recognition set her pulses racing, the flashing, daredevil grin that had challenged her so many times in their childhood, never failing to drag her into every adventure he set his mind to.

Now, as he drew level and circled her, showing off the paces of the horse, the dark eyes shone in his tanned face. Every hero of romance should look like this, Chloris found herself thinking.

"What do you think of this beauty?" he called. "A fine fellow, isn't he?"

Chloris knew what was expected of her and she smiled. "Superb, and certainly not your mother's carriage horse. I doubt if Sir Lionel himself could boast such a one. Who owns him?"

"I do," said Matt.

Chloris could barely keep her surprise hidden. How on earth could Matt afford such a creature? "Where did you get him?"

Matt laughed and swung himself out of the saddle. "Come down and I'll tell you."

She slid from her saddle into his arms and he looped the reins of the two horses on adjacent bushes. They walked along the cliff top and descended to a rocky place where they had met in childhood. A convenient ledge of rock formed a seat.

"Went into Somerset for him," Matt said. "I had some business with a couple of landlords that way. There was a horse sale on and this fellow caught my eye. Belonged, they said, to a young lordling who died of the fever in the West Indies. Remember the night we had to swim for it?"

"Very well," said Chloris. "An adventure I have no wish to repeat."

"Six kegs of the finest brandy and we got them ashore safely. A good profit with only the two of us to share it, and all things being fair, since Croker did not swim for it, the profits were split sixty-forty."

"A fair division," Chloris said. "Where was

106

Sefton, by the way? I thought he always came with you."

"Well, he would have, chill or not, but Mother stopped him."

"Your Mother! Don't tell me she knows what's going on!"

"Of course not, but the cottage we gave him after he survived the sinking of our ship is so close to ours that Mother keeps an eye on him. Stupid fellow asked Mother for some cough mixture, so what does she do but order him to bed. If that wasn't enough, she promised to call in every hour with hot soup and the like." He gave a derisive chuckle. "So poor Sefton could do nothing but keep to his bed. He'll be a mite more careful next time."

"I see," said Chloris. "Well, you're welcome to my share too."

Matt turned a look of surprise on her. "Your share? But you're a girl."

"Why, so I am," she said mildly. "How kind of you to notice, but does that fact make me ineligible? I swam out too, you remember."

"So you did." His dark eyes laughed into hers. "We'd have lost the kegs if you hadn't. You were the only one willing to risk your life for them."

Chloris was silent. Did Matt really think she had risked her life to save those brandy kegs? Matt put an arm about her shoulders and gave her a hug.

"I knew you'd help me like you've always done but thanks anyway." He removed his arm and sat with hands clasped between his knees, staring out to sea.

Chloris studied his profile, noting the dark brows under the wind-swept hair. He relied on her support, she knew, but his casual acceptance was a relic of childhood. Surely he saw her as a young

107

woman now? Or was she still in his eyes the child who followed his lead without question?

He turned to her. "There'll be no more swimming for I've got my eye on a boat. Down payment on a fast little craft at a yard in Plymouth. Another good run and I'll be able to buy her."

"A boat? Well, I hope your man, Croker, is a better sailor than he is a swimmer."

Matt grinned. "He should be. He jumped one of H.M's ships in Gibraltar and worked his passage home on a Welsh coaler. With my own boat, who needs the middleman? We'll do the entire run ourselves and double the profits."

Chloris knew that she should feel happy for Matt was achieving what he wanted but she had a nagging fear in the back of her mind. She had always loved his recklessness, but how many smugglers plied their trade with such indifference to the law? And how many lived to profit by their endeavors? If the last run had reaped such a rich reward, would it not have been better to invest the proceeds in something that meant security for his mother and young brother instead of indulging in a fine horse and the purchase of a boat? But she knew that Matt would not take kindly to any interference on her part.

To bring him out of his brooding silence she said, "Did you know that Quentin Field has bought a reaping machine? It performs beautifully, for I have seen it cut the lucerne grass."

"A reaping machine! God, how dull!" His mouth twisted. "I'll bet that cost a packet of money."

"I've no idea, but it will save the scythe men a lot of hard labor."

"And put them out of work, I don't doubt."

"I don't think Quentin has that in mind. He

cares for his workers and will not turn them off, I'm sure."

Matt shrugged, then gave the grin that always touched her heart. "You seem to know a lot about friend Quentin's plans. A dull fellow by my reckoning, but he's rich which makes him a catch." His eyes regarded her mockingly. "Do you fancy yourself as a Squire's lady?"

"Don't be ridiculous," she said, flushing. "There is already a contender for that position at Field House."

"Ah, yes. I heard there was a girl staying with them. They say she's quite a beauty." His brows rose in question.

"Yes, Georgina is very beautiful. She would make an ideal Squire's lady."

"Better than a girl who consorts with smugglers, I'd say." Matt's smile was lazy and full of confidence. "You'd not give that up in favor of good works, would you?"

"It would be a more comfortable existence, to be sure," Chloris said, smiling. "But don't describe me so horribly. I don't consort with smugglers like some female pirate. I've helped you twice, that's all."

"Enough to tar you with the same brush, my dear Chloris. But you don't care about that, do you?" He had risen and was looking down at her with his challenging grin. "Remember the adventures we had as children? Well, this is real and we're in it together."

Chloris rose too and stared into his face. "It's real, yes, and I'm not sure that I like it any better, especially since you tell me that Croker is a deserter from the Royal Navy. He could be violent if he's in danger of recapture."

"Don't worry about Croker. I can handle him."

"I'm sure you can," she said smiling down as he helped her to mount. He swung himself into the saddle of the black horse and gathered up the reins.

"Are you going to Quentin's harvest supper, Matt?"

"Of course. I want to take a look at this gorgeous Georgina of his." He smiled and raised a hand in farewell. "And incidentally, my dear Chloris, I had already noticed that you were a woman." He kneed the stallion and galloped away, leaving Chloris bemused, staring after the lithe figure moving easily to the rhythm of the horse.

8

"Dear Chloris, do advise me on what to wear tonight. I have never attended a harvest supper before, and Mama says that a lady must always be dressed as the occasion demands. How am I to know what is suitable when such an occasion has never arisen before, since I cannot recall being once invited to a harvest supper in London?"

Georgina's voice trembled a little and she stared at Chloris from agonized blue eyes. "I should be dreadfully mortified if Quentin or dear Sir Lionel raised their brows when they saw me, but they would say no word, I am convinced, for their manners are most genteel, but I would sense their disapproval and be thrown into gloom."

Chloris, sitting on the bed in Georgina's room, smiled into the troubled face. "Forget all about London parties, Georgina, for I dare say your Mama has never been to a harvest supper herself, unless in her childhood she was acquainted with country life."

"Oh, I doubt it, for she has spoken only of being taken in her baby carriage to St. James's Park—or was it Hyde Park—by her nurse, or when she became older, by her governess."

"Then you have nothing with which to reproach yourself, for your Mama cannot advise you, even were she here. It is the simplest of occasions so you need wear only your simplest gown. Not one scrap of jewelry must you wear, in case the people think you are putting on airs. And make sure that your shoes are comfortable for there will be a little country dancing."

"How kind of you, Cloris." Georgina flew to her wardrobe and began sorting through her extensive array of gowns. "This? Oh, no, it has seed pearls round the collar, and this has too many satin flounces. Oh, Chloris, dear, do help me, for my mind is quite in turmoil."

Chloris crossed to the wardrobe and cast her eyes along the hanging gowns. "Good heavens, Georgina. Did you entirely strip your bedroom in London? You have as many gowns as if you were the Queen herself, setting out on a State visit."

"Mama is so particular, you see. She insisted I pack morning and afternoon dresses, dinner and ball gowns, walking costumes, and, oh so many, for every occasion that should arise."

"Except harvest suppers," murmured Chloris. "How could your respected Mama have overlooked such a simple occasion, for it comes round every year?" She glanced into Georgina's stricken face and laughed. "Forgive me, Georgina, I was only teasing. How could your Mama possibly know that corn has to be reaped long before it is delivered to your kitchen door by the baker's boy? When you return to London, you will be able to dazzle your friends by your knowledge of farming."

"I doubt that very much, for I could not understand at all when Quentin and Sir Lionel spoke of the new reaper and what it would mean to farming. I confess that my mind wandered away when I saw it and Quentin tried to explain about lucifer fields."

Chloris gave a gurgle of laughter. "Not lucifer, Georgina, but lucerne."

"I still don't know what it is, whatever it is."

"You don't have to know, Georgina. Leave it to Quentin and Sir Lionel. They have been farming for hundreds of years. All you need to do is to look pretty tonight and you will have no difficulty there. How about this muslin dress with the little autumn leaf design. It is quite simple but elegant with the round neck and puffed sleeves. The color of the leaves matches your hair. A light shawl about your shoulders and you'll be perfectly dressed and no brows will be raised, I assure you."

"Oh, thank you, Chloris. You're so clever and it sounds exactly right. I thought the pattern pretty myself, but Mama was not at all pleased when it was made up. She said I looked like a milk-maid for it had panniered sides and it was not a kind thing to remind people of poor dear Marie Antoinette."

"Marie Antoinette?" Chloris stared into the grave blue eyes. "What's has she to do with anything?"

"Don't you remember how the poor dear queen used to go to her model village and dress as a milkmaid, pretending to be a country girl, just like the peasants?"

"Yes, of course, but the poor dear—I mean the Queen of France—was guillotined over fifty years ago. And we are not in France."

"But the emigres, dear Chloris. It would be insensitive to remind them of their poor dear queen. And one does still meet them in Society."

Chloris laid the muslin dress on the bed. "I can promise there'll not be a single French emigre at the Fields' Harvest Supper, so you may safely wear the gown, without ruffling anyone's sensibilities."

Georgina beamed at her. "What will you wear, Chloris?"

Chloris smiled and glanced at the brimming wardrobe. "My choice will not be so difficult. And who will look at me when the beautiful Miss Davenport is gracing the scene? People . . ." she paused, thinking of Matt. "There are people most eager to see the Field House guest. Your fame has spread abroad, my dear, and as in most villages, they gossip and speculate."

"Speculate? On what?" Georgina's eyes were so wide and innocent that Chloris was tempted to ask if dear Mama had not made her intentions for this visit clear enough. Surely Georgina was aware that dear Mama's hopes were pinned on Quentin coming up to scratch with a proposal of marriage?

Instead, she shrugged and smiled. "Oh how long you will stay and how you like the country life, I suppose."

Georgina looked out of the window into the blue sky. "It is a most delightful day and the countryside is beautiful. I am so looking forward to this evening and to meeting everyone. The country is most beneficial, just as Mama said it would be."

Chloris's own preparations for the evening celebration were untroubled by thoughts of Marie Antoinette or any other queen, for her wide-skirted dress was plain and lacked panniers. It was of white muslin with pale green stripes and like Georgina's, the sleeves were puffed and the neckline simple. She tied back her hair with a matching green ribbon and slipped her feet into sandals. Her father had given her permission to use her late mother's accessories, and Chloris chose a fine white shawl of soft cashmere.

He was waiting for her in the hallway and she was pleased to see that he no longer stiffened at her approach, recognizing the likeness to her mother with a touch of pain. His own outfit was of well-cut tweed, rather somber in shade, but lacking the magisterial effect of the unrelieved black he usually wore.

She smiled and reached up to kiss his cheek, glad that the lines of taut suffering had softened and his eyes were more at peace, feeling his loss less keenly.

"We'll go to Field House in the carriage, my dear, then walk over to the farm. Sir Lionel swears that his gout is better but he may prefer to take the trap. Since he has never missed a harvest supper yet, he is determined to arrive one way or the other." As he handed Chloris into the carriage, he gave her a look of approval. "Very pretty you look, my dear, but that is only natural, after all."

Chloris smiled. "Thank you, Father." She understood his meaning but knew that she could never achieve the perfection in his eyes that her mother had.

As they travelled towards Field House, she tucked her hand under his arm. In this relaxed state, she decided to probe a little into the progress of the coastguards' plans.

"And have her majesty's ministers finalized their schemes yet for our coastal protection, Father? It is a long time since you mentioned a new scheme, but then," she shrugged carelessly, "government offices move slowly, don't they? The plan may still be years away."

"Not years, my dear. Months perhaps, but hopefully only weeks. Questions in Parliament are increasing in volume, I hear, so that plans may be sprung upon us at any time. We are far from

London and may receive notice only when the scheme is in operation."

"You mean that you will not be told until then? That is hardly fair since you are requested to administer whatever they decide." Her voice sounded too indignant and she checked herself, but her father was smiling.

"Dear child, to be so concerned with my feelings. I am only a country Justice of the Peace. Great decisions are made in the capital and do not carry with them any demand for full consultation of minor officials."

Chloris subsided, feeling rather ashamed. She had not been thinking of her father's position as he supposed, only of how she could help Matt. She glanced up at her father and found his eyes upon her. He was smiling.

"This is not a night for such reflections, my dear. We celebrate the harvest safely brought in. What a splendid young man Quentin Field is. I doubt if Sir Lionel would have invested in new machinery but now that it has proved a success, he is overjoyed at being able to crow over his competitors."

Chloris said, "Before long, I expect Sir Lionel will take all the credit and convince himself that he sent Quentin to the Great Exhibition with that sole purpose in mind."

They laughed together as Field House came in sight. How nice it was, Chloris thought, to see her father beginning to take an interest in life again. She half-expected that he would refuse the invitation to the harvest supper, but Sir Lionel had added his own message to the card, declaring that the affair would be intolerable without a companion who could be trusted not to kick up his heels with the rest. The appeal had worked for Gerard Blair had known Sir Lionel in the days when he was first into the country dance with the prettiest girl in the village on his arm.

They entered the hall of Field House to be greeted by Sir Lionel, who was testing a selection of walking sticks, followed patiently by his valet bearing the complete selection from silver-headed canes to sturdy ash sticks. Sir Lionel chuckled affably.

"Gout nearly better, thanks be to God and not to that young sawbones, but I'll take a stick just the same. You and I, Gerard, will go in the trap and let these young people make their own way. Up the stairs with you, Chloris, and help our young Miss who has appeared twice, then disappeared as suddenly with some nonsense about curls." He looked at Chloris's thick dark hair, tied back with a ribbon. "No primping of curls for you, Miss, but you're the prettier for it. 'Tis London ways, of course, and that Mama she's always prating about. Sounds a regular dragon to me but hold your tongue on that, Miss, if you please, for I'd not want to hurt the lass." He grinned and winked at Chloris. "Off you go and bring her down before the night's over. A glass before we go, Gerard?"

As usual, Sir Lionel awaited no reply from anyone and turned towards the study while Chloris mounted the stairs to Georgina's room.

"Oh, Chloris, how good to see you. Is it not ridiculous, but since Mama disliked this dress so, I have never worn it, though the panniers were removed. In consequence I cannot think which hair style suits it best. Sir Lionel has glared at me twice, I swear, and he must be losing patience, so please tell me what I must do."

Her blue eyes were so full of appeal that Chloris hid her amusement. "Far from being impatient, Sir Lionel has taken my father off into

117

the study to have a glass of something, so you may rest easy on that score." She looked at Georgina's reflected face in the looking glass. "I am convinced," she said solemnly, "that the poor dear queen would have worn the simplest of hair styles when she played country girl. A ribbon anyway, but matching her gown, of course."

Georgina's russet hair was brushed and secured by a golden ribbon, the bow high on the nape of her neck, then the two girls descended to the hall.

Quentin came out of the study and paused, watching their descent. He was dressed in a plain white, open-necked shirt and dark trousers, his thick hair looking fairer against the tan of his skin. His throat was a tanned column, smooth and strong, and Chloris thought how handsome he looked. He greeted both girls with the same courtesy, showing no added warmth to either, and Chloris wondered if Mrs. Davenport's plans had not been perfectly understood by Georgina; if they were, then Quentin was not playing by the accepted rules. If he intended Georgina to be his wife, he was not showering her with flowery compliments, but then, Quentin was always one to keep his feelings and thoughts to himself.

Sir Lionel and Mister Blair came from the study and Sir Lionel smiled at the girls. "If you've got your curls in place, m'dear, we'll be off to the supper. As pretty a pair as I ever saw, eh, Quentin?"

"Quite so, Father," Quentin agreed. "And with Ruth to complete the trio, why, we shall be graced by the Three Graces, indeed."

He offered an arm to each girl and they set off for the farm, while Sir Lionel and Mister Blair climbed into the trap.

Long before they reached the field close by the

118

farmhouse, and set aside for the gathering, the scent of roasting meat and hot bread reached them. A low murmur of voices drifted towards them and the lanes leading to the field were full of hurrying people, colorfully dressed and Sunday-suited villagers. Children dashed fore and aft of their parents, shining, fresh-washed faces split into grins of delight as they shouted and jostled each other.

Georgina stared about her in amazement. "Does your father employ all these people, Quentin?"

Quentin laughed. "I doubt it, but if the whole village comes, they'll be welcome. We shan't count heads and turn away those we don't employ."

Sir Lionel was already there and talking to the farm manager, Joss Darling, who glanced over at the newcomers and touched his forehead. Meggie Darling, his fifteen-year-old daughter, was standing back, smiling shyly, her eyes open wide at Georgina.

Quentin beckoned her forward and she gave the girls a little bob as she murmured a greeting.

"Will you show us where we are to sit, Meggie?" Quentin asked. "Since you are our hostess, we are in your hands. From the delicious aromas coming from your kitchen window, you must have had a busy day."

"Yes, Master Quentin, but there's been a lot of help from the wives and young Tom and his boys have been fetching and carrying all day."

Quentin grinned at Chloris. "What did I tell you? Young Tom wants Mister Darling's job as well as my own. I must walk carefully with that young man."

They reached a long trestle table, surrounded by stools and set a little apart from the rest.

"Here, sir," said Meggie. "This table is for

Squire and his party. You'll get a good view when it begins and there'll be dancing after the food, like as not."

"Thank you, Meggie. Is your own young man coming?"

Meggie blushed. "I haven't got a young man, sir."

"You will have after tonight, I'm sure. When they find out you can cook as well as look pretty, why they'll be swarming up to your front door."

Meggie giggled, turned and fled back to the farmhouse.

"What a sweet child," said Georgina, looking about her with interest. "She spoke of dancing. Where is the orchestra, Quentin?"

"Over there," Quentin pointed.

Georgina looked puzzled. "I can see no-one save the old man sitting on a barrel, smoking his pipe."

"That's him, or it, if you prefer. The finest fiddler in these parts and much in demand, I can tell you. The Cornwells and Randalls wanted him for their own suppers tonight but he preferred my offer."

Georgina still looked doubtfully at the old man. "Your payment was higher?"

Quentin grinned. "Lord, no, he doesn't play for money. He likes our ale better than theirs and I promised him a barrel of our finest to be delivered to his cottage tomorrow."

"Goodness me," breathed Georgina, round-eyed. "He must be very good, then, to know all the music for waltzes and polkas."

"No such thing, my dear. This is not London Society and our people don't bother with newfangled dances. They do what they have always done, dance country style. Look, Chloris, isn't that Ruth coming over the field? Who is she with?"

Chloris looked. "Oh, it's Matt with her. They must have met on the way. I'll go and greet them."

Matt waved as Chloris neared them and Chloris thought again how handsome he was in his white frilled shirt and black riding breeches. His dark eyes were brilliant and his smile made her heart beat more quickly. Chloris kissed Ruth's cheek, complimenting her on the pink cotton dress that went so well with her brown curly hair. Ruth, too, was bright-eyed and smiling, her cheeks becomingly flushed.

"I haven't seen your Neil Kernick yet," Chloris said on a teasing note.

"Neil Kernick?" asked Matt, looking down at Ruth, whose flush deepened.

"People will matchmake so," Ruth said with a hint of crossness in her voice. "I have told you, Chloris, that he is not my Neil Kenrick. I visit his mother, that's all." She glanced up at Matt and there was appeal in her voice. "Even your own mother, Matt, wil have me being courted by Neil Kernick, when it is no such thing, and you know that very well!"

Matt smiled. "Well, he's not such a bad catch, after all. A girl could do worse."

Ruth shook her head impatiently and hurried off to greet Georgina and Quentin.

Chloris gazed after her for a moment. "Oh, dear, I'm sorry I teased her, but I do think that Neil Kernick is fond of her, but naturally Ruth may have other ideas."

"I don't doubt it," Matt said lazily, and shrugged the matter away. He looked over to the trestle and his gaze fell on Georgina. "So that's the beautiful Miss Davenport! I'd say the reports haven't lied. What a stunning girl!"

"Come, let me present you," Chloris said in a carefully controlled voice.

"Present me, be damned! I can do that for myself." He strode up to the table and swept Georgina a bow. "How do you do, Miss Davenport? I am Matthew Trevelyan and beg the honor of partnering you in a considerable number of dances throughout the evening." He grinned mockingly at Quentin. "Since you have the lady as house guest, you will not deny lesser mortals the pleasure of Miss Davenport's company, will you?"

"That decision rests with the lady herself, Matt," Quentin said coolly.

"I shall be happy to partner you, Mister Trevelyan," said Georgina. "Providing I have knowledge of the dance. I believe I learned some in my schooldays."

"Which are barely behind you, I'd guess," Matt said cheerfully and took a seat beside her.

Chloris noted the slight compression of Quentin's lips but he turned to Ruth and engaged her in conversation. For a moment Chloris felt an outsider. She had hoped that Matt would seek her company that evening, after his last remark on the cliffs, but she acknowledged, somewhat wryly, that his aim was to disconcert Quentin with his attentions to Georgina. She knew Matt well enough to realize that hidden deep within him was an envy of Quentin's position, though he would never have admitted it. When he tired of that game, she knew he would turn to her as he always had done.

More people were arriving as dusk became evening. The fire in the middle of the field was set alight and Sir Lionel and Mister Blair joined them.

Noise died away as the opening ceremony began.

From the darkening fields a procession of men came into the firelight. Leading them was young Tom, holding aloft the corn dolly plaited from the husks of the last cropping of the corn. He strode forward proudly, a small sheaf of corn under his arm. There was applause as he took his place before the fire. The file of men who had taken part in the reaping ringed the fire. Young Tom raised the corn dolly and the men roared in chorus " 'Tis made," then Tom took the sheaf of corn from under his arm and tossed it into the fire.

"Why does he do that?" whispered Georgina.

"To burn out the witch who follows every sheaf that is bound," explained Quentin. "She hides in the last one, so we burn it and she has no power to harm the corn harvested."

The circle of men gave three hurrahs and stood back, their eyes sliding expectantly towards the farmhouse. From the kitchen door issued a file of women, each bearing a tray of tankards, the frothing ale brimming over the edges. Three times the men reached for the tankards and three times each tankard was emptied.

Young Tom, swelling with pride and beaming self-consciously, passed the main trestle, the corn dolly still held aloft. He disappeared towards the farmhouse.

"It will be hung in the kitchen," Quentin said. "To ward off evil spirits over the year until it is replaced by a new corn dolly from next year's reaping."

The men left the fire and grouped themselves before the trestle. Every tankard had been replenished and tankards of ale stood on the table in front of Sir Lionel and Quentin.

The spokesman for the workers raised his tankard. "A toast for the Squire."

They drank deeply, then the tankard rose

again. "A toast to Master Quentin."

Sir Lionel and Quentin Field both rose to their feet, tankards in hand.

"And I give you," boomed Sir Lionel, "a toast to the best harvest yet. To Joss Darling and to everyone of you who made it possible. May we prosper together." His head went back and the contents of a full tankard disappeared down his throat. He wiped his lips with the back of his hand as the men had done and beamed on them happily.

Quentin held up his own tankard. "My thanks and congratulations to you all for a great harvest. And let us not forget our gallant band of stone-pickers, led by young Tom there. Since they are overyoung to join us in ale, they may drink their fill from the five gallon jar of fresh-made lemonade that came over from Field House in the Squire's trap." Like his father, Quentin tilted back his head and downed the ale without pause.

Quentin's manner towards the men of the fields was so easy, and his words were as one man to another, not master to employee. Chloris felt a surge of pride as if she too was part of the Field family and shared with the men the happiness of a good corn harvest. She glanced at the faces about the top table and her gaze caught Matt's.

He was smiling but one eyebrow rose in derision. He murmured so low that only Chloris caught the words. "God save us from worthy men and lords of the manor."

The workers cheered and clapped as Quentin sat down, then there was a rush to get places at the long trestles set round the fire, where plates of beef and ham were steaming in unison with great dishes of vegetables. Bread and more ale was brought and the field settled into the business of eating and drinking.

9

As the dishes were cleared away and the trestles moved back to create a large enough area for the dancing, the fiddler's barrel was rolled to one side of the top table. The old man bowed to the Field House party and again to the assembled villagers before seating himself once again on the barrel. A quart jug of ale was between his feet and from the shine on his face, it was obvious that he was already well fortified to endure an evening of fiddle-playing. He drew his bow across the strings, then launched into a simple tune.

"Oh, I do know this one," Georgina said, clapping her hands. "We form eights, do we not?"

"Eights it is," said Matt, reaching for her hand. "Allow me to be your partner, Miss Davenport."

Georgina withdrew her hand and smiled brightly at him. "Perhaps another one, Mister Trevelyan." She glanced at Quentin who rose.

"It is the host who leads out, Matt, and since Father has declined to frolic, it is my pleasure to partner our special guest, Miss Davenport. But do help us make up the set."

Georgina was well-versed in the courtesies

due to her host and she had no intention of relaxing them, even though she was in the country. Chloris watched the two elegant figures move into the center of the ring and she smiled, glancing at Matt. His mouth still held a smile but his eyes were narrowed on the couple. He lifted his tankard and drained it, making no attempt to join in the set. She glanced towards Ruth and saw the figure of Neil Kenrick moving towards her. Ruth might deny any attachment on her part but Neil's determined approach did not signify·indifference on his part. Chloris waited for Matt to invite her into the set being formed but he made no move, save to fill his tankard from the jug on the table. She knew he had been piqued by the rebuff but he had counted without Georgina's sense of duty.

"When you are better acquainted with Miss Davenport, Matt," Chloris said, "you will learn that her mother's strictures on etiquette are second nature to her. She will not deviate one inch from them." As Matt turned his gaze on her, she smiled. "She will dance next with you, I am convinced."

Matt shrugged. "If I ask her again, that is." He returned his gaze to the dancers.

"I'm sure you will," Chloris said softly and Matt looked at her sharply.

"What does that mean?"

"A challenge, and you will not refuse it and give Quentin the victory—or the lady."

Matt grinned, his good humor restored. "Confound you, Chloris, you know me too well. The girl's pretty enough, and I'd give a keg of brandy to see Quentin furious with jealousy, but if she's starched up with etiquette, she'll do nothing to displease Quentin. She means to have him, does she?"

126

"I imagine so, but as far as I can tell, they haven't yet reached an understanding."

"An understanding! My God, what a term to use! Have they no fire in their blood?" He laughed suddenly and pulled Chloris to her feet. "I cannot imagine a demure miss like that flinging herself into the sea like you did."

"Hush, Matt, for pity's sake. My father might hear you."

Matt gave her his old reckless grin as they joined the new sets assembling. "Wait till you see my boat, the Heron she's called, and you'll not think of your father when we put to sea in her."

The movements of the dance separated them before Chloris could declare that she had no intention of putting to sea in a freetrader's boat. She would admire it, certainly, but not even Matt could tempt her to cross the Channel on such a dangerous pursuit.

The evening lengthened into night and the fire was constantly rebuilt, paling the moon and stars into insignificance. Hot food and quantities of ale had the dancers red-faced and perspiring but none thought of leaving, save the mothers of small tired children, together with the most elderly of the villagers. The fiddler played on, and if some of his notes grew discordant, no-one noticed or commented on the frequency with which his quart jug was lifted. Harvest Supper came only once in a year and the workers and their families intended wringing out of it every last drop of enjoyment.

Matt took Georgina into the dance many times, occasionally inviting Ruth or Chloris to partner him, but his attentions were for Georgina.

Sir Lionel and Mr. Blair had returned to Field House, thus enabling the younger element to become a little more riotous, though still held back from complete abandonment by Master Quentin's presence.

Chloris and Quentin had returned, breathless, to the trestle and were sipping cider and watching the dancers. Quentin turned a smile on Chloris.

"I think Georgina has enjoyed herself and Matt has certainly put his best efforts into attaining that end."

Chloris glanced at him. "Do you mind that he has partnered Georgina so constantly?"

"Not in the least, since he had it in mind from the start."

"You knew that?"

"Of course. Georgina enjoys flattery and if Matt wishes to play the gallant, she will enjoy the evening even more." He smiled at Chloris. "We both know Matt. His attentions to Georgina are a challenge to me." He gave an amused chuckle. "But he reckons without our esteemed Mrs. Davenport. Georgina may appear fluffy-headed but she is well aware of the rules laid down by her dear mama. Enough talking, Chloris. We're here to dance." He rose and took her hand and they joined a new circle forming on the grass. They danced apart most of the time, coming together when the rings met. Hands clasped left and right as the dancers changed partners until at last, Quentin and Chloris were once more facing each other. Chloris curtseyed to Quentin's bow.

She saw Georgina and Matt, flushed and as breathless as they were themselves. They joined together and began to walk back to the trestle table.

"Goodness, how warm it is," said Georgina, fanning herself with a lace handkerchief. "You are such an expert dancer, Mr. Trevelyan, I am quite overcome and must sit quietly and take a cooling glass of cider. Do sit with me, Chloris, for I am

sure we are both completely out of breath." She
smiled up at Matt. "Will you not take cider with
us, Mr. Trevelyan?"

"Thank you, Miss Davenport, but cider is not
to my taste tonight." He grinned at Quentin.
"Your ale now, that is to my taste and I'd best go
before your men empty all the barrels." He
bowed. "Ladies." Then he turned and crossed the
field.

"I think we must gather our party together
and take ourselves off. Rest here, Georgina, while
Chloris and I find Ruth. I'll take her home in the
trap when we reach Field House."

He took Chloris's arm and they skirted the
dancers. The fire was still blazing but beyond its
reach the night was dark, though stars were vying
with the firelight. A few farm vehicles made pools
of shadow but Quentin saw no-one there. He
smiled, guessing that with the full coming of darkness, the mothers of female offspring were
keeping them well in view. The strong ale of Field
House farm had been known to result in at least
one unwelcome child.

A slight movement beyond the last farmcart
caught his eye. He almost paused, but on reflection, decided his best course was to make a
casual inspection without Chloris by his side. He
thought he had glimpsed the swing of a skirt and
heard a vague murmur of voices. As landlord, he
felt compelled to check that no young female was
in danger through overindulgence. He glanced
back as they passed. A bursting spark from the
fire illuminated a smiling face above a white
frilled shirt. At the same moment Chloris pointed
ahead.

"Isn't that Ruth?"

Quentin took a firmer grasp of Choris's arm
and they walked quickly after the slow-moving

figure of a girl, pink dress swaying as she moved.

"Yes, that's Ruth. Do go on ahead, Chloris, and tell her what we've decided. I just want a word with someone back there."

Chloris nodded and Quentin released her arm. Not until he saw the two girls meet, did he turn back into the darkness.

"Ruth, I've hardly seen you all night," Chloris said. "Hasn't it been a splendid affair?"

"Splendid," answered Ruth in a muffled voice. Her gaze was on the grass and her face turned from the firelight. Chloris was puzzled by the flat tone.

"Haven't you enjoyed it, Ruth? Is there something wrong?"

"Wrong? What could be wrong?"

"I—I don't know, but you sound a little—a little unhappy."

Ruth raised her gaze. "Unhappy? Oh, no, certainly not! A splendid affair, as you said. I am just tired, that's all. I shall go home."

"Quentin says he will take you in the trap if you come back with us to Field House, unless you have made other arrangements."

"Other arrangements?"

"With Mr. Kernick, perhaps—"

Ruth whirled away, her pink skirt flying. "Not Mr. Kernick, nor anyone else, and I don't want to go to Field House. Please thank Quentin for his offer but I'll see myself home. Please leave me alone, Chloris."

Then she turned and ran into the darkness, hair bobbing and skirts swaying as she ran. Chloris stared after her, perplexed. This was not the calm, unruffled Ruth she had always known. What had upset her, for surely something had. Had that flashing upward look held tears? Neil Kernick was not amongst the dancers, she noted.

130

In spite of all Ruth's protestations, could he have been the cause of her distress? Chloris turned away and walked slowly back to the trestle to rejoin Georgina. Ruth had seemed very gay all evening. Chloris had seen her dancing and laughing with many of the young men, including Quentin and Matt. She could think of no reason for her refusal to go to Field House.

Quentin was relieved to leave Chloris with Ruth. He strolled back, soft-footed on the grass. Matt, he knew, had drunk a great deal of ale. Quentin had noted the brilliance in his eyes and the rakish tilt of his smile. There was a vibrant vitality about Matt. He was the kind of man that even the most demure girl would look at twice from under lowered lids, and the type of man fond mothers eyed warily. Quentin thought of his meeting with Matt outside the tavern in Weymouth, and he remembered the sight of Matt's arm encircling the barmaid's waist. Matt might have drunk just enough to forget that the estate workers' daughters were not in the same category. He reminded himself that not only estate workers were here but a number of village people too. The girl inside the dress he had glimpsed may well be from the village and no real concern of his but he would feel easier in mind if he made sure of that.

He had reached the spot and his glance was casual. It was Matt all right. He heard the soft teasing laugh and saw that Matt's hands were spread wide, both palms on the wood of the wagon. Whoever stood between those arms was temporarily imprisoned. A female voice reached Quentin.

"Is it late, Mister Matt. There'll be a whipping from my dad. Please, Mister Matt."

Quentin stood very still. The young scared voice was interrupted by Matt's teasing laugh.

"What a little rabbit you are. Didn't I catch you kissing young Joel when your dad had his back turned?"

"Joel is kin, Mister Matt. 'Tis different."

"So what's a kiss between friends? There's no-one to see you, now is there?"

Quentin forced himself to move. "Save me, Matt. And Meggie's right, it's different with kin."

Matt straightened, his gaze turning to Quentin. Without taking his eyes off Matt, Quentin spoke.

"Go back to the house, Meggie. Your father will be looking for you if you stay out any longer."

There was a rustle of skirts, a gasp of relief, then Meggie was gone. Neither man turned to watch her go. Quentin felt cold with anger and his eyes raked Matt's flushed face.

"Good God, Matt! What the devil do you think you're doing?"

Matt returned his angry look. "What I do is my own concern. Go to hell!"

"I make it my concern when it involves the daughter of my farm manager."

"I know she is. She told me that."

"Did she also tell you her age? Good God, man, she's a child, barely fifteen."

"I wasn't proposing to rape the girl, dammit! You sound as if you'd like to string me up, and all for teasing the young chit about a simple kiss."

"I think you've had too much to drink."

Matt's temper erupted. "Damn you to hell! You and your kind think to lord it over the confounded county. Can't think why I bothered to come anyway, save that Chloris asked me."

"Chloris? You've spared her little attention tonight in your bid to show Georgina what a dull fellow I am. Calm down, Matt. Sleep it off and you'll feel better tomorrow. Let's not have an argument. It's been too good an evening. I'm taking the girls back to Field House now, Chloris included."

"Chloris included? Why do you stress that? Do you think I shall force my attentions on someone else, after being thwarted in the matter of the farm wench?" Matt gave a short, hard laugh. "You sound like a broody hen, counting her chicks."

Quentin's lips tightened. "Since Mr. Blair is at Field House with the carriage, it seems logical to take Chloris there, wouldn't you say?"

"She could walk home with me."

"She could, and probably would if you asked her, but I prefer she comes to Field House and goes home with her father. Leave her alone, Matt, she's not your kind."

Perhaps his voice had held too much vehemence and Matt's eyes narrowed in speculation.

"Isn't the beautiful idiot enough for you, old friend? Do you have an interest in Chloris too?"

"For her happiness, yes, and I doubt she'll find it with you."

Matt grinned. "She's in love with me, always has been. She'll come when I call."

"More's the pity, since you prefer lower company. Don't involve her in that. She has more to lose than you have. Leave her out of your plans, if you've any regard for her."

"Oh, I have the greatest regard for Chloris. Probably more than you think."

Matt was grinning again, but Quentin caught the mocking note in his voice. He nodded curtly and turned on his heel. "Goodnight, Matt."

He heard Matt's chuckle behind him as he strode away.

10

Two weeks after the harvest supper, Sir Lionel gave his customary dinner party for his personal friends and neighboring landowners. The time was chosen to fall between the end of the corn harvest and just before the barley gathering. The sheaves of corn, now safely under cover in the barns, were spread to dry before the flailing and winnowing could begin.

All the large rooms of Field House were opened and Belling, with his legion of maids and cleaning women, washed and polished until every item of furniture and silver sparkled and shone. Sir Lionel, his gout further improved, looked forward to the coming of his rival estate owners, Joseph Randall and William Cornwell, with their wives and sons. One son apiece, as he had himself, but neither young Charles nor James had the flair of Quentin, he was convinced. Fine young fellows, of course, but not in the same class when it came to new innovations, like that hand-operated winnowing fan Quentin had designed with the local ironsmith and carpenter. He forgot his own first rejection of the reaping machine and had now convinced himself that he had favored it from the

135

start. He smiled at his reflection over the cravat as he dressed for dinner. Randall and Cornwell should be in no doubt that Field House led the county in all things new.

He descended the wide staircase into the hall to await the first guests. Quentin was already there, a tall, fair-haired but younger edition of himself and both in dark frockcoats and spotless linen.

"Georgina not down yet, eh?" Sir Lionel asked. "Hope she'll not pop up and down like she did for the harvest supper." He chuckled and Quentin smiled.

"She knows the form better for these occasions. Harvest supper outfits don't figure much in London. She'll be here any minute."

Both turned to the stairs as the soft tapping of slippers sounded on the uncarpeted stairs treads. Georgina swept down to them, a vision in cloudy blue gauze, silk ribbons threaded through her russet hair and sapphires winking.

"Delightful, my dear," said Sir Lionel. "You'll put every lady in the shade. Can't think why you've not been captured already by some royal prince."

Georgina beamed on him. "Thank you, sir, but as to royal princes, why they're all still in the nursery, are they not?"

"Why—er—yes, I suppose they are." He was nonplussed for a moment. "But just a figure of speech, my dear. I dare say London abounds with coronets, nevertheless." He patted the hand resting on his sleeve and then turned to the doorway as carriage wheels rolled up the driveway.

Chloris and her father were the first to arrive. As Sir Lionel greeted Mr. Blair and Chloris kissed Georgina's cheek, Quentin let his eyes rest for a moment on the girl in rose silk, dark shining hair piled on her head and secured by rose-bud decorated combs. A string of creamy pearls round her slender throat highlighted the honey-gold skin. Quentin had the urge to draw his fingers lightly across the bared neck and feel the warmth of that fine skin, but he did not move until Chloris turned her smiling green eyes upon him. He bowed over her hand, keeping his expression calm and welcoming.

"I will echo Father's words to Georgina. Delightful, my dear. Quite ravishing." His eyes met hers. "You once accused me of not saying pretty things to you like the young gentlemen of Dorchester. I stand accused and beg pardon. You have grown up quite beautifully and I promise never to call you helter-skelter again."

"What a pretty speech, Quentin. Thank you for it." Chloris's eyes laughed into his. "You have grown up tolerably well yourself, and I will never call you sober-sides again."

"Touché." Quentin grinned and tucked her arm in his. "For that small mercy, you may now help us greet our guests, for you're as much at home here as anyone. I rely on you and Georgina to entertain our young gentlemen for I don't doubt Father will monopolize his contemporaries."

"And who will you pay court to?"

"Since we have Mrs. Trevelyan and Mrs. Kernick, together with the Cornwell and Randall ladies, I shall dance attendance dutifully and hope they'll succeed in getting their heads together after dinner, allowing me to withdraw gracefully." He cocked an eyebrow in mockery at Chloris. "See how well-trained I am with not a Mama Davenport in sight."

Chloris laughed. "How unkind we are to the poor lady. I'm sure she is an excellent person but do let me know if she ever engages to visit. I shall try and have business elsewhere."

"Coward," he murmured. "You would leave me alone on the barricades?"

"You will be in my thoughts," she promised solemnly, though her green eyes laughed.

Although Quentin still smiled, his eyes met hers with an expression she could not read, a strangely intent look that belied the humorous words. It held softness and warmth and her heart was touched but she was distracted from further conjecture by the arrival of more guests.

Ruth Baxter, small and dark in a wide-skirted dress of cream taffeta, came in with the tall, redhaired Neil Kernick and his mother.

"We met on the way over," Ruth said, slightly defensive under Chloris's smile.

"And why should you walk when we had the carriage?" said Mrs. Kernick, a tall gentle lady whose upswept hair was a paler shade of red than her son's. "How do you do, Sir Lionel? So kind of you to ask us." She shook hands with Quentin. "Ruth has been telling us of the success of the new reaper. We grow only a little corn ourselves. Neil is more interested in horses."

"We must talk later, Neil," said Quentin. "I would value your opinion on a chestnut I've just bought."

More guests arrived, including Matt and his mother, and Quentin escorted the ladies, Mrs. Trevelyan and the wives of Mr. Cornwell and Mr. Randall, into the sitting room. Sarah Cornwell, just sixteen years old, was beckoned to sit beside Georgina on the couch, her shyness quickly abating under Georgina's artless tongue, though she stared, as if intoxicated, at Georgina's beauty.

"How sweet of Miss Davenport to take pity on my Sarah," whispered Mrs. Cornwell to Chloris. "But one can understand it when she is acting as

138

hostess for Sir Lionel. Sarah can be tiresomely mute at times."

Chloris looked over towards the couch and smiled. "I would hardly call her mute at this moment. She is quite animated, and I assure you that Georgina is enjoying the conversation. She is the kindest person and her enjoyment is quite genuine."

The room began to fill as the men joined them. Chloris caught Matt's eye and he gave her a grin as he stood with Charles Randall and James Cornwell, the large sons of Sir Lionel's neighboring landowners.

Wine trays were circulated by Belling and the maids, Quentin moving amongst the ladies, smiling and talking. Chloris watched him as he paused in front of young Sarah Cornwell. She knew he would treat her with the same courtesy as he would any full-grown lady and she admired him for it. It did not make him a dull dog as Matt would have said, but then Matt was not one to hide his feelings out of consideration for others.

Chloris leaned back in her chair, sipping her wine and comparing the two men. How unalike they were and how strange that Matt, the careless adventurer, should retain first place in her mind when Quentin was equally handsome and cared so much more for people.

Then the dinner gong was sounded and they entered the splendid dining room in pairs, Sir Lionel and her father escorting the Randall and Cornwell wives. Quentin took in Sarah and Matt bowed to Georgina. Chloris and Ruth were offered escorts by Charles Randall and James Cornwell. Both young men took after their fathers and there was no mistaking them for anything else but gentlemen farmers. Their fathers entered with

Mrs. Trevelyan and Mrs. Kernick and Neil, partnerless, brought up the rear, a rueful grin on his face.

The table was magnificently laid with crystal goblets, gleaming silver cutlery and covers of lace-edged linen. The walls were panelled in wood, but shone like satin through years of careful polishing, and the tall windows stood open to allow in the perfumed breezes from the garden beyond the terrace.

Since the wives of Sir Lionel's friends were seated one on each side of him and the order of seating ran by age down the table, Chloris found herself between James Cornwell and Neil Kernick. Ruth Baxter, beyond James, was being entertained by Charles Randall. Quentin, Chloris noted, had young Sarah beside him and Georgina across the table from him. It was a measure of Quentin's concern that he had thought to place the young girl in a position of certain inclusion in the conversation. She sensed this and gave him a warm smile as he caught her eye. Matt saw the exchange of smiles and raised a sardonic eyebrow at Chloris. Chloris knew that look. Matt would not have wasted his time on Sarah but sought out the prettiest girl for his gallantry. Since he was seated beside Georgina, he had no problem, she mused, yet it was all a great glorious game to Matt and she knew he would seek her out when he tired of it. He always had and she saw no reason why he should change. She turned to James Cornwell.

He was an amiable, ruddy-faced, quite genial young man and she flirted mildly with him, delighting in his clumsy gallantry. Neil Kernick she found an amusing and quick-witted table companion. Like Quentin, he had inherited responsibility early and was of a more serious nature. She also noted that his eyes rested

140

interest in Ruth, though Ruth herself had denied any attachment most volubly. A pity really, Chloris thought. Neil had much to offer a girl and was a man of kind dispostion.

The meal was a happy one, since the harvest had been good, and although the conversation centered on the activities of the county, it was only natural since they were, after all, a farming community. Mr. Blair, though no farmer, was almost as knowledgeable for he was a countryman, too.

Georgina, the perfect hostess to her fingertips, knew the exact moment to gather the ladies and escort them to the drawing room, leaving the men to relax and draw closer over their wine.

In the drawing room, the housemaids served tea and coffee, light cakes and biscuits. As Quentin had hoped, the older ladies joined forces to compare recipes and discuss domestic matters. The four younger girls grouped themselves on couches set in an alcove beside an open window and Georgina held court on London fashions. Chloris had never admired her so much, for fluffy-headed as she might be, she never made the mistake of monopolizing the conversation. Young Sarah was enchanted and blossomed visibly under Georgina's spell.

Sir Lionel, replete with good food and wine, leaned back in his chair, eyeing the tip of his cigar. Then he raised his eyes to William Cornwell.

"Did you get your reaper blade fixed, William?" he asked with malicious amusement.

Quentin glanced at his father, knowing that Sir Lionel's moment of triumph had come. He smiled inwardly and rose.

"With your permission, gentlemen, I will join the ladies and see that they have everything they need." He glanced questioningly at the younger men. "Perhaps you'd care to stroll down to the stables, Neil, to look at my chestnut?"

Neil rose. "I would indeed."

"Bought a stallion myself recently," Matt said casually and grinned at Quentin. "I'll take a look at your cattle, too, and see how they compare."

"Do that," said Quentin, grinning back. "How about you two? Want to stay and talk about reapers?"

Charles Randall and James Cornwell rose. They left Mr. Blair and the three landowners together and strolled outside, taking the path to the stables. Quentin led them to a small stable set a little away from the main one.

"He's young yet and a mite nervous of Father's hunters so I keep them apart until they're better acquainted."

"Good idea," said Neil. "Let them meet in the paddock. They'll accept each other then."

Quentin opened the stable door and the young chestnut whinnied with pleasure and came easily to Quenton's hand. Neil ran an expert eye over him.

"Very nice. Good set head and strong shoulders." He ran his hands down the legs and flanks. "He'll breed well, I'd guess, if you've a mind to mate him."

"I've thought of it, which is why I'd value your advice."

Neil nodded. "I've a couple of chestnut fillies at my place. Good blood line and no viciousness in them. Should suit this fellow. Come over to High Ridge and take a look at them."

"Thanks, Neil."

As they strolled back to the house, Matt told them of his black stallion. It was in character, Quentin thought, smiling, that Matt should choose a black stallion. Not for him a brown or even a golden chestnut. A hero on horseback, a dashing fellow set above the satin sheen of horse hide. He did not envy Matt or his horse, only the picture he must present to Chloris. He shook away the thought as they walked into the drawing room to be greeted by the ladies.

11

The saloon bar of the Royal Oak was full that evening. Blue smoke from the clay pipes eddied about the heads of the men who thronged the low-ceilinged room; the murmur of voices and the clank of pewter tankards filled the air. The corn harvest was completed, the grain sacked and on its way to the corn-merchants. A good harvest meant a bonus and not even the most hard-pressed wife resented her man joining his fellows at the Royal Oak, to spend a few precious coppers on a cele-bratory drink.

Dominoes were played with slow deliberation by old men whose working days were over, but even they listened with half an ear and nodded sagely, recalling great harvests of their own time. Since Gilminster land had been farmed for centuries, the common topics of conversation remained unchanged. Festivals and country fairs added to the rhythm of their lives, and in all things, the men were content to serve that land.

No-one paid heed to the stranger sitting by the window, sipping the strong dark beer morosely. A thin-faced man with calloused hands, he was dressed roughly, a kerchief knotted about his neck, a flat tweed cap on the bench beside him. The men had nodded to him but he seemed indisposed to conversation and his presence had all but been forgotten.

Laborers from the three estates of Cornwell, Randall, and Field talked together, their laughter spilling out when the tale of the broken blade of Mr. Cornwell's reaper was repeated. Their rivalry was mild and good-natured with the Field estate men declaring stoutly that Mr. Quentin had the right idea from the start and took the risk on himself, not like others who left the job to their managers.

Joel Darling, the eighteen-year-old cousin of Meggie, stretched out his long legs under the table and took a gulp of cider. He wiped his mouth with the back of his hand and remarked, "Uncle Joss thinks a fair deal of Mr. Quentin. As good a master as Sir Lionel but with a sharper eye on the future." He nodded wisely. "I've heard tell of his plans."

"Aye, and you'd know all about them, wouldn't you, young 'un?" a man teased. "For you as near as nothing sit in maid Meggie's pocket."

Joel reddened, looking every inch the gangling youth he was. "She's my cousin, isn't she? What's wrong with visiting kin? She's a rare hand with the mutton pies, too."

There was a roar of laughter and the man slapped Joel's shoulder. "So, it's mutton pies, not sheep's eyes that take you to the farm?"

Joel grinned, seeking to change the subject. "I was a mite curious about the new reaper and asked Uncle Joss to show it to me. It's a sight and no mistake. All the way from America, my uncle says."

"That's right," one of the Cornwell men said. "And I did hear tell that Master was so pleased he might order another in time for next summer's crops."

The thin-faced stranger lifted his head and spoke for the first time. "Machines!" he said with such abhorrence in his voice that the men round the table turned to stare at him.

"What's wrong with machines?" The innocent question came from Joel.

"What's wrong with them?" the man repeated. "They lead to starvation, that's what!"

"What do you mean?"

"They take men's jobs, that's what I mean."

"How can they do that?" persisted Joel.

The man sighed and spread out his rough hands. "See these? They've worked in the mill for nigh on twenty years. I was took on as a lad of ten and learned my trade in the spinning sheds. Then some fellow invented a machine. Mill master was pleased as Punch for it did the work of ten men. So what happens? I'll tell you. Nine men get turned off. Master don't want them anymore 'cos he's got this machine, see?"

'But somebody's got to work it—"

"Of course, but not ten men. Machines don't need wages, do they? Not like men who've got wives and hungry babies."

The men were all staring at the stranger, noticing his thin shoulders and shabby clothes. They stirred uncomfortably. One spoke his thoughts.

"We did hear of troubles in the north. Is that where you're from?"

"Aye, it is, Jack Oldroyd's the name. Those Mill Masters deserve all the trouble they're getting for putting decent folk out of work."

"Couldn't you get another job?" asked Joel.

Oldroyd scowled. "With hundreds more on the streets, all looking for jobs?" He ran his gaze

147

over Joel. "You talk of mutton pies, young fellow, but how would it be if you'd a scrag end of mutton to last a family for a week? There's women begging bones from the butcher to make a soup and lasses picking up dropped cabbage leaves in the market. There's folks starving up there and who cares? Let me ask you that."

"Well, I reckon other folks would help out, like they do here."

Oldroyd's lips twisted. "Oh, aye, save like as not, they be starving too."

"What are you doing down here?" asked Joel. "Looking for a job?"

"Something like that, but I don't reckon there'll be any going soon."

"What does that mean?"

"You'll find out soon enough. Machines and men don't mix and it won't be the machines that lose out, you mark my words." His voice had risen, drawing the landlord's attention. The man moved slowly from behind the bar, a large ex-seaman with heavily tattooed arms. He halted beside the table.

"Mister," he said flatly. "I do be hoping you're not going to cause a disturbance here."

Oldroyd looked up. "I'm not causing a disturbance," he said hotly, then his eyes took in the thick muscles under the tatooed skin on the man's bare arms.

"For if you keep raising your voice like that," went on the landlord, "I'll think you're a mite drunk and I don't hold with that in my establishment." He peered into Oldroyd's tankard. "Ah, I see you've an empty tankard. Will you be wanting another?"

Oldroys was conscious of his meager supply of coin. He shook his head and rose as the big landlord regarded him impassively. Oldroyd looked down at the circle of faces. Not exactly unfriendly but not friendly enough to buy him a drink. Well, he hoped he'd frightened them with his talk. At least they had something to think on and when the day came for man to rise against master, they would be that much more willing.

"Machines don't get empty bellies. Just think on that, lads." He brushed past the solid body of the landlord and strode out of the Royal Oak. Daniel Moffat, ex-gunner's mate on a ship of the line, and now the owner of his thriving tavern, watched his departure thoughtfully.

"What do you think, Dan?" asked one of the drinkers, a line of worry on his forehead. "I'd not be wishing to lose my job at Cornwell's, with four young mouths to fill."

Danny pondered and the man waited, eyeing him with respect. Dan Moffat had travelled the world, unlike most of them who had spent their lives in Dorset, going no further than Dorchester.

"A man with a grudge, if you ask me," he said at length. "A lower deck firebrand, always wanting to go at the officers. Pay no heed, lads. Folks up north are different, more hot-headed like. If they go about breaking machines as I've heard tell 'tis no wonder masters come down hard on them." He scratched his chin, a sound like sawing wood. "Still, I do grant 'tis powerful sad to see the young 'uns go hungry and none to care."

He moved back to his bar and the men dispersed early, all of them slightly affected by Jack Oldroyd's warning. But the industrial north was a world apart from the agricultural county of Dorset and the faint uneasiness stirred up by the northerner soon faded away.

But Jack Oldroyd himself did not fade away. His narrow, discontented face was often glimpsed at street corners and in the Royal Oak.

Daniel Moffat glimpsed him one morning as he went into the yard to unlock the heavy trapdoors leading to the beer cellar. Oldroyd was leaning on the wall, hands thrust deep into his pockets.

"Best move yourself from there, mister," Dan called. "I'm expecting a wagon and those brewery horses have rare big hooves. You'll not be wanting a crushed foot, now will you?"

Oldroyd moved reluctantly as the wagon came into view. Dan frowned but held his tongue until the driver negotiated the two steaming horses into the yard and halted the wagon neatly by the trapdoors.

"Where's Ned?" Dan demanded. "Can't shift this lot by yourself, or was you thinking Daniel Moffat, being a big strong lad, might take kindly to humping his own barrels?"

The wagoner grinned. "Can't be helped today, Mr. Moffat. I did tell Ned he should have more sense than to climb trees, even if his lad's kite was stuck up there." He shrugged. "Paper and wood, that's all. He could have made another."

"Fell out of the tree, did he? What's the damage?"

"Kite's fine." He grinned. " 'Twere Ned came down heavy. Just bruises. Be back next load."

Dan saw Oldroyd watching. He beckoned. "Give a hand, lad, and your dinner'll be free, with a pint of best thrown in."

Oldroyd advanced, eyeing the stout wooden barrels. He sniffed. "Make it two pints. This is laboring work."

Dan checked a hot response and said with sarcasm, "Well, of course, Mr. Oldroyd, if you've been offered a ladylike position at haberdasher's, I'll not expect you to soil your delicate hands with

150

such common toil. It's for you to decide." He turned his back and removed the pins of the tailboard.

Oldroyd shrugged his bony shoulders and moved towards them. Dan set the planks in place as Oldroyd climbed up into the body of the cart amongst the upright casks.

"Let them down nice and easy," Dan instructed, looking at Oldroyd. "Then roll them to me. I'll have the ropes ready in no time."

The barrels were far heavier than Oldroyd expected and he was sweating profusely after three were rolled off into Dan's chute.

The wagoner swung them competently, forgetful of Oldroyd's inexperience, and it was the fourth barrel that proved his undoing. Oldroyd caught his foot on a cart bolt and stumbled. His flailing arms knocked the rolling barrel into a spin.

"Hold up!" yelled the wagoner and he made a wild grab to bring the barrel about. He grunted with pain as the edge caught him on the kneecap and fell back on Oldroyd. The two men struggled for balance, then went down together in a sprawl of limbs.

Dan flung himself aside as the heavy cask missed his chute and thumped solidly onto the flagstones of the yard. A stave splintered and forty gallons of best dark ale swept in a torrent over the backyard of the Royal Oak.

Dan, breathing heavily, glared wrathfully. "If you've a mind to stay hereabouts, you'll need a stronger back than you seem to have."

Oldroyd stared resentfully. "Aye, a strong back and a weak head, it seems to me. You all think that life will go on the same it's done for a hundred years. Masters get richer and workers get poorer. That's machines for you, taking the bread

151

out of our mouths . . ."

"That's enough," snapped Daniel. "You've no cause to tell your tales over and over again. We've no Mill Masters here so don't go stirring up trouble. You and your machines. There's no machine to get these barrels into my cellar and stack 'em right and tight, is there?"

Oldroyd was aware of the grinning wagoner watching the altercation with relish. He flushed darkly.

"Well, you'll have naught to worry about, that's for sure, for you're your own master." He scowled at the wagoner. "You'll be having dozens like him soon, when the men get laid off. Just wait and see if I'm not speaking true . . ."

"And what would you have the men do about it, may I ask, for a clever fellow like you must have the answer, though it seems you weren't too successful up north." Daniel was a man slow to anger but Oldroyd's persistent harping on the same theme made him speak with unusual sarcasm.

"There's an answer all right." Oldroyd turned away but his gaze still held Daniel's. "It's for the men to ask and they'll be looking for me before too long." His lips twisted into a sardonic grin. "And maybe I'll oblige them." He strolled away, hunching his bony shoulders.

Next door to the Royal Oak stood the general store, a long, raftered-ceiling building with whitewashed walls. Even in the hottest weather it stayed cool. It was here that housewives came for their flour and rice, sugar and dried fruits. The air was always exotically scented with spices and herbs from foreign parts. A saucepan, a fish kettle, a wooden spoon or a tea caddy, they were all to be had in the Gilminster store but more importantly, village gossip was exchanged whilst debating the merits of a bone or wooden-handled knife.

Joe Darling worked here and despite his loose-limbed youthfulness, he never spilled a pinch of red pepper or cinnamon when he weighed out. He enjoyed his work, especially as cousin Meggie was a regular customer. Miss Blair and Miss Baxter often dropped in too and occasionally young Miss Cornwell. Standing in the center of the village street, the store was used as a place where messages, special recipes, and pots of preserves could be left and collected by the stated parties, saving many a long walk to outlying farms. Joel was always first to know when folks fell ill or needed a hand. A word to Miss Blair or Miss Baxter was usually followed by practical help.

Jack Oldroyd was intrigued by the tightness of village life. Nothing went unremarked here and he made it his business to listen to gossip. Within the week, his sharp mind had discovered that almost every inhabitant of Gilminster was dependent on the goodwill of one of the three masters, Field, Randall or Cornwell. He also made it his business to wander round these estates and look at the machines being used. His thoughts were sour as he heard the laborers joking amongst themselves. Aye, he told himself, there'll not be much to joke about when autumn comes and the machines are laid up for the winter. That's the time the masters count the cost and make their plans for next season. These thickheaded fellows would listen to him then when masters cut costs at the expense of the farmhands. They had done it up north. Why not here?

His mind went back to that day in Manchester when he had barely escaped with his life. There's none so queer as folks, he mused bitterly. Thrown out of work himself, he had sought to mold the

153

workers into a force to fight it out with the mill owners. They had cheered him in the taverns and on the street corners, hiding him away when the constables had stormed the meetings, but who had rushed back to the mill gates, when the Mill Master had threatened a lockout? They'd needed a scapegoat then and the pointing fingers picked him out.

He drew in a deep breath and stared over the countryside. It wasn't right that a single man should own so much and rule over the lives of men. Fate had sent him, for the machines were here, too, and these thickheaded men had no notion of the threat they represented. It was his duty to organize them into a solid movement, his mission to bring light into this benighted village.

He jingled the small change in his pocket. Enough for a loaf and a sup of beer. Odd jobs he could do, but not the sort that bovine landlord expected. He was a craftsman, not a thick-muscled peasant. During his wanderings, he had come across a small wooden lean-to, deep in the heart of what they called Prior's Wood. More like a copse than a wood, for the large trees had been felled years ago, judging by the growth of briar and bramble. The lean-to shack was almost buried by bush, some old woodsman's shelter, he supposed, when the felling had been going on. It was an ideal hiding place and there was any amount of dried old wood to keep a fire going. The only sign of life he'd seen thereabouts was rabbit and the odd lad collecting firewood. The place might come in handy if he needed to disappear in a hurry. He grinned. No prattling landlady to inform on him when the masters realized what was happening and sent the constable looking.

Chloris met Quentin Field on the road from

High Ridge Farm. He was riding the chestnut horse slowly along towards the village. He saw her and raised a hand. Chloris turned Bessie towards him and they met on the outskirts of Gilminster.

"Good morning, Chloris. Where are you off to today?" He was hatless and his fair hair tossed about his tanned brow.

"Nowhere in particular. Bessie needs a daily ride. She is getting too fat. What a pretty color your chestnut is. Georgina said you had a new horse and were very proud of him."

"Am so I am." He patted the chestnut's neck. "I've just come from High Ridge where Neil Kernick has been showing me a couple of beautiful fillies. I shall probably buy them for this fellow."

Chloris raised her brows. "A harem, indeed, or do you mean to create a dynasty?" She smiled across at him. "Do you have time to breed horses, too?"

"It has been in my mind for some time and now with the reaper all set for the barley field, and Joss well able to oversee it, I can train spare hands to care for the horses. Most of them are familiar with the heavy horses and some might like the chance of working in stable or paddock."

They walked their mounts through the narrow streets of the village with its bow-fronted shops and cobbled side streets. Few people were about but they were greeted by cheerful shopkeepers and shyly by children playing on corners. Through the village, Quentin turned the chestnut onto the Field House road.

"Come for coffee," he suggested. "Georgina's idea. Every morning at precisely eleven o'clock. Father is beginning to enjoy it. At least he's drinking less wine, which is good for his gout. Almost gone, he says."

"Thank you. I'd like that. It's a week since I've seen her. How is she?"

"As beautiful as ever. Young Sarah Cornwell has taken to visiting and you'd think that Georgina is no more than sixteen herself to listen to them."

"We shall all miss Georgina when she goes back to London. If she does, that is." She looked speculatively at Quentin, who met her gaze solemnly. Then he smiled a little wryly. "Don't look at me like that, Chloris. Not you, too. The whole village has us married already in their minds. Any excuse for a celebration."

He quickened the pace of his horse as they left the village behind and Chloris knew that he wanted no more remarks on the subject. At Field House, a groom took their horses and Chloris entered the sitting room while Quentin went in search of his father. Georgina and Sarah were sitting on the couch, surrounded by fashion books. Georgina glanced up.

"Oh, Chloris, dear. Do come and give us your opinion on this style of gown for Sarah. Her mama has given permission for her to have a special one made up for their Christmas party. I know there are weeks and weeks to go but the seamstress who makes all Sarah's gowns, and Mrs. Cornwell's too, might well be inundated with orders later on and it is always a good thing to be prepared, don't you think?"

"You are perfectly right as always, Georgina. How we have contrived without your advice for so long, I cannot think."

Georgina looked at her suspiciously, then her mouth curved into a smile. "Very well, I would say, judging by that rose silk creation you wore at Sir Lionel's party. Quentin remarked on how superb you looked and I agreed entirely with him."

156

"Quentin did?" asked Chloris in astonishment.

"And why should he not? He is most perceptive and very noticing about everything. Now do stop teasing and look at these pictures. The Brussels lace is exquisite but so is the white Tarleton with embroidered flowers."

Chloris drew up a footstool and joined them, smiling into Sarah Cornwell's animated face. "Dear Georgina," she protested. "Your taste is vastly superior to mine. I have never been to London and have not the faintest notion of the fashion there. Both Sarah and I must bow to your judgment." She looked at the sketch of a crinolined lady in white lace. "A trifle fulsome, perhaps, for a country Christmas party." She shot Sarah a mischievous glance. "A little cumbersome, wouldn't you say, for hiding in cupboards."

Georgina's gaze came up sharply as Sarah giggled. "Really, Chloris! If you intend to make fun of me, I shall become most seriously angry."

Chloris reached out and took her hand. "Dearest Georgina! Not for the world would I make you seriously angry. The very thought makes me quail though it would be an experience to see you really cross."

"Then kindly explain what you mean by hiding in cupboards. What have cupboards to do with anything?"

Sarah intervened. "It is just a silly game we play at parties. The children love it. Hide-and-Seek, Sardines, that sort of thing is what Chloris means."

"Sardines?" Georgina was unconvinced. "You are making it up. I have never heard such nonsense." She looked sternly at her companions.

"No, truly we're not teasing," Sarah said. "It's

157

like Hide-and-Seek but when you find the one who was sent off to hide, you must join him until the last person finds the hiding place and everyone is packed as close as sardines in a tin. Of course," she added grandly, "it's really a game for the children, but at Christmas we all play it."

"Well," said Georgina, "it sounds most uncomfortable, especially in a cupboard. Still," she added brightly, "I dare say you have very large cupboards in your house, Sarah."

12

Joel Darling listened with only half his attention on the gossiping housewives of Gilminster. Tonight he was going for supper at the farm. It was quite a common occurrence but each time he was invited, it sent a glow of happiness through him. Meggie's flushed face over the stewpot or rabbit pie, Uncle Joss's slow drawl as he told of the day's work made him feel good. A pretty one was Meggie and a rare good cook too. They were cousins but not exactly first cousins, for his own father had been cousin to Uncle Joss. He knew Meggie was fond of him but was she fond enough? She was only fifteen, after all, and maybe saw him as a sort of elder brother. He was too shy to ask outright. Maybe one day, unless of course some handsome fellow took her fancy first. It depressed him to think of it but he was cheered by the fact that she was too young for marriage at present. He knew he was not a dashing fellow himself, towheaded, freckled, all arms and legs, but age might improve him at least to the extent of getting his limbs in better control. But what could you do with the face you were born with? Could time improve that?

He was idly contemplating the problem when his ears picked up a phrase.

"After the barley, 'tis said."

Joel looked about the store and identified the speaker. A middle-aged woman he'd known for years, the wife of a Cornwell employee. He moved along the counter and smiled at her.

"After the barley, Mrs. Pritchard? What's that then? Your Millie getting married or Grace having another little one?"

Mrs. Pritchard stared at him. "Nay, Joel. That'd be cause for a smile but you don't see me smiling, do you?"

Joel's own smile died and he flushed. "Sorry, missis. I just caught the words and thought. . . ."

The woman sighed, her tone softening. "I've no call to snap at you, lad, for it's none of your fault. 'Tis bad news and my man not yet fifty. We've still got three at home."

Joel looked puzzled. "What's wrong, Mrs. Pritchard?"

"You've not heard then?"

"Heard what?"

"That Master Cornwell is laying off after the barley. Nothing's been said but there's rumor."

"There's always rumor, missis, and what makes you think your man will be one to go?"

"Stands to reason. It'll be the older ones first. I'm afeared, I can tell you, and it's a tied cottage too."

There were sympathetic murmurs from the other women.

Joel frowned. "Where did you hear it, Mrs. Pritchard, if it's only a rumor?"

"My man came back from the Royal Oak last night in a fair old taking. Could hardly eat his supper for worrying."

"I see," Joel said slowly. "And I'll bet he mentioned a fellow from the north."

Mrs. Pritchard stared. "Why yes, he did. Ever so sympathetic for he'd been thrown out of work himself. Knew all about it, he said. And a lot worse coming, he said, for masters were the same the country over. Greedy for profit and never a care for the workers."

"That's a bit strong, missis," Joel protested. "Your man's been at Cornwell's for as long as I can remember. Hasn't Master always been fair?"

"That he has, but these machines now. 'Tis progress backwards for some of us if we're thrown out of our cottage and no money coming in. We'll be on the parish for sure." She swept up her shopping basket and hurried, tight-faced, towards the door.

Other women made their purchases in silence and drifted away, leaving Joel unhappy and thoughtful. It was only rumor, he told himself, and that man, Oldroyd, was a carping kind of fellow, bitter because he'd lost his own job. But that was different. It had all happened hundreds of miles away. These weren't factory people, they were farming folk. Masters were not the same as up north. But these machines, Mrs. Pritchard had said. Joel wrinkled his brow. He supposed a reaper was a machine, but it wasn't like filling a factory with dozens of them, all going full stretch. A reaper couldn't be used all year round like those spinning things Oldroyd had talked about. Just like him to start rumors. Nothing to worry about, he decided, and yet he might mention it to Uncle Joss at supper that night, since Uncle Joss rarely called at the Royal Oak.

He put the matter from his mind as he measured out a pound of brown sugar for another customer. It was so far back in his mind that he never thought of it during supper that night. Meggie was wearing a bright pink cotton dress with small blue flowers in the pattern. With her brown hair brushed to a silky finish, she faced him over the pine kitchen table, smiling as he recounted his day in the store. He knew it was a dull account, for nothing eventful had happened, but her smile encouraged him and after a long draught of homemade cider, he stumbled through his first complimentary remark.

"Pink suits you, Meggie. You look like a grand lady from London." He felt his cheeks redden as Meggie laughed.

"A grand lady, indeed! If 'tis only the dress that makes me look so, well no wonder, for Miss Sarah Cornwell gave me the material and I made it up. She said she'd bought far too much and there was enough length left on the roll to cut up a plain dress, and it was too good to stitch into dusters. A kind heart has Miss Sarah."

"Aye, well, but take off the dress and I reckon you'll still be a lady underneath."

Meggie's eyes opened wide and Joel realized what he had said. "I didn't mean—I wasn't saying . . ." he stammered, his hands growing damp. His words trailed away and then he heard Uncle Joss's low chuckle and a peal of laughter from Meggie.

"We know what you meant, son," said Joss. "And Meggie is very sensible of your compliment. Isn't that so, Meggie?"

"Yes, Father." Meggie gave Joel an affectionate smile. "Dear Joel, I thank you kindly. I sewed all day in order to wear it tonight. You are the first one to see it finished."

The heat subsided from Joel's body and he

grinned sheepishly. "I'm no hand with the words. My tongue is as thick as my wits."

"Nonsense," said Meggie and rose to clear the dishes. "You'll learn the way of it when you come to be courting. They do say a man gets a powerful urge to say sweet things when he's an eye for a maid. Maybe it comes natural when the fancy's on him."

Joel watched the slim form of Meggie in the swaying pink skirt move across the kitchen. He realized that Uncle Joss was looking at him. He cleared his throat and sought for a new topic of conversation. The face of Mrs. Pritchard came into his mind. He frowned, remembering her distress.

"Uncle Joss, have you heard anything about laying off at Mister Cornwell's?"

Joss squinted at him from over the bowl of the pipe he was filling. "No. Why?"

"Mrs. Pritchard was in the store today. She's convinced that her man is going to lose his job and her in a tied cottage and all. Very upset, she was."

Joss lit his pipe and blew out a cloud of blue smoke. "I've heard nothing. Has Ted Pritchard been told for a fact?"

Joel shook his head. "She says she's convinced he'll be laid off. Not just him. Others too."

Joss took the pipe from his mouth and stared at Joel. "Where did she get that idea?"

"From the Royal Oak, I'd guess. Leastways, not her but Mr. Pritchard. There's a queer sort of stranger hanging round. Name of Oldroyd. Comes from the north and goes on and on about machines putting folk out of work."

"I reckon there's some truth in that from what I've heard but what has making cloth to do with us?"

Joel shrugged. "He just goes on about

163

machines." He looked at his uncle. "The reaper's a machine, isn't it?"

"Likely it is, but it's not the same."

Joel searched his memory trying to recall the conversation on the first night Oldroyd had appeared. He found what he wanted.

"One of the men said Mr. Cornwell was going to get another reaper. That's when this Oldroyd started on about machines."

Joss frowned. "This fellow must be after something. Do you say the men are listening to him?"

"Must be," said Joel. "Mrs. Pritchard was in a rare talking as if it were gospel truth her man had told her."

"I've a mind to drop into the Royal Oak myself tomorrow and take a look at this fellow," Joss told Joel as he opened the front door for Joel to leave.

Meggie dropped a light kiss on her cousin's cheek and Joel walked home, his mind devoid of everything but the memory of Meggie's soft lips on his face, now a brighter pink than Meggie's new dress.

Sir Lionel Field closed the farm accounts ledger with a smile of satisfaction. Quentin rose from his position on the other side of the wide mahogany desk and stretched his shoulders.

"You've done well, Quentin," said Sir Lionel. "Top quality grain and first to the merchants and onto the ships. We'll make a good profit this year. Maybe cover the cost of the reaper we installed. I knew it would be a good idea. Don't hold with all newfangled things but I must say this American fellow, McCormick, invented something useful. I could see it at once."

Quentin smiled with amused affection at his father. "A wise investment, Father. Always the best kind." He ran a hand through his disarranged hair. "A drink, sir? I think we may indulge in a cautious celebration. Claret or whiskey? Let's hope the weather holds for the barley."

"Claret please, my boy. This bookkeeping gives one a thirst. Get Belling to light the lamps, will you? It must be past nine o'clock. Did we have dinner? Must have done but I fancy a piece of chicken pie or cold cut. See to it, will you? Now, where did I leave my cigar case?"

Quentin moved to the bellrope but before his fingers reached it, there was a tap on the door and Belling's reluctant face appeared.

"Excuse the interruption, gentlemen," he said. "But Darling from the home farm has called and begs leave to see you. Shall I tell him to come back in the morning, sir?"

"Where is he, Belling?"

"In the hall, sir. I suggested he leave a message as you instructed me not to disturb you, but he was quite insistent." Belling looked apologetic and affronted at the same time. "He is—er, sitting on one of the hall chairs."

Sir Lionel's brows rose. "Isn't that what they're there for?"

"Well yes, sir, but—but he's wearing corduroy breeches. The covers, sir . . . "

"Good God, Belling," Sir Lionel exploded. "It's the farm manager, not some raggedly evil-smelling tramp crawled in off the road! His breeches'll be as clean as yours."

"Send him in, Belling," cut in Quentin. "It must be important for him to come at this hour. You can argue about breeches some other time."

"Yes, sir." Belling retreated with stiff dignity and moved into the hall, his aura of disapproval almost tangible.

Quentin looked at Sir Lionel, who grinned.

"Confounded fellow! Been here so long you'd think he owned the place, let alone the damned chairs in the hall."

Quentin laughed. "Probably thinks we're a pair of slipshod fellows, letting Joss into the house at all."

"Good man, Joss. I wonder what's on his mind?"

"We'll soon know." Quentin glanced at the doorway. "Come in, Joss. Sit down, won't you?"

Joss took the chair indicated, sitting carefully on the forward edge. His face was unsmiling, deep furrows marking his brow.

"Meggie all right?" queried Sir Lionel in quick concern. "You're looking mighty serious. What's wrong?"

Joss relaxed a little. "Meggie's fine, sir. 'Tis about these rumors in the village. Young Joel put me on to it so I dropped into the Royal Oak earlier tonight to hear for myself."

"And what did you hear?"

Joss looked uncomfortable. "Nothing definite, just rumor. Dare say it's nothing but I thought I'd best tell you."

"Well, tell us then," said Sir Lionel. "What rumors are these?"

Joss drew in a deep breath. "That masters are laying off men after the barley on account of these reapers. The men at the Royal Oak asked me but what could I tell them? I don't know anything save Mr. Quentin talked of putting men to the care of the new breeding stables."

Sir Lionel looked bemused. "Laying off? What nonsense! Are the men doubting my son's intentions?"

"No, sir. They were mostly Cornwell and Randall men there tonight and only a few of our own, but they're worried all the same, living in

166

tied cottages and all." He hesitated. "There's talk of a deputation."

"No need for that, Joss," Quentin said. "Gather the men at the farm first thing tomorrow. I'll be there to talk to them and set their minds at rest if that's what they need."

Sir Lionel leaned forward over his desk and fixed his gaze on Joss. "I confess to surprise and disappointment that you saw fit to come here at all, Joss. You've been with us a long time, since before Meggie was born. You've had our complete trust all these years. Why should you doubt us? If I'd thought one reaping machine was going to give rise to discontent, I'd never have bought the damned thing in the first place! It's true we'll not need as many scythemen, not for the harvest anyway, but with horses and a flock of South Down sheep, there'll be work for all of them if they lay by their scythes. Can I say fairer than that?" His gray eyes held steadily on Joss's face.

A smile twisted the corner of Joss Darling's mouth. "I reckon not, Master. For myself, I never doubted it."

Sir Lionel sat back, his color fading to normal. He frowned. "Then what the devil is this all about?"

Joss hesitated. "Well, sir, I'd be obliged if you'd maybe sound out Mr. Cornwell and Mr. Randall. 'Tis none of my business you'll be telling me and right enough, but it'll be a sad day in the village if the rumors have substance. It's said that Mr. Cornwell has ordered a second reaper and that's ill news for his scythemen."

Quentin looked inquiringly at his father. "Do you recall any mention of it when we had the families here after the harvest? I left you in the dining room and took the younger men to look at the chestnut."

Sir Lionel pondered aloud. "We talked of crops and the price of corn, winter planting, the usual things when farmers get together. Cornwell talked of setting more land to corn..." He stopped and regarded Quentin interrogatively. "That's maybe it. He'll need a second reaper if he turns all his fields to corn and buys his fodder in instead of growing it. More profit that way." He drummed his fingers on the desk top for a moment, then looked across at Joss. "I'll be over to see Mr. Cornwell tomorrow, maybe Mr. Randall too. Can't promise anything, mind, for a man may do what he will with his own land, deputation or not."

"Yes sir, but there's something else I haven't told you yet." He glanced up to meet two pairs of intent gray eyes.

"Well?" demanded Sir Lionel.

"There could be a troublemaker in the village. A man from the north, called Oldroyd. Might even have started these rumors himself."

"How could he do that if he's no knowledge of the land?"

"By listening, sir. A sharp man can pick up a lot by just sitting there and Dan Moffat says he's a sharp one all right and he's dead set against machines."

A glance passed between Sir Lionel and Quentin. "Then I'd better be over to Cornwell's and Randall's first thing tomorrow," said Sir Lionel heavily. "If the men are on edge already, this fellow won't improve matters, unless that's his intention. Did he look like a rabble rouser, Joss?"

"He looked like a bitter man, sir, but that's only natural since he lost his job up north."

"What the devil has he come to Dorset for?"

asked Sir Lionel irritably. "Is he looking for work?"

"Not noticeably, sir," said Joss dryly. "An odd job here and there, but only half finished and not proper done before he wanders away, folk tell me."

"Let's hope he wanders away for good when he finds nothing worth his attention."

Joss rose. "Let's hope so, sir, for I wouldn't like to see men do things they'll be sorry for when the heat's gone out of them."

Sir Lionel nodded and rose, holding out his hand. "Thanks for coming, Joss. I'd not like it either. We must put a stop to it before it begins."

Quentin arrived early at the farmhouse the next morning. He had dressed hurriedly in old breeches and faded shirt, neglected to shave in his efforts to arrive before the earliest worker. Joss eyed him over the pine kitchen table with amusement. "Best take a sup of tea, Mr. Quentin, and a plate of Meggie's rashers, for I doubt that Frost-face up at the house bethought himself to rouse the cook on your behalf. Not even the cock's astir yet!"

Quentin rubbed his rough chin and grinned. "To tell the truth, Joss, I never thought to mention my early rising and found the kitchen range cold with yesterday's ashes and no hot water for shaving." He glanced up as Meggie set a mug of tea before him. "Thank you kindly, Meggie, and I wouldn't say no to a rasher."

"It'll be but a moment, sir," Meggie said, her face fresh and glowing from the morning's cold water wash.

Joss sat down by the hearth and began to fill his clay pipe. "I set young Tom by the crossroads to tell the men to gather here. Those dredging the stream in the lower field by Prior's Wood might go straight there else." He packed his pipe with a broad thumb and reached for a spill of wood from over the mantlepiece. "The men'll rest easier in their minds if they have the word from you, Mr. Quentin." He gazed reflectively at the flame on the spill before touching it to the tobacco. "Sir Lionel'll be off to see the other masters today, won't he?"

Quentin nodded. "As soon as—er—Frostface fills him up with bacon, eggs, kidneys and an abundance of coffee."

Joss smiled and Meggie gave a muffled giggle as she set a plate before Quentin.

"You mustn't mind Belling, Joss. He's been at Field House for so long, we'd have to auction him along with the furniture if we ever left, but it shouldn't ever come to that."

"There'll be Fields up there long after we've gone," Joss said with quiet certainty. "And a houseful of young 'uns beforetimes, I'll warrant." His eyes rested shrewdly on Quentin's impassive face and he smiled. "But you'll not be pushed, I know. A Field always did plough his own furrow."

The sound of voices reached them and both men rose.

"Thank you, Meggie," Quentin said. "A man thinks better on a full stomach." He drained the tea mug. "Especially if you're the cook."

Meggie smiled. " 'Tis welcome you are, Mister Quentin." She turned back to the stove, her cheeks pink.

Young Tom put his head round the open door. "They're all here, sir." He looked at the empty plates on the table and sniffed the aroma of fried bacon. "Reckon you're ready to see the men, sir,

170

since you've had breakfast, like. Bacon I suspicion. Fair puts an edge on a fellow's appetite."

"It does, indeed," Quentin agreed, straight-faced.

Tom's gaze roved the kitchen. "Reckon I'll be off then, if there's nothing else, sir. School starts in two hours."

"And it's all of half-a-mile away. Shouldn't you hurry?"

Tom sighed. "Yes, sir."

Meggie turned from the stove, trying to keep her smile from showing. "Would you have a minute or two to spare, Tom? I know you're eager to be at your books but it does seem a shame to waste this plate of bacon, since we've all had enough."

Tom looked round with mock innocence. "Well, I dare say I've the time really, and if you've got some over, I'd be glad of a bite for it was a mite chilly by the crossroads." He grinned ingenuously at the two men and Quentin laughed, punching the boy's shoulder lightly as he followed Joss into the yard.

The Field estate workers stood in a group, watching Quentin's approach. He moved slowly, hands in pockets, and halted before them, grave and unsmiling.

"Do you have a spokesman?"

The men looked surprised and heads were shaken.

"I ask because it is usual to elect a man to speak for all of you when there is some area of dis-content. Like fear or flame, discontent spreads quickly if it is fanned into life by a hot tongue or ill-chosen word. Calm talk is better than hasty action, when a man may do something he regrets later. I regard you as sensible men. Tell me of your discontent."

"We've heard tell of laying off, sir," a man in the forefront mumbled.

"I have no authority to speak for any other estate but our own," Quentin said crisply. "I speak only for Sir Lionel in this matter when I say there'll be no laying off here. Any man who has heard different has been keeping too close company with Dan Moffat's best ale."

A few grins appeared as Quentin went on. "You'll have heard from Mr Darling, I don't doubt, of Sir Lionel's plans in regard to horse breeding and new sheep stock." He surveyed their faces steadily. "I tell you this as fact, not rumor." A few boots shifted uncomfortably. "We'll be setting on, not laying off. Horses and sheep need a deal of caring for and we've stable blocks and sheep pens to build first."

"What about machines, sir?" An anonymous voice came from the back of the group. "Machines don't get empty bellies."

"Machines can help fill empty bellies if they're used right. The harvesting was quicker than ever before and none of you suffered by our using a reaper. Remember last year when half the corn went rotten because we couldn't cut it fast enough?"

Heads nodded, men remembering the late summer storms of last year. They looked at each other, beginning to feel a little foolish. One of the older hands scratched his head and took a step forward.

"Well, I reckon that's all, Mr. Quentin. Seems like us been wasting your time. The word of a Field is good enough for us, eh, lads?"

Heads bobbed up and down, the men grinned and nudged each other, relief evident in every face.

"We'd best get back to work, sir," said the spokesman.

"Just one thing," Quentin said. "If any man here has a likely lad who'll have finished his schooling by Christmas, and he's a fancy for being a stableboy, I'll be well pleased to see how he measures up."

The men moved off cheerfully and Quentin went back into the farmhouse to find Tom mopping up his plate with a crust of bread. He raised a red, shiny face, and slid from the kitchen stool.

"I'll be off now. Thank you for the bite, Meggie."

"Bite, indeed!" she scoffed. "More like a pound and a half all to yourself."

Joss Darling ruffled Tom's hair. "He's a growing lad, Meggie," he said, grinning.

"Well, don't you come here when you've grown, young Tom," Meggie said severely though her eyes were laughing. "For it'll be three pounds on your plate and a dozen eggs, I shouldn't wonder!"

Tom grinned, unabashed. "And when I'm grown I'll marry you so you can cook it."

"Get off to school with you before I throw something."

Tom put himself the other side of the back door and strode off whistling shrilly.

Meggie brewed a fresh pot of tea. Quentin and Joss sat down again.

"I'm glad you spoke to the men," said Joss. "Though to be sure their heart's aren't in revolution, but they'll rest easier." He frowned. "I wish I felt easier about the other estates."

Quentin nodded. "Let's hope Sir Lionel has talked sense into them. This man, Oldroyd, is dangerous but it's no crime to talk. There's little we can do about it."

When Quentin reached Field House, he was greeted in the hall by a hovering Belling whose expression showed relief as he walked in.

"Is my father home yet?" Quentin asked.

"Yes, sir. Sir Lionel has just returned. He is in the study. He—he took in the decanter of brandy, sir, with orders not to be disturbed."

"Brandy?" Quentin paused. "Not Claret?"

"Well no, sir. I had just brought up a fresh bottle from the cellar but it was not ready for drinking, so Sir Lionel took the brandy instead. He is in a fearful temper, sir."

"Is Miss Georgina in?"

"No, sir. She went for a carriage ride with Miss Cornwell."

"Good." Quentin walked down the hall to his father's study and tapped on the door.

"Go away, damn you, or I'll break this decanter over your head!"

Quentin grimaced and opened the door. "Surely not, Father. It's one of a set and quite priceless." He closed the door behind him and surveyed the flushed face and snapping gray eyes of his father.

"Oh, it's you," growled Sir Lionel. "Come in. Brandy?"

"No thank you. I've had a couple of pints of Meggie Darling's tea." He sat down. "You've no need to tell me how you fared this morning. It's pretty obvious you weren't successful."

"Randall saw the sense of my argument for he's ever been cautious. He'll wait and see, like always. But Cornwell . . . "

Quentin waited patiently while Sir Lionel wreathed the name of Cornwell with unflattering epithets.

"That—that crackbrained fool won't listen to reason. He's riding high with his new reaper ordered. Talking of serving notice on nine tenants, after the barley's in, to be out of their cottages by the end of the year. What the devil do you think of that?"

Quentin stared, appalled, at his father. "Dear God, that could mean upward of twenty people since the tenants are family men. He can't turn out families in the middle of winter. What the devil is he thinking of?"

"He's thinking he wants those cottages empty before Spring planting. A coat of whitewash apiece and he can rent them out to casual labor. He's thinking further than Spring, too. Full of plans for hiring these travelling bands of farm laborers next Summer."

Quentin's brows drew together. "Run the whole season on casual labor?"

"He'll keep his manager and a handful of his best men to keep the casuals in order but he'll not be paying men's wages all year round. Necessary cost cutting he calls it." Sir Lionel's voice was gruff with exasperation. "I'd never have thought even William Cornwell could be so confounded penny-pinching."

"I think he's taking a great risk," Quentin said slowly. "Nothing can justify turning out nine families who've committed no offense."

"Greed can. Dammit, Quentin, he's no better than those Mill Masters up north."

"Dear God—Oldroyd!" breathed Quentin. "The men may have dismissed his tales before but they won't when the news gets out. This is just what he's been waiting for." He rose abruptly and began to pace the study floor. "Damn the man! He's a troublemaker and this will be a godsend to him. Damn Cornwell too! He's giving Oldroyd the weapon he's after." He stopped and whirled on his father. "Did you tell Cornwell about Oldroyd?"

Sir Lionel lifted a weary hand. "I told him and he says he'll have his gamekeeper watch out for Oldroyd if he puts so much as a foot on Cornwell land." He looked up into his son's taut, angry face. "There's nothing we can do, Quentin. Cornwell is within his rights. We've no empty cottages ourselves so we can't shelter when the time comes."

"Then he must be persuaded to change his mind."

Sir Lionel smiled wryly. "Not by me. We parted on the worst of terms, bellowing at each other like a couple of old bulls. He'd have had me thrown out, head over ears, if he'd dared." He stopped talking as both men heard the sound of carriage wheels. "Georgina and Sarah returning from their drive," commented Sir Lionel. "I believe I shall stay unavailable until lunchtime. I'm in no mood for idle chitchat."

"Neither am I." Quentin rubbed his unshaven chin. "Neither am I fit to be seen in polite company. I believe I'll head back to the farmhouse. Take a stroll round the fields. If I shave now while I'm thinking of Cornwell I'll probably cut my throat. I'll back for lunch."

Quentin left quietly by the back door and took the old roan from the stable. The farmhouse was empty and Quentin tied the reins loosely to a field fence, allowing the horse the freedom to graze.

The morning had warmed a little but a cool breeze tossed his hair and played round the open neck of his old shirt. He breathed deeply, feeling the soothing effect of fresh country air. Who in their right minds could live elsewhere but amongst these fertile fields and rolling hills? Yet many did live elsewhere, he reminded himself, for the choice was not theirs. Families lived in cramped alleys throughout all large towns, depending on masters for their living, and with machines to replace men were then tossed casually aside as being of no further use. It could not be denied and Oldroyd had every reason to feel bitter if one faced the truth. But bitterness fed on itself and violence was not the answer. Did Cornwell not understand the risk he was taking, with a man like Oldroyd in the neighborhood?

Quentin broke off a stalk of grass and stuck it between his teeth as he leaned over a fence to watch men in thigh waders dredge the stream. He was tempted to take on the men Cornwell planned to dismiss but Field estate had enough workers and could not provide accommodation. And if Sir Lionel was somehow able to could not provide accommodation. And if Sir Lionel was somehow able absorb these nine families, would it not encourage Cornwell to turn that nine into ten, or twelve, or even more?

"Damn Cornwell for a cold-hearted . . . " he growled aloud but stopped abruptly, hearing the swish of a step on the grass. He glanced over his shoulder, expecting to see Joss, but it was not the farm manager.

A man stopped a few paces away, sharp eyes darting over Quentin's old breeches, faded shirt and the overnight stubble on his chin. Quentin returned the gaze, seeing a thin-faced man, medium height and build, a soiled neckerchief flapping between the hunched shoulders. Neither man spoke and Quentin returned to his contemplation. Was this Oldroyd? No farmworker by the look of him and certainly a stranger. He would let the man make the first move.

"I heard you," came the flat tones of north

177

country speech. " 'Damn Cornwell,' you said."

"So?" Quentin spoke without turning his head.

"You stand there right calm, mister. Aren't you afeared your master'll catch you idling?"

For a moment Quentin stood motionless. When he turned, his face wore an expression of vacancy. He chewed the grass stem noisily then spat it out, choosing another with care.

"Cornwell's not master here," he said in a slow Dorset drawl.

"All the same, aren't they? Masters, I mean."

Quentin regarded him blankly for a few moments, then let his face assume a wary expression. "Did Master send you?"

The man's lips twisted in a sneer. "Send me? Not likely."

"What you want, then?"

"Just a few words."

" 'Bout what?"

"My name's Oldroyd." He watched Quentin's face keenly. There was no reaction, not the slightest flicker that the name meant anything.

Oldroyd gave an inward sigh and bared his teeth in a smile. This was a useful-looking lad, broad in the shoulders and well-muscled. Strong enough to heave over a cart and throw a good-sized rock. He looked into the amiable but vacant face. Thicker than most, this one.

"You've heard, I suppose, that Mister Cornwell's turning off men?"

Quentin shrugged. " 'Tis only rumor. Cornwell's not master here."

"I know. You said so." Oldroyd tried again. "But you said 'damn Cornwell' so maybe you've kinfolk 'mongst those that'll be losing their jobs?"

"No."

Oldroyd felt his patience ebbing. "Then why'd you say it?" he snapped.

The fair young man looked at him. "Don't seem right to do that."

"Exactly. What are you going to do about it?"

Quentin shrugged. "Nothing. He's master. Can do as he likes. Stands to reason."

"And what if your master starts turning men off? Won't you do anything then?"

"Oh aye, I will."

Oldroyd felt hope returning. "What will you do?" He watched the almost painful frown of concentration on the tanned forehead, then the brow cleared.

"What?" asked Oldroyd eagerly.

The young man beamed. "Get another job."

Oldroyd leaned his arms on the fence and fought down his exasperation. "Don't you want to do nothing to help these poor folks? Don't it make you angry enough to want to fight somebody?"

"Who?"

"How about Mister Cornwell?"

Quentin let his jaw sag. "Mister Cornwell? Why would I be wanting to do that?"

"To pay him out for sacking those people. Somebody's got to show him it isn't right."

Quentin raised his gaze and stared into the distance over Oldroyd's head. "You mean, go right up to Mister Cornwell and hit him?" He looked down at Oldroyd. "He'd send for the constable."

"I didn't mean like that," Oldroyd spoke through gritted teeth, feeling the sweat of anger on his palms. "I don't mean hit the man personal like, but go in the dark and break something. This reaper he's so proud of, for instance. Or maybe burn a hayrick."

Quentin removed the grass stem, looked at it

for a moment, then stuck it back in his mouth. "That'd be bad."

"But not as bad as throwing folk out of work and out of their homes."

The fair head nodded. "That's bad too."

"Then will you help us teach Mister Cornwell a lesson? There's others feel bad too."

"What do you reckon to do?"

Oldroyd looked round the field. "There's a fellow coming this way. Can't tell you now. Come to the Royal Oak tonight." He glanced over his shoulder.

"Who'll be there?" asked Quentin.

Oldroyd looked athim, then tapped the side of his nose and grinned. "Brave enough lads, but best you don't know, just in case."

He turned and hurried away. Quentin watched him go. The hunched figure followed the stream that paralleled Prior's Wood. Beyond the wood, the Cornwell estate began. It seemed likely that his brave lads were employees there but Oldroyd would get a warm reception if he was spotted by Cornwell's gamekeeper. A pity Oldroyd hadn't confided any names to him for he could have had a quiet word with them. It was no use him going to the Royal Oak. They'd know him there.

He was frowning as Joss reached him. "Morning, Mister Quentin. Wasn't that Oldroyd here a moment ago?"

Quentin nodded. "Tried to enlist me, too."

Joss stared. "You?"

Quentin looked down at himself and laughed. "Dressed like this, I'm not surprised he took me for a son of the soil." His face grew serious. "It seems there's going to be a meeting tonight in the Royal Oak. I'd like to know the company he keeps."

Joss nodded. "I'll have a word with Dan

Moffat. He'll keep an eye on Oldroyd.'' He paused. ''How did Sir Lionel fare?''

''Badly. Randall is holding back but Cornwell is hell-bent on issuing those notices. It would serve him right if we gave Oldroyd his head.''

''It's not Oldroyd who concerns me but the young hotheads he gets to do his bidding.''

''You're right. God knows what the penalty would be if they wreck something.'' They walked in silence back to where Quentin had left his horse.

Jack Oldroyd crossed the stream well out of sight of the dredgers and Quentin Field. Instead of taking the footpath to Gilminster, he turned back and entered Prior's Wood. His sharp eyes darted about but the wood was silent. Walking as softly as he could, he moved cautiously towards the stand of trees he had chosen as a vantage point to gaze into the Cornwell land. From this position he could see the barns and farmhouse. In the distance stood the residence of the master. Hedges and trees lined each field, windbreaks, he had been told, but they could also serve as places of concealment for running figures. He tried to gauge the distance between the last hedge and the group of barns. They'd keep the reaper in one, for sure. A telescope would have helped, for he thought he glimpsed stacked hay under far roofs of slatted wood. Dry it would be in this weather.

He felt a surge of excitement as he pictured creeping flame lick up the dry straw, then the breath-holding moment when the whole stack bloomed into gigantic life. He had never taken part in anything so magical as firing a rick. Breaking machine looms was one thing but to see a great billowing cloud of fire and smoke was another. A wondrous and spectacular sight, telling the whole village that a man could fight his master. After the barley crop, the rumor went. He stared over the fields. Which was the barley and when was it to be cut? Why wait for that? Let the barley burn too, if it would. He must get the lads moving. They were too frightened of their masters here. What they needed was a man of experience. They needed him!

His stomach rumbled in the silence. He was hungry and could do with one of those mutton pies the lanky youth at the Royal Oak had talked of. He thought of Dan Moffat's otter of a meal. No chance of that now since he'd got the blame for knocking over that great barrel of ale. He took a last look at the distant barns and moved along the bushes hedging the wood. He stopped abruptly, his heart thumping, as he heard a sharp snapping sound. Not a twig, too metallic for that. He peered round. Nothing to see, then he did see something. The breeze, stirring a brush, allowed a chink of sunlight to fall on a glinting object. He approached warily, eyes darting about. It was a metal trap, an animal snare, and its victim lay lifeless within it. Oldroyd licked his lips, his stomach growling anew.

Roast rabbit on a spit, he could almost smell it. The trap was on the edge of the woods in a small clearing about ten yards ahead of him. Whose land was it on? He grinned. Since there was no-one about to claim ownership of land or trap, then Jack Oldroyd would be assured of his supper if he moved quickly. A last look towards the fields and then he was sprinting into the clearing, his gaze fixed on the rabbit.

Memory became confused then. A movement in the bushes, some long rough-barked branch leapt between his running legs and he was cartwheeling through the air, arms and legs flailing. He landed on his back with a thump that shook the breath from him. Leaf-filtered sky looked down into his bemused face and his mind was full of confusion. Then the sky was gone and in its place was a huge darkness that masked the sun. From the center of this darkness two perfectly rounded steely grey eyes protruded. He blinked, his senses clearing, and he began to sweat. A twin-barrelled shotgun pointed with rock-like steadiness a bare ten inches from his face.

Oldroyd lay very still, feeling the sweat gather along his back. The hairs on the back of his neck prickled. Without daring to stir, he said in a whine, "I done nothing." His throat rasped dryly.

After an eternity, the figure stepped back and the twin barrels receded but held their aim.

"Get up," a man's voice ordered. "But mind, no tricks. I've both barrels loaded with birdshot."

Oldroyd crawled slowly to his feet, his eyes fixed on the shotgun. Then he allowed his gaze to travel up the barrels to the face. Weathered and ruddy, it belonged to a man of early middle age. A leather sleeveless jerkin over check shirt encased wide shoulders. It was the eyes that caused Oldroyd to cringe inwardly. Pale blue and hard like flat pebbles, they watched him and the finger of one thick hand never left the trigger of the shotgun.

Oldroyd swallowed the lump in his throat and wished the man would point those lethal barrels away from him.

"Well?" The voice held mockery. "I always like to hear a good story from a poacher. Tell me yours, now."

"I'm not a poacher," Oldroyd said weakly.

"Caught you red-handed, didn't I? Master doesn't like folks to lay traps hereabouts."

"I didn't lay the trap," Oldroyd protested. "I heard it go off and . . ."

"Thought you'd help yourself to a nice fat rabbit."

"Well—er—I'm hungry and saw no harm in it. There must be hundreds of them."

"If anybody's the right to empty traps, it's me, not some come-lately fellow I don't even know and like the look of less." The voice had gone cold and Oldroyd flinched.

"All right then. I'll leave it be and go on my way." He stared hopefully into the hard face.

"I doubt if Master would thank me for letting go a poacher. He'd maybe like to see you in front of Mr. Blair."

It was a new name to Oldroyd. "Who's he?"

The man laughed. "You must be a stranger round here. Mr. Justice Blair, the local beak. Court sits tomorrow. He may not be too hard on you, providing you've not been in trouble before, that is."

Oldroyd began to sweat in earnest. If this Mr. Justice made inquiries up north—oh yes, they knew him there. Transportation maybe or years inside.

" 'Tis not my trap and I never touched the rabbit. You were too clever there. I didn't see anybody about. I'm a stranger looking for work. Give me a chance."

The man pondered. "What's your name?"

"Jack Oldroyd."

"Oldroyd?" The man straightened and his eyes narrowed. "So you're Oldroyd." The twin barrels of the shotgun rose. "You're the troublemaker I've been asked to keep my eye on."

Oldroyd watched in stupefaction as the barrels lined up on his chest. He licked dry lips. "Who—who asked you?"

"Master, of course. Mister Cornwell."

"What's he want to do that for? I've done nothing to him."

"Not yet you haven't, but he's not keen on you stirring up the men. He thinks you should go away."

"I will, I will," croaked Oldroyd. "Don't point that gun at me, please."

To Oldroyd's surprise, the man lowered the gun and laid it on the grass. He straightened, grinning. It was not a grin that commended itself to Oldroyd. There was a wolfish anticipation about it. He backed away, his eyes darting about for a way of escape.

"Aye, you go away, lad, like you said, but I'll give you a little present from Master first, then you'll know not to come back for his gamekeeper'll be watching out."

He launched himself with sudden ferocity and Oldroyd stumbled back, twisting to avoid the swinging arms. A blow on the cheek made his head swim but he dodged a second blow. He'd run enough up north. If he could stay upright under those wild blows, he might outrun this man. He kicked and hacked back, much as he had done as a boy in the back streets of Burnley. But the man was stronger and more powerfully built than Oldroyd. A crack on the shoulder and a punch in the midriff numbed his arm and left him gasping, but he kicked out instinctively. The gamekeeper grunted as Oldroyd's boot met a shinbone.

In that moment of withdrawal, Oldroyd saw his chance and leapt for the trees. His breathing was ragged from the midriff blow but he dragged in great gasps until the pain eased. He ran, zigzagged through the trees, unsure of his direction and not knowing on whose land he was. He slowed, listening. There was no sound of pursuit and he stopped to lean against a tree. Perhaps he had left Cornwell land behind. He wiped his wet face and winced at the pain in his shoulder. A right bruise he'd have on his face, maybe a black eye too. He staggered on, feeling his stomach muscles cramp with pain and hunger. So, Mr. Cornwell had set his gamekeeper to watch out and give him a beating if he showed. As he walked, a fierce determination grew in Oldroyd. Mr. Cornwell should suffer for this day's work. Oldroyd dragged himself up the incline onto the footpath to the village. He'd beg a crust from the first cottage he came upon. They couldn't refuse him that.

The sole of his boot skidded suddenly on a flat stone and he lurched off-balance. A tree root tripped him and he fell heavily onto his bruised shoulder. Twisting away from the pain of it he found himself falling, rolling uncontrollably of the road edge. With a thump he landed on his back in a deep, moist-earthed ditch. He closed his eyes and let the pain and dizziness take him.

"I'll try him higher, Chloris," shouted Matt from across the paddock beside the Trevelyan cottage. "Set up another bar."

Chloris Blair shook back her hair and hurried to do Matt's bidding. The stallion Matt had named Black Prince crabbed sideways, shaking his head irritably. Matt forced him into a tight circle to face the fence he had constructed. To Chloris's eye, Black Prince was not a born jumper but Matt was determined to turn him into a steeple chaser. She set the three-foot bar into place and ran back to the paddock fence where Matt's mother and Sefton stood.

Mrs. Trevelyn smiled. "Don't overheat

yourself, Chloris. The weather has turned a little sultry and you have been running about after Matt for the last hour."

Chloris wiped her damp palms down the side of her old skirt and smiled back.

"Well, he is so proud of Black Prince that I haven't the heart to refuse my help."

Sefton took the pipe from his mouth. "Yon horse has a mean streak and I'm thinking he's not enjoying being put through his paces."

Mrs. Trevelyan gave him a worried look and Chloris interposed, "Nonsense, Sefton. Matt is handling him perfectly. The horse will respond when he has grown used to what is asked of him."

She turned to watch Matt prepare the horse for the three-foot jump. It was little enough height when compared with the hedges the hunters took but this horse was not a hunter. Even Matt knew nothing of its history, save that it was young and handsome and had taken his eye. The jump was perfect, Matt close to the strong neck as the horse flowed over bar with feet to spare.

Matt brought the horse circling back, tight jaw relaxing and a glow of triumph on his face.

"Well done, Matt," called Mrs. Travelyan, her fears forgotten. "Is it not time for a cooling drink? I, for one, am quite parched. Will you join me, Mr. Sefton? Come soon, my dears, it will be cool indoors." She turned towards the cottage.

Matt looked down on Chloris and she thought again how handsome he was with dark looks and irresistible charm.

"Had enough, Chloris?" he asked, raising a mocking brow.

"Not at all," she said. "How can you suppose me wearied of scurrying back and forth across this paddock, raising bars at your command and replacing them when that dear horse kicks them away without consideration?"

Matt laughed. "I never supposed it for a minute." He patted the horse's glossy neck. "But Black Prince, here, is growing a shade hot. One more jump and we'll stop training for today." He paused, considering. "Set up a five-foot jump, Chloris. Let's see what he makes of it."

"Five-foot?" Chloris stared up into the brown eyes. "Isn't that too soon? He may refuse it."

She knew as she met Matt's gaze that it was pointless to argue. She recognized the glinting excitement she had seen on their smuggling forays, the challenge of danger he could not resist. He glanced at the retreating form of Sefton and his mother.

"You saw how he cleared the last bar, at least by three more feet." He wheeled the horse about. "Set it up, Chloris." Then he was off across the paddock.

Chloris walked to the fence and raised the bar, eyeing the height with misgiving. It was too high for a novice jumper but Matt was determined and would raise it himself if she refused. She moved back to the paddock rail and watched, her heart beating a little faster.

Matt guided Black Prince twice round, showing him the bar, then cantered to the far end of the paddock field. The stallion moved swiftly, man and horse flowing as one. For a moment the horse appeared to be gathering itself for the jump, then it hesitated fractionally and swerved aside. Chloris gasped as Matt, already high in the saddle to complete the jump, hurtled over the fence. The stallion, free from its rider, took off in a wild career round the paddock.

Chloris began to run, her gaze divided

between the still figure and the cavorting stallion. An excited and loose horse could be dangerous to anyone in its path. She reached the end of the jump fence and looked down.

Matt lay flat on his back, eyes closed, dark hair falling over a flushed face. Without touching him, Chloris knelt down, running her gaze over his still figure. None of his limbs lay in contorted positions to suggest broken bones. Internal injuries or broken ribs would need a doctor's attention before anyone moved him. She leant forward, lightly running her fingertips along each shoulder. No evidence of dislocation. Her gaze rose to his face again. The brown eyes were open and watching her with suppressed amusement.

"Just winded," he said calmly, and Chloris sat back on her heels, feeling her face flush as a spasm of anger shook her.

"It's usual to keep the horse with you when you jump a five-foot fence!" she snapped. "But Matthew Trevelyan elects to be different!" She glared down at him. "Why didn't you say you were all right, instead of letting me think you were concussed or had some internal injury?"

He climbed to his feet, brushing the hair out of his face and grinning down at her. "Curious, I suppose. Just wanted to see if you'd scream or faint when confronted with a mangled corpse."

"Very considerate of you. At least your mother was spared the sight of your play-acting."

He put an arm about her shoulders. "Don't be cross. I hate cross women. Let's go and have that cold drink." He glanced about to see the stallion, now quiet, cropping the grass. "Refuse me, would you? I'll attend to you later."

"Don't be too discouraged," Chloris said in tones of mock comfort. "One out of two over the jump is halfway there. With a little more practice, you could make it together and double your score."

Matt gave her a sideways grin, his eyes bright. "Had you worried, did it?"

Chloris drew a deep breath to calm herself. He would never know how worried she had been and she wouldn't give him the satisfaction of knowing it.

"Of course I was worried," she said lightly. "The stallion could have broken a leg and heaven knows what you paid for him."

Matt laughed and gave her shoulder a squeeze. "That's my Chloris. Always on target with her tongue." He dropped his arm and held open the cottage door as they moved into the cool interior to join Mrs. Trevelyan and Sefton.

Oldroyd came out of his dazed coma slowly and in some confusion. He tried to sit up, then fell back, groaning. A sound reached him and he tensed. Hoofbeats. Somebody was riding slowly along the footpath. Was it that gamekeeper, now mounted and searching for him? But he couldn't still be on Cornwell land, could he? He shivered as he remembered the way those two gun barrels stared down at him. Lying flat on his back in a ditch, as he was now, might prove an irresistible target for the man whose shin he had hacked.

Chloris Blair, riding Bessie from the Trevelyan cottage, was taking the short cut home along the fringe of the Field estate. She frowned, staring about her. Was that a groan? She could see no-one. A movement from the ditch drew her attention and she slowed Bessie to a walk, peering down. Her first thought was for a trapped animal but the groan had sounded human.

"Who's down there?" she called. "Are you hurt?"

Oldroyd relaxed as he heard a girl's voice. Not the gamekeeper, thank God. He began to heave himself out of the ditch. His face and shoulders still hurt but he had the use of his legs. He could still run if needs be.

Chloris stared at the mud-streaked shabby man watching him warily. He held one shoulder awkwardly and the side of his face was swollen and beginning to bruise. He saw a dark-haired girl, green-eyed and smooth of skin. She was well-mounted and despite the well-worn riding habit, he detected the look of quality.

"What happened to you?" she asked. "Can I help?"

Oldroyd shrugged. "Fell in the ditch. I'll mend."

"You've hurt your shoulder. There's a doctor in the village—"

"I don't want no doctor," Oldroyd stated, then a wave of dizziness overcame him and sank down on the grass verge.

"I'll ask him to bring his trap if you can't walk that far. He is most obliging."

Oldroyd peered up at her. "Fetch a doctor? For me? Why should you? You don't know me."

"What has that to do with anything? You're hurt, that's obvious. May I ask who you are?"

Oldroyd's eyes narrowed in suspicion. "Who wants to know?"

Chloris eyed him in surprise. "My name is Blair, if it makes any difference."

An alert look crossed Oldroyd's face. "Blair? Kin to Mr. Justice Blair?"

"He's my father. Now, do you wish me to ride for the doctor?"

"You ride for the doctor and come back with the constable. Is that it?" He grinned without mirth. "Think I was born yesterday?" He dragged himself upright, crossed the footpath and began a stumbling run towards the stream, leaving Chloris frowning in puzzlement.

13

Daniel Moffat watched Oldroyd sidle into the
Royal Oak that night. The man had hesitated by
the door first, his sharp eyes darting about, as if
he had reason to avoid someone in particular. Dan
glanced about too but only his regulars were
there. Oldroyd seated himself, apparently satisfied.

Daniel had been reflecting on his summary
dismissal of Oldroyd yesterday when the ale
barrel had spilled its contents over the yard. He
had promised the man a meal and a drink and it
wasn't entirely Oldroyd's fault since the man was
inexperienced. Dan felt bad about not keeping his
word. He filled a pint tankard, took a plate containing a large meat pie, placed both on a tray and
moved out from the bar.

Oldroyd jumped as Dan's bulk blotted out the
light. He looked up nervously. Dan put down the
tray.

"This is for you, on the house."

Oldroyd looked at the tray, then up at Dan.
"What for?"

Dan shrugged. "I promised you a pint and a

bite yesterday. I'm a man to keep my word, like it or not."

Oldroyd's eyes flickered to the pie and he licked his lips. "And you don't like it, do you? Being beholden to me, I mean?"

"Can't say that I do," Dan said steadily. "So I've given you what I owe and there's an end to it. For myself, I'd be a whole lot happier if you moved along somewhere else."

Oldroyd grinned savagely. "So would a lot of people but why should I?"

Dan noted the way Oldroyd held his shoulder. He glanced at the purpling bruise on the man's face.

"It seems," he said dryly, "that I'm not the first to suggest it, though I'm not a man of violence, myself."

Oldroyd lowered his gaze and reached for the pie. "Like you, Mister Moffat, I'm a man who likes to keep a promise and pay what's owed."

His jaws closed round the crust of the pie and Dan turned back to the bar. Someone had given Oldroyd a beating. He had not denied it, and by his own words, he was not a man to forget it. There'd be trouble when Oldroyd took his revenge. Dan had no doubt that Oldroyd planned something. He nodded to himself. Yes, he would do as Joss Darling had asked, and note who joined the Northerner at his table. During the evening, it puzzled him to see that apart from a few nods and muttered words, no-one took notice of Oldroyd. The man, himself, left early, after finishing the pie and ale Dan had given him. Was he taking the hint and moving on? Dan had the uneasy feeling that his words had been a waste of breath.

Meggie Darling was up early next morning to cook her father's breakfast. With a large apron protecting her new pink dress, she packed the lunch baskets for those who were entitled to receive farmhouse food at the midday break. Her own basket stood on the sideboard. Wrapped in a napkin and surrounded by small pots of home-made chutney and jam was a rabbit pie.

Joss smiled into his daughter's pink face as he laid down his knife and fork.

"Give my regards to the Widow Brownlow, Meggie, and tell her I'll be along with a barrel of apples by month end."

"Yes, Father." Meggie looked round the kitchen. "You'll manage without me for a few hours?"

"With a pound of farm cheese, a shelf of pickles, and a batch of new bread, I reckon I'll not starve, lass, and neither will Widow Brownlow by the look of that basket."

Meggie smiled. "She's a good soul and likes a bit of company since she can't get out much now with her rheumatics. I'll be back to brew your tea."

"I'll be off myself, then," Joss said as Meggie took her straw bonnet from the hook behind the door. He shrugged into his working jacket and patted the pockets. "You'll be passing Joel's store, won't you? Bring me a couple of ounces of tobacco, will you?"

"Of course, Father." She kissed him on the cheek and Joss thought again how pretty she looked in the pink cotton dress with its little sprays of blue flowers.

They left the farmhouse together, Joss turning to the fields and Meggie setting out to walk the two miles to Widow Brownlow's cottage. She could have taken the old horse but his pace was no faster than walking and she didn't want to crease her new dress.

By the time she reached the village store, the morning was well-advanced, and Meggie's basket had acquired several bunches of wild flowers she had gathered on the way to brighten Widow Brownlow's tiny parlor.

Joel Darling saw her first and the roll of webbing he had just lifted from the shelf dropped out of his hand. He still clutched one end and the roll bounced along the floor, unwinding itself like some serpentine creature until it was halted by a pair of ladies' elegant sandals.

Chloris Blair looked down at the now exhausted roll, then followed its trail to the hands of Joel Darling. He was pink-faced with embarrassment, coming crabwise round the counter to gather up the webbing in a flurry of gangling arms and legs. Chloris gave him a grave smile of sympathy, stifling the urge to giggle as she saw the reason for Joel's sudden loss of co-ordination. Meggie appeared not to have noticed and was gazing with fixed intensity at a display of iron kettles. Joel stood as if his boots were nailed to the floor.

Chloris reached out a hand and lifted a loop of webbing from Joel's clutching arms.

"Brown webbing is all very well, Joel," she said. "But do they make it in green or blue? Brown is so somber. Do show me your stock, if you will."

Joel blinked and Chloris took him casually by the elbow, leading him back to the counter. "I cannot, for the moment, think what use it is put to, but I dare say the groom has his reasons or why would he be so particular as to color?"

Chloris had no idea what she was talking about but it served to bring Joel out of his trance. He began to rewind the webbing.

"Only brown, Miss Blair," he managed as Meggie approached the counter.

"Thank you for showing it to me, anyway," Chloris said and turned. "Hello, Meggie. We don't see you in here very often. I don't need to ask if you're well, for you look a picture of prettiness."

"Thank you, Miss Chloris. I hope you and Mr. Justice are in health, too. I'm on my way to the Widow Brownlow with some few things but I called here to get tobacco for my father." She looked at Joel. "His usual, if you please."

As Joel hurried to do her bidding, Meggie gave a tiny chuckle. "I pretended not to see," she whispered. "It seemed kinder."

Chloris nodded. "You have a kind heart, Meggie."

"So have you, Miss. What would you be wanting with webbing?"

Chloris looked into the dancing eyes. "I haven't the faintest idea," she admitted, a wavering note of laughter in her voice.

Joel came back and Meggie tucked the small packet into her basket, smiling kindly at Joel. "Father says to invite you for supper tonight, if you can manage it. Six o'clock?"

Joel nodded and mumbled something indistinct. He lowered his head to hide the pleasure on his face and concentrated his attention rewinding the heaped webbing on the counter.

Outside, on the sunny street near the store, a young girl in a straw bonnet and flowered cotton dress paused, catching the eye of the old man sitting in his cottage doorway. She smiled and raised a hand.

He peered, then his face cleared. "Good morning to you, Miss Cornwell."

Lounging in the shadowed alley between the store and the wall of the Royal Oak stood Oldroyd. The tavern was not yet open and he waited, jingling the few coins in his pocket. He craned his neck, seeing the swirl of pink cotton skirts as the figure of a young girl went into the store.

Miss Cornwell, he mused. Daughter of the man who had ordered his gamekeeper to give him a beating. His shoulder gave a vicious throb as he thought of the gamekeeper and the high and mighty landowner. They'd not be so smug when the ricks went up in smoke and he, Oldroyd, got his revenge for that beating.

Sarah Cornwell stepped into the dim interior of the store. "Good morning everyone," she said cheerfully. "I'm sorry I'm a little late, Chloris. I told Father at breakfast that I was to meet you here and walk over to Field House together but he argued I should take the carriage. I really can't think why as it is a lovely day, but Mother persuaded him in the end. Have you been bored, waiting for me?"

"Not—not at all," Chloris said, avoiding Meggie's mischievous eye. "One learns a great deal about—things here."

Meggie lifted her basket from the counter and turned into a shaft of sunlight streaming through the door. Sarah Cornwell blinked. She and Meggie regarded each other gravely, then both girls began to laugh.

"It's almost like looking into a mirror, Meggie. Both of us wearing our pink dresses and straw bonnets. How clever of you to make such a pretty dress from that small piece."

"Thank you, Miss." Meggie's smile dimpled. "I must be off now or Widow Brownlow will think I am not coming." She moved to the doorway as she spoke. "Goodbye, everyone."

Chloris smiled at Joel. She and Sarah moved to the door, pausing to pull the brims of their bonnets a little further forward. Chloris saw Meggie turn onto the bridle path disappearing from view behind the field hedge. A few old men sat outside their cottages and an assortment of dogs and cats lay stretched in the sun. Not a soul but themselves seemed to be astir in Gilminster.

Sarah paused at the haberdashery shop. Through its bowed windows, Chloris caught a reflected glimpse of movement. Someone was astir, after all. She looked over her shoulder back to the store with the Royal Oak tavern beyond. A figure detached itself from the side shadows of the store and wandered down the street, away from them. A man, angular-boned, capped head and with hands thrust deep into pockets, moved towards the bridle path. His pace was slow, as if on a leisurely stroll. Chloris tried to place him for there were few she was unacquainted with in Gilminster. She forgot about him as Sarah exclaimed. "Oh, look, Chloris, that pink velvet ribbon. It's just the shade I want. Do let's go in before it's bought up."

Joss Darling walked into the farmhouse, wiping his face on a large cotton handkerchief. The day was hot but a touch sultry, he thought. Maybe a shower tonight to cool things down, and the orchards could do with it. He crossed to the stone sink to wash his hands. It wasn't until he was drying them on the roller towel behind the backdoor that he became aware of the stillness. He touched the kettle with a tentative finger. It was cold. The stove beneath was cold too, no flicker of warmth from the ashes, usually made up by Meggie to boil the kettle. Widow Brownlow must have kept her talking.

He filled a tankard with cider and sat down to

smoke his pipe. She'd come dashing in soon, full of apologies, as if his tea was that important. He finished the cider and as he tapped out his pipe, he glanced at the clock over the mantlepiece. Going up to five o'clock, it was. Well, she wouldn't delay longer with Widow Brownlow for with Joel coming to supper, she'd want to get started on it. He laid his pipe on the mantlepiece and went back to the fields.

It was almost six o'clock when he returned. Joel Darling was sitting on the bench under the parlor window, his long legs outstretched, a gloomy expression on his face. He scrambled up as Joss approached.

"Evening, Uncle."

"Hello, Joel. Has Maggie thrown you out for getting in her way?"

"Meggie's not here, Uncle. I thought she might be with you."

Joss's smile faded. "Not here? She said she'd be back to make my tea but she wasn't." He frowned. "Was she in the store this morning?"

"Yes, Uncle. She bought your tobacco. Said she was going on to Mrs. Brownlow's."

"So she intended. Has anyone been taken sick, sudden like?"

Joel shook his head. "Nothing said in the store." He thought for a minute, then looked at his uncle with alarm in his eyes. "Perhaps Meggie's had an accident."

Joss stared. "We'll soon find out," he said grimly. "She'd take the bridle path from the village. Saddle up the old horse, Joel, and follow the path to Widow Brownlow's. If something held her up, she'll come that way home. Keep a sharp lookout and ask Mrs. Brownlow what time she left. If we find her I'll send a lad to the Royal Oak."

Joel nodded and flung himself towards the

stable. Joss hurried back to the fields. Some of the men would be leaving to go home. He'd ask them all to keep their eyes open for Meggie. She was well-liked by the farm workers and if she'd had an accident, they'd be only too eager to help find her.

Half-an-hour later, Joel Darling brought the old horse to a halt after emerging into the village street from the bridle path. He dismounted, gazing up and down the street, like a man in a daze. The Royal Oak, now open for business, caught his eye and he led his mount towards it. He stumbled inside.

Daniel Moffat looked over at the wild-eyed youth and frowned. "What's to do, lad? You look as if you've seen a ghost."

Joel stared about him, then moved to the bar in a rush. "Has anybody come in here from Field's just lately?"

Dan shook his head. "Now you mention it, there's not a one from there yet. Only the Randall and Cornwell fellows." He looked at Joel's white face. "What is it, lad?" His tone was so gentle that Joel felt like bursting into tears. His tale was disjointed but Dan seemed to gather the relevant facts. He reached above his head and brought down a heavy pewter pot. The crash as he banged it twice on the counter, brought utter stillness and a craning of necks. Dan surveyed the questioning faces.

"Now listen, you lot. Joel here has brought mysterious news and it's my belief you'll all be wanting to help." He glanced at Joel but the boy seemed incapable of speech, so Dan continued. "Meggie Darling's gone missing, and you all know she's a good lass and wouldn't do anything to upset her dad. Fact is, she left the village store well afore noon to go to Widow Brownlow's place. Joel's just come from there." He paused, watching their faces. "Widow Brownlow says she never arrived. Meggie Darling has disappeared!"

There was a murmur of voices, a scraping of stools as men rose. Dan raised his hands to quieten them.

"From here, you'd suppose she took the bridle path, but maybe she didn't."

One of the domino-playing old men looked up. "She did that, for I saw her myself. Turned down the bridle path, she did, with a basket on her arm. Saw the other lasses too." He returned to the contemplation of a domino in his hand.

"What lasses, Billy?" asked Dan patiently.

"Eh?" Old Billy looked up. "Miss Blair and Miss Cornwell. They left the store together."

"With Meggie?"

"No. They two went the other way."

"Did you see anyone else?"

Billy shook his head. "I was dozing a bit in the sun 'til my old dog rolled onto my feet. 'Twas maybe only a shadow I saw. Can't say for certain it was that fellow."

"What fellow, Billy?"

Billy glanced up surprised, into the intent faces of the men crowding round his table. "That fellow Jessop and Dormer are so thick with. The one who goes on about machines."

Dan stared at the two men named. "Oldroyd? We'd best get him over here and find out if he saw Meggie on the road to Widow Brownlow's. Since you two are so thick with him, go and fetch him. Where's he staying?"

Jessop and Dormer looked uncomfortable. "Don't know. Said he had a tidy little place somewhere and nobody to see him come and go. No landlady, like."

"Living rough, you mean?"

"Reckon so. Safer, he said, 'specially after his

tangle with . . ." An elbow in the ribs silenced him.

"Go on," said Dan with dangerous quiet. "Who gave him that beating? You'd best tell me."

The man answered sullenly. "It was the Cornwell gamekeeper." He looked defiantly at Dan. "He'll get even, he said so. But that's nothing to do with Meggie Darling. We're just wasting time talking."

"Reckon you're right," Dan said thoughtfully. "But keep an eye out for him, all the same. We've got to find Meggie Darling first. Get on to it, lads, and we'll have her safe home before dark."

Dan stood on his doorstep, shouting after the men streaming down the street. "Any news and you take it to the Field farmhouse and Joss Darling." He turned back to confront Joel. "Get back to your uncle, lad, and tell him I'll rouse every man in the village if needs be."

Joel nodded dumbly and Dan helped him onto the back of the old horse.

The drawing room at Field House was a place of light and laughter. The glow of the sun fell across the small baize-topped table Quentin had set up, highlighting the chestnut glint of Georgina's hair as she leaned forward over the cards.

Quentin had been persuaded to make a fourth with Chloris and Sarah. The game was light-hearted with blatant cheating accepted cheerfully. Georgina was fast learning that her mama's strict behavior pattern was a pliable thing in country life and she was not in the least shocked by Chloris's denunciation of the character of gentlemen like Quentin who cheated most outrageously.

Sarah glanced at the carriage clock on the mantlepiece as it chimed. "Oh, my goodness," she exclaimed, her cheeks pink with the excitement of the game. "Can it really be half-past six? I said I would be home by teatime. I shall have to rush if I'm to be there for dinner." She smiled round the table. "I have so enjoyed this afternoon and the time has just flown by."

"I'll take you home in the trap," Quentin said, rising. "It will only take ten minutes."

"May I beg a lift to the village?" asked Chloris. "Sarah and I walked here together."

"Of course. I'll see you both safely home."

They said goodbye to Georgina and moved into the shadowed porch to await the trap Quentin had ordered. The sun was still bright but low on the horizon, its hazy glow a fierce deep pink.

"Rain, perhaps," observed Quentin, his eyes on the sky.

Carriage wheels sounded and they turned. It was not the trap but a heavy carriage being driven at speed through the entrance gates. It bore down on them and halted in a swirl of gravel and dust.

"Why, it's our own carriage," Sarah exclaimed from behind Chloris. "Father must really be cross to send it here. He didn't want me to walk in the first place."

Quentin glanced over his shoulder. "Why not?"

Sarah shrugged. "I don't really know. He had words with the gamekeeper yesterday and has been bad-tempered ever since. I've no idea why that should upset him."

Quentin thought of Oldroyd and the remark of William Cornwell's of setting the gamekeeper to turn him off Cornwell land. If the instructions had been taken too literally, physical violence might drive Oldroyd into some vengeful response.

The door of the carriage swung open and Mr.

Cornwell himself climbed down unsteadily. He stared at Quentin.

"Sir Lionel. Is he in?" There was the slightest of quavers in his voice. "I must see him."

Quentin stepped off the porch. "I believe so, sir. Will you step inside? I was about to bring Sarah home in the trap and apologize for keeping her so long. We were playing cards and quite forgot the time." He stopped, aware that William Cornwell was not listening to him. His eyes had found Sarah.

"Are you all right, Sarah?" asked her father.

"Of course I'm all right." Sarah was puzzled at the abrupt tone. "Is something the matter, Father?"

William Cornwell seemed to pull himself together. "Nothing, nothing. You were late. I was worried. Get into the carriage, Sarah. I will take you home." She obeyed and he climbed in after her and closed the door.

Quentin moved forward. "You wished to see my father."

"Not important. Another time. Drive on, coachman."

The carriage swung in a wide arc and swept out between the gates. Quentin and Chloris looked at each other.

"What was all that about?" she asked.

Quentin shook his head. "No idea."

The trap came round the side of the house and Quentin helped Chloris onto the bench seat. She laid her bonnet beside her, letting the evening breeze play through her hair. The golden chestnut horse between the shafts high-stepped along the lane.

"Have you brought his wives yet from High Ride?" Chloris asked.

Quentin gave her a grin. "Not so loud. I haven't told him yet what delights are in store."

Chloris laughed and shook back her dark hair.

Quentin eyed the streaming hair with amusement. "You're like a wild young filly yourself with that mane of hair. Your Miss Sinclair did not succeed in taming you, I'm glad to say."

"Why, Quentin, I always supposed that you disapproved of my wildness and bade me conduct myself in the manner of Georgina."

Quentin laughed. "I rather thought this afternoon that Georgina was modelling herself on you. I'll swear she had cards tucked in both sleeves and on her lap, too."

"How appalling!"

"Quite outrageous."

They grinned at each other, then Quentin looked past Chloris. "Hello, that looks like Joss Darling coming this way on one of the field horses. In a hurry, too." He urged the chestnut into a swift canter and closed the gap between the trap and Joss Darling's horse.

"I was coming to the house, Mr. Quentin," Joss gasped and they noticed the grayness of his face and the haunted eyes.

"What's wrong, Joss?"

"It's Meggie. I've got the men out searching for her. She's been missing since this morning. Never showed for tea nor supper. Dear God, where can she be?"

"Meggie was in the store this morning," Chloris said. "She was going to Widow Brownlow's."

"She never got there," Joss said grimly. "Joel's been out there already. I wanted to ask Sir Lionel if we could have permission to search the other estates too."

"You've got it now, Joss. Let's get back to the

farmhouse and I'll send messages to Mr. Randall and Mr. Cornwell."

Joel Darling jumped up from the bench by the wall as the trap drew to a halt by the house door. In the darkening light his face was pale, his clothes dusty from the search. A few farmhands stood about looking awkward and sweat-streaked.

"We've searched down by the stream and in Prior's Wood," they said. "No sign of Miss Meggie. Dan Moffat sent men down the bridle path, the way she is supposed to have gone, but she wasn't there. Maybe she cut off and went elsewhere but it's mortal hard to think where else she could have gone."

"She wouldn't let down Widow Brownlow. That's not like Meggie," Joss said emphatically.

"We need more helpers," Quentin said. "It's going to rain and if she's hurt, it won't help. We need Cornwell and Randall men out too."

"They're out already, sir. Dan Moffat put the word about."

"Good. Though I can't think for the life of me why she should have gone on either land there's no harm in looking." He looked at Joss. "You look all in, man. Get inside and sit yourself down. Take a mug of cider." He took Joss's arm, forcing him into the kitchen of the farmhouse. Chloris filled tankards for Joss and Joel. Quentin shook his head and Chloris sat down.

Joel spoke first. "Old Billy at the Royal Oak said he saw that stranger, Oldroyd, go down the bridle path same as Meggie."

"Oldroyd?" Quentin looked at him sharply. "And what has he to say about that?"

Joel shook his head. "Nobody's seen him since then. They say he's living rough." He lapsed into silence.

Quentin frowned at the cider jug. "I can't fit Oldroyd into this. His grudge is against Cornwell, not Joss or us. It wasn't our gamekeeper who gave him a beating. No, it must be some simple accident."

Chloris said slowly. "Do you remember Sarah talking about her father having angry words with the gamekeeper? Supposing he hadn't intended the gamekeeper to go so far and was worried that Oldroyd might do something drastic in revenge."

Quentin was watching her closely. "Like what? Damage to Cornwell's property?"

Chloris lowered her voice so that the two dull-eyed men could not hear her. "A little more personal I was thinking." She saw the shock and understanding come into Quentin's eyes.

He too spoke in low tones. "Sarah was late going home. He knew where she intended going this morning, and the urgency to see my father diminished rapidly when he saw her. Could he have feared—? But dammit, Chloris, if Oldroyd's involved, why Meggie? Why not Sarah? I don't think he even knows either. No, it's nonsensical!"

Chloris's heart gave a sudden jerk. "Oh my God, it couldn't be!"

Quentin gripped her wrist. "What couldn't be?"

Chloris swallowed. "This morning in the store." She recalled the laughter. "Sarah and Meggie were dressed alike in sunbonnets and pink dresses. The same material, for Sarah gave Meggie the length that was left over."

"You mean he might have followed Meggie, thinking she was Sarah?"

Chloris nodded, her face pale. "Someone did call a greeting to Sarah as she came in. I heard it."

"And a pink dress is a pink dress," Quentin said grimly. "My God, the men will tear him limb

208

from limb if he's harmed Meggie." He rose. "You'd best stay here with—" He turned as back door opened.

Young Tom stood there, a wide grin on his face, a large bunch of wild flowers clutched in a grimy fist. "Evening, all," he said. "I brought these for Meggie." His smile faded as he caught the atmosphere and saw the pale, strained faces. "Wh—what's wrong?" he stammered.

No-one spoke. They all stared wordlessly at the boy, whose freckles stood out like golden spots on his suddenly pale face. The flowers dropped from his fingers and lay colorful but a little wilted on the floor. Monkshood, snapdragon, tufted vetch.

Chloris's eyes followed their fall. What was it about those flowers that held her attention. Wild flowers, growing on every hedge, lurking in every ditch, adding splendor to the vistas of green. She drew her gaze up with an effort to Tom's still face.

"When did you gather those, Tom?" she whispered.

He looked surprised. "On the way here."

"When, Tom? How long ago? Please tell me truly."

The boy dropped his gaze and shrugged. "Well, I didn't really. Gather them, I mean. I sort of found them, all nice and neat, so I brought them."

"Where did you find them?"

"In a field. Why?"

The question was in all their eyes as they watched Chloris.

"Those flowers," she said, "were lying on the top of Meggie's basket this morning. I distinctly remember those snapdragons and the ferns around them."

Quentin moved towards the boy. "Tell us

exactly where, Tom. Meggie's lost and it gives us a point to start from."

"Meggie's lost?" The boy looked incredulous. "How can she be?"

"Never mind how, just tell us."

Tom thought for a moment. "Can't exactly tell you but I'll take you there." A mulish expression fixed itself to his face. "Meggie's my friend. I'll help by showing you the place and we'll find her together. Can't say fairer than that."

Joel was on his feet. "I'll come too. Meggie's my cousin."

When Chloris stood up, Quentin sighed. "I suppose you want to come too?"

"Certainly. Meggie will need me." She stared at Quentin, willing him to understand that in certain cases another female was most necessary.

His eyes looked into hers and he nodded. "Yes, you're right." He looked down on Joss. "I think there's a good chance here with Tom's help. We'll find her, never fear."

Joss nodded dully. "Please God," he muttered.

The four of them climbed into the trap and Quentin set the chestnut into a brisk trot through the lanes. The village came and went, then they were on the bridle path. It was raining a little as Quentin drew the trap to a halt beside the field Tom indicated.

"I came over the heathland," he stated. " 'Tis a mite shorter than going down through the village to our cottage."

Chloris looked at the lane that curved in the opposite direction towards Widow Brownlow's. There was a great deal of heathland, rough, stony, and with dips and hollows.

"Why should Meggie have taken to the heathland?" she asked. "Are you sure, Tom, that you found those flowers out there?"

"Certain sure," answered Tom and pointed. "Over there, beyond that falling down cottage."

They began to walk to the ruined building. Very little of it was left and the roof had fallen in. Joel and Tom climbed over the fallen masonry but there was no place of shelter within.

The sky was darkening and the rain had turned into a drizzle. They hurried their steps, spreading out, the unspoken thought in each mind that Meggie must be found before darkness fell.

Tom pounced on a drooping fern leaf. He held it up and frowned. "I found the others back there," he said with a jerk of his head. " 'Tis like a trail we're following." He looked ahead. "There's nothing over there till you reach Randall's."

"Nothing you can see unless you're looking on purpose," Chloris said. "This heath is chalky soil and you can find fragrant orchids if you're determined on it."

"And Meggie was collecting wild flowers for Widow Brownlow," Quentin agreed. He raised his head to listen.

Far in the distance they could see and hear the searchers from the Randall estate. "We'll meet up with them," he said. "Let's move on."

They went on in the increasing rain, Tom circling like a sheep dog eager to bring in a stray lamb.

Quentin pointed to a dip in the land, shadowed and surrounded by bushes. "What's down there, Tom?"

Tom glanced over. "A bit of a cleft in the rock, a sort of hidey-hole the children play in." From his advanced age of ten years, his tone was scornful.

"We'll look just the same," Quentin decided and they moved down the incline.

"It's not very big," Tom said. "Room for little 'uns when they're playing, I suppose." He reached the place and pulled on a bush.

Joel stared, then hot black anger tore through his body. In two strides of his long legs he was through the opening, his hands reaching like claws. They fastened on the collar of the startled man, lifting and shaking him like a stringless puppet before flinging him over backwards.

Meggie stared up, her eyes wide and awestruck. "Joel!" she breathed. "Don't do that to poor Mr. Oldroyd."

Joel blinked and looked down at Oldroyd crouching by the rock wall. "We—we've been searching for you all evening." He stood there, unable to say anymore.

"Of course, dear Joel. I knew you would when you heard. Mr. Oldroyd said so."

Chloris knelt beside Meggie. "Are you all right? What happened?"

Meggie smiled. "Of course, but it was my own silly fault for trying to reach those orchids. I put my foot in a hole and twisted my ankle." She looked ruefully down. "It was lucky that someone else was on the lane for I couldn't walk." She turned her smile on Oldroyd, still crouching by the wall and watching the entry of Quentin and Tom with trepidation. "Mr. Oldroyd has been most kind."

Chloris saw the grubby wet neckerchief bound tightly round Meggie's ankle and she recalled where she'd seen it before, around the neck of the man she had tried to remember from the village street, the man she had heard groaning in the ditch. She glanced up as Quentin eased into the cleft.

"Mr. Quentin," gasped Meggie. "Oh dear, what a lot of trouble I have caused. Mr. Oldroyd said he'd sent a message and I knew someone would come but it has seemed a long time. Poor

Mrs. Brownlow. We had to eat the pie I'd made for her."

Quentin looked hard at Oldroyd. "You sent a message? Is that right?"

Oldroyd nodded. "Aye, I did. Sent a lad to her father. Before six it was. Didn't ask for much, like, save what I felt he owed me for the beating. Might have known he'd send men, the old skinflint," he finished bitterly.

"You sent the lad to Mr. Cornwell, I presume."

Oldroyd pulled himself cautiously to his feet, a wary eye on Joel. "And now you'll have me in front of the Justice though I never intended harming the lass."

"Step outside with me, Oldroyd," said Quentin. "Joel, can you and Tom carry Meggie to the trap?"

Joel nodded and scooped Meggie up into his arms. He came out of the cleft, his face hard set and started over the heath, Tom trotting beside him.

"You, too, Chloris," Quentin said, laying a hand on her wet cheek and smiling. "I've a little business with Mr. Oldroyd. I won't be long." On an impulse he dropped a kiss on her forehead. "Dear Chloris. Wet and bedraggled but careless of it for a friend. No fashionable vapors for you, thank God."

Chloris smiled through her wet curtain of hair and turned to cross the heath.

Quentin was not smiling as he turned back to the shivering Oldroyd. The man was eyeing him curiously.

"I've seen you before. In the fields it was. I reckon you were having me on, acting stupid. You're not a farm laborer by the look of you now."

"No. My father is Sir Lionel Field."

213

Oldroy'd shoulders sagged. "One of the bosses. So now you've got me. What are you going to do?"

Quentin looked over his head. "If you listen, you'll hear the sound of men searching the area. Men from all three estates, Oldroyd, all searching for a missing girl. You may take it from me that the estates combine together when one of their own is threatened, like Meggie Darling disappearing."

"Who?"

"You thought it was Miss Cornwell you followed on the bridle path, I believe? You were wrong. It was the daughter of the Field estate manager." He paused. "Tell me exactly what happened."

Oldroyd shrugged. "When I followed her, I didn't know what I was going to do. I saw her go onto the heath, poking about for flowers, then she seemed to slip. I heard her cry out. I was about to make off when she saw me and called for help. I couldn't leave her there alone." He peered up wetly into Quentin's face. "I never did harm a lass in my life so I wet out my neckcloth in a puddle and tied it round her ankle 'cos it was swelling. When it started to rain, I helped her into that shelter. I went away for a while and told her I'd sent a message to her father. I waited for the lad to come back with a guinea or two, but he didn't. I went back to her then. Thought I could run for it if anybody came—she'd be all right. Never heard you come at all. The rain was making a din on the rocks." He stared morosely towards the advancing men. "That's the truth of it, guv'nor. The lass'll tell you no different."

"I believe you but will those men when they hear of it? You'll have no friends left in the county. There'll be no-one to listen when you plan your revenge on Mr. Cornwell."

Oldroyd laughed harshly. "I'll not get the chance, will I? In jail for trying to—what is it they call it?"

"Extort money?"

"Aye, that's it."

"If you've any sense you'll move back up north."

"I wish I'd never left it!" He stopped and looked from narrowed eyes at Quentin. "What do you mean—if I've any sense?"

Quentin weighed his words carefully. "The men don't know your involvement yet. Only four of us, including Meggie, have that knowledge. I'll make a bargain with you. Get well out of Dorset and we'll keep quiet. Show your face round here again and I'll bring a charge of kidnapping. If I do, you'll be safer in jail than out of it. Do you understand me?"

The barking of a dog made Oldroyd flinch and change color. "I understand you fine. You don't want nay talk about the lass and I don't want to go to prison. All right, Mr. Field. If you give me a chance, I'll go." He straightened his shoulders. "I'll not be down this way again. Folks stick together too much." He hesitated. "I never met a gent like you before. One who'll give the likes of me a chance."

Quentin smiled thinly. "Put it down to my kind heart, but don't presume on it. Don't suppose my head's soft too!"

Oldroyd turned. "I'll thank you for your heart, then. I'll be off."

"A moment," Quentin said and reached into his waistcoat pocket. "Here's a couple of guineas to help you on your way."

Oldroyd stared down at the gleaming coins, then looked up into Quentin's hard face.

"If I ever see you again," Quentin said in a voice that matched his expression, "I'll take them back. Understand?"

Oldroyd nodded, a flicker of fear in his eyes. Quentin turned abruptly and strode away from him. Oldroyd didn't wait to see him climb into the trap.

When Quentin reached home, his father was not in. He arrived as Quentin was descending the stairs, dry and freshly clothed. Sir Lionel was looking very pleased with himself.

"Join me for a drink, Quentin," he said, reaching for the bellrope. "This is cause for celebration, wouldn't you think?"

Quentin followed him into the library. "I quite agree but didn't realize you'd heard so soon."

"Got a message from Cornwell soon after you'd set off with the girls."

"Cornwell? But he came himself in the carriage and took Sarah home. Wouldn't stay and see you, though he seemed keen at the time."

"Second thoughts, my boy. A bit evasive is our William but the upshot is that he's not going to issue eviction notices after all."

"I see." Quentin smiled at his father. "Did he say why?"

"Not in so many words. Talked about not wanting to bring hardship on his workers and maybe he'd acted a bit hastily. It's my belief something frightened him into changing his mind."

"Or someone."

Sir Lionel was silent as Quentin recounted the evening's activity.

"Well, I'm damned," he said at length. "The old fox never said a word about any message."

"You may be sure he's thought about it since," Quentin said dryly. "He may have Sarah safely in the house at the moment but he can hardly keep her prisoner forever."

"But when you tell him Oldroyd's gone for good?"

"Mm. In a day or two, maybe," Quentin said.

Sir Lionel grinned. "Let him fret a bit?"

Quentin nodded. "Long enough to assure those nine tenants in writing they've nothing to fear, wouldn't you say?"

Sir Lionel laughed. "You're a sly dog, my boy."

"It goes with the inheritance, sir."

Sir Lionel sat back beaming. "Like father, like son," he chuckled.

When Chloris ran from the open trap to her front door, she was soaked through as they all had been on the way back to the farmhouse. Joss had had to be told of Oldroyd, for Meggie would speak of him in all innocence, but since Quentin and Chloris were the only ones to know of Oldroyd's true intent, the matter was treated as an accident and the search called off.

Chloris ran upstairs to be met by a horrified Molly. "Good heavens, Miss Chloris," said her maid. "Get out of those wet things at once or you'll catch your death of cold. And your sandals . . ." She stared at the mudstained leather. "Anyone would think you'd been stamping about the fields to look at them."

"So I have," said Chloris, kicking them off. "I've been out looking for Meggie. We found her, sprained ankle and all."

"I'm pleased to hear it, but surely there were enough men searching without you."

"I expect so, but I just happened to be there."

"And ruined your sandals into the bargain."

"Stop fussing, Molly. Help me change for dinner. I don't want to keep Father waiting."

Mr. Justice Blair put aside the papers he had been studying as Chloris entered the sitting room.

"Official papers, Father?"

He smiled. "Yes, my dear. Matters seem to be well in hand now with our small coastal problems."

Chloris's heart beat faster. During this glorious summer, she had not given much thought to the men who moved by night in the pursuance of their secret trade. The long light nights were not the ideal times. Autumn and winter gave better cover. All her old uneasiness about Matt came rushing back.

"And what have our Lords of the Admiralty decided?" she asked lightly.

"The scheme is basically the same as the one we talked of, all those months ago." He smiled. "I shouldn't have told you of it then, but you have repaid my confidence by allowing no hint to escape your lips. I thank you for it, my dear."

His eyes were so trusting that Chloris felt her throat go dry. Could she turn traitor on her own father for Matt's sake? Dear God, but she had to know.

"And when do they plan to start? Or is that a deep, dark secret?"

"It is not a father's duty to burden his daughter with secrets." Mr. Blair smiled. "Shall we say soon, and leave it at that?"

"Am I not to be trusted, Father?" She could not help feeling that her tone had become childishly petulant.

"Of course I trust you, my dear, but I hoped for a little less serious talk tonight for I see little of you, due to these meetings I am bound to attend. I have no wish to drive you away by my boring topics of conversation."

Chloris felt ashamed and reached out a hand to his. "Forgive me, Father. I am being quite thoughtless." She realized how lonely he must have been since her mother died in that still mysterious clifftop accident. What could a man do but immerse himself in his work?

Chloris smiled into the beloved face and began to tell him of the day, starting in the store with Joel chasing the errant roll of webbing and finishing with the successful finding of Meggie.

Mr. Blair was amused, then concerned, but Chloris assured him that a few days of rest would have Meggie back on her feet again. She omitted all mention of Oldroyd since his lawyer's mind might have seen Quentin's action in a different light.

When they parted for the night, it was raining heavily, thunder rumbling distantly. Chloris stared out of her bedroom window morosely. There was still nothing she could tell Matt to dissuade him from further activity. She shivered a little as she remembered Quentin's words on what happened to smugglers. They had made a greater impression than she realized. Perhaps if the sun shone again and summer returned . . . She turned to her bed, knowing Matt would not heed her pleas unless she had sound evidence to offer him.

14

It was two days before she saw Matt again. Unable to extract any information from her father without making him suspicious of her reasons, she had thrown on a cloak, changed into stout shoes and climbed the headland. The wind was cool as she sat hunched on a rock, hugging her knees. The sea was as gray as the sky with wind-whipped feathery crests lining the heavy swells. Like the sea she felt restless and the monotonous and repeated withdrawal of water across the pebbly beach below sounded like a slow drumbeat at some desolate place of mourning.

The weather was worsening. Ideal weather for smuggling, she supposed. She glanced over her shoulder, hearing the skid of booted feet on the rocks. Matt was coming towards her, the strong planes of his face revealed as the wind flung back his hair. He stopped, gazing down at her moody face, then he grinned. "I thought I'd find you here, Chloris. A good night for a run, don't you agree?"

She looked at him in astonishment. "Just look at the weather. Surely you're not so mad as to arrange a run tonight? They're more likely to be drowned than taken by the revenue officers.

There's a gale in the offing as you should know."

He dropped to sit beside her on the rocks, stretching his long legs before him. He was so close she could feel his heart begin to pound as it always did when he was near but she maintained her disapproving stare.

"It's madness, Matt, and you know it. Let them go if they want to. It's their business but for you it's sheer crack-brained folly. What would happen to your mother if you were caught?"

He lifted her chin with a long finger, turning her face to his. "Well, then, my little Cassandra," he said, his eyes full of amusement. "I would commend her to your care."

She pulled her chin away crossly. "Be serious, Matt. How would she go on if you were in prison?"

"Comfortably, I hope. Father's money is running out and Philip still at school. This way I hope to provide for them both for many years."

"Well, I'm sure she would be happier on less if it kept you out of prison," she returned sharply.

The look he turned on her was quizzical. "What happened to the wild adventuress who helped unload and even swam to help me that night?"

A touch of color tinged her cheeks. "I've had time to think. It was exciting, I don't deny, but I dare not join you again."

"Has your father been talking to you? Pointing out the evils that befall the lawless?"

"Not exactly," she began reluctantly. "But I realized earlier when Father and I dined at Field House that I must not bring disgrace on him. He has had enough sorrow to bear since Mother died."

Matt's eyes narrowed. "I would not for a moment imagine your father to have the slightest idea of your involvement, but there is someone else at Field House who might."

"Who can you mean? No-one knows I was there on the beach."

"Not with any certainty, to be sure, but there's one who might connect you with me. I suspect that Quentin Field knows what's going on."

"Oh, Quentin. But he's an old friend and would never betray us."

"Don't be too sure, my dear. He has become remarkably strait-laced since he came back to take over the estate. If anything happens on this coast, he'll know of it. If one of his grooms yawns all day, Quentin will want to know why he's so tired and with half the County involved, there'll be a deal of yawning. It wouldn't take long for a man as sharp as Quentin to discover the reason."

"But I won't believe he could ever inform on them."

"No, I agree, but a quiet word to the grooms and farm workers would do the trick just as well and we should then be short of helpers for Sir Lionel is the biggest landowner around. Quentin is determined to run that estate to perfection. He won't tolerate half-awake men operating his precious machinery or tending his stables."

Chloris thought uneasily of Quentin's searching questions. Could he be so base as to drop a hint in her father's ear of her support for the free-traders? She rather doubted it. On the other hand, she knew that Quentin respected her father. He might take it upon himself to keep a watchful eye on her in his stead.

"It wouldn't surprise me," Matt commented, shying a pebble into the sea moodily, "if he intends making the estate a showplace, comparable with the Chalmers land in Norfolk."

"Chalmers?"

"You wouldn't know him. It was while you were in Dorchester, but he used to stay often at Field House. One of Quentin's London friends, I believe. They had a common interest in the latest farm machinery."

"Was he a Lord Chalmers?"

"That's right. Come to think of it, I haven't seen him lately."

"What was he like?"

"About Quentin's age. A tall man with a primrose head on him."

"Primrose? What do you mean?"

"His hair. As like to the color of an early primrose as ever I've seen. But dangerous to remark on it. For all his delicate looks, I once saw him throw a man across the room for calling him a dandy-puff."

Was it possible, Chloris wondered, that Lord Chalmers had been the man on the cliffs riding after her mother? He had been at Field House too, that night. Quentin or Lord Chalmers? Or someone else completely, someone of whom she knew nothing.

"Sefton thinks we'll manage it before the storm breaks," Matt said, his eyes on the gray clouds. "According to the fishermen, the bad weather is moving fast across Europe. Shouldn't hit us until late tonight. We'll be back by then."

"You're not going with them, Matt?" She could not hide her anxiety.

"Yes, I am. I've had enough of Croker's sly comments."

"What sort of comments?"

"About taking risks at sea while gentlemen reap profits ashore. I put him in charge of the Heron, for he's a professional seaman, after all, while I organize the shore party. Now, he's taken to calling me Young Master, which is why I'll show him tonight that he's not the only one able to sail a lugger."

"Oh, Matt. Does it matter what he says?"

"Of course it matters! You don't understand, Chloris. You're a girl. I'll not have the team sniggering behind my back while Croker sings under his breath about lily-white boys. Shockingly off-key, too!"

She refused to respond to his grin. "Don't go, Matt. I have a premonition that something dreadful will happen."

"Don't be a goose, Chloris. And don't tell me you have the gift of prophecy or you see it all in the stars."

"But Matt . . ."

"Now don't go all gloomy and foreboding on me. I thought you had more spirit than that!" he interrupted impatiently. "If you don't have a better reason than just a silly old premonition, then I'll see you tomorrow after the run. It'll be dark early tonight. We'll be away just after sunset."

It was no use arguing with Matt when his mind was made up. She recognized the stubborn, almost sulky look that showed his dislike of being thwarted, and acknowledged that pride would not allow him to remain on shore with Sefton while Croker made slighting references to his courage. All she could do was hope that arrangements for the new measures were not yet complete.

They parted near the village and Chloris walked home deep in thought, trying to recapture the excitement that had made her eager to join him before. It had been a glorious adventure but strangely, not one she cared to repeat. What had changed her mind? she wondered. Matt was still the same so the change must be in herself. Or perhaps it was all Quentin's fault with his description of the horrid fates awaiting those who were caught.

That evening she dined quietly with her father. As soon as the table had been cleared he took his coffee into the study, leaving Chloris to wander moodily from armchair to bookcase to piano. A few chords struck, a few pages read, a period of staring into the flames of the fire still left her restless and uneasy. Through the mullioned windows she could see the sky darkening. A patter of rain like soft running footsteps blurred the view and the leaves of the elms at the boundary wall shivered in the rising wind.

In search of company she ran upstairs, knowing that Molly would be turning back her bedclothes and sorting through the clothes she had worn that day. Molly was always cheerful and her gossip might lighten the somber mood into which Chloris had fallen. She found her maid examining with a critical eye the hem of the riding skirt she had cast off hurriedly.

"I wish you would tell me, Miss Chloris, when you catch your heel in one of your skirts, for how can I mend it if I don't know of it? Think of my shame if I saw you ride off with the hem of your habit all hanging down in tatters. Why, I'd be the talk of the village!"

"I didn't know of it myself, Molly, and I would hardly describe that little piece of hem come loose as tattered."

"Well, it's time you had another riding dress made. This one is getting threadbare and won't last much longer. You should speak to Mr. Justice, too. Your mother's habit is still in her wardrobe and you're of a size now, so there's no sense in not using that one."

"Yes, I will, Molly, but not just yet. He is very busy with his legal affairs."

"That's true enough, poor gentleman. It's enough to wear out a younger man than him, all this coming and going to Dorchester. Then that business with the Royal Navy."

"The Royal Navy?" Chloris asked, staring. "Are you sure?"

"It was the linen draper told me. He said he'd seen Mr. Justice standing by his carriage outside the Customs House talking to some naval officers. The draper was on his way to the warehouse. While his wagon was being loaded he chanced to fall into conversation with a couple of chandlers who told him a strange thing."

"What was that?"

"They said they'd been ordered to provision a ship due to sail on the tide and there was but a handful of sailors aboard."

"Did he say where they were bound?"

"No. The men didn't know that but they weren't provisioning for a long voyage, just enough for a few days."

"That seems quite a normal thing," Chloris said slowly. "Why should the draper and the chandlers think it something to comment on and consider strange?"

"He used to be a sailor himself, did Tomkins, and he said the ship had seen better days and wouldn't bet on her coming through as much as a high wind in the Channel, not without a deal of repair which she was not getting, let alone a rough sea. She's not for sea duty, the chandler told him, but for something else nobody else knows anything about." Molly gave a grin as a thought struck her. "Tomkins says some of the men on board were as green as the sea and they'd not even upped anchor."

227

"What! The sailors?"

"No, Miss. Those revenue men who joined them at the last. And one of them was that inspector who tried to find lodgings in the village last month. Never been to sea in his life, Tomkins reckoned."

"For heaven's sake, Molly, why didn't you say that before?"

Molly stared at her. "What is it, Miss?"

"When did Tomkins tell you all this?"

"Why, not more than an hour ago. He'd had a bit of trouble with the wagon axle and couldn't get home last night. He called on his way to drop off a roll of linen for the sewing woman to make up the new kitchen tea towels."

"That means he was in Weymouth yesterday and the ship due to sail on the next tide." Chloris ran to the window. It was already dark. Her fingers gripped the stone sill and she tried to think logically and calmly. Was it just a frightening conicdence, her father's visit to Weymouth and the sailing of the old ship? Or was it the new scheme, already under way? Could it be coming here? She had to know. But was there time to warn Matt before he sailed? Without warning of the possible arrival of the ship, he was likely to return with a full load of contraband and run straight into the arms of the Royal Navy!

"Quickly, Molly, my cloak."

"Where are you going, Miss?"

"Never mind. I must go out."

Snatching her cloak from Molly's hands, she flung it about her shoulders and ran for the door, ignoring her maid's astonished face. Down the stairs and across the hall she fled, fumbling a little with the large bolt, then she was out in the garden. In evening slippers the stones cut into the thin soles but she ran without feeling the discomfort, her breath coming in gasps as she raced for the shore. Only the faint light from the horizon guided her, the moon all but invisible behind banked storm clouds. The wind snatched at her cloak, teasing it into the grasping points of the hawthorn bushes, but she dragged it roughly from all obstructions, her eyes intent on the path to the headland. From the high ground she would be able to scan the beach, then drop swiftly down one of the winding paths to intercept Matt. There was little hope of persuading him to abandon the venture but at least he should be warned of the likely presence of a naval ship and could contrive to return to some safer landing.

Her eyes, now accustomed to the dark, picked out the shape of the Martello Tower standing sentinel over the Channel, and her feet slowed in the rough grass of the cliff top. The beach lay below in shadowed silence. Nothing stirred, no sound of muffled oars or creaking canvas. She knelt, grasping the wiry grass, peering desperately along the coastline. A dark bulk held her gaze. Trying to identify it, she caught the faint winking light as of a dimmed lantern and her heart rose. Why had't she brought a lantern of her own? Her flight had been too precipitate to think of it but it would have been more sensible. They would have been sure to investigate a waving light.

She began a rapid descent to the beach, stones and earth showering down to bruise her feet. Only as she reached the level ground did she realize with a hollow feeling in her stomach that the object she was making for was far too large to be Matt's boat. She heard too the rattle of an anchor chain and the thud as it hit the water. It had to be Mr. Tomkins's old ship, full of sailors and revenue men, newly arrived and lying dark and menacing in the cove, waiting like some enormous cat for the unsuspecting mice to present themselves.

Standing motionless, her shoulders drooping, she felt for the first time the chill breeze and the soreness of her feet. The climb back to the headland was laborious. From there she cast a despairing look out to sea. For a second the moon emerged, then sank back defeated into the blackness, but in that second she imagined she saw, far out, the glimmer of a sail and the tiny flicker of a masthead light.

Whatever it was she was too late with her warning and Matt was gone, unaware of the danger that faced him on his return.

15

Chloris clutched her cloak tightly about her shoulders, numbed by the chill night, her heart cold within her. It was no use standing shivering on the cliff top. There was nothing she could do now. Matt had sailed to France, happy to refute Croker's jibes and intent on bringing back a full load of contraband. She had no doubt that the naval vessel had secretly moved into position under cover of darkness, anchoring in deep water beneath the sheltering cliff. Perhaps even now the lookouts had their telescopes trained steadily on sea and headland. She gave a gasp. Someone might be watching her this very moment, wondering why a girl, muffled in a heavy cloak, should be standing motionless on a bleak cliff top. She turned drawing the hood forward to conceal her face and began to retrace her steps.

By the Martello Tower she paused and looked back. The ship lay in darkness. If Matt and his crew used the same beach as they had on the night she joined them, they would fall into the clutches of the Preventative men before they knew it. A vague idea began to take shape in her mind and she gazed considerably at the steep wall of the

Tower, trying to work out the time it would take them to cross the channel, load up and return. What speed had a two-masted lugger? Matt had described the boat to her proudly, saying she skimmed the water like a heron, the bird she was named after. A rough or choppy sea would reduce their speed but with the impending storm, it was essential they return before it broke. They could not take the risk of waiting out the storm near the French coast or delaying their return until daylight. She considered briefly the helpers who ordinarily waited to unload the boat. The sight of the Royal Navy anchored in the bay might easily persuade the prudent ones to return to their homes. Would any of them consider it their duty to attempt a warning? She could not risk leaving it to chance. In the early hours before dawn she must be in the Tower, the highest point on the coast, ready to flash a warning to the Heron. There had to be a windowed lantern in the stable somewhere. Waved from the Martello Tower, it must make them suspect danger. But not only Matt and his crew would see the light, she realized. The men on the naval vessel were on watch too. How could she avoid alerting them at the same time? At the moment it was a minor problem and she dismissed it as such. As soon as she knew that Matt had received her signal, and she would know from a sudden change of direction by the lugger, then darkness and fleetness of foot must be her allies in evading the searchers.

There was no light in the stable as she crossed the grass, only the stirring of horses and the smell of liniment and carriage polish greeted her. Easing her way past the stalls, she cast a quick look around. There on a shelf stood a lantern, wax candle newly trimmed, ready for use as the groom always left it. She lifted it down, murmuring softly to Bessie, who had turned her head at the intrusion and whickered a welcome. The big carriage horse ignored her after one glance, returning to his silent contemplation of the well-filled stall. She slipped a box of friction matches into the pocket of her cloak, then silently withdrew. These, together with the lantern, she placed by the wall, ready to be picked up later.

As she entered the house her mind reviewed her possessions. Something red to cover the lantern was needed. Thin enough for the light to penetrate, silk or gauze, perhaps a scarf or handkerchief. The red chiffon swathed around her tall riding hat would be ideal, she decided. Now she must let Molly see her to bed but whatever happened, she could not allow herself to fall asleep.

Molly was waiting, every line of her plump face registering disapproval.

"Well, miss. I surmise you've been to see for yourself if the ship's arrived. Now that your curiosity is satisfied, I'd be obliged if you'd get out of those wet shoes and let me prepare you for bed. Mr. Justice would not approve of your careering over the countryside at this hour of the night. Whatever's going on out there, you'll do well to keep clear like any sensible person."

"Yes, Molly," said Chloris meekly, allowing her maid to remove her dress. She was unwise enough to mutter as Molly brushed her hair later, "If only I'd been a boy, no-one would question what I did." She caught Molly's eye in the looking glass and surprised a real air of worry on the older woman's face.

"I wish you wouldn't talk in that fashion, miss. You remind me too much of your mother. She wouldn't heed me either and look what unhappiness that caused."

"But that was an accident. It could have happened to anyone."

"The cliffs fascinated her too, especially that Tower. She was always riding up there where it's dark and lonely. Not many people will venture that far at night but your mother loved the moonlight and the freedom she said she felt. But it can be dangerous too as we know. When I warned her of the danger she just laughed. She looked on it as some sort of challenge."

"Did she always ride alone?"

"She never would have the groom with her."

"But her friends—who were they?"

"Mostly it was Sir Lionel and Mr. Quentin, then Lord Chalmers and other guests at Field House. Some of the neighboring families too. Occasionally they made up riding parties to places like Lulworth Cove and Corfe Castle."

"Did she never speak of anyone riding with her on the cliffs at night?"

"Not to me but I don't say she couldn't have come across somebody during one of her rides. That night, though, she must have been alone."

"How do you know?"

"Well, it stands to reason. If somebody had seen her fall, they must surely have brought her home or gone for help."

Unless, thought Chloris, that someone had good reason to wish his presence unknown. But with what motive? Fear of involvement with the authorities or plain hatred? But Mrs. Blair was popular and well-loved. Her death had been declared an accident. Chloris had accepted that verdict herself until her meeting with the boy gathering mushrooms by the Martello Tower. He could have been imagining things but his fear of her and his account of the unknown man had been too real for invention.

After Molly had gone, Chloris lay for a while in the high bed watching the flickering candle, willing the hours to pass quickly. She must have dozed for she woke with a jump of the heart as a distant church clock trilled the quarters, and with a swift glance at the clock on the mantlepiece, she confirmed the hour as midnight. Alarmed by her lapse from wakefulness, she threw back the bed-clothes and climbed from the bed. The clothes worn on the two nights she had joined Matt were still tucked into the back of her wardrobe and she dragged them out, laying them before the dying fire. A small log coaxed the fire back to life as she threw off her nightgown and struggled into the trousers and linen shirt. Her strong winter boots, the reefer jacket, her hair netted and tucked into the cap completed the transformation. At the last moment she remembered the length of red chiffon.

It was raining a little and the wind had risen, sweeping the clouds across the face of a moon weak and fitful but struggling to cast down a small illumination. For this she was grateful. It was one thing exploring the Martello Tower in broad daylight, but quite another fumbling a way aloft on an old rusty ladder in pitch darkness without daring to light the lamp.

Easing open her bedroom door she paused, listening. There was no sound from Molly's room. The house lay slumbering in darkness, save for the hanging lamp left aglow in the porch, a custom never discontinued since her mother's death. Riding the cliffs at night, Estelle Blair liked to see the distant amber glow. Chloris remembered her once calling it the wanderer's beacon and saying laughingly that as long as it shone from Blair House, justice lay unsleeping, a remark her daughter found incomprehensible at the time.

Only now did Chloris wonder if her mother had been making reference to her father's habit of never retiring until he heard the returning horse.

The well-oiled bolt of the front door slid back easily and Chloris, holding the large knob tightly, in case a wayward gust flung the door shut with a crash, transferred herself swiftly to the other side, closing the door behind her. She stood motionless for a minute in the shadow of the wall, away from the porch, then, as her eyes became accustomed to the dark, picked her way carefully towards the wall where she had left the lantern and matchbox. It was darker than she had expected but it made no difference. Matt had to be warned. The thought of the unsuspected danger that awaited him urged her into a fast trot across the rough ground beyond the garden, but after stumbling twice she realized that speed was impossible. A wrenched ankle would be of no help to anyone. Only during the intermittent gleam of the moon could she progress easily. At other times it needed a great deal of close peering at the ground to avoid rocks, straggling roots and the occasional rabbit hole.

The looming mass of the Martello Tower was before her. She paused to rest, leaning her shoulder on the cold brickwork. Now that she was here she felt her nerves tighten and her palms grow damp. Every rustle became a stealthy footstep, every sound of the night a creeping danger. Could there be a clifftop patrol? Was she even now being watched? Perhaps the cliffs were alive with revenue men awaiting her next move! For a second she was overwhelmed by a sick fear. Only a quickly-grasped thought of Matt made her relax her rigid grip on the handle of the lantern and drag her mind back from that encroaching atrophy.

Feeling her way around the walls she came upon the ladder, rising twenty feet towards the narrow opening. She began to climb. Level with the entrance she halted, listening. There was no sound and her senses told her the silence was of emptiness not ambush. Once inside, the dank air caught in her throat. Sunlight had never penetrated or warmed these cold walls. Abandoned, except by nesting rodents over the years since the threat of invasion by Bonaparte, its walls felt damp. Her fingers moved over mossy pockets and coarse roots that struggled for life on its inhospitable brick. Her vision was helped slightly by the drifting glimmer through narrow openings and she set down the lantern and moved along the wall, judging her best vantage point. Far below, the bulk of the naval ship lay crouching, silent and dark.

She eyed it uneasily. For all its quietness she had no doubt that it was prepared to burst into fierce activity at a given command. Could she, from her superior height, see the approaching lugger first? If only the moon would break through, just a little. It would, of course, help the naval detachment too, but with luck and already moving, Matt might swing his boat away and be out of sight before any small craft could be launched. The element of surprise was on the side of the navy—unless she could alter that.

Storm clouds chased each other across the sky. The wind whipped her face as she craned forward scanning the horizon. Let them come before all courage fails, she prayed silently as time dragged by.

A faint luminance on the horizon suggested that dawn was fast approaching. She stared hard, straining her eyes. There was something far out, breaking the even line between sea and sky. At the same moment the wind carried a sound across the cliffs, a word, a sentence, so brief and indistinct she hardly caught it. Far below something moved and settled. A solid click, as if a bolt had been rammed home, drifted upwards. She sought to identify the sound. It reminded her of Sir Lionel when rabbit shooting. The click of the stock and barrel of a shotgun being levelled up after the cartridges had been loaded into place.

A carbine or weapon of some sort had just been readied beneath. How many armed men were crouched amongst the rocks, their eyes on that shape far out at sea? The wind was blowing inland, a southwesterly, she gauged, bringing the Heron skimming shorewards. The outline of the lugger was clearer now. No need for a telescope. It had to be Matt, running swiftly on the wind, unaware of what waited.

She knelt by the lantern, trying not to fumble the act of striking the phosphorous stick on the box. The wick of the thick wax candle caught and blossomed. Hoping that at this moment no-one had the Martello Tower under observation, she closed the hinged door, diffusing the light. The length of red chiffon wound and knotted round the body of the lantern, gave it the necessary red glow. Sinking back on her heels she slipped the matchbox into her pocket and considered her next move. Sefton had swung his undimmed lantern three times that night. If she did the same with the red light, surely Matt would understand. There was nothing else she could do.

The lugger was closer now. No sound or light issued from the naval vessel. With the cliffs behind, it was not outlined by the sky as was Matt's ship. Now was the moment to hold up the lantern. The Heron's lookout man, if it was indeed the Heron, must spot it instantly.

She rested the lantern on the sill of the slitted window. The wind tried to drag it from her grasp, teasing the flying ends of the knotted chiffon into streaming pennants. She had expected to see the Heron change course immediately but nothing happened. It sailed steadily to shore. Thrusting her arm far out of the window she swung the lantern wildly, heedless of anything but the need to warn the approaching lugger. Someone must be on watch! Matt could not be such a fool as to take no precautions. In an agony of fear she watched the Heron sail into the range of fire. What had happened? Were they all blind? Was it the Heron or just an innocent fishing boat? No, it couldn't be that. No fisherman would attempt this coast without signal lights and a reliable lookout. Only a smuggler would run in the darkness.

She was unprepared for the shot. The lantern blew up in her hand. Metal and shards of glass flew in all directions. Blood trickled over her empty fingers. Her cheek, hit by rock chips, stung sharply. The noise, reverberating against the rocks, sent nesting seagulls screaming and whirling into a battering of wings overhead.

She fell back gasping against the wall, her brain numb until realization came. The lantern had been shot out of her hand. They knew she was here and they would come seeking her.

The moon had gone. Shock and blind panic hurled her into headlong flight. Careless of her footing she flung herself towards the entrance. The wall struck her shoulder. Through her pain and panic, common sense stirred and reasserted itself. She had only to find the ladder and slip away across the clifftops before any climbing man reached the Tower. Hand over hand she felt her way down the ladder. The steps seemed endless but then the wind was full in her face and her feet touched grass. To her left were the cliffs dropping to the sea, to her right was the stretch of land to the village and safety.

Metal striking on rock and the slither of boots coming closer sent her flying towards the village in renewed panic. Someone shouted and a bullet whistled over her head. Then the firing started, farther away, down on the beach. No time to watch her footing. Only one aim in mind. By-pass the village and reach the beacon and sanctuary of Blair House. Thank heaven for the freedom of trousers. She could not have run at this pace hampered by skirts. Her feet flew over the grass as if the hordes of Genghis Khan were on her heels.

Within sight of the welcoming porch light, panic slowly receded, leaving only a cold fore-boding. She must return and find out what had happened to Matt.

Still running she veered in a wide circle until all sounds of pursuit had died away. The beacon of Blair House was gone, only the endless cliffs lay before her as she came to a stumbling halt on legs that threatened to collapse beneath her. For a moment she rested on a rock, shivering violently in the aftermath of terror, huddled into a jacket that felt like tissue paper. Gradually her breathing calmed. The firing was less than it had been. Voices reached her, shouted orders and something that sounded like a groan. Forcing herself to the cliff edge she lay flat, then focused her gaze on the scene below. The naval ship was fully lit and lanterns stood on the beach. The Heron lay quiet, her drooping sails riddled by shot, several crumpled forms visible on her deck. A group of booted and jerseyed men were being manacled together by dark uniformed sailors while other naval personnel stood, carbines to shoulder.

Chloris scanned them swiftly. Pray God that Matt was amongst the captured and not one of those sprawled forms on the Heron. He was there! Tall, his dark head erect, there was no expression on his pale face. He looked at nothing but gazed over their heads out to sea. What was he thinking? If only he had not answered Croker's jibes and gone on the expedition, he would have been safe. But he was alive and that was important. In her relief she had not considered the consequences of this capture. They came to her now with appalling clarity and she dropped her face to the grass to stifle her cry of anguish. A trial and a term of imprisonment? But resisting the law carried an even greater penalty. A smuggler could be hanged or transported for life! Even without the ultimate penalty, Matt was not a man to take kindly to confinement. Reckless and daring, he had scorned her warning. Would he think of it?

Her head came up at the shouted command. The prisoners were moving, up the cliff path to where, in the light of a lantern, a farm cart waited. And farther on prison walls waited. Oh, Matt, my love, why didn't you listen to me? Tears coursed down her cheeks onto her clenched hands, mixing with the blood from the cuts caused by the flying shards of the lantern. Only by burying her face in the thick material of her jacket collar could she stop her sobs from becoming audible.

It was a long time before she moved. The farm cart had gone. The lamps from the beach had been removed. The naval ship lay, dimly lit, its officers no doubt congratulating themselves on the operation, she thought bitterly. Would she ever know what went wrong? Why had her signal been useless? She rose to her feet. Even in her distress, she thought to move warily. Men might still be on watch, hoping for more than one catch this night.

Widely skirting the looming walls of the Martello Tower, she spared a thought for the ruined lantern. It was a common type, no identification there, but its absence must be explained to the groom before he reported it missing. Just past the Tower her steps faltered and she froze into immobility, gripping the cloth of her jacket with suddenly rigid fingers. A shadow, darker than the brickwork, moved and was outlined for a fleeting second against the sky. Then it disappeared. There had been no clink of metal or scrape of boot. Was it only her nervous imagination? Or had one of Matt's men evaded capture on the beach and was now seeking a hiding place? Whichever it was she had no wish to make her own presence known and to this end she turned away and put all the distance she could between them.

The matches she returned to the stable, then crept into the house and up to her room. The fire still burned but it was much later before its warmth stilled the shaking reaction from her experience. At last she had the boys' clothes bundled and returned to the back of her wardrobe and the worst of the dirt and blood washed off with cold water from the jug on the washstand. Dragging the enveloping nightdress over her head she climbed, almost mindless with fatigue, into bed, ignoring the tangled mess of her hair. Within minutes she was asleep, deeply sunk into blessed nothingness.

The rattle of curtain rings woke her. Sun streamed through the window, illuminating the face of Molly staring at her from the foot of the bed. Turning her face into the pillow, Chloris sought to avoid the reality of a new day.

"Not yet, Molly," she muttered. "Go away."

"Here's your tea, Miss Chloris. It's nine o'clock and I've been trying to wake you this past half-hour." Receiving no response from the bed, Molly set down the cup and saucer with a thump. "Mr. Justice has up and gone to Gilminster in a rare old hurry so you'll not be needing to explain yourself to him."

Opening one eye Chloris regarded her maid cautiously. "I don't know what you are talking about, Molly."

"No, miss, but perhaps you'll tell me why your hair is full of grass, which I know wasn't there when I left you for I brushed it myself."

"I couldn't sleep so I went for a walk. Now do stop asking questions, there's a dear."

"Oh, well, that makes it all perfectly clear," replied Molly with awful sarcasm. "Taking a walk and getting grass on your hair is nothing out of the way for a young lady, I'm supposed to believe. Funny how I never noticed it happen before. It accounts as well for everything else, you'll be trying to tell me."

"What else?" asked Chloris wearily, her eyes shut.

"Why, those grazes on your hands and face, of course. Not to mention the blood on the towel and a pair of boots that look as if they've been dragged behind the Gilminster Hunt on a wet day."

Chloris sighed and leaned up on one elbow, knowing from past experience that she would not be allowed to drift back into slumber. She drank her tea in silence. Molly remained at the foot of the bed.

"I fell down," said Chloris through the curtain of her hair. "And I broke the stable lantern so you can tell the groom not to go searching for it."

"I see, miss." Molly's voice was flat but Chloris knew better than to suppose she was satisfied.

"Why has my father gone to Gilminster?" she asked.

"I couldn't say, miss, and it's not my place to guess at his reasons." She began to lay out fresh clothes, turning only to ask with unusual formality, "And will you be wearing a morning gown or your riding habit?"

Through the open door of her wardrobe, Chloris's gaze rested on the shelf where her bonnets were kept. The silk hat she wore for riding seemed to stand out from the rest, suddenly stark and ribbonless. She caught her breath. The red chiffon she had used to bind the lantern had gone with the rest of it, tumbling down the cliffs. But where? Could the searchers have found it? An expensive length of chiffon was hardly the thing one commonly came across lying on the beach. She would have to search for it—but not this morning! The sailors and revenue men might be there, going through the Heron's cargo, even placing a guard on the whole area to keep the village folk away.

For the sake of her father, she decided, she must profess complete astonishment as to the events of the night. Molly might suspect something but she would never betray her. But Molly's mood was not promising. Even her back looked offended! Chloris ached to know what they were saying in the village, for nothing much went unremarked in Gilminster, but she could not ask without revealing her own knowledge that something had happened. There were times, she reflected, when an old and faithful person like Molly, who had shared her life and thoughts for years—and expected still to do so—was rather too uncomfortable to have around. She loved her dearly but there was no denying that Molly was an inveterate gossip. The less she knew the better.

An hour later Chloris was in the small sitting room trying to keep her mind on the embroidery lying untidily on her lap. She had tried to read but after several pages of non-concentration, she realized the book might as well be written in Greek for all she had absorbed, so she laid it aside.

The uneven stitches she had set in the rose silk of the antimacassar she regarded with disfavor. It was just not one of her accomplishments, she decided, but then, what was? A taste for adventure? Last night's events were enough to convince her that she lacked the spirit of the girl, Mary Read, who took to the roistering life of a pirate with remarkable gusto. Quentin had been right to ridicule her words the night she dined at Field House.

In a rush of bad temper, aimed chiefly at her own inadequacies, she lifted up the embroidery and hurled it violently across the room, just as the door was opened by a maid who announced that Mr. Quentin Field was wishful to have a few words with Miss Chloris. As the sitting room was situated immediately off the hall, and Quentin was standing in the hall, there was no way he could have avoided seeing the embroidery and tangle of silks flying through the air.

From under those slightly hooded eyelids he regarded her impassively with an air, she felt, of bored disdain. Her color rose as she stood to receive him.

"Thank you, Sarah," she said, with more coldness than she realized. "You may show Mr. Field in."

'Yes'm." Sarah bobbed an uneasy curtsey

under the unconsciously stern gaze of her mistress who was struggling to recover her composure.

Why did Quentin always make her feel like a child—an idiot child come to that! It must be the way his lips suddenly compressed, as if he was trying desperately not to rend her into shreds with scornful words. Not for her the gentle treatment he meted out to Georgina. For her it was usually what he thought, unadorned by any flattering veneer.

He came into the room and bowed, his gaze flickering briefly over the heap of embroidery before resting blandly on her face.

"I seem to have chosen a bad moment to call but perhaps I have arrived in time to save something of greater value from imminent destruction." His eyebrows rose questioningly.

"And perhaps not, Mr. Field," she returned sourly, "Unless you care to take a seat and enlighten me as to your unexpected and rather early visit."

"I shall make haste to do so if this is your usual morning mood, although I must admit it surprises me for I imagined you to be a lark-rising early morning exercise girl. You know, out for a canter on Bessie before breakfast."

"My morning habits are surely of no relevance to this conversation, Mr. Field, or indeed of any interest to you at all?"

"Not in the least but, shall we say, your nocturnal habits might be." He sat down on a hardbacked chair close to where she had resumed her seat.

There was a short silence. Knowing those keen gray eyes were on her Chloris strove to control the sensation of having received a sudden blow in the region of her stomach. Quentin waited.

"Really? I am at a loss, sir," she managed on a dragged breath, striving for mockery. "In what way do my simple habits interest you?"

He leaned forward, his brown hands loosely clasped between his knees.

"What happened last night, Chloris?"

"Last night? I've really no idea. Did something happen?"

"Don't play games with me, Chloris, I am not in the mood. You're lying."

He spoke quietly, almost wearily, and her emotional state, tossed between despair and foreboding all morning, erupted into blazing anger. She sprang to her feet, her green eyes glinting with passion.

"How dare you speak to me that way? Please leave this house."

"Sit down, Cloris. This is no time for childish behavior."

"Are you going to leave or shall I summon the servants?"

He leaned back in his chair. "Don't be a fool. Do you expect any one of them to toss me out of the front door? What reason would you give? I'm here to avert gossip, not to provide it."

The words, forcefully spoken, dimmed her anger and she sank back into her chair, noting for the first time that his eyes held dark shadows under them.

"I'm sorry. Why did you come, Quentin?"

"I suppose with some vague idea of saving you from your own folly."

"How very thoughtful of you," she said with a hint of sarcasm. "A branch to be plucked from the burning, whatever that might mean?"

"Something of the sort, but unless you tell me

the truth I can do nothing."

"I appreciate your offer but as I don't yet know what you are talking about, there seems little point in this conversation. As far as I know I do not stand in need of your protection."

He made an impatient movement. "I am not here for your sake but to safeguard the reputation of your father and in memory of your mother, for whom I had the greatest affection. What you choose to do with your life is your own affair, but have you considered—in your stubborn selfishness—the effect any revelation might have on your living parent?"

"Revelation of what?" she asked coldly.

Quentin rose abruptly and as she met his eyes she was shocked by the glacial look he turned on her.

"This, for instance." His hand left his pocket and he flung a length of crimson chiffon across her lap. It lay, scorched and creased, before sliding like some living thing, to the floor. Her eyes, wide with sudden shock, watched it curl up on itself, blood-red and glowing. She felt herself pale and was reluctant to bring up her gaze to Quentin for fear of seeing the contempt on his face, but when he spoke it was without anger.

"You were not the only one on the cliffs last night."

She recalled the shadow she had seen near the Martello Tower. "Why—why were you there, Quentin?"

"I hardly know, even now. After the arrival of the naval vessel I sensed some uneasiness amongst my workers and this led me to suppose that someone had planned a run for last night but had no foreknowledge of the coming of the navy. That was the only explanation I could think of to account for their consternation, although they did their best to hide it from me."

"They knew you would disapprove."

"Of course I disapprove but I am not blind to the fact that half the district is involved. I don't know who was taken last night but I believe you do."

She was silent, seeing again in the light of the lanterns that proud head lifted in quiet acceptance. At last she spoke. "Why do you wish to know? What good can it do?"

"I have no idea, perhaps no good at all, but I intend to be at the hearing. At least I can bear witness to their characters if I know who they are."

She gave him the names of all those she could remember seeing, except one.

He thanked her and waited for a moment, watching her face. "Two grooms and one farm laborer, apart from the boat's crew. I see. But none of these men would bring you onto the cliffs at night, Chloris. You put yourself in danger of being shot or captured with that foolhardy attempt at a warning from the Tower. You would only take that risk for one person. Matt was involved, wasn't he?"

In a voice of rising anguish she cried, "Oh, why didn't he see my signal and turn away? They were near enough, heavens knows. If only they'd made a run for it."

Quentin shrugged. "I don't know why not. They weren't expecting a reception party, that's certain. Perhaps the lookout, if there was one, took a bottle with him, or they were too confident to bother. Matt's a fool, a headstrong fool."

She raised her eyes at the bitter note in his voice but he went on with the troubled look still on his face. "There may be nothing I can do but I'll see that he has the best man I can find to defend him if it goes to the Assizes. You do realize, Chloris, that smuggling is a very serious offense? If any of the sailors or revenue men were hurt, things will go badly for them all."

As if an icy hand had been laid on the back of her neck, she shuddered involuntarily. "Please, Quentin, do what you can. Matt would hate being confined in prison, even for a short time. Is there any way I can help?"

"His mother will have to be informed by the authorities. You might be on hand to comfort her when the news arrives."

"I'll go at once. Poor Mrs. Trevelyan. This will break her heart." She rose and tugged the bellrope, giving an order to the maid who answered that she required her mare saddled immediately.

Quentin rode a little way with her, promising to return with what news he could, then their paths diverged and he took the road to Gilminster. Chloris urged Bessie to a gallop and skirted the village, hoping that Mrs. Trevelyan was still ignorant of Matt's part in the affair. Coming up to the gray stone house, she was overtaken by another rider apparently headed for the same destination. Glancing over her shoulder she recognized Ruth, whose gentle face held a look of distress. Chloris reined in her horse.

"It seems we are on the same errand," she remarked. "You've heard?"

Ruth nodded, her usually fresh complexion paled by worry. "I met Quentin in the High Street. He sent me here. I'm glad of your company, Chloris. I don't think she knows yet and she is still not fully recovered from the effects of her ailment."

They dismounted in silence, tying the reins of

their horses to the iron rings set in the wall. Ruth knocked at the door.

"How on earth do you comfort a person whose elder son has been arrested for a crime?" she asked. "What can soften that blow?"

"I don't know," answered Chloris. "But she will not be alone when the blow falls."

Old Martha led them into the sitting room that looked over the garden.

"I'll tell missus you're here. She's not been too well but she'll be down presently."

Left alone the two girls exchanged helpless glances. Ruth sank onto the couch biting her lip. "I've been afraid of this," she murmured, almost to herself.

"You knew?" asked Chloris in surprise. "You knew what Matt was doing?"

"Yes, of course, but he wouldn't be talked out of it, whatever I said."

Chloris stared at the downbent head with its cluster of curls framing the heart-shaped face. She experienced a stab of jealousy. Why had she supposed that she alone shared Matt's confidence? Because she loved him? But Ruth was a friend from childhood too. Matt would know that his secrets were as safe with her as with Chloris herself. And yet, somehow, she resented Ruth's knowledge.

Ruth glanced up, and as if reading her thoughts, smiled. "It was when he came back from college in Weymouth last year. You were in Dorchester at Miss Sinclair's Academy and he needed to talk to someone sympathetic. He told me it all started there as a lark. Some of the boys at college earned pocket money by helping to hide the contraband inland but Matt went farther than that. He used to go to the beach and help unload the boats. You know how reckless he can be. I think something happened in Weymouth but he would never tell me what it was, just that it would be best if he came home for a time. I hoped he would settle down and have nothing more to do with those people but he became restless for adventure." She glanced towards the door but there was no sound. "He always said I worried too much about consequences. He was forever telling me that you would understand for you had the spirit of adventure I lacked." Her gentle smile showed briefly. "I know that's true. Unlike you and Matt, I never hankered for exciting things to happen."

"And you were the wisest of us all, Ruth. Except for Quentin, who would never take any risk at all." As soon as she had said the words she was vividly aware that they were untrue. He had come to the cliffs last night to see if his suspicions were correct. He had witnessed her attempts at a warning, afterwards risking his own liberty in retrieving the length of chiffon under the noses of the revenue men. But not for her sake, she recalled him saying, but for the sake of her parents. Or perhaps more particularly for the sake of her dead mother whose image she was! Could he have been in love with her mother? Was he the light-haired man described by the mushroom-gathering boy? Had he been there when Estelle Blair met her death and was he now seeking to make restitution of some kind by protecting her daughter? Her eyes focused on Ruth. "I'm sorry. What did you say?"

"I said I think you misjudge Quentin. Sir Lionel has always leaned heavily on him since Lady Field died five years ago. Quentin had to take over the burden of the estate completely from his father who was ill for a long time after her death. Quentin was barely twenty at the time. It was a lot to ask of a boy that age but he worked like a laborer until his father was recovered. All that responsibility made him perhaps more serious-minded than most."

Chloris sat down abruptly. She had never given a thought to that aspect of Quentin, considering him more in the light of a friendly, but disapproving and distant elder, than a companion in their adventures. She knew the events of the village as well as Ruth, but unlike Ruth, had never looked beneath the surface of people. Her interest had always been with Matt. Nothing in her life had been difficult. Protected by her father and Molly, even the death of her mother had at the time left no deep scar. Ruth had no such guardians, yet she was so much wiser, perhaps because of it.

Mrs. Trevelyan entered the room. Both girls rose to her smile of greeting and nothing was said until they had Mrs. Trevelyan seated in an easy chair with a light shawl cast round her shoulders.

"What a lovely surprise, my dears. Both of you at once. I wonder Matt is not down this instant, playing the host." Something in their expressions made her break off. "What is it? Your father, Chloris?"

"No—no, he is quite well." Chloris's voice choked and she glanced at Ruth, who took the thin blue-veined hand in a warm clasp, kneeling at the older woman's side.

"Tell me quickly, Ruth. Has something happened to one of my sons?" Mrs. Trevelyan's hand twitched in Ruth's grip. "Which—which one?"

"It's Matt," said Ruth quietly. "But he's not hurt. Please be calm."

"Then what is it?"

There was no easy way of breaking the news to his distraught mother so Ruth said quite simply, "He was with a band of smugglers last night and they were taken by the revenue officers."

Mrs. Trevelyan's head fell back on the chair, all color leaving her face. "Taken—then he's in . . ."

"I'm afraid he's in custody. Quentin has gone to see what he can do. I understand there is to be a preliminary hearing in front of the Justice this morning."

The faded eyes turned to Chloris. "Your father, Chloris? He will be on the bench?"

"He left early this morning. I haven't seen him yet but I will speak to him as soon as I can. He will know what is to be done." She spoke in a rallying tone, convinced that her father, in some miraculous way, would extricate Matt from this situation.

"I can hardly believe it," whispered Mrs. Trevelyan. "Matt—a smuggler! I know he spent nights away from home—and I never asked him where—for he is after all a grown man, but I really thought he stayed with college friends or at Mr. Sefton's cottage." She dropped her face into her hands. "Oh, my poor Matt. I should never have troubled him with all the bills I have. I might have known it would make him feel he had failed me. He always said I should have the best one day but I thought he meant from the shipping firm he was due to join this winter. We could have managed till then," she finished on a desperate note.

"Hush," said Ruth, pressing the trembling hands. "You will make yourself ill. Let me take you back upstairs and Martha shall make you a hot drink."

Mrs. Trevelyan allowed herself to be persuaded, leaning heavily on Ruth's arm. Chloris, about to follow and speak to Martha, was detained by a sharp knock on the front door.

"I'll attend to it," she stated firmly, her eyes meeting Ruth's. She waited until they had turned the bend in the stairs before opening the door.

As they had suspected, the constable stood upon the doorstep regarding her uneasily for he was a Gilminster man and related to half the families in the area and the bringing of this kind of news was never to his liking.

"Is Mrs. Trevelyan at home, Miss Chloris?"

"Yes, but she is most unwell and not able to see anyone."

"It is my duty to inform her of certain distressful facts, miss, and there is no way I can wrap it up in clean linen, however wishful I be."

Chloris felt sorry for the man's obvious discomfiture. "There is no need for you to see her personally, constable, if it concerns Mr. Matthew Trevelyan. She knows all about it. That is why she is unwell."

The man's expression was relieved. "I'm glad I haven't to break it to the poor lady, miss, for I take no pleasure in this part of my job. Proper villains I can handle and gladly but youngsters out on a spree is something different. And yet," he said, suddenly recalling his official position, "this free—er, this smuggling business is unlawful and must be put down. I'm only sorry that a fine young gentleman like Mr. Trevelyan has got himself mixed up with it."

"Has he appeared in court yet?"

"Not yet, miss. The hearing is set for eleven o'clock in front of Mr. Justice Blair. It is for him to decide whether they be remanded in custody until the Dorchester Assizes or not. Your father is a good, fair man, miss, but he has to go by the evidence and administer the law with impartiality."

"Yes, of course, but we must hope the charge

255

will not be too heavy."

"Yes, miss." He saluted her and turned away, dragging from his pocket an outsize handkerchief with which he mopped his shining face.

As Chloris closed the door, Ruth came down the stairs. "She's resting now and Martha put a little laudanum in her chocolate so she may sleep for a while."

"Then there's nothing else we can do."

"Nothing, except find out what is happening. Was that the constable at the door?"

"Yes. The hearing is at eleven o'clock. It's only half-past ten now."

"And Quentin will be there. Chloris, I promised to go to High Grange Farm to take some quince jelly to Mrs. Kernick. I'll be back in an hour or so. I'll call on you to see if Quentin has any news."

They rode from the quiet house, past the village, then Chloris turned for home. There was nothing else to do but wait although waiting was irksome. She thought of riding over the headland but decided that she must be at home when Quentin called.

Some ten minutes after her arrival she heard the sound of a carriage and flew to the window. It was too early for either Quentin or her father to return and she was in no mood to indulge in polite morning call conversation. Her scowl changed to surprise as Georgina stepped from the carriage, daintily elegant in sea-green gauze with a small straw bonnet perched on her shining russet hair. In one kid-gloved hand she carried a neat bouquet of bronze chrysanthemum buds arranged in a nosegay with silver-edged lacy paper. Their rich color matched almost exactly her hair.

Chloris opened the door herself, greeting her visitor with pleasure. Better Georgina, a stranger to the village, than someone she was well acquainted with. The conversation would not be exacting, Georgina herself quite happy to supply most of the girlish chatter.

"Dear Chloris," she said, "I had to come and see you for you are the only one in sympathy with my dilemma."

Chloris ran her mind swiftly over their brief conversations as she led Georgina into the sitting room and ordered coffee to be brought. What dilemma was this? She had no recollection of being asked her advice.

Georgina accepted a seat, sinking gracefully onto the couch, the gauzy folds of her dress floating in picturesque array on either side. Chloris took a chair opposite and watched Georgina lay the nosegay with great care and a lingering glance onto the wine table beside her, thereafter folding her hands and fixing Chloris with a limpid blue stare.

"They're from him," she said simply as if that explained all.

"Well, they're very beautiful," replied Chloris. "But hardly the sort of thing one might expect unless he sent to London for them or found a florist with a hothouse in one of the larger towns hereabouts."

"From London—yes," breathed Georgina. "Just imagine—all that way just for me."

"Unimagined depths," Chloris said dryly. "I would never have thought Quentin capable of it."

"Who? Oh, not Quentin, my dear. How could you think that? No, no, they were delivered this morning with a verse on the back of the card and the dew still fresh on them. Bronze chrysanthemums mean 'friendship' he says, for much as he would like, he cannot presume to send me red roses at this time."

Understanding came to Chloris. "Of course, how stupid of me. From your poet, naturally."

Georgina nodded. "He said I put every flower to shame."

She spoke with such artlessness that what Chloris had previously put down to vanity was merely the innocent remark of a girl so used to her own beauty that she accepted it as other girls might accept sallow skins or mouse-colored hair for which there was no cure.

"And what is the name of your faithful knight?" she asked in amusement.

"Robert—Robert Courtney. Only think! If Mama knew of this, she would read me a severe lecture and say I must return the flowers immediately. But how can I? I don't in the least know how it should be done."

"They would certainly be a trifle withered if they had to go all the way back to London."

"And Mama is not here to arrange it."

"I suppose you could throw them away but Mr. Courtney would not be aware of it so there would be no significance in the gesture."

Georgina cast her a beaming look. "I knew you'd understand. There is no help for it so I must keep them."

Chloris laughed. "Was that the dilemma you spoke of? If so, then I hope your Mama will never hear of my part in it. She sounds a very formidable lady."

"She is very strong-willed and determined that I will make what she calls a good marriage."

"And that will not be with your poet, I gather."

"Oh, no. He is most unsuitable. I can see that."

"Then you are not in love with him?"

"Mama says it is not to be thought of. Just because a man is handsome and says such flattering

258

things and writes poems to one's eyes. She says I could not be comfortable with a poor man who cannot afford a town house and carriage. She is always right, you know, and I can see that one might just as easily fall in love with a rich man as a poor man. A poem is very nice but not as lasting as a private income."

"How very true," said Chloris gravely, accepting the realism of Georgina's impeccable logic. Romantically flattered by Mr. Courtney's ardor, Georgina was too well versed in the ways of society to believe there could be lasting happiness in a liaison with a penniless poet, however handsome.

For a short while Chloris's own troubles had been overlaid by Georgina's small dilemma but she was soon brought back to realty by the sound of a rider coming up the drive.

This time it really was Quentin who strode into the sitting room, checking abruptly as he saw her visitor. He recovered swiftly and bent over her hand, then turned a faintly inquiring look on Chloris.

"Would you care for coffee, Quentin, or perhaps a glass of wine? Georgina has only just nicely arrived; in fact we have barely begun our own coffee. We were discussing flowers and poetry."

Thus warned that Georgina was ignorant of the nature of his errand, Quentin subsided into a chair, opting for coffee. Chloris tried to read his expression but gave up speculating on the outcome of the hearing as Quentin became the polite and agreeable guest that convention demanded.

It was only after he had handed Georgina into her carriage, nodded to the coachman and waited while his own horse was being brought from the stable, that he spoke. By this time Chloris was almost speechless with anxiety, wanting nothing so much as to see the Field House carriage disappear, allowing Quentin to turn to her.

"There's very little to tell yet," he said, looking down at the green-eyed girl with her heart in her eyes. "The naval officer gave his account of what happened, then the prisoners made a brief appearance and were identified. The only thing we can be thankful for is that none of the sailors or revenue men were injured. The fellow they all say put up the most resistance, a big, black-bearded fellow, got away. Happily, the villagers surrendered immediately and that will count in their favor."

"What will happen now?"

"Your father will examine them again tomorrow at a fuller hearing. Depending on what emerges—like evidence of previous involvement—it will then be decided whether or not to proceed to a higher court."

Chloris clasped her hands together tightly. Her voice shook slightly as she asked, "And if they accept that it was Matt's first time, what will they do to him?"

A spasm of irritation crossed Quentin's face. "Well, how should I know, Chloris? I'm not the justice. Ask your father."

He took the bridle from the approaching groom at that moment and nodded dismissal to the man. Looking into Chloris's white face, his expression softened. "I'm sorry. I didn't mean to snap at you. I'm fond of Matt too, the young fool, but I can think of no way to help him. He was arrested in the course of a criminal action and there's no getting around that, but I'll talk to the family lawyer and see if we can come up with any extenuating circumstances."

"Thank you, Quentin. I shall be eternally grateful."

"Well, don't build on it. There may be nothing he can suggest." He swung himself into the saddle. "The court was adjourning as I left so you may expect your father any time." He saluted her briefly with his riding crop and cantered down the drive.

For a moment she stood in the cool autumn air watching the broad shoulders and the easy grace of his riding. The sun touched his bare head and the fair hair glinted silver. She knew he would do his best. One could always rely on Quentin. He had not the reckless dash of Matt, perhaps because he had nothing to prove. Perhaps his dreams were realized, unlike Matt's, and there was nothing to reach out for. The estate of his ancestors was his. All he lacked was a mistress for that home, a wife and chatelaine to continue the line.

And even there it seemed he would be lucky. Georgina was perfect for the part. Mrs. Davenport knew it, and for all Georgina's talk of her poet, it was obvious that she knew it too.

Chloris turned and went into the house, feeling a sense of desolation. There was no perfect ending for her. Matt was the only one she had ever loved. What was their future? Or was there even a future at all?

16

Chloris glanced up swiftly as her father entered the room. Since Quentin's departure and Georgina's brief visit she had faced the possibility of a lengthy separation from Matt with acceptance but still with a struggling hope that things might not be as bad as she anticipated. One look at the face of Mr. Justice Blair dispelled most of that hope. He seemed to have aged in the few hours since she had seen him, more than she could have believed possible. The look of exhaustion on his lined face had drawn the skin tautly over his cheekbones and his eyes were shadowed by frowning brows.

She guided him gently to a chair and without speaking poured a glass of wine, placing it in his hand. He sipped it with an air of abstraction, gazing into the fireplace as if he might discover some ease of spirit within the glowing coals. His attitude stilled the outpouring of all the questions that seethed in Chloris's mind. Pity filled her and she realized for the first time the responsibility that was his. To pass judgment on anyone was an act requiring the greatest integrity. How much more difficult it must be for her father to see before him people from his own village and still remain impartial. No man could be completely unmoved.

At last Mr. Blair stirred and placed the empty glass on the table. A slight trace of color had returned to his face and his body relaxed. He turned to Chloris.

"The longer I live the more I dread familiar faces appearing before me, but my hands are tied for the law allows little clemency in such crimes. Thank God I am only a magistrate and not an assize judge." He reached to take her hand. "I am sure you have already heard of the capture of the smugglers last night from the servants. News travels quickly in a small place." He hesitated, his eyes on her. "My dear, young Matthew Trevelyan was amongst them."

"I know, Father. Quentin called earlier and suggested I go to Mrs. Trevelyan to offer any comfort I could."

"I'm glad. These headstrong young men who go their own ways never stop to consider the anguish they bring to their families."

"I'm sure he only took part for the adventure of the thing, Father," she offered, haltingly. "You know he is not really bad."

"You may be right but that is no excuse in law."

"What will happen to him?"

"If I accept that it was his first crossing to France and that during the capture he raised his hand to no arresting officer, then it will not be a capital crime. Even so, he is guilty of smuggling."

"But he will not be hanged or transported?"

"It is unlikely but there will be punishment."

"What will that be?"

"My dear child, I cannot say. I should not be discussing the case with you at all except for knowing of your friendship with Matthew. You must let me consider all the statements and evidence offered first. They will be examined again tomorrow. Meanwhile they remain in custody."

It was some comfort, thought Chloris later, to know that Matt would not be hanged but he might face years of imprisonment, years through which she must live and wait. What would imprisonment do to Matt? Would it dim or change the proud arrogance she loved? How she wished she might be there tomorrow but her father had never encouraged her to attend the court. But Quentin would be there and he was not as closely concerned as she was. Why should she not go? The small courthouse was always open to the villagers and nothing out of the ordinary would be thought of her presence. It might be her last chance to see Matt anyway and for that reason alone she determined to be present.

Early the next morning she rose and breakfasted with her father. He left the house and she delayed until the carriage had disappeared before running upstairs for her cloak.

The benches in the courthouse were crowded with early arrivals but she managed to squeeze between a farmer's plump wife and a red-haired young man. Across the heads of the crowd she could see Quentin, deep in conversation with a bearded man she assumed was his family lawyer. Quentin's gaze moved across the courtroom and Chloris ducked her head, sliding low in her seat. In the sudden movement her gloves slid off her lap. The red-haired man bent and restored them to her and she looked at him for the first time.

He smiled. "Good morning, Chloris."

She looked at him for the first time. "Oh, Neil, it's you. Forgive me, I hadn't noticed you beside me. Ruth is with Mrs. Trevelyan."

He nodded. "Ruth is always ready to help."

"Unfortunately—yes!" His rueful smile was attractive. "I wish I could say she came for my sake."

"She is a dear person and I am not surprised you are fond of her."

"More than that, Chloris, and for my own selfish reasons I hope to convince her that her visits to Mother are an essential part of her recovery and convalesecence."

Chloris laughed. "And what will you do when your mother is completely recovered?"

"I have given that problem much thought. I can only think that I must succumb to some rare complaint that leaves me looking healthy but subject to bouts of deep melancholia which can only be soothed by Ruth's presence."

"I hope you succeed in convincing her but at the moment her attention is concentrated on soothing Mrs. Trevelyan."

"Yes, I know. And the boy who is to appear this morning with Matt and the rest is one of my people. That is why I am here and not at High Ridge."

There was a stir at the front of the court as the Justices entered and took their places. A hush descended on the assembly and Chloris felt her breathing quicken.

Mr. Justice Blair sat between two dark-suited gentlemen, equally austere-looking. The constable called for silence and the proceedings began. The prisoners, eight in all and handcuffed together, were led in. Chloris craned forward as Matt led the way, his head erect, no trace of fear on his face. In contrast, the boy who followed hung his head and his freckles stood out starkly on his white face.

Neil Kernick drew in his breath sharply and muttered angrily. "Poor little devil—he's not more than fourteen—what possessed him? Damn Trevelyan!"

Chloris took her gaze from Matt to glance at the boy. She was shocked by his youth and obvious terror. Preliminaries over, the case for the prosecution was put by the clerk of the court. It soon became apparent that few of the prisoners were first offenders and court records quickly disposed of the two grooms and the Heron's crew. All were discovered to have previous convictions and so were removed from the court to await the Dorchester Assizes. Only two remained in the dock, Matt and the young boy.

Her father was looking directly at the boy but she could read nothing in his expression. She prayed he would be easy on the child, for that was all he was. After the charge was read, Mr. Blair asked the boy if he had anything to say. The boy, Billy Carpenter, shook his head dumbly.

"Sirs," came a clear voice. "May I speak for the boy?" Heads swivelled towards Matt as he leaned over the rail.

The Justices regarded him for a moment, then Mr. Blair nodded. "Proceed."

"Billy," said Matt, "is too terrified to understand anything that has been said today. He is, at the best of times, slow-witted and incapable of deceit. He did not sail on the Heron that night. He was on the shore, I admit, but only to help take away the contraband. He was swept up with the rest of us merely because he was too frightened to run for it. He never had the opportunity to lay hands on any of the contraband—thanks to the clever tactics of the naval lieutenant." Here he

267

bowed in mock praise to an erect figure at the side of the court. "So I am at a loss to know what you are charging him with. Is it against the law to walk on the beach at night? If so, then many young couples in the county who do their courting by moonlight on the cliffs and beaches have committed crimes. Not to mention some respectable gentlemen I know . . . "

"That will do, Trevelyan," interrupted Justice Blair sternly. "You are not here to preach a lecture on morals. If you have nothing else to say in Carpenter's favor, be silent."

Matt bowed his head meekly as a murmur ran through the court. Chloris glanced at Neil Kernick. "Was it Billy's first time?"

"I wish I knew but if Matt is speaking the truth, then perhaps they will release him through lack of evidence."

The Justices conferred together, and Mr. Blair spoke to the boy. His voice was kind, encouraging the boy to raise his head. "Why were you on the beach that night, Carpenter? Tell us in your own words."

The boy fixed his gaze on Mr. Blair and blurted out, "I dunno, sir. Mr. Matt never told me nothing, just said if I wanted to earn five shillings leading a donkey, to be on the beach afore dawn. He never did ask me before."

"And where were you to lead this donkey?"

"Don't know, sir, for I never saw the donkey anyhow. I just needed five shillings for my mother." His head drooped again.

Chloris heard a swift intake of breath and the man beside her rose.

"Your Honor, Mr. Justice, sir. May I speak? I am the boy's employer, Neil Kernick of High Ridge farm."

"Come forward if you have anything pertinent to say."

Neil pushed his way through the onlookers and stood before the bench.

"Sir, Billy Carpenter is a child from a large family. He will always be a child and as such, easily led. If no charge is found against him, will your Honors release him into my custody? I swear that he will never appear before you again."

There was a hum of speculation as the Justices conferred again. At last Mr. Blair spoke. "I think it would serve no useful purpose to sentence the prisoner to be detained. We accept the evidence given on his behalf, that he was ignorant of the reason for his presence on the night in question and was being used by older and more capable persons. If you, Mr. Kernick, are willing to stand surety for his future behavior, then we will accede to your request."

He sighed to the constable, who led the boy from the court. Neil Kernick bowed deeply to the Justices and hurriedly left the courthouse. An approving ripple ran round the court. Chloris was proud, both of her father and Matt. The crowd settled. All that remained now was the sentencing of the final wrongdoer, Matthew Trevelyan.

Mr. Blair began to speak. "Your consideration of the boy does you credit, Trevelyan, but in no way mitigates your own crime. You have admitted taking part in an illegal act of smuggling contraband from France. You stated in the earlier hearing that it was your first excursion into crime, a statement corroborated by your accomplices. You may have been under the influence of hardened runners in the trade but the law takes no account of that fact. The only thing to be said in your favor is that you surrendered to the law officers without a struggle." He paused as a slip of paper was handed to him. He sat, staring at the words, and Chloris, who knew him so well, had a feeling of unease. Although his expression never altered, she sensed that he had been dealt a blow. His pale skin whitened and the hand holding the note grew rigid. He was silent for so long that the crowd stirred impatiently. Both Matt and Quentin were watching him, Quentin with an intent frown and Matt, head up, with a slight smile on his lips.

Mr. Blair crushed the paper into a ball, his knuckles showing white. He stood abruptly. "This court is adjourned until ten o'clock tomorrow morning." Ignoring the surprised look on the faces of his fellow Justices, he strode through a side door and disappeared. In stunned silence the officials stared after him. Voices rose, questioning, about Chloris.

"Whatever made him rush off like that, do you suppose?"

"And before passing sentence, too."

The Courthouse buzzed with question and surmise. Chloris stared at Matt as the constable laid a hand on his shoulder. He still wore the slight smile. No hint of puzzlement showed on his face. Could he have known the contents of the note that sent her father hurrying from court? Quentin and the lawyer were pushing their way from the courthouse. Chloris struggled to follow them. It didn't matter now if Quentin saw her. She must find out what was happening.

Outside in the sunshine on the stone steps, she caught them up. "Quentin," she called.

He turned, breaking off his conversation and frowning. "Chloris. What are you doing here?"

"I had to come. What happened? Why did Father rush away like that?"

"I don't know. It took us all by surprise.

Something in the note—I don't know what—new evidence perhaps. We won't know until tomorrow. I thought you would be with Mrs. Trevelyan."

"Ruth is there." She turned to the man standing silently beside Quentin. "I do beg your pardon for interrupting. I had to speak to Mr. Field."

"I'm sorry, James," said Quentin. "Let me present you to Miss Chloris Blair. Chloris, this is James Gregory, the lawyer I asked to come along."

"How do you do, Mr. Gregory. It is probably very presumptuous of me to ask but you will have experience in these cases. What sentence do you suppose Matt will receive?"

"It is difficult to say, Miss Blair. It all depends on the Justice who presides. I know your father for a compassionate man but even so, his hands are tied to a certain extent by the law. Smugglers have received as much as five years detention before now."

Chloris gasped. "Five years?"

"It depends, of course, on their records and what violence was offered and what position they held in the operation. Their general character is also considered. But let us hope for the best, Miss Blair. I understand that Trevelyan has no previous record of smuggling so perhaps his sentence will be shorter in view of this one episode."

Ruth's words floated through Chloris's mind. Something about a happening in Weymouth. Matt had been involved with contraband even then. She pushed aside the thought. He hadn't been caught so he had no record. No evidence connected him with Weymouth, it must have just been a close call he had. After this experience and a term of imprisonment he would surely give up the game and settle down to a career.

She rode home wondering if her father would

271

be there but the house was silent. He did not return until late that night and his expression was so forbidding that her questions died unspoken. She had rarely seen him so unapproachable. He took his meal in his study with orders that no-one was to disturb him.

Several times Chloris woke in the night, hearing him pace the floor below. She longed to go down but feared to anger him. What could have been in the note to upset him to such a degree?

When she awoke the next morning, he was gone. She had overslept. Where was Molly? Her maid appeared in answer to her summons, informing her that it was by her father's orders she should not be disturbed.

"What time is it, Molly?"

"Gone half-past nine, miss."

"Oh, Molly, I wanted to be up early."

"To go to court, I suppose." Molly gaze was severe. "It's not the sort of place for you to be, miss. I know you are concerned for Mr. Matt and I heard you were there yesterday. Very likely your father did too, which is why he particularly said he would be happier if you visited Mrs. Trevelyan today. Someone should be with her when the case ends."

In her anxiety over Matt, Chloris had given little thought to anything else. Now she felt a stab of guilt. Not once had she thought of Ruth, coping with Mrs. Trevelyan's distress alone. After she had dressed and breakfasted she rode through the village avoiding the courthouse in case her resolve weakened. Quentin could be relied upon to come to the house of Matt's mother with the verdict.

Ruth answered the door. She was heavy-eyed and showed signs of recent tears but she welcomed Chloris gladly. They had a few minutes together in the hall but Chloris could shed no light on the reason for yesterday's abrupt scene in the courthouse and they moved into the sitting room.

Mrs. Trevelyan sat as one carved from marble, pale, cold and motionless. Chloris's heart went out to her. The sea had robbed her of one man. Could fate be so unkind as to rob her of another? No hint of emotion showed on her face. It was as if she had conserved all her strength into one tiny spark, shielding it from outside influence until she had learned what it had to withstand.

They sat in silence as minutes lenghtened into hours. Martha came and went on silent feet, placing coffee and biscuits before Ruth and eyeing her mistress uneasily. Mrs. Trevelyan's coffee grew cold beside her. At midday Chloris raised her head and listened. Her eyes met Ruth's. From the lane came the sound of hooves. Chloris rose and moved quietly to the door, letting herself out into the hall. The sound stopped and Chloris had the front door open before the rider had swung himself out of the saddle.

Quentin came close. "How is she taking it?"

"Like a statue. She hasn't spoken for hours and won't even take a drink. What—what news is there?"

"Not good but better than we expected. Matt has been sentenced to one year's imprisonment. The revenue man demanded a heavier sentence. He said that one year was hardly a deterrent and would make the law a laughingstock. I must admit that I was surprised too, in view of the hard attitude the government is taking these days, but your father was adamant."

"So there was no new evidence in the note passed to him yesterday?"

"He didn't mention any; in fact he was rather sharp with the revenuer, something I've never

273

seen in your father before. Incidentally, he gave Matt the choice of serving his time in Dorchester prison or aboard one of his majesty's men-of-war. If no violence was involved, there is always this choice." He paused, a reluctant smile on his lips. "You might guess which sentence Matt chose."

"The sea?"

Quentin nodded. "Well, it could have been a lot worse. According to the naval officer, only the black-bearded man who escaped was armed and none of the others appeared to be. That is what really saved them from hanging, Chloris, and the fact that they surrendered without a fight."

"I saw bodies on the Heron."

"Two of the crew were injured in the first burst of firing ordering them to heave to, but minor injuries only. Erratic firing, I suppose, from the naval detachment. It was dark and they were eager to make a capture. One of the ratings spoke of a light in the Martello Tower but nothing was found when they searched so there was no evidence to support his statement."

"Thanks to you." She raised her eyes to his with a grateful look but there was no answering warmth.

"I told you my reasons. You would do well to remember in future just who your father is before setting out on some mad adventure."

She lowered her gaze, chilled by his words.

"And now let us go in and see how we can help Mrs. Trevelyan." He held the door open for her, his expression noncommittal, making her feel that her selfish concern for Matt and herself was of no importance compared to the suffering his mother must undergo through no fault of her own. It was quite true that Matt had brought this disaster on his own head but even so, Quentin did not have to be so insufferably righteous, she thought in resentment.

But with Mrs. Trevelyan his attitude was gentle and comforting. At times he could be as kind as Ruth, but only if the object of his attention merited it, she supposed, and she herself did not come into that category. She watched them both talking softly to Mrs. Trevelyan, discussing her future. It was unthinkable for her to remain here with only old Martha. She needed people and company to banish the long hours of thought. With Mrs. Trevelyan's consent it was decided to convey her to Bridport to spend her waiting time with her widowed sister, Quentin offering to ride there immediately with a letter. There were children to lighten that household and an invitation of long standing to visit for as long or short a time as she wished. As sisters they were close so no difficulty was envisaged there. Until the travel arrangements were made, Ruth announced her intention of staying with Mrs. Trevelyan as house guest.

To all these suggestions Mrs. Trevelyan agreed with composure, except for one point on which she was adamant, and that was to visit Gilminster jail before Matt was taken away.

Quentin smiled. "Of course. I had no intention of hurrying you away before that. I will arrange for a carriage to convey you there as soon as possible."

"I could not be easy if I did not see him for the last time and encourage him to keep up his spirits. One year is not such a long time after all and he will enjoy being at sea like his father did."

For a moment there was silence, none of them wishing to point out the difference in station between an officer in the Royal Navy and a convicted felon. Naval life was hard, even for those who had chosen the profession. How much harder it would be for men forced by law to serve in the fleet, subject to brutal punishment with no redress as for free men. Matt's spirit, Chloris felt, could never be broken but the harshness of the life might scar his mind and body. But Mrs. Trevelyan must be encouraged to keep her illusions.

"Yes, indeed," said Ruth. "Matt is already something of a sailor so the experience can only give him greater knowledge of the sea."

Chloris caught the approving look Quentin bestowed on Ruth and felt herself a little ill-used. No-one considered that she might be suffering too. At that, she chided herself. It was a selfish thought as Quentin had inferred. She was young and strong, able to bear it more than Matt's mother.

Quentin left soon afterwards, bearing a letter from Mrs. Trevelyan to her sister. Old Martha was then brought into the discussion and they fell to deciding on what should be transported to Bridport. The house must be closed up for a year and young Master Philip Trevelyan informed that henceforth his holidays from school were to be spent with his cousins in Bridport. Mrs. Trevelyan was almost cheerful as Chloris said goodbye, the household tasks occupying her mind and lifting her spirits considerably. Although Matt was to remain in Gilminster jail for a few days yet, Quentin was of the opinion that his mother's farewell visit should not be delayed. The less time she was allowed to brood on the matter the better and so, at the first opportunity, Quentin escorted her to Gilminster.

Mother and son met in the office of the chief warder, both unaware that only Quentin's persuasive tongue and well-filled notecase achieved the setting and removal of the manacles from Matt's wrists. On the face of it, there was little to disturb Mrs. Trevelyan, Quentin standing surety for the warder's relaxing of the rules. It was almost a cheerful meeting, Matt's unquenchable spirit persuading his mother that far from dreading his punishment, he merely looked on it as another adventurous episode in his career.

Quentin managed a few words with him alone as Mrs. Trevelyan was thanking the warder. "That was well done, Matt," he said. "Your mother's mind is at rest and she'll go happily to Bridport knowing that you're not suffering."

"Not even remorse, Quentin," answered Matt, his eyes dancing. "I knew you'd be rallying to the rescue while I served my time before the mast. You'll make an ideal squire of the village when your time comes."

"I hope to do it with a little more responsibility than you've shown," said Quentin dryly.

"Well, you always were more of a one for duty than I, but I thank you all the same."

"Ruth and Chloris have been of great help in supporting your mother. Any messages for them?"

"Just my thanks and kind regards to them both."

Quentin's gray eyes rested enigmatically on Matt for a moment. "That's all?"

Matt laughed. "There's little else I can send, is there?"

There was no time for any more conversation, the warder hurrying them out after a last embrace between mother and son. Mr. Justice Blair was expected shortly, said the man a little nervously, and it would serve no purpose to have him find one prisoner favored above the others on account of his own kind heart and sympathy for the lady. Quentin smiled but made no comment, escorting

Mrs. Trevelyan back to the carriage that was to take them to Field House. Sir Lionel had insisted on Mrs. Trevelyan taking her last luncheon with him. Martha and the boxes had already been dispatched early in the morning to Bridport and rather than allow the emptiness of her own house to undo all the good work that had been done to the lady's spirits, Chloris and Ruth agreed to meet them at Field House instead of at the Trevelyan home.

It was almost a party atmosphere as six people took their places around the large oval dining table. Georgina had been apprised of the situation and her own excellent manners kept in check any curiosity she might be feeling. Chloris had to admit that she graced the table, deferring to Sir Lionel almost as a daughter-in-law and being treated by the servants as the hostess, which, in the absence of any other female in the household, she undoubtedly was.

Mrs. Trevelyan talked happily of her nephews and nieces in Bridport and of her own childhood in that town, and encouraged by Georgina even spoke of her own two sons as children. The others had carefully avoided all mention of Matt but Georgina's unaffected interest in their affairs eased the tension and struck exactly the right note. With anyone else, Chloris thought, one might consider it a contrivance by a clever hostess but with Georgina it was simply a kindness of heart and an innocent delight in the escapades of others.

By the time dessert was served it was obvious that the success of the luncheon was due entirely to Georgina. That Quentin was sensible of her qualitites was also obvious to Chloris as she caught his glance resting increasingly on the russet-haired girl. She was glad for she had come to realize her own affection for Georgina. From considering her a mannered fashion plate, quoting only her mother, Georgina's own personality had expanded with her sojourn away from London. She would never be a clever woman but her instinctive kindness would serve her better, should she become Quentin's wife. The unhappy love affair of Quentin's, mentioned vaguely by Molly, was in the past. Georgina was here and now, highly suitable from everyone's point of view.

The farewells to Mrs. Trevelyan were not protracted. The journey to Bridport was less than an hour by carriage and in the company of Quentin she would have no time to dwell on the sudden change in her life.

Sir Lionel, who had come into the hall with them, was walking more easily.

"My gout is as well as it ever will be," he said jovially. "So I'll be in the saddle with the Gilminster by the start of the season. I'll look to see you both join me."

"Not me, Sir Lionel," answered Ruth. "You know very well I don't hunt for all you've been inviting me for years."

Sir Lionel boomed his great laugh. "No harm in asking. I always fancied myself between a pair of handsome women in the field yet I invariably end up opening gates for the Misses Ford. Nice girls really but no spirit for throwing themselves over fences. Not like my little Chloris here. You'll not disappoint an old man, will you, my dear?"

"You've no need to go playing on my sympathy by pretending you're an old man or I shall be opening gates for you and that you wouldn't like for you're not above forty-five."

Sir Lionel, who owned to a few more years than Chloris's estimate, gave her a gratified grin, his ego flattered by a pretty young thing and offered her, in a magnanimous gesture, the pick of his hunters.

Chloris was not deceived. "And woe betide me if I pick yours," she said, laughing.

As they rode away, Ruth said musingly, "It will be strange not to have Mrs. Trevelyan to call on."

"And Matt, too," Chloris added.

"Yes, of course." Ruth's gaze was long and considering. "Chloris, do you love Matt?"

Chloris was startled by the abrupt question. "I—I always have."

"I know you were inseparable as children but now we're all grown up. Is he still the most important person in your life?"

"Yes, he is. And I'll wait for him."

"Has he asked you to?"

"I haven't seen him since the arrest but I shall ask my father if I may. Why the question?"

"I just don't want you to be hurt. Matt can be a little careless of people's feelings without even realizing it."

"What are you trying to tell me? That Matt is in love with someone else?"

"No. I'm sure that isn't so. Just don't commit yourself too deeply, Chloris. We can all change in a year."

"I know I shan't."

Ruth smiled, then said almost on a sigh, "Well, we shall see. People do change although they never think they will."

She wheeled her horse and galloped ahead, leaving Chloris gazing after her. Was Ruth speaking from a hurtful experience of her own? Or was it just a reminder that a year was a long time and Chloris should not spend that time in dreaming and waiting? She took the cliff road home. Perhaps Ruth was right and she should keep her feelings for Matt secret. No-one had asked that question openly before. The whole village knew of their childhood closeness but to flaunt her love at this point might embarrass people and distress her father.

Near to the Martello Tower she glanced down into the bay. The naval ship was still there and in the distance she could see a line of mounted revenue men crossing the far hills. The coast would be quiet for a time, she supposed, none of the villagers daring to carry on with the trade. Where was Croker now? After his resistance and escape, the most sensible thing for him to do would be to leave the Dorset coast entirely, returning to Cornwall or wherever he came from. Just past the Tower and within sight of the path leading home, she heard her name called. A man dressed in rough tweed and leather gaiters and leaning on a stick raised his hand. As she drew level she recognized him as Sefton, Matt's mentor, a man she hadn't given a thought to since the fateful night.

"Well, Mr. Sefton. I see your position is somewhat freer than your erstwhile companions."

"Aye, miss. I wasn't out that night, having a bit of trouble with my leg, but I'm right glad to hear things haven't gone too hard on Mr. Matt."

"Hard enough, I would say."

"No denying that, miss. Have you seen him?"

"Not yet but I hope to visit him soon."

"Tell him I'll be putting a bit by for him. He'll not be forgotten."

Chloris frowned. "That sounds remarkably like an intention to carry on with the trade."

Sefton grinned, eyeing her with complete assurance. "You have it right, miss."

"But you're mad to think of it! The ship, the guards, and look there over the hill—can't you see the revenue men?"

Sefton kept his eyes on her, not deigning to spare a glance in any direction. "We'll not be surprised again. I know a few spots they'll not be looking in."

"But half of your men are in prison."

"Plenty more willing to pit their wits."

"Well, I think you're mad to try so soon. Can't you wait until things have quietened down?"

Sefton scratched his chin. "That's where we hit the problem, miss. Our shareholders, as you migh call them, are wanting to know what happened to their dividends. We've no choice but to make it up to them."

"Then I'm almost glad Matt was taken on the last trip. You'll have much more dangerous opposition next time. You might all be killed out right."

"We'll have a few more tricks up our sleeves this time. Take my word on it." He saluted her and stepped back, his smile so confident that it filled Chloris with foreboding. She nodded curtly and urged her mare forward. The village could ill spare any more men for such a foolhardy enterprise. The only comfort to be had was the thought that volunteers, seeing the ship in the bay might decline the adventure in the face of that threat.

Mr. Blair was at home when Chloris arrived but it was not until after dinner that she saw him. He called her into his study and the look he had worn in the courthouse was on his face. She felt a sense of shock as she gazed into his troubled eyes and saw the new deep lines scored across his brow.

"Father, what is it?" she asked, crossing swiftly to his side and taking his hands. "You look so ill. What has happened? Was it something connected with the case and the note you received?"

"You saw that, did you? Yes, it was a note from Matthew Trevelyan asking me for an urgent interview before passing sentence."

"You granted his request?"

"Yes. I should not have agreed to it, I know, but he said it was vitally important and that I would regret not acceding to his petition."

"What did he mean?"

"I thought at first to dismiss the note as impertinence but something about the wording made me pause. He begged me to consider it a sincere plea. I spoke to him in my chambers straightaway. He told me of your love for each other and how he was afraid of losing you if he was locked away for years. Chloris, my dear, he wants to marry you before he goes away. Do you love him enough for that?"

"I have always loved him, Father, but I would have waited." Never before had Matt declared his love for her, she thought, but what a time to reveal it!

"So I told him but he—he convinced me that delay would be harder on you than on him." He passed a hand tiredly across his brow. "What is your answer, Chloris? Do you agree?"

"Oh, yes, Father." She frowned suddenly. "But why should this upset you so much?"

"My fellow Justices were decided on a three-year sentence for him—mainly as a warning to other offenders—but I overruled them and passed a lenient sentence—far too lenient in law. I am deeply ashamed of going against them but I could do no other. I should have given up the case—but there were reasons. I am minded to resign from office rather than be accused again of partiality. My sentence was swayed in part by the thought of

283

you waiting for three years. I admit my fault but cannot alter it now." He smiled grimly. "Sent ment has no place in law, my dear, but as I looke at that note I could not help but recall you mother."

"My mother?" she asked in bewilderment.

"I fear she grew to dislike the dull life I ha given her. How could I sentence her own daughte to suffer a similar period of unhappiness when had the means at hand to shorten that period?"

"No, Father! You underestimate yourself an her. She was happy, I am sure."

And yet as she said the words she wondered i they were true. The man on the cliff—the partie at Field House—the lonely moonli rides—perhaps not always alone. She could no bring herself to believe that her mother was a unfaithful wife but she was gay and willfu perhaps flirtatious and a little bored with he serious husband. But Estelle was dead. Her fathe must not hold himself responsible for her action prior to the accident.

Her father was speaking. "Tomorrow he wil be sent to Portsmouth to join the fleet so it mus be tonight."

Chloris stared at him. "Tonight? We mus marry tonight?"

"I could wish it otherwise, my dear, but yes tonight—and in secrecy. You must promise m that, at least!"

17

The small stone prison of Gilminster stood on the edge of the village facing the moorland. It was an old building, far older than the courthouse it served. A depressing place, thought Chloris, as the Blair coach drew to a silent halt beside the solid studded door with its brass bell-handle green with verdigris from the cold salt winds. She shivered and drew her cloak closer. The flickering gleam of a candle illuminated the window of the jailer's small room.

Chloris and her father descended from the coach and a horseman reined in beside them. No words were spoken as the bell was rung. The door opened and the three of them were ushered inside. Chloris kept her veiled face turned away from the curious gaze of the jailer and his wife. Witnesses to my wedding, she thought bleakly. How different from what she had imagined her wedding day would be. She saw her father raise his eyebrows in inquiry to the strange horseman who nodded briefly and patted the pocket of his ulster.

They were led into a small room adjoining the entrance, where a sea-coal fire glowed dimly, outlining a battered horsehair sofa beneath the window. The jailer made to light a lantern but Mr. Blair shook his head, indicating that the one flickering candle was sufficient. The horseman removed his beaver hat and muffler, revealing the face of a complete stranger, smooth and bland above a clerical collar.

Chloris swallowed dryly and turned her gaze to her father. He spoke through stiff lips. "It is best this way—if it must be." He moved towards the jailer and she heard Matt's name mentioned.

The three of them stood silently in the shadowed room until footsteps were heard. Mr. Justice Blair crossed swiftly to the door and spoke in a low tone to the three people halted there. Chloris's heart leapt as Matt walked into the room. He smiled and raised his eyebrows but said nothing.

Her father returned. "The witnesses will stand in the hall, out of earshot but within view of the—the ceremony." He seemed to find the words hard to say and his eyes flickered over Matt with a strangely hostile light in them. He dislikes Matt, Chloris realized suddenly, but he is allowing this marriage simply out of love for me and in memory of my mother; yet it is hard for him to accept.

The strange vicar cleared his throat and produced a prayer book from his jacket pocket. Matt moved close to Chloris and raised his hand to the veil she still wore, but a sharp word from her father caused the hand to drop. Matt shrugged. Later, his smile said. Despite his incarceration, he seemed unchanged. He was still the laughing, daring hero of her every dream. Tanned and handsome, the thick dark hair falling slightly over his brow, she wondered if anything could dim that proud, almost arrogant, spirit. A year on a man-of-war would be as nothing to him, his own personality sufficient to surmount the hardship endured. And at the end of the year a reunion, and nothing would be changed.

The vicar was speaking, so softly they had to lean forward to catch the words. It was a far from romantic setting but it bound them together as surely as if the words had been spoken by her own vicar in the little Norman church of Gilminster, before a congregation of friends and neighbors.

It was over—and she was Mrs. Matthew Trevelyan by special license and his signet ring was on her finger. They moved to sit gingerly on the horsehair sofa, Matt's arm about her shoulders.

"However did you persuade Father to agree to this?" Chloris whispered, gazing around the room with distaste.

Matt grinned. "I have a persuasive tongue and your father approved my line of reasoning."

"Your note must have been very moving to account for his leniency."

"Oh, it was! I threw myself on his mercy and pointed out the sorrow he might be causing you."

She looked into his dark dancing eyes and smiled shyly. "You mean if I had to wait for perhaps three years? I—I never knew I was so important to you."

"My dearest Chloris," he said, his gaze holding hers steadily, "you'll never know just how important you have become to me. Your father and I had a long talk and I can safely leave all my affairs in his hands. He will not fail me now that you are my wife."

"It seems so strange. All this secrecy, I mean."

"Marriages in prison are not unusual. Besides, I want to be sure that you will be waiting for me when I am released. I cannot do with you being swept off your feet by some dashing man-about-town. That would not suit me at all." He looked round. "I told that jailer fellow to fetch a bottle of brandy, then we can be cozy when the others have gone."

Chloris looked about her at the bleak room. Apart from the sofa, there was nothing but a table and a couple of straight-backed chairs with a strip of tattered rug before the fire. A depressing room in which to spend one's wedding reception.

The strange vicar had gone. She heard the sound of hooves fade into the distance. Then her father turned from the door and looked at them. His eyes glittered strangely in his pale face.

"Jailer," he said, "remove the prisoner."

Matt's head came up with a jerk. The jailer approached, wooden-faced and determined. No-one argued when Mr. Justice used that tone.

"Remove—!" Matt was on his feet, staring at Mr. Blair. "What is this?"

"The ceremony has been performed. Now you return to your cell." Chloris hardly recognized her father's voice, it held such a gritty quality.

"But this is our wedding night," Matt protested. "Surely you will allow us to spend it together?"

"I agreed to a wedding and that was the extent of my agreement, I think you will recall."

"But this is inhuman!" Matt hesitated, glancing at the jailer. "My—my wife . . . "

Mr. Blair regarded him glacially. "Yes? What about—your wife?"

The two men stood face to face, their eyes looked in silent challenge.

"You have something to say—or tell?" asked Mr. Blair softly.

Matt's gaze fell first and he shook his head savagely. "No, damn you," he said in an under-tone. He turned to Chloris, who had risen in

288

bewilderment. With an effort, Matt controlled himself. "I'm sorry, my dear, but I am not, it seems, even allowed to toast my bride. Mr. Blair's word is law. I have no choice but to obey."

Chloris looked appealingly at her father. The face he presented was that of some grim stranger. "Surely a few hours—is that too much to ask?"

"I will not compound one felony with another. It is enough that I have erred once. I cannot go farther than my conscience allows." He nodded sharply to the jailer who was standing in incomprehending silence. The man laid a hand on Matt's shoulder. He shook it off irritably.

"Very well. You force me to accept your terms, sir. Goodbye, my dear." He bowed stiffly, making no attempt to kiss her. She saw the anger and frustration on his face as he swung about and marched to the door, not glancing again at Mr. Blair.

For a few moments there was a strained silence. Chloris was appalled by her father's behavior. She was at a loss to understand his reasons for parting them so cruelly within five minutes of their marriage. How could he do it? Never—never would she forgive him for this heartless act! Even when he spoke in a voice of unbearable weariness, she did not look at him.

"Chloris, forgive me. I had to do it."

A few moments elapsed, then she turned, her eyes hard. "Did you? I don't understand why. What harm could a little time together have done?"

"A little time? You heard him speak of spending the night here."

"But we are married, Father!"

Mr. Blair looked round with disgust. "Do you seriously think I would have left you here in this company, with the cells full of felons and cutpurses who are no doubt aware from that loose-tongued jailer that a marriage has taken place? Do you relish the thought of that fact being discussed in a lewd fashion by half the scum of the county?"

She colored hotly. "Of course not!"

"This being the only room outside the cells," he went on harshly, "to where would you suggest the jailer and his wife remove themselves while the celebrations take place?"

"Stop, Father, please!" She turned from him, unable to bear the hurtful tone any longer.

In a calmer voice he said, "Come, let us go home. We serve no useful purpose by staying here."

"Of course," she said coldly. "By all means. You have carried out your part of the agreement as you stated, without deviating one unlawful inch. I must thank you for going so far as to allow the marriage to take place at all for it is perfectly clear that you dislike Matt."

"What I did was for you but I cannot pretend that I am happy about it. This is not what I had hoped for you. Not this way."

"I love Matt and when this is all over you will come to see that I was not wrong in doing so."

"Then we must pray that this coming experience will have a salutary effect upon him and he will prove worthy of your confidence. Until then, we must agree to differ on the subject."

He held the door open and she passed into the hall where the jailer hovered. He took a quick look at Mr. Justice Blair's stony face and hurried to open the outer door.

They journeyed home in silence and Chloris went straight to her room. She removed her cloak and veil and sank into an easy chair before the fire. The chill she felt was not entirely due to the cold night air. Her mind was full of bewilderment

over her father's attitude. If he so disliked the idea
of her marriage to Matt, why had he allowed it? She
would not have changed in spite of Matt's fears, but
if her father had hoped for a change of heart it
would have been to his advantage to refuse consent
until Matt was free again. It was not as if she had
persuaded him into it, that had been Matt's doing—
and yet if her father disliked Matt—how then had
Matt succeeded in obtaining his consent?

She fell asleep that night with Matt's ring on
her right hand, no nearer to solving the riddle of
how it had come about.

The coldness between father and daughter
persisted in the days that followed. Nothing, it
seemed, would ever heal the breach. The wound
was too deep and bewildering for Chloris to
dismiss and her father threw himself into his work
with the desperate air of a man trying to regain his
peace of mind.

Mrs. Trevelyan was gone. Ruth spent most of
her free time at High Ridge farm with Neil
Kernick and his mother. Quentin was occupied
with his duties and at other times was to be seen
driving about the country with Georgina. Chloris
had no wish to make an unwelcome third party in
their outings. Sir Lionel's gout had flared up
again, forcing him to leave his hunters in the
stables, and on the occasion of her last visit to him
he had bemoaned his ill-luck so frequently that she
was not sorry to leave.

She took to riding alone, mainly on the
clifftops where the Martello Tower stood. The
wreck of the Heron, cut to pieces as was the
custom with smugglers' crafts, lay in ruins down
in the cove. How, she wondered, did Sefton
envisage a continuation of his trade?

The answer came to her the following evening.
The dry weather had broken, there was a hint of

thunder in the air and the wind chased black clouds across the sky. Darkness came swiftly with a light scattering of rain, catching her a mile from home. Reining in her horse on the cliff path, she stared out to sea, watching the breakers swell and crash on the shore. The naval ship, shrouded in volent shadows, rocked and swung at anchor.

The mare flung up her head and stamped, impatient for her dry stall. Chloris urged her forward into an easy canter, the thud of hooves muffled by the wet grass. The mare responded eagerly, increasing her stride as Chloris bent forward, exhilarated by the damp breeze flung in her face. Near to the Martello Tower the mare shied suddenly, so unexpectedly that Chloris almost lost her seat.

"Steady, girl," she said. "Nothing to frighten you. You've seen the Tower a hundred times before." As she spoke she was aware of a difference in its outline. A shadow detached itself from the wall. She gathered the reins tightly as Bessie laid her ears back.

"Miss Blair? Is that you?"

She looked down at the face that appeared by her knee. "Sefton! What are you doing here?"

He chuckled. "A little business you might say. A good night for it, too."

"You're making a run tonight? Isn't that rather risky with the trial scarcely two weeks back?"

He squinted up at her in the gloom. "That's why they'll not be expecting us to go out again so soon. They're still full of success over the Heron. Maybe think we'll be lying low for a space."

"You're mad! The naval ship is no more than a quarter mile away. They're bound to see a boat beached below, or anywhere, for miles."

"Ah, but it won't be beached below. Just

round the corner, you might say, in the next bay. A nice, tight little anchorage, overhung by rock. There's a tidy track in the shadows from it, too. We'll use the donkeys to carry the stuff here."

"Here? To the Tower, you mean? How will that help? There's fifty feet of rock to the shore. You plan to drive the donkeys vertically?"

"No need for that, they'll unload below," he said, unmoved by her sarcasm. "Since our last adventure we've made a discovery." He looked at her slyly. "But should I be telling? You're Mr. Justice's daughter, after all."

"I'm also—," she stopped. "I'm also Matt's friend and you've nothing to fear from me." Even less than before, she told herself with a stab of bitterness.

"Well, miss, we've been doing a bit of exploring like, and we've found a cave down below. The main passage rises near as high as the cliff and is wide enough for two men to walk it. We've been hacking away at the rock these past ten days and nearly got ourselves through into the base of the Tower. I reckon that cave was used long before they built the Tower, only nobody knew it was there, it was all overgrown. I came on it by accident when I dropped my pipe in the bushes one day. We'll store our goods in the cave and bring them up out of the Tower while those blue-jackets are watching the shore below."

"And what if they decide to examine the Tower or even man it?"

Sefton laughed. "They'll see nothing more than a pile of rock by the wall and they'll not think to move it. Why should they? As for manning the place—not them! Too wet and cold and they can scan the sea just as high from their masthead."

Chloris glanced at the sky. "It'll be a dark night."

"Aye. There'll be nothing but a sliver of moon and the tide'll run out strong with this wind."

"Well, I wish you luck. Goodnight."

"Goodnight, miss. Maybe you'll join us sometime. For old time's sake."

She stared down at him for a moment and checked the curt refusal that rose to her lips. "Perhaps. I'll think about it."

She shook out the reins and Bessie, who had been fretting in the wind flurries, sprang forward, the echo of Sefton's chuckle spinning away on the breeze.

In the days that followed she found her mind dwelling more and more on Sefton and the gamble he was taking. That the expedition had been successful there was no doubt, for no arrests had been made and she noticed, here and there, a fine pair of French kid gloves, a lace jabot and the whiff of a perfume that had not been purchased in Gilminster. A slight rise in the drunk and disorderly charges, mentioned briefly by her father in one of their rare conversations, indicated a plentiful flow of cheap brandy and Dutch schnapps.

The fine dry autumn weather dissolved into a weeping, bone-chilling foretaste of winter, leaves swept raggedly from the trees, leaving only the beech to flaunt its copper pennons. Chloris's mood matched the weather, there seemed no lightness anywhere. She knew her father watched her anxiously but a wayward streak in her nature ignored the openings he gave to return their relationship to its previous footing. The gold ring with the engraved lettering—M.T.—was seldom absent from her finger, only common sense and her promise of secrecy holding her back from wearing it on her wedding finger in public.

It was three weeks after the trial when she

met Quentin again. Georgina was still in residence at Field House. They had called on her several times, according to Molly, but each time she had been on one of her long lonely rides. She had gone out of her way to avoid contact with old friends but at the same time had taken a perverse delight in considering herself neglected. So it was with mixed feelings that she viewed the invitation to dine at Field House. Knowing her father to be in Dorchester for a few days, Sir Lionel hoped that Chloris would spend that time in their company.

There seemed no way to refuse and Chloris knew she had no real wish to refuse. It was all very well having reasons for feeling ill-used, but if others were unaware of the reasons, it was pointless to cut one's own throat by retiring into seclusion. The whole winter must be lived through somehow and an evening with Georgina and the Fields would be a pleasant change.

As if approving her decision, the weather did another about-face and she rode to Field House under a warm, cloudless sky with only a slight breeze off the sea. The ripples from the slow green swells clutched the pebbles in a desultory manner, hissing gently back, spreading foamy lace ruffles across the shingle.

Field House was a warm glow on the landscape, the french windows thrown open onto the terrace, where stone urns full of bronze crysanthemums complemented the mellow stone of its walls. A lovely house, she thought, with its high-ceilinged rooms, curving stairway and elegant Georgian furniture. A fit setting for Georgina as the first lady of the neighborhood, should she desire it.

Quentin met her in the hall as she removed her cloak and shook out the folds of her dress. He appeared to scan her face closely and she lifted her chin and smiled.

"Welcome, Chloris. You've become quite an elusive person to contact. Georgina has missed you."

"Put it down to the delicacy of my nature," she replied lightly, peering into the gilt-edged mirror. "An overabundance of females can prove an embarrassment at times, I'm sure you'll agree, but Bessie has been my constant companion these past days."

"Yes, we were told each time we called that you were out riding. Bessie must be getting a deal of exercise. Is she up to it? You may borrow any of our horses, you know that."

"Oh, Bessie does very well, only she likes to be home before dark. She's taken to shying at any object in her way after dusk, whether a tree or the Martello Tower. I have to be sure I see it before she does or I'll be over her head one night."

Through the looking glass she saw his face tighten, then he turned away. What have I said? she wondered. Surely my riding, day or night, is of no interest to him?

He turned back, his expression smooth again. One couldn't read Quentin as easily as Matt—which reminded her.

"Did you get Mrs. Trevelyan happily settled in Bridport?"

"More happily than I thought possible. To hear her talk, you'd think that Matt joined the Royal Navy of his own accord. She is expecting to hear from him anyday."

"Are they allowed to write letters?"

"I suppose so but it may prove rather difficult as I hear the ship is to sail to the West Indies within a few days."

"Really? Well, I do hope he manages to write to her before they sail. It will ease her mind enormously to know he is well." Mine too, she added silently, although she was convinced that Matt would appear in a year's time exactly the same as when she last saw him.

"Let us hope it crosses his mind to think of his mother," Quentin said, equably.

Chloris felt a spurt of anger but she controlled it. "You have never thought a great deal of Matt, have you?"

He looked surprised. "On the contrary. I'm quite fond of him but he is apt to fling himself into adventures without considering the consequences to others." He smiled. "A little like yourself, wouldn't you say? Now, don't glare at me like that, you know it's true."

She laughed suddenly. "Perhaps it is but there is no need for you to say it, is there? Sometimes you are really too righteous, Quentin. It's not fair on us less noble folk."

He stared at her, then caught his breath on a choke of laughter. "Righteous? Good God! Is that what you think? Perhaps I should be glad you didn't say 'pompous.'"

She eyed him with a considering light in her eyes. "No—not yet—but when you become the squire and have a lady wife and a brood of children about you, and are deferred to in the first circles—then the word may apply."

He sighed. "Well, now that you have settled my vastly boring future, I suggest you come into the drawing room and meet our friends. Try your hand at fortunetelling with them."

They fell into step and moved through the double doors of the drawing room. Sir Lionel boomed his greeting and she turned smiling to the counch where Georgina sat with Ruth. Beside them, on a high-backed chair that appeared too delicate to hold his weight, was a young man who rose easily and lithely to his feet. She stared at him, knowing before Quentin's introduction that this was Lord Chalmers. His hair of palest gold, almost the primrose color Matt had mentioned, identified him. It was as distinctive as his slender height and breadth of shoulder. A strong man for all his slim build, she surmised, one who could throw a man with ease as Matt had said. Or a woman, said a tiny voice at the back of her mind. She blinked swiftly, dismissing the notion, and held out her hand. It was only then that she realized he had been regarding her with just such a careful scrutiny.

The heavy lids dropped as he bowed and offered her his chair. She accepted, trying to avoid wondering what his hair would look like by moonlight.

"Forgive me staring, Miss Blair. It was very rude of me but you are so like your mother I was stunned for a moment."

"You knew her well, Lord Chalmers?"

He hesitated as if gathering his thoughts for a careful reply. "We met a number of times here and in the neighborhood when I stayed with Quentin last year. I was distressed to hear of the accident. Please accept my belated sympathies."

"You were not here when it happened, then?"

"I must have left only hours previously. I was due out of Weymouth and have just recently returned to England."

"How did you come to hear of it?"

"Quentin wrote to me. I was in Italy."

Time enough to ride to Weymouth afterwards, she thought. But how could one ever reach the truth after all these months? Perhaps the whole thing was in her imagination only and it was nothing more than a tragic accident. And yet the

oy on the cliffs had been so sure that Estelle was
ot alone.

Her attention was claimed by Georgina,
ommenting that now autumn was upon them, she
ust think about returning to London. As one
ecently come out of the capital, Lord Chalmers
ll into conversation with Georgina on the subject
f entertainment now being offered to returning
ociety after their country sojourns.

Chloris was able to ask Ruth how the young
oy, Billy Carpenter, was settling down after his
rrifying court experience.

"Very subdued, according to Neil," explained
uth. "They have taken him to live in on the farm
nd he's proving very handy but no power on earth
ill get him out after dark. He's afraid of being
ken up by the revenue men again."

"Poor lad. Matt should never have involved
uch a child."

"Neil has been very good to him. He's such a
ind man and so thoughtful."

"I had that impression when I sat next to him
court." Chloris gazed at Ruth with interest.
You're spending a great deal of time at High
idge. Isn't his mother better?"

"Very much better but she likes company so I
greed to keep calling. Neil says she looks forward
my visits."

"I'm sure they both do."

Ruth glanced at her, a smile on her gentle
ce. "I don't see that much of Neil, he's far too
usy, so don't try matchmaking."

Chloris laughed. "He is very fond of you,
evertheless."

Ruth looked away. "I wouldn't want to hurt
im but it is out of the question. Perhaps if I'd met
im earlier."

"Are you telling me you already have . . . "

Ruth interrupted with an unusually sha[rp] note in her voice. "I'm telling you nothing, Chlori[s] because there's nothing to tell."

Chloris was silenced. Had there bee[n] expectations which had come to nothing? Ho[w] cruel life could be to someone as deserving [as] Ruth.

After dinner Georgina was persuaded to pl[ay] the piano. She had been well-schooled and h[er] touch was light. The pieces she chose were gent[le] ballads, in keeping with the late summe[r] fragrance that drifted in from the garden. Th[e] tender notes of a Scottish air touched Chloris wi[th] an unbearable poignancy and she moved soun[d]lessly from her chair and slipped out of the frenc[h] windows onto the terrace.

What was Matt doing now? Was he on dec[k] staring up at the same stars, thinking of her? S[he] drew his ring from the chain concealed in t[he] bosom of her dress and slipped it on. The engrave[d] letters M.T. blurred as she gazed at her thi[n] finger. This was all she had of him. This and h[er] memories. Her mind shied away from the ug[ly] scene on her wedding night. That was somethi[ng] for which her father would never receive fo[r]giveness.

She raised the ring to her lips. "Deare[st] husband," she whispered to the stars, [so] engrossed in her thoughts she was unaware of t[he] cessation of music and the outbreak [of] conversation.

A voice spoke her name. She jumped, turnin[g] Quentin stood there, a hand gripping t[he] balustrade, his eyes fixed on the ring. Th[e] lettering was clear in the moonlight. She droppe[d] her hands, clasping them together. For a mome[nt] they stood silent, gazing at each other. Fro[m] under the lazy eyelids Quentin's gray eyes were sharply questioning.

"Matt's signet ring?" he asked.

She nodded. "He—he gave it to me the last time I saw him in—in—prison."

"Don't worry about Matt," Quentin said gently. "He is one of life's survivors. He'll be back next year to claim your hand—if that is what you still want."

"I'll never change. I shall always love Matt."

He smiled at her vehemence. "We all say things like that but sometimes time proves us wrong."

She looked at him curiously, remembering Molly's words of long ago. "Were you ever in love, Quentin?"

"Once I thought I was but love cannot survive on its own."

"She didn't return your love?"

"No. It could never have been anyway. Too many obstacles."

"I'm sorry."

"Don't be. It was sheer infatuation and one recovers as from a fever." He leaned his elbows on the balustrade. "Tell me, why do you wear Matt's ring on a chain round your neck? Why not on your finger?"

"I promised Father I wouldn't . . . " she began, unthinkingly, then stopped, aghast.

Quentin's eyes narrowed. "You promised? A secret engagement perhaps? Why would that need to be secret? Everyone knew your sentiments concerning Matt."

"No—no," she replied, stammering, the blood rushing to her face. "We're not engaged. It's not that. It's just a ring—a gift."

"To plight your troth?"

"Yes—no—leave me alone, Quentin. I can't

tell you any more."

"You don't need to now. My God, Chloris! You never married him in prison?"

"Why shouldn't I?" she retorted defiantly.

"And your father allowed it? He would have to have, you're underage. He was there, wasn't he?"

"Of course, but I don't want to talk about it."

He stood silent for a moment. "That would explain a lot of things. The lenient sentence—your father's haunted looks—and all for you. He didn't owe Matt a thing. Why did he allow it?"

Chloris felt compelled to explain. "He said he didn't want me to be unhappy like Mother. He felt he had failed her—their ages—this quiet place . . ."

"I see. I wonder."

"Wonder what?"

"If that was all."

"What else could there be?"

"I don't know—perhaps nothing." He shrugged. "You could be right." He looked over his shoulder. "I think we should rejoin the others."

"You won't say anything, Quentin, please?"

"I promise."

As they passed through the french windows into the drawing room, a darker shadow moved from the little stone bench beneath the balustrade, hands reaching blindly to cling for a moment to a marble birdbath before entering the house by a different door.

Over the hard winter months, Chloris's restlessness increased. She had little contact with her father, rebuffing his overtures of friendship until he retired into his study for hours on end. She began to hate herself for this attitude but the gulf between them was too wide to bridge.

Perhaps when Matt came back she could forgive him but until then she must live in this frozen half-world where nothing else mattered.

Her constant riding had worn her habit skirt thin and remembering Molly's words, she decided the time had come to go through her mother's clothes, still hanging in the wardrobe as they had done since the accident. Her father was out the evening she went into her mother's room. A faint fragrance still permeated the garments, evening gowns, day dresses and soft furs. She withdrew the riding habit. It was of black broadcloth, the jacket braided at collar and lapel. On the shelf above stood a top hat of velour, bound by a black and white spotted chiffon round its crown. She remembered seeing her mother wearing it many times.

The habit fitted well. She must ask her father's permission to wear it. As she was returning it to its place, the skirt slipped from the coat hanger and fell to the bottom of the wardrobe. Reaching in and parting the long dresses in order to retrieve the skirt, her fingers disturbed a small leather suitcase. It fell over with a thud. Curiosity caused her to draw it out and its heaviness intrigued her. The clasp sprang open immediately. It looked like an overnight bag, the sort a lady might take when travelling some distance but not requiring to take a trunk.

A nightdress, dressing gown, toilet requisites, a day dress and a small case of jewellery spilled from the bag. Chloris sat back on her heels and regarded the contents. Now why would her mother have packed a bag and left it undisturbed in the wardrobe? Was she planning a trip or had she returned from one? The clothing was clean and pressed, not crumpled from use.

What had prevented her from going somewhere? A pulse in her head leapt violently. Had sudden death cancelled this trip? Was her mother planning to leave soon after that last visit to Field House? To come home, change into travelling clothes, collect this bag and leave her husband? Alone? Where could she go alone? Her family was dispersed, most of them dead. That destination seemed unlikely. With a lover perhaps, someone who offered her a gayer life than her husband could give her? Someone she met at Field House? Lord Chalmers, who had left only hours before the accident—or so he had said! Quentin, who had loved some mysterious lady? They were both fair-haired. Could one of them have been the companion on the cliffs, fleeing in panic to avoid involvement on finding Estelle had fallen to her death? Could either be so base?

Another possibility presented itself. Supposing her mother had agreed to run away and then changed her mind, informing her lover that night at Field House of the change of heart. A spurned lover might be so enraged as to promise vengeance, even murder! A deliberate act, arranged to look like an accident. Mad as a wet hen, the boy had said. Mad indeed, if it was so.

Had her father any suspicion? she wondered. Did he know of this packed bag? She looked closely at the leather. Two faint marks were scored on its sides, as if it had been strapped to a saddle behind the rider. Had Estelle then taken the bag to Field house? Was that why she refused the carriage to convey her there? But then, her own husband had found the body. He must have found the bag too if it had been on the saddle. Silver-haired? Could he have been on the cliffs already?

Chloris dropped her head into her hands. No, it was absurd! He had loved her mother very much. He was not a man of violence. But if he had known she was leaving him—what then?

The questions spun madly in her brain. Would he have stood by and let her go or made some move to prevent her disgracing his name and profession? By returning the bag to the wardrobe, he would have forestalled any question of why his wife rode the cliffs with an overnight bag strapped to her saddle.

Accident or murder? Which one and by whom?

18

Chloris replaced the bag carefully in the wardrobe. A feeling of unreality, like living in the middle of a nightmare from which there was no awakening, clouded her mind. Was it just the strain of parting from Matt and the alienation with her father that created these terrifying fantasies? Were they really fantasies or had she stumbled upon the truth? If she had never met the boy on the cliffs and her father had unpacked the bag, then none of these doubts would ever have occurred. Estelle's death would have remained an accident to her.

It was a long time before she slept that night and even the morning brought no joy. The day was cold and wet and her head ached. Who could she turn to? Not her father or anyone at Field House, not until she had discovered the truth. But how to do that?

When Molly came to call her, she eyed her maid thoughtfully, and came to a decision.

"Molly? That night Mother died—the night she went to Field House—did she take a bag with her, a small leather bag fastened to the saddle?"

"Good heavens, child, how should I remember?"

"Try, Molly, please."

"I don't remember any bag. If she needed a pair of shoes, then like as not she had them in a cloth drawstring bag that she hung on the pommel."

"Did she ever stay overnight at Field House?"

"Not to my knowledge. Now, don't go fretting about something that's over and done with. No good will come of raking up the past."

The advice was sound enough but Chloris knew she would never rest until she had solved the mystery—if mystery there was. After breakfast she saddled Bessie and rode out. Turning her back on the Martello Tower and the naval vessel, she cantered her mare along the descending slope of the cliffs towards the long pebbly beach. Deserted, save for a few upturned boats, she moved parallel to the sea until the landscape met dunes topped with spiky wind-whipped grass. Too many dips and hollows made riding hazardous at this point so she halted. About to dismount, her gaze was caught by a flash of scarlet above her on the dunes. Something taut and circular, moving in the slight breeze, like a—yes, like an umbrella or parasol.

She left Bessie cropping a small patch of grass and moved towards the object. Cresting the last hillock, she found herself staring down at two people. Too late to retreat for she had been noticed. Georgina, twirling a red umbrella, was seated on a rock, while slightly below her and oblivious of anything but the face he gazed at so eagerly was a young man, a complete stranger to Chloris.

Georgina looked up and gave a gasp. The young man, following her gaze, sprang to his feet.

"I beg your pardon for intruding," said Chloris. "For some reason I thought to find an abandoned or runaway umbrella. Forgive me, Georgina." She turned away with the intention of returning as quickly as possible to Bessie.

"Wait!" It was Georgina calling. "Don't go."

Chloris halted and looked back. Georgina was hurrying towards her, hands outstretched.

"I'm so glad it was you, Chloris. I haven't seen you for ages."

Chloris smiled. "Well, I'm not the best of company these days."

"But I've missed you at Field House with only the men for company. I thought we were friends."

"So we are." Chloris smiled into the appealing face. "But to be quite truthful, I thought you would be gone back to London by this time."

"I would have been but I caught a chill and Sir Lionel insisted I stay until I was recovered."

"Should you be out like this then, unprotected from the sea breeze?"

Georgina's face turned pink. "No, I should not but I had to see Robert."

"Robert?"

"Robert Courtney. Don't you remember? I told you of him."

"Ah, yes, of course. Your poet."

Georgina beckoned the young man to her side. "I'd like to present him to you. Robert, this is my good friend, Miss Chloris Blair."

Chloris had time then to consider the man. Very young, a little too thin, with wide intense blue eyes under an untidy wind-blown sweep of dark hair, he looked as one imagines a poet should look. Barely able to take his gaze off Georgina, he bowed, then stood silent, his heart in his eyes.

"I'm happy to know you, Mr. Courtney," said Chloris. "I hope you are achieving success in your profession."

"Isn't it wonderful," said Georgina, clasping her hands together. "Robert came all the way to Dorset from London, just to tell me that, at last, his poetry is to be published."

"Congratulations, Mr. Courtney. You must be very pleased."

"Just a small volume, Miss Blair. Nothing like Lord Byron's." He spoke in a deprecating tone.

"Not yet, perhaps, but one day you may be as famous," Gerogina said, giving him such a sweet smile that the young man almost reeled with the beauty of it. "Robert wrote to me at Field House, but I could hardly invite him there, because of Mama, you see."

"Yes, I see that. Well, I hope you make a great deal of money with your book, Mr. Courtney."

"It's most unlikely," he said, gloomily. "Not enough to make any difference." He lapsed into silence again. Chloris felt sorry for him. Compared with the money and position Quentin was possessed of, one slim volume of poetry would hardly weight the scales in his favor with Mrs. Davenport.

"I really must be going," she said, feeling an unwelcome third, as far as Mr. Courtney was concerned. "I intend to call on Ruth this morning."

She left them on the dunes, promising to visit Field House very soon. Mounted on Bessie, she looked back and saw them moving slowly over the dunes to the path above. They made an attractive couple, but had it been her own choice, she would have picked Quentin, not for his position in life but for his character and strength. At least—she qualified that thought—as long as he had not been involved in her mother's death.

A few minutes' riding brought her to the

village. Past the now shuttered and deserted Trevelyan house, she rode on to the edge of the village where Ruth lived alone. There was no answer to her knock. The back door was also locked and through the kitchen window she saw that all was clean and tidy, as if the occupant had departed on holiday.

A neighbor, seeing her standing indecisively on the front path, volunteered the information that Miss Ruth had been gone for more than a week.

"Gone? Do you know where?" asked Chloris.

"I did hear she's gone to stay at High Ridge farm. Maybe Mrs. Kernick's been taken bad again."

"Thank you. Then I'll call on her there."

High Ridge farm was three miles on the other side of the village. Chloris delayed her visit until after lunch in order to give Bessie a rest. The farm was on a hillside facing inland, protected from the sea winds at its back by solid stone walls. Sheltered in the valley below were the cattle. It was an attractive old building, the tiles russet-hued and sweeping down to the mellowed stonework below the high chimneys. Neat, white-painted shutters framed mullioned windows, behind which one glimpsed spotless curtains. Surveying the tended hedgerows and solid field gates, Chloris could only conclude that Neil Kernick was a hard-working young man with the inborn pride of land of his yeoman ancestors.

She dismounted in the yard. Before she had time to approach the door, it was opened by Ruth herself, wearing a loose enveloping apron on which she wiped floured hands. As Ruth met her eyes, Chloris had the strange feeling that her presence was unwelcome, but in the next second the impression was gone as if it had never been.

311

Ruth smiled. "Hello, Chloris. What brings you so far out?"

"I called at your cottage. They told me you were here. Is Mrs. Kernick ill again?"

"No, she is quite recovered."

So, the faint lines of strain on Ruth's face were not due to caring for Mrs. Kernick.

"I'm glad. But you look rather tired yourself, Ruth. Are you quite well? Is there anything I can do?"

Ruth's lips twisted a little. "No, there is nothing you can do. I'm perfectly well and am not in need of anyone's help. Give my regards to your father." She turned away as if the interview was at an end. It was unlike her to be so cursory and Chloris was taken aback. Ruth had always been the gentle, undemanding friend, called on by everyone in trouble. Had she now tired of this role to the extent of rebuffing old friends? What had brought it to a head?

"I'm sorry, Ruth. I must have called at an inconvenient time. Perhaps later, when all the excitement is over."

"What do you mean?" The question came sharply.

"You're in the middle of baking, that's obvious, and you don't need visitors when you're busy, especially with Christmas coming on. Are you staying for that or will you go back to your cottage?"

"I don't know. I'm here indefinitely. It all depends." She was silent then, her expression so withdrawn that Chloris hesitated to question her further.

As she rode away, she reflected on Ruth's changed attitude. High Ridge farm was far enough away from the village to eliminate any chance meeting. Was that Ruth's intention—to cut herself off from all contact with her previous circle? With her mother dead and Mrs. Trevelyan in Bridport, there was no-one left she need concern herself with. Neil Kernick was obviously in love with her and in spite of Ruth's denial the last time they met at Field House, it could be that something would come of it after all. More than anyone else she deserved some happiness.

At Christmas the Blairs were invited to Field House. It was the only light moment in a period of depressing wet weather but even that visit could not be called a success. They had gone together, Chloris and her father, in the carriage and the little conversation they had was strained and formal. Even Field House, full of light and warmth, could not dispel the feeling that she stood alone. Georgina and Quentin were as friendly as usual, Sir Lionel a benevolent host, but underlying her own forced gaiety, she was conscious of Matt, heaven knows where, so far away with eight months of his sentence still to run.

In spite of Sir Lionel's bluff kindness, Mr. Justice Blair would not be drawn into his circle of good humor, seeming to have sunk even deeper into a sober world of his own. Lord Chalmers was still a house guest and a sober world of his own. Lord Chalmers was still a house guest and only he and Georgina, with their talk of London, eased the long silences of the dinner table.

It was a relief to Chloris when she and Georgina finally left the dining room. Over coffee, Georgina asked, "What do you think of Francis Chalmers? He is very charming, don't you think?"

Chloris shrugged. "I barely know the man."

"But you watched him quite a lot over dinner. I saw you."

Chloris was startled. For all her simplicity, Georgina sometimes surprised one with her perspicacity. She smiled. "I was wondering what kind of man he was." Or what he might be capable of, she said to herself. "I understand he has recently returned from Italy. Was he there for his health?"

"Yes, poor man. I think he went there to forget. He didn't actually say so but I believe he had an unhappy love affair." She sighed, her blue eyes full of sympathy. "It is always sad when things don't work out."

"Don't waste your sympathy on Lord Chalmers," Chloris returned dryly. "With his looks and fortune, there will be no shortage of applicants for his favors when he returns to London."

"Dear Chloris, don't talk like that. It shows an unbecoming hardness of character."

"I suppose so but what have I got to look forward to over the next eight months? It is so long to wait for Matt's release."

"I would not have mentioned it first but Quentin told me how fond of Matt you were. I never knew him well myself but I do feel for you in your grief. But the days will be longer if you cut yourself off from all your friends as you have done. You must do something more than just ride the cliffs every day."

"Yes, you are right." Into Chloris's mind there came a sudden recollection of Sefton's invitation to join them. Well, why not? It would ease the unbearable waiting if she were to carry on where Matt left off. And what if she was caught? She gave a mental shrug. Who would care? Not her father, who had shown his power that night at the prison. Besides, it would show her contempt for him and the stupid laws that kept Matt from her.

Georgina gave an exclamation and rose from the couch, crossing towards the french windows.

"Chloris, look! What is that bright light out there?"

Before Chloris had reached her side, Georgina gasped and said in a high frightened voice, "My God, they're flames! Chloris! A fire—below in the stableyard. What can it be?"

They stared for a horrified moment, watching flames shoot skywards, hearing the crack of tiles splintering in the heat, to fly across the lawns below the terrace.

Georgina was the first to recover. "The stables, Chloris, the stables! Tell Quentin—the horses—can't you hear them? Go quickly!"

At the urgency in her tone, Chloris turned and fled across the room into the hall. She burst into the dining room and the door crashed back against the wall. Four startled faces turned to her. "The stables. They're on fire. The horses are trapped!" she half-screamed.

Quentin and Chalmers were out of their seats before she had finished speaking. Sir Lionel's face turned purple as he struggled from his chair. "Damn this gout!" he snarled. "I'll rouse the servants to make a bucket chain, Quentin. You go and get out the horses. Hurry, for God's sake!"

But the two younger men had already gone, their feet racing down the hall as they hurled themselves out of the house.

"I'll call Belling, Sir Lionel," shouted Chloris. She flew across the hall to the kitchen door, calling in a loud voice. "Belling! Belling!"

He was halfway up the stairs as she flung wide the door. "Get buckets, bowls, anything—get all the servants—the stables are on fire."

For a man of his bulk, Belling moved with speed. Without a word he turned back, his voice rising in command, issuing orders to the house-maids, sending one flying to alert the gardeners

315

and off-duty grooms. A crashing of metal indicated that buckets, hot water cans and whatever else came to hand were being mustered in quantity to fight the fire.

Chloris let the door swing back behind her. She caught a glimpse of her father and Sir Lionel hurrying out of the front door as she turned back to the sitting room.

"Everyone has been alerted, Georgina. Georgina?" The room was empty, the french windows standing wide open. "Where are you, Georgina?"

There was no reply. A cold wind billowed the curtains. She stared out at the flames. Figures had begun to converge, staggering along under the weight of heavy buckets. A garden hose snaked across the grass, its end being hastily connected to an outside water tap. But where was Georgina? Surely she hadn't rushed to the stables while Chloris was alerting the men? In a sudden agony of fear, Chloris ran across the terrace, down the stone steps and over the lawn.

"Georgina!" she called, hoping to find her friend on the fringes of the disaster, but there was no sign of that tall elegant figure of green brocade. She ran until she could see the stable doors. They were open but smoldering and sparkling with tongues of flame licking up the wood. Belling and his team were hurling water over the roof, steam and smoke making it difficult to see what was happening. The stable was empty of horses although she could hear them whinnying nearby in the paddock. Thank heavens the hunters were safe. Quentin and Chalmers must have gone like the wind to get them out in time.

A shower of sparks caused her to draw back. There was nothing she could do here. Grooms, gardeners, even estate workers from the cottages on Field land had turned out to join the bucket chain. She had better prepare the house for casualties. But first, Georgina. Where could she be? From the stables she ran down to the paddock. She reached the gate—and her heart stopped!

A small group, Sir Lionel, her father and Lord Chalmers, was staring down at Quentin, kneeling on the ground and cradling a limp figure in his arms. Towards this group she walked on unsteady legs, the sickness of horror at what she might find rising in her throat. It was Georgina, wrapped in Quentin's jacket, who was lying so peacefully in his arms. Her eyes were closed, the lashes making a crescent of darkness across her smoke-streaked face.

"Oh, God, not dead?" groaned Chloris, dropping helplessly to her knees beside Quentin.

The lashes quivered and the eyes opened. "N-not dead, Chloris," whispered Georgina in a thin voice. "But sleepy and so prickly." She reached out a hand and Chloris saw the burn marks scored on the white skin. The sight sent the blood rushing back into Chloris's heart.

"Get her to the house, Quentin, quickly. Her burns must be dressed at once."

He roused himself swiftly at her tone and with a strangely haunted look on his chalk-white face strode towards the house, cradling the girl as he might a child or a newborn lamb.

Chloris followed and, pausing only to call the housekeeper and bid her bring warm water, clean clothes and ointment, ran up the stairs to Georgina's room. Quentin had laid her on the bed and Chloris removed his jacket carefully, her eyes searching her slim body. The thick brocade of her dress had served as some protection but her arms and hands were blistering and scorch marks showed on her face and neck.

The housekeeper arrived and Chloris turned to Quentin. "Leave us now. I'll call you when we have done what we can."

He nodded and left the room. The housekeeper produced a large pair of scissors. "Best cut off her dress, miss, just in case."

Chloris agreed and held the fabric as the scissors cut the beautiful brocade from neck to hem. Moving Georgina as little as possible, they removed the dress, together with her corselet and stockings. Between them they sponged off the smoke and grime on the unburned skin, then bound her hands and arms with cloths thickly smeared with cool healing ungents. Her neck and cheeks were gently covered with the ointment and as Chloris smoothed the tangled russet hair from the forehead, Georgina's eyes looked up at her and she smiled faintly.

"Thank you both. Not prickly anymore." And she fell asleep with a small sigh.

There was a lump in Chloris's throat as she looked across the sleeping girl at the housekeeper. That lady's eyes were bright with unshed tears.

"Always such a polite young thing she is, miss. Whatever one does for her, she is ready with a smile and a word of thanks. A well-brought-up young lady, that she is."

"Yes, indeed."

"Would you tell Mr. Quentin, miss, that I'll be happy to sit up tonight with Miss Georgina, if it should be required?"

"I will, and thank you. He'll be most grateful."

The housekeeper gathered up the things they had used and left the room. Chloris covered Georgina with a sheet and a soft light eiderdown, lifting the bandaged arms over the covers. After closing the window, she built up the fire. Warmth and hot sweet drinks, she thought. Wasn't that the treatment for shock? Georgina was sleeping peacefully at the moment but there could be some reaction to her frigthening experience. The doctor must be called. Yes, she would ask Quentin to send for the doctor. She opened the door quietly. Quentin sat on a bench near the stairhead, his head in his hands. For a moment she regarded him with pity. Had he, for one terrifying moment, faced the possibility that the girl he loved was gone forever?

"Quentin," she said softly.

His head came up sharply. His face no longer held that deathly pallor but his eyes retained the haunted look. "How is she?"

"Sleeping. We've done all we can and her injuries are not too severe but it would be wise to send for the doctor. She might still go into shock."

"I've already sent a groom to fetch him. Can I see her?"

"Of course, but let her sleep. It will be helpful to her system."

He went past her swiftly and she saw him bend over the bed, his fingers gently touching the spread of hair on the pillow. Chloris placed a chair behind him.

"Would you like to stay until the doctor arrives?"

He nodded and sat down, his eyes never leaving the face on the pillow. At that moment, Georgina's eyes fluttered open. Her gaze met Quentin's and she smiled. "Is that chestnut safe?" she asked.

Quentin's brows came together crookedly and his voice held a gentle note. "Perfectly safe. What a crazy child you are. Risking your life to get the chestnut out of that stable."

"I knew how fond you were of that colt. He was frightened and—and I was leading him out when—when the beam fell on me." Her lips quivered. "I never thought to wait. Please don't be cross."

"Cross?" His voice was choked. "I'm not cross, but you might have been killed. When I saw you lying there, I thought . . . " he broke off. "I would never have forgiven myself. Never!"

"I'm not much hurt, I think. I did it for you and there was no-one else about . . ." her voice trailed tiredly.

"Don't talk anymore, my dear. When you're well again, I'll make it up to you, I promise. You shall have whatever you want."

"Oh, Quentin, you're so good and kind." Tears trembled on Georgina's eyelashes. "I would like above all to stay here forever, unless, of course, you hold me in dislike."

Quentin stared silently into the flushed face. "I do not hold you in dislike, my dear. On the contrary, you are a brave and beautiful girl." He glanced up at Chloris and she was startled to see the look of pain in his eyes, then he glanced at Georgina again. "I have waited too long already and to no purpose. I will try to make you happy, my dear." He leaned forward and kissed her lightly on the brow. "Your mother will hear from me soon."

"Mama will like that." Her eyes closed again and Chloris slipped out of the room.

Yes, Mrs. Davenport would like that. She must have been grateful for Georgina's chill to delay her departure from Field House and now, with Quentin's proposed letter to inform her of the betrothal, her plans had come to fruition. No need to worry anymore over penniless poets. But did Georgina really love Quentin? Mama will like that—not—I will like that. A strange remark to a man who has just laid his heart at your feet.

320

She continued downstairs and asked one of the maids to take a teatray to Miss Davenport's room. Sir Lionel and her father were standing in the hall looking up at her.

"How is she?" They were both pale and concerned.

"She's quite comfortable. The worst burns are on her hands and arms. Quentin is staying with her until the doctor comes."

The rattle of a carriage announced the hasty arrival of the doctor. Chloris took him upstairs, explaining on the way what she and the housekeeper had done. A quick examination and he said, "Good, good. I won't unwrap the bandages then until tomorrow about nine o'clock when I start my rounds. Meanwhile, I'll give her a sleeping draught. A good night's sleep is the best cure for any kind of shock. I'll instruct you in what to do if she wakes in pain during the night."

Chloris caught Quentin's gaze of appeal. "Could you stay, Chloris? She would be happier with you if she woke and I should be very grateful."

"Of course I will. I'll slip down and tell Father to go home without me."

Later, in a borrowed dressing gown, the fire made up and a supper tray beside her, Chloris leaned back in the big easy chair. The housekeeper, on being apprised of Mr. Quentin's request, had insisted on taking her share of the vigil, promising to come up at four o'clock with a nice large pot of tea for Chloris and for Miss Georgina if she should feel like a cup.

The house was very quiet with everyone abed. It was barely one o'clock and the only sounds were of the distant owls and the faint sighings of the wistaria clinging to the walls. Georgina had slept soundly since the doctor's visit but on the beside table was another sleeping draught, along with a jar of ointment, in case the pain brought her awake.

Chloris closed her eyes, not intending to sleep, but as the church clock struck twice, she was roused by a soft whimper from the direction of the bed. Georgina was awake, her bottom lip gripped between her teeth, her eyes staring fixedly at the ceiling. Chloris bent over her and the stare was transferred to her face.

"Does it hurt, darling? Let me mix you a sleeping draught."

Georgina gasped. "I'm burning up, burning up!" Her voice rose, shaking, and the perspiration stood out on her forehead.

"Drink this. It will help. I'll change the dressings."

Georgina drained the water glass containing the sedative thirstily and moved her head restlessly from side to side, moaning softly with the pain. Chloris swiftly changed the dressings, spreading the cool ointment thickly on the cloths. It seemed to bring a little relief but Chloris was alarmed by the red flush and heat of the girl's skin. She dipped a cloth in the water basin and wrung it out, placing it across Georgina's brow. She continued this treatment until the sedative took effect and Georgina sank into an exhausted sleep, punctuated by sighs and tossing. By four o'clock, Chloris was herself exhausted, trying to keep Georgina from hurting her arms as she flung them about in search of coolness.

She welcomed the tap on the door and the sight of the housekeeper bearing a teatray. Pushing back her own damp hair, Chloris smiled and stretched her aching shoulders. "What a welcome sight you are. Miss Georgina had another sleeping draught at two o'clock and I've changed the dressings. She has been very restless but is quieter now. Do you think it natural she should be so hot? Her skin is extremely heated."

The housekeeper laid a hand on Georgina's forehead. "Unusually hot, quite feverish I would say. What time did the doctor arrange to call?"

"Nine o'clock, he said," answered Chloris, helping herself to a cup of tea.

"Well, I'll stay here until then, while you, Miss Chloris, must go and rest. You're looking worn out. The room next to this has been made up for you."

"Please call me if you need any help."

"Of course, but I think the poor dear might settle now for a while."

Chloris entered the next-door bedroom and collapsed gratefully onto the bed. For an hour she lay between waking and sleeping. On the verge of falling into a deep sleep, she came upright with shock, her heart thudding painfully as a sound like tearing linen split the fabric of the night. The cry echoed and re-echoed in her head. Georgina! What torment was she suffering? Chloris flung herself off the bed and moved unsteadily to the door, fighting her own sleep-drugged state. In the corridor she met the flying figure of Quentin, white-faced with dread.

Without a word they entered the sickroom. Georgina, sitting bolt upright, was feebly warding off the housekeeper's attempts to lay a damp cloth on her brow. She was sobbing as if her heart would break. With an arm lightly around her shoulders, Chloris talked soothingly to the girl, taking the housekeeper's place with the damp cloth.

"So hot! So hot!" complained Georgina. "Why is it so hot, Chloris?"

"Lie still, my dear, and you'll be cooler,"

answered Chloris. "Let me put this cold cloth on your head. Now, isn't that better?" She was alarmed by the intense heat of Georgina's skin and looked worriedly at Quentin. "She's burning with fever. We must have the doctor again. I don't know what else to do."

"I'll fetch him," Quentin said.

"It's so early, only five o'clock. Will he come?"

"He'll come—whether he likes it or not," said Quentin in a voice of steel. "Give me half-an-hour."

Chloris nodded and turned back to her patient, utterly convinced that in half-an-hour Quentin would have the doctor in this room—in his nightshirt if need be.

Georgina clung to Chloris, sobbing like a child. "He was frightened—I didn't want to . . ."

"No, my dear, but that makes you very brave. The bravest girl I know. You did it for Quentin and he loves you. Try not to think about it. It's all over and you're safe."

But Georgina refused to be comforted. There seemed to be something more on her mind. Her words were becoming incoherent, feverishly entangled with each other.

"Tell him I couldn't help it. He won't understand—oh, it's too hard!"

"Of course, my dear, but he'll be back soon. He'll understand."

"No, he won't. He'll never come back when he knows."

Chloris exchanged a puzzled glance with the housekeeper. "She must be delirious. I wish the doctor would hurry."

True to his word, Quentin was back in half-an-hour with a hastily dressed, very irritable doctor. One look at Quentin's stony expression and Chloris knew why the doctor had answered his summons so speedily. One didn't take time out to

324

argue with a man who looked capable of dragging one at the rope's end if necessary. However, there was little he could do but suggest plenty of liquids and lighter bandages.

Between them, Chloris and the housekeeper devoted the next six days to caring for Georgina. The hours ran into each other as Chloris moved back and forth from this room to the next, snatching a few restless hours of sleep between coaxing Georgina to drink and eat a little. Her father had thoughfully sent over a small bag containing a change of clothes, together with a few toilet requisites and her nightdress.

Georgina made progress. Her fever abated and she threw herself about less. The stabbing pain of fresh burns had eased into bruised and tender flesh that began to heal. Delicate pink skin showed itself as the burned skin peeled away. The scorch marks were almost gone from her face and neck.

Quentin was a constant visitor, content to sit silent or assist Chloris in urging Georgina to drink fruit juice or take a little soup. Chloris was careful not to change the dressings in his presence. The sight of the disfigured arms was something she could not inflict on him. She found his eyes on her own face several times. They held a slightly puzzled expression. She had no time to consider its meaning until the first evening that Georgina seemed more herself agin. She had opened her eyes, clear blue unclouded eyes. Her skin was cool, too.

"I feel better," she said. "Can I have my hairbrush and looking glass?"

Chloris laughed in sheer relief. "Now I know you are better, my love. Do you feel up to changing into a pretty nightgown before your visitors arrive?"

"Visitors?"

"Quentin and Sir Lionel have called many times while you've been ill."

Georgina gazed into the looking glass with horror. "You let them see me like this?"

"Well," said Chloris mildly, "I could hardly turn them out of their own house, could I?"

"I look terrible," said Georgina with a squeak of anguish.

"Nonsense! A little rouge and a ribbon in your hair will have your fiance in transports of joy."

"My what?"

"Don't tell me you've forgotten! Quentin promised you the earth but you asked only for his love. He has already written to your mother. By this date it will have been announced in The Times."

The blue eyes were large in the pale face as she stared at Chloris. "I don't remember. It was all confused."

"Well, you did say 'Mama will be pleased,'" Chloris said, a little dryly. "Don't you remember that?"

"Ye-es, I do now. She will be pleased, you know."

"And you?"

"Yes, of course. Quentin is so—is so very eligible. We shall be extremely happy. He is good and kind and thoughtful. He is everything one could wish for and I am a very lucky girl." Her lashes hid her eyes as she stared down and Chloris could read nothing in the pale withdrawn face.

When Quentin came in later, Georgina greeted him brightly. She wore a nightdress of pink chiffon that added color to her face and her hair, brushed by Chloris, was confined in a satin band of the same color. She was still pale with shadows under her eyes but looked like a delicate flower, slightly buffeted by an April shower.

Chloris escaped and treated herself to a long luxurious bath. Tonight, she was having dinner downstairs, the housekeeper insisting that she relax for once, now that Miss Georgina was well on the way to recovery.

An hour later she stood in the sitting room, looking out across the lawn. In the distance, the roofless stable had a forlorn dejected appearance. She wondered where the hunters were now stabled.

A step behind brought her round to face Quentin.

"Georgina is having supper. She sent me down to join you and Father for dinner."

"Don't put yourself out on my account, Quentin."

He smiled. "Six months ago if you'd have said that—and you probably did—I would have thought you were being sarcastic. But now I know you really mean it. You've shown me another side to Chloris Blair."

"Thank you, kind sir."

"I always considered you young and rather selfish but even my opinion can change."

"What an admission—coming from the next Lord of the Manor," she mocked.

He laughed. "Beneath your viper's tongue, you are a remarkable girl."

"No compliments please, Quentin, or I'll lose all respect for you! There's nothing remarkable in looking after a friend. Your housekeeper did as much as I did."

"I shall remember that too, but you had no need to stay and yet you did and, I suspect, spent most of your nights by her side."

"I am very fond of Georgina."

"So am I."

"Only fond? But you are going to marry her!"

"Yes. It seems the best thing to do. I'll try to

make her happy." His brows were drawn in a slight frown as if he looked into the past. Chloris suddenly remembered his words on her last visit to Field House, the night she had confessed her marriage to Matt and he had spoken of a lost love.

She touched his arm gently. "We have to forget the past, Quentin, and look to the future. Georgina will make you a delightful wife, she's so gentle and elegant."

"Like a summer breeze," he said, smiling. "Not a cold lashing wind, like you."

"I have my summer moments too," she began indignantly, and he suddenly bent and kissed her hard on the mouth.

When he released her she gasped, as if she had herself been lashed by a cold but scorching wind.

He smiled. "I've wanted to do that for a long time. This seemed an appropriate moment." He held out an arm. "Shall we go in to dinner?"

She accepted the arm in silence, her ready tongue deserting her in the wake of an emotion she could not, as yet, define.

Dinner was a gay affair. Only the three of them, as Lord Chalmers had gone, but the burden of worry over Georgina had lifted, making them, if anything, more talkative. Chloris learned from Sir Lionel that the hunters were now housed in a barn, little the worse for their night of terror.

"Did you discover how the fire started?"

"We think a travelling tinker was looking for a night's shelter and lit a candle in the stable. Unfortunately, he chose the wrong stable. Those horses won't have anyone near but the people they know. I imagine he got too close and one of them lashed out. No sign now of the tinker of course, but we found his bundle and a burned out candle end. We only use enclosed lanterns there ourselves to eliminate any such accident."

"Well, thanks to Georgina's warning, only the stables suffered."

Sir Lionel nodded. "Considering that she has always kept her distance from the hunters before, it was exceedingly brave of her. They could have stampeded out while she was freeing the colt. She was near the paddock before collapsing."

Chloris slept that night like a log, the first full night of sleep she had had since the fire. At the breakfast table, Quentin suggested they take out the horses.

"It's a beautifully dry day and the fresh air will do you good."

It was exhilarating to ride one of the Field House horses after old Bessie. Quentin smiled at her enthusiasm and kept pace as she flung the roan mare into a headlong gallop along the cliffs. They reined in high above the beach and sat smiling at each other as they regained their breath. The exertion had brought fresh color to Chloris's cheeks and her green eyes sparkled under the windswept fall of dark hair.

"You always were one of the best riders in the county," said Quentin.

"For a girl?" she asked, giving him an amused look.

He smiled and shook his head. "No qualifications whatsoever to that statement. I mean it. I wish—," he paused.

"You wish what?"

"It sounds disloyal I know, but I wish Georgina liked a mad gallop. I didn't realize how long it was since I'd been out like this. Usually it's a gentle canter on a couple of hacks or a carriage ride."

"A great deal more elegant, Quentin, and in

keeping with Georgina's upbringing. Mrs. Davenport would think me quite hoydenish, I'm sure, and be very disapproving."

His lips came together in a straight line. "She had better not show it or make any such remark in my hearing when she comes to visit."

Chloris stared at him in mock alarm. "Quentin Field," she said faintly. "Can I really believe that Quentin Field would spring to my defense against such a formidable opponent as Mrs. Davenport? I think I must be delirious through lack of sleep! You have always treated me like a half-witted child."

He laughed. "A gross exaggeration, my dear, but as I told you last night, I have discovered a new Choris Blair, one I never knew existed." He held out his hand. "Whatever the future brings, I'll come if you need me. Wherever I am," he added.

Oddly touched, she gripped his hand. "Thank you, Quentin. When Matt comes home, I might hold you to that."

He nodded and they turned for home, both a little quieter than on the outward journey. As they dismounted in the stableyard Chloris said, "I called on Ruth a few weeks ago. Did you know she had removed to High Ridge farm?"

"Yes. I took her there myself."

"Really? I wonder why she left the village. Did she say?"

"We discussed it and she thought it best to go away for a time. She'll be well cared for by the Kernicks."

"I'll go and see her again now that Christmas is over, although her welcome wasn't too warm the last time I went."

He looked at her strangely. "It may not be any warmer next time."

She was astounded. "Whatever do you mean? We're old friends."

"Perhaps for that reason she won't want to see you. Chloris—Ruth is pregnant."

19

"Ruth! Pregnant? I—I don't believe it!" Chloris stared at Quentin, whose face had become quite unreadable. He said nothing. "Well, yes," she said finally. "Of course I believe it if you say so but I would never have thought—it's so—."

"Out of character? Yes, I agree, but there it is and all we can do is help her through it."

"Yes, of course. Poor Ruth," She looked up swiftly. "Is it Neil Kernick? He is in love with her, I know."

"No, it wasn't Neil, more's the pity. He's a good man."

"Does he know of her condition?"

"Yes. He was the one to suggest she move to the farm, away from the gossiping tongues of the village. I went to see Ruth last month at her cottage because I was worried about her living alone with winter coming on. While I was there she had an attack of sickness. She finally confided in me as she had no-one else to turn to and allowed me to speak to the Kernicks in confidence."

Chloris listened with a feeling of shame. Too full of her own unhappiness over Matt, she had not spared a thought for others. Even an old friend like Ruth had not called on her for help but had gone instead to Quentin, knowing that he was a person to be trusted to put things right. Just as he had for Mrs. Trevelyan. Just as he had when he returned her scarf after that reckless night in the Martello Tower, the night of Matt's capture. He did these things, not out of righteousness as she had once accused him, but out of friendship and an inborn desire to help.

"Quentin, I'm so ashamed," she admitted, trying to explain her feelings. "I should have been more concerned instead of turning my back and thinking my own troubles were greater than anyone else's."

"Don't blame yourself, Chloris." He gave her a swift encouraging smile. "You've made a good start, only this week with Georgina. Who knows? Before long your services may be as much in demand as Ruth's were."

"I wish there was something I could do for her."

"Leave her for a few weeks until she gets used to the idea of the child. At present she is very sensitive and doesn't want to see anyone. Give her time to accept the situation. I'll let her know you are aware of it and would like to see her. She'll be more comfortable, knowing we share her secret and are still her friends."

"Matt always said you would make a perfect Lord of the Manor when your time came."

His face darkened. "Yes, Matt would. Little he cares for people, even his own mother."

"That's not fair, Quentin! He was only trying to make extra money for her."

"And look where that led. A broken home and Matt on his way to the West Indies as a convicted felon."

"I know, but it will be different when he

comes back. He won't be so reckless after that experience."

"I hope you're right, Chloris. I don't want to see you unhappy."

"He did try to make it up to me by asking Father's permission to marry before he left. That showed he cared for me."

"It still puzzled me why your father agreed. But let's not argue over that. I'm too grateful to you to risk our new relationship. Let's go in to lunch and see our invalid."

Georgina was so much improved that Chloris felt she should return home the following morning. With the aid of a long-sleeved dress and cotton gloves to cover the healing skin, Georgina felt well enough to be driven out for an airing by Quentin.

Before she left and while Quentin had gone to order the carriage, Georgina drew Chloris into the privacy of her bedroom. She stood for a moment twisting her gloves between her hands as if unable to put her thoughts into words. Her cheeks were pink under downcast eyes but at last she looked up and drew a deep determined breath.

"Dearest Chloris, you've been so good to me. Can I make one final request before you go home?"

"Yes, of course. What is it?"

"It's about Robert."

"What about him? Don't tell me he is still here!"

"Well, that's just it. I don't know. I did say I would meet him on the beach the day after you came to dinner but with the fire and my being ill, I couldn't go, of course."

"I imagine he would hear all about the fire in the village and understand why you couldn't keep your appointment."

"But when he hears that I am about again; he will expect me to get in touch with him. I am convinced he will not just go back to London. He is the sort of man who waits for hours without getting the least bit cross."

"Well, why don't you take a walk to the beach and let him know you are quite recovered. I'm sure he would be most happy to see for himself."

"But Chloris, don't you see? He may not know I am engaged to Quentin. How can I tell him? He will be heartbroken."

"It seems to me you have no choice."

The blue eyes gazed appealingly at Chloris. "I can't! I just can't face him and break his heart like that. He feels things so deeply."

"Well, he must be told, that's certain. The poor man can't spend the rest of his life sitting on the beach waiting for you to appear."

"I knew you'd understand, Chloris, dear. You will tell him, won't you?"

"Me? You want me to tell him?"

"I'd be most grateful. I know I'm a coward but I can't bear to hurt people's feelings."

"His feelings will still be hurt, even if I tell him."

"I know. Poor Robert. But if I go he will plead with me to change my mind." Tears sparkled in her eyes. "He has a most poetic turn of phrase, quite irresistible," she finished with a damp smile.

"Are you sure, Georgina," asked Chloris, "that you really want to be engaged to Quentin? It's not too late to change your mind."

"Oh, I couldn't do that!" There was almost a hint of fear in the blue eyes that stared at Chloris. "Mama would never forgive me. It is an ideal match and I am a very lucky and extremely happy girl."

Chloris eyed her doubtfully. It was indeed an ideal match, as Mrs. Davenport would be the first to agree. Quentin had the strength of character and mind to make an excellent husband, apart from being rich and handsome. Georgina would come to realize that life with him was preferable to an existence dependent on the vagaries of poetry sales, however fascinating the poet.

Having agreed, reluctantly, to seek out Robert Courtney and deliver the blow to the heart, Chloris saw them on their way before packing her bag and going to the makeshift stable. The old mare who had been brought over that morning showed her pleasure at their reunion by breathing gustily down the neck of her jacket and behaving generally like a frisky young filly.

The stableboy grinned as Chloris tried to avoid Bessie's exuberant nuzzling.

"Here, miss, let me strap your bag on the back. There now, old girl, be still while miss gets into the saddle. For an old 'un, she's got near as much life in her as that white horse Missus Blair used to stable here when she came to the House."

From the saddle Chloris looked down at him and her heart suddenly beat faster. "You remember my mother?"

"Oh, yes, miss, only too well."

"What do you mean—only too well?"

He ruffled his hair awkwardly. "No offense, miss, but the only time Missus Blair spoke sharpish to me was the last time I saw her—or the horse."

Chloris tried to space her words evenly. "Really? What was that about?"

"She had a bag strapped on the back of the saddle—smaller than that—and when she'd gone to the house I thought she'd forgotten it so I set off after her. She gave me a cross look and told me to put it back where I'd got it from and if she'd wanted it, she'd have said so." He looked up at Chloris. "Sometimes the gentry speak sharpish, like Sir Lionel when the gout bothers him, but we know they don't always mean it. They got lots of things to worry 'em in their sort of lives," he finished stoutly, in defense of the gentry.

Chloris smiled. "Yes, I'm sure it must have been something like that to make her speak so."

Out of the gates and onto the path leading to the cliff road, Chloris rode Bessie hard, partly to calm down the horse and partly to avoid contact with anyone else until she had time to think. She knew now that the packed bag had accompanied Estelle to Field House that night. It was obvious by her words to the stableboy that she wanted it kept secret. Only one other person must have known her plan, but was he the one to cause her death? Or had it really been an accident with her father discovering the bag and hiding it to protect her reputation? Perhaps they were all innocent and she was reading too much into the finding of a packed bag. But until she knew the truth, she could never accept Estelle's death as purely accidental.

Bessie's pace slowed along the cliff road, her first wild surge being spent. She settled into an easy canter and Chloris looked about her, breathing in the fresh sea air. The view was marred only by the naval vessel still anchored in the bay. Within sight of her home she came upon a solitary figure trudging towards the village. His head was bowed and his hands were thrust into the pockets of an ulster. A slight breeze disturbed the dark curls above the classical-featured face that turned at her approach.

Drawing rein, Chloris looked down into the eyes dark with suffering and understood why

Georgina had not dared see this man again. To a tenderhearted girl, the thought of inflicting pain was insupportable but, gazing into the sensitive face, Chloris herself regretted having been commissioned to deal the blow.

She slid from the saddle."Mr. Courtney, will you walk a little way with me?"

He bowed. "Miss Blair. We met on the dunes, I believe."

"I—I want to talk to you about Georgina."

"Is she well?" His expression was haggard and she felt desperately sorry that she must increase his distress.

"She has recovered very well. A few burns from the fire but in time the marks will be unnoticeable."

"I hardly liked to inquire at the house as I am not acquainted with the family there, and I should get back to London but I couldn't leave without seeing Georgina again."

"Mr. Courtney," said Chloris gently, "I think you must go back to London and put all thought of Georgina behind you. It will do no good to stay here."

His pale face went even paler. He did not pretend to misunderstand her and for that she was grateful. He was intelligent enough to know why Georgina was in Dorset.

"I see. She has accepted Sir Lionel Field's son?"

"Yes."

"I really can't blame her. My own prospects are such that I could never hope to be acceptable to her family." His mouth twisted wryly. "This son—Quentin Field—what is he like? Rich and proud, I suppose? I only hope he is good to her."

"He is not that rich and not at all proud but yes, he will be good to her. You need have no fears on that level. I have known him all my life and she could not have chosen better, I assure you." For some reason she found herself defending Quentin with unwonted heat but it seemed to satisfy Robert Courtney.

"I'm sorry," he said. "I should not have criticized him. I saw him once and he looked a decent enough man. I'm sure she will be very happy." He looked at Chloris and she was aware of a calm acceptance on his face. "Thank you for telling me. I didn't dare hope that Georgina would come herself."

"Goodbye, Mr. Courtney. I'm sure you knew in your heart that it could only end this way."

He nodded. The glimmer of a smile crossed his face, giving him a look of such charm that she understood his attraction for Georgina. "Goodbye, Miss Blair." He turned and strode away, his shoulders erect, his chin raised, like a man who has looked into the face of adversity and come to terms with it, she thought. Now that the uncertainty of his relationship with Georgina was at an end, she had the feeling he would advance to new heights with the strength of mind she had glimpsed.

Remounting Bessie, she continued on her way. Mr. Justice Blair was crossing the hall as she entered. He stopped abruptly and the joy of seeing her lit his face for the briefest of moments, then was gone, replaced by the well-schooled mask she had encountered over the last few months.

"Welcome home, Chloris," he said in a voice of careful precision. "I hope you left them all well at Field House?"

"Very well, Father." She came towards him, her gaze noting the new lines round his eyes and the slight receding of silver hair at the temples. She placed her hands on his shoulders, gently kissing his cheek. "Forgive me, Father. I have caused you pain with my selfishness and I am sorry."

Without a word his arms encircled her and she felt the frailty of his body and the thin bones under her hands. For a moment he held her in silence.

"Welcome home, Chloris," he repeated with a new meaning and smiled into her eyes. "You look tired, my dear. Come into my study. Molly has just now brought a pot of coffee."

While they drank coffee, Chloris brought her father up-to-date with the happenings at Field House—Georgina's recovery and her engagement to Quentin—but she made no mention of Robert Courtney or of her talk with the stableboy. The suspicion that her father was connected with his wife's death she dismissed as ridiculous.

Once back at Blair House, she settled into a routine but saw more of Georgina and Quentin than she had done previously. Her father too, was often in Sir Lionel's company and since her return had ceased to look so somber and care-ridden.

Spring came suddenly. After the long grey winter, it was with a sense of astonishment that Chloris noted the burgeoning bushes and the petals of the early primrose under the hedgerows. Her spirits soared and she set Bessie into a gallop. Matt would be home in the summer and everything would be as it used to be, except that she was now his wife. She had not thought beyond Matt's return. Would he have changed? Did he still love her?

She drew rein near the Martello Tower and gazed unseeingly across the water to where the sun edged the whitecaps with gold. Her mind went back to that night in prison—the night of the wedding. Matt had told her she was important to him, but not in so many words had he said he loved her. She frowned. He wanted her to be waiting for him on his release, she recalled him saying, but—the thought nagged—never once had he said, "I love you, Chloris."

She shook the thought away. Of course he loved her! Who would insist on marrying in such difficult circumstances if it was not to one's choice? There could be no other reason.

"Well now, Miss Blair," said a familiar voice below her. She started, and gazed down at Sefton. Not having given him a thought for several weeks, she was surprised to find him looking just the same, almost like a prosperous gentleman farmer, she thought.

"Well, Sefton," she said. "Still in business?"

"Right, miss. And with Mr. Matt due home in a matter of months, I wondered if you'd given further thought to my proposition."

"To join you?"

He eyed her speculatively. "You'll maybe not have heard but down in the village there's a story going round that the lady on the white horse has 'come again.' "

Chloris recognized the country expression. If the villagers believed that the ghost of her mother haunted the place where she died, that fact would be enough to keep the cliffs deserted after dark. How had such talk started? Was it possible that her meeting with the boy on the cliffs so long ago had been the seed from which the rumor grew until it flourished into a full-blown haunting? People were superstitious and it could well be that the story had been embellished in the telling until it entered into legend.

She looked down at Sefton. "Go on," she said. "What do you have in mind?"

"Well, miss. You're as like to your mother as

any daughter could be. You'll no doubt still have her riding habit and this mare would pass for the other at night."

"So you want me to impersonate my mother in case any brave soul should disregard the story and venture up here on the wrong night?"

"You have it first time, miss. If anyone should challenge you, why, you're Miss Blair who has as much right as any to ride the cliffs for an hour whenever she pleases."

"And what will you be doing while I ride about up here?"

"We'll be moving the goods into the Tower from the cave below. All we want is for no-one to be about while we're doing it. The sailors don't go near the Martello nowadays. They're too busy watching for boats."

"I see." She gazed over his head at the brick-built Tower, then down across the bay where the naval vessel swung at anchor. A warm glow of excitement began to grow in her. "You are still putting aside Matt's share of the proceeds?"

"Of course. I'll see he's not done out of his rights."

"If I agree to do this, Sefton, I shall want a share too. Don't think to fob me off with a silk handkerchief or a piece of lace."

"Agreed." She reached down a hand and he shook it firmly.

"Tonight all right, miss? About eleven?"

She nodded and he stood back as she shook out the reins. Riding home Chloris wondered at her sudden impulse, but the handshake had committed her, there was no drawing back. As far as she could see there was little risk. As Sefton had said, her only task would be to patrol the cliff by the Tower, and that was no crime.

Over dinner she broached the subject of her mother's riding habit. Mr. Blair agreed that she might wear it until such time as she paid a visit to Dorchester to be measured for a new outfit.

The night was cloudy, the moon overcast as she let herself quietly out of the house and hurried to the stable. Leading Bessie across the grass, she delayed mounting until they had passed into the shadow of the trees at the edge of the lawn. Her heart thudded uncomfortably as she positioned Estelle's distinctive top hat, with the long black and white spotted streamers of georgette, upon her head.

At first she walked Bessie slowly, only urging her into a canter as the last stroke from the church bell-tower died away. The clifftop was dark and deserted. Sefton, she supposed, was conducting his business below but no sound of any kind reached her. She kept a wary eye on the anchored vessel, but apart from a few dimmed lights, saw nothing to cause alarm as she began her vigil.

An hour, Sefton had said, and as time moved on and the church clock began to strike midnight, she cantered slowly past the Martello Tower and along to where the cliffs dropped sheer to the beach, forming ragged inlets and bays, too small and rocky for boats to beach there. But laden animals might follow the sandy path at the base of the cliffs for quite a distance before the track petered out into the cliff face. And that, she assumed, was where Sefton's cave was.

She stared down, a motionless figure, except for the streamers of georgette, teased into movement by the breeze that was strenghtening. It had grown cold. Sheet lightning lit the sky and a few drops of rain pattered down. For a moment the moon was clear of clouds, and in that moment she found herself staring down into the face of a big, black-bearded man. Shock held her rigid. But it was more than shock she read on the face of the man below. His lips were drawn back in a grimace, his mouth opened wide and a strangled wail of sheer terror pinned her momentarily to the saddle. She could only stare at him, fascinated. It was then that she noticed the blindly fumbling hands were not empty as they left his belt. A pistol appeared, the barrel rising, albeit waveringly, towards her.

Then, like a theatre curtain's sudden descent, blackness fell. The moon disappeared in a scurry of clouds and a sharp rattle of thunder flung itself across the sky. The sound of a pistol shot joined the dying echoes.

In that moment Chloris unfroze and wheeled Bessie sharply away from the cliff edge. She smiled grimly. If the moon should come out again and show a deserted clifftop, the man would be convinced that what he had seen was truly an apparition.

A thought jarred her. She knew that face! It was Croker, the man she had helped on both of those nights Matt had taken her dressed as a boy to the beach. So he was still free and operating in the same area. Sefton had obviously not confided her impersonation to him. Why, he could have killed her had the night not so suddenly been plunged into darkness!

A new thought occurred. Why had he been so terrified? What had her appearance signified to him? Surely a girl on a horse could not inspire such blind terror as she had witnessed? The next time she saw Sefton she would question him about Croker.

By morning there was no sign of the previous night's storm. When Molly called her, she rose quickly for she was promised to Georgina for a

gentle ride over the Field estate, Georgina's firs
outing on horseback since the accident. Th
morning was fresh, the air a mixture of damp
leaves and the scent of flowers. Bessie tossed he
head skittishly, her ears pricked in anticipation a
Chloris led her from the stable. A quick gallop t
Field House and Bessie would have settled enough
to join Georgina's quiet pony in a sedate ambl
over the fields.

Since Chloris had reported on her meeting
with Robert Courtney, Georgina had neve
referred to the subject again. Her attitud
towards Quentin was unchanged, but behind it all
Chloris detected a certain strain in the blue eyes
Was it the lingering aftermath of her experienc
or did she still carry in her heart an affection fo
her poet?

In the stableyard at Field House, Chloris'
eyes rested on Quentin as he helped Georgina int
the saddle. Once married to him, the girl woul
soon forget her romantic little episode. There wa
really no comparison, apart from Quentin'
position and income. Had she herself been aske
to choose between them, Quentin would hav
stood head and shoulders above any other man o
her acquaintance. Generous, deeply caring, ther
was no-one she would rather have at her side in
any crisis than Quentin. Her train of thought
halted abruptly. The words "even Matt" had
somehow floated into her mind. What she had
meant was "except Matt." Naturally, she would
prefer Matt by her side. He was her husband. And
yet—she faced it honestly—would he have gone t
so much trouble had the situations been reversed?
Knowing her to be in love with Quentin, would
Matt have risked the cliffs to seek out and return
her scarf and in order to keep her out of trouble?
Would he have brought in a lawyer in the event of

346

the case going to the assizes, or put himself out to
comfort Sir Lionel? She tried to convince herself
that he would, but remembering Matt's careless
reliance on Quentin to support Mrs. Trevelyan,
she wondered. It was a treacherous thought and
she dismissed it as being unworthy. Matt had
always been the one she loved, his very
recklessness an endearing trait. He would remain
the one she loved in spite of this temporary
parting.

Quentin raised a hand in salute as they left the
yard. It was about ten minutes later that Chloris,
busy with her own thoughts, realized Georgina
was unusually silent. She looked across at the girl.

"Are you finding the ride too tiring,
Georgina?"

The blue eyes turned to her with a startled
expression in them. "Oh, no, not at all. I'm sorry. I
was thinking."

"Of your approaching wedding, I suppose?"
Chloris said, smiling.

"What? Oh, yes, of course." She looked at
Chloris with a sudden concentration. "Quentin
wants a quiet wedding here but Mama wants a big
splash in London."

"And what do you want?"

"I think I prefer Quentin's idea. I—I see no
need to go back to London. I'd rather not have
everyone staring at me."

Especially Robert Courtney, Chloris surmised. "I agree with you," she said gently. "A
simple wedding in the parish church would be so
much more comfortable. Your mama is bound to
agree if that is what you both want." And if Mrs.
Davenport is wise, she added to herself, she will
not make an issue of it in case the fish slips off the
hook. She smiled. "Don't worry about it, Georgina.
Your mama will do whatever Quentin wants. You

may rely on that!"

Georgina giggled. "You make him sound ver
masterful."

"And so he is. He never fails to tell me of m
mistakes and failings. He's been doing it for years
but even though I hate him for it, I know he's righ
It's never flattering to be treated like the villag
idiot, even when you deserve it!"

"You don't really hate him, do you, Chloris?"

"No, of course not, but sometimes he's ur
bearably right—or perhaps I'm unbearabl
wrong. Whichever way it is, I never win an argu
ment with Quentin."

"You're probably too much alike. A clash o
personalities like—like two rain clouds on th
same course."

Chloris laughed. "And everyone gettin
drenched in the downpour. Everyone but you fo
you'll be safe and dry under Quentin's umbrella.

"When I first met you, Chloris, I wondered i
you were in love with Quentin. The way you talke
to each other and the sense of humor you bot
share made me think you would make an idea
couple." She looked apologetically at Chloris. "O
course I didn't know about Matt then."

"What a strange thought. I'm sure Quenti
never considered me in any other light than as
rather harebrained girl he had to keep draggin
out of trouble. More of a nusiance than anythin
else."

"He is very fond of you, I know, from the wa
he talks."

"He is fond of his horses and dogs too.
probably come after them." She looked teasingl
at Georgina. "But of you he is more than fond. Yo
are the girl he will marry. Are you prepared for
strong, masterful husband?"

Georgina gasped, losing a little color, and Chloris reassured her swiftly.

"I was only teasing you, my dear. The last person in the world to be domineering is Quentin. He will treat you with great consideration and kindness. It is in his nature."

"There are times when I feel so ignorant and simple-minded in his company that I cannot help feeling he should have chosen a clever girl."

"But he chose you, my dear, and that surely is all that counts."

Georgina nodded. "I will do my best to make him happy," she said, but the words had a desperate sound to them.

They rode back slowly, Chloris wondering if the thought of marriage to Quentin was a terrifying prospect to Georgina but a lesser evil than returning to London, unbetrothed, to face her mother.

Quentin met them on their return. A glance at Georgia's pale face made him urge her to take a rest in her room before lunch. Chloris followed him into the sitting room, accepting the sherry he offered. They sat in silence for a moment and Chloris studied Quentin's downbent head as he gazed fixedly at the carpet, his untouched sherry glass in his hand. He was frowning. Was he worried about Georgina's health?

"Give her time, Quentin. We mustn't expect too much of her at first."

His head came up and he stared at her as if she had spoken Greek. His eyes focused sharply on her with a strangely intent look. "What? What are you talking about?"

"Georgina, of course. Perhaps she is not yet ready for riding. It seems to have tired her. Isn't that why you were looking so worried?"

His face went blank as if a shutter had dropped. "Of course. She mustn't overdo it. It is not that long since the accident." He smiled—with an effort, it struck Chloris. "Drink up your sherry and have another glass. Will you stay to lunch?"

"No, thank you. Father expects me home. But I wanted to ask you if you had seen Ruth lately. May I call on her yet?"

"Ah, yes, Ruth. I rode over to the farm and had a talk with her. At first she was loath to see—to see anyone." The hesitation was slight but Chloris wondered if he had been about to say "she was loath to see you." "However," he went on smoothly, "she has agreed that you may pay her a visit one afternoon. But remember, Chloris, no questions. That is her only stipulation."

"I wouldn't dream of it!" she said, indignantly. "Although I must admit it seems a despicable thing for her lover to do, to cut and run like that."

"If he knows," said Quentin. "Otherwise, I agree with you but my concern is only for Ruth at present."

It was later that afternoon when she drew rein outside High Ridge farm. Ruth was alone and greeted her pleasantly, if not with the same warmth she had once shown. But as Chloris talked of Georgina, the Field family and various happenings in the neighborhood, Ruth seemed to relax and enjoy her visit. Over tea and scones Mrs. Kernick joined them and Chloris found her to be a comfortable, motherly woman, just the kind of person to care for Ruth in this crisis.

On the doorstep, as she took her leave, Chloris asked, "May I come again? I have so enjoyed this visit."

Ruth nodded. "I've missed you too. The Kernicks have been wonderful to me and so has

Quentin but it's nice to gossip with a girlfriend now and then."

Chloris gave her a quick hug. "It has done me good too. Goodbye, Ruth."

Just before she reached the open heathland beyond the fences of High Ridge, she came upon a red-haired man jumping down from a stile. He looked up as she halted Bessie.

"Neil. How are you? I've just been taking tea with your mother and Ruth."

He nodded, eyeing her coolly. "Hello, Chloris. We last met in the courthouse, I believe."

"That's right." She swung down from the saddle and faced him. "I'm glad I've met you." He waited without answering and she went on. "Ruth and I are old friends. I'd like to help all I can."

His expression didn't change. "What makes you think she needs help?" The pale blue eyes regarded her steadily and she sensed a hostility in him.

"Forgive me, Neil. I'm not prying but Quentin said I might call with Ruth's permission."

"I see. Well, if Ruth and Quentin say it's all right, then I won't argue. I just don't want any more hurt coming to that girl."

"Neither do I. If I can help in any way, please call on me."

"Thank you, Chloris, I will, but she'll be all right with us for as long as she wants to stay and I hope that will be for good."

Chloris felt a stab of pity for him. To discover that the girl you love is carrying another man's child must hurt deeply, but to go on caring for that girl required strength of a high quality.

He patted Bessie's neck as if taking the opportunity of changing the subject to cover the moment when there was nothing more to be said on the matter.

"Fine horse," he said. "Not too young but still strong. Reminds me a bit of that mare of your mother's. Same family?"

"An elderly relative," Chloris answered, smiling. "You remember then that splendid white horse my Mother rode?"

"Too well. I moved her from the cliffs."

At Chloris's startled expression he explained. "Your father asked me to move the corpse. I did it with a couple of Shire horses and a farm gate." He shook his head. "Sad to see such a fine horse broken up like that."

"It was a bad fall."

"But not that bad. It always puzzled me why her kneecaps were broken when she only fell on the grass."

"Isn't it possible to sustain that kind of injury in a fall?"

"Yes, but I reckon the kneecaps went first before she did. Nobody took any notice when I mentioned the scorch marks. They said she must have torn her knees going down."

"Scorch marks? How do you mean?"

"I'd swear it looked to me as if she'd run into something that whipped her suddenly across the knees, fast enough to burn the hairs of her forelegs. There were bits of rope fibers in the wounds too. It's my belief something caught and tripped her and that's what made her fall. Mrs. Blair was an excellent rider. I've seen her riding the cliffs many a time. A wrong-footed step by that horse and she'd have pulled her out of it right away."

"You are saying the horse got tangled up in a piece of rope?"

"It looked like that to me but don't ask me how it happened. I've no more idea than you and there wasn't any rope found up there when I removed the horse."

All the way home Chloris tried to discover a reason to explain Neil's theory. A discarded length of rope left carelessly on the cliffs and into which the horse had stepped? But the rope would have been found afterwards. Neil was an expert on horses. He would not have made a mistake. No rope had been found and the verdict was accidental death. But a simple accident did not explain the rope-burns.

20

Whichever way she turned, Chloris felt she faced another question. Although she no longer suspected her father of involvement in Estelle's death, she had not ruled out the mystery man on the cliffs that night. But here was another link in the chain. How did it all fit together and would she ever know the truth of it?

Her next meeting with Sefton took place two days later. She found him perched on a rock, contemplating the ocean, an empty pipe gripped between his teeth. His sidelong glance rested on her as she cantered Bessie towards him and she noticed the self-satisfied expression on his face.

"You're beginning to look as prosperous as Sir Lionel, Sefton," she said. "How was the run?"

He removed the pipe. "Very good, miss. Our best yet. There'll be a tidy packet waiting for Mr. Matt."

"Then you can add my share to it."

He stretched out his stiff leg and nodded. "It's hard work for an old man. When Mr. Matt gets back I'll take my share and put it into a few acres back home."

"Where's home?"

"The other side of Weymouth."

"Do you have any family?" He had been so long in the cottage near the Trevelyan house, she had never thought of it before.

"I've got a half-brother somewhere. He worked with us for a minute, then he went off on his own. Mr. Matt told me he got tired of the game so he took his share and left. That was over a year ago while Mr. Matt was still at that college in Weymouth and just before we moved here. Funny, though, him just going off like that without a word to me."

"Maybe he'll turn up again when you set up as a farmer and he hears you've become law-abiding."

"Maybe he will at that. I was always fond of him."

"By the way, Sefton, will you tell that man of yours, Croker, that I take great exception to being fired on? I'm supposed to be on your side."

Sefton looked startled. "He never said a word about it, though I remember he looked mighty queer when he rushed into the cave."

"Then you'd better tell him the truth if you expect me to carry on."

"I'll have a word with him, miss. Though it's a rum thing for Croker to be scared for he's put away one or two in his career and not let it upset him."

Chloris frowned in sudden thought. "Do you remember the night my mother died?"

"Very well, miss. We were out on a run but heard nothing of it until next day when Mr. Matt told us." He shook his head and bent to fill his pipe. "Poor soul. A real nice lady she was."

"Was Croker with you on that run?"

"Aye, he was. Why do you ask?"

"I really don't know. I just wonder if he could have seen her."

"Take my advice and keep away from him, miss. He's an ugly-tempered fellow."

Something still nagged at the back of Chloris's mind. "You said he looked queer when he came back to the cave. As if he'd had some kind of shock, would you say?" She looked at Sefton intently.

He squinted up at her, then went back to filling his pipe. He shrugged and his voice was casual. "Maybe he thought you were a ghost. Seamen are superstitious folk, Miss Chloris. It's likely he heard the story in the village, then seeing you up there so sudden-like, it gave him a nasty turn."

Chloris nodded. A reasonable explanation, she supposed. "When is the next run, Sefton?"

"Friday, miss. You'll do it again?"

"As long as I have nothing to fear from Croker."

"Don't worry. I'll see he doesn't bother you again."

He was as good as his word and for the next few weeks Chloris roamed the cliffs on the appointed nights without seeing a soul, smuggler or coastguard. After the first novelty had worn off, the duty became tedious, for none of the villagers showed signs of tempting fate by venturing near the Martello Tower at night. When next she saw Sefton she complained of the boredom.

He grinned, then eyed her speculatively. "If you're wanting a change, maybe I can arrange it."

"In what way?"

"Friday week, that's the third of April with the moon in it's first quarter, we're picking up a special big consignment and using two boats. We're trying to find extra hands for the unloading. A good strong lad like—er—Clem, was it—could double his pay that night."

Chloris laughed and felt her blood quicken at the thought of an adventure. "I'll get him over," she promised.

At the end of March, Quentin sent over a note to inform her that Ruth had been delivered of a son. Although the birth was premature, both Ruth and the boy were well. Chloris was pleased. Perhaps now, Ruth might marry Neil. Her code would not have allowed her to do so while pregnant. This way, she clearly indicated that Neil Kernick was in no way responsible for her predicament.

As Chloris waited for the April night to arrive, her thoughts turned to Matt. How proud of her he would be and how pleased to know that money was being kept aside for him. Through her father she learned that the ship on which he was serving had left the West Indies and was bound for Plymouth, due to dock sometime in May or June. Although his sentence would not be completed by then, she hoped he might be transferred to some smaller vessel and not be compelled to undergo another long voyage, extending his time away from her.

On one of her visits to Field House, she spoke of her hopes and fears to Quentin. He had been walking alone in the gardens when she came across him and she joined him in his search for signs of the early crocus, planted the previous year around the trees. He listened with his usual courtesy and she found him easier to talk to than she had ever done before. He has changed, she thought, not realizing that it was she who had changed. From a reckless and sometimes thoughtless girl, she had become more caring of other people and had risen in Quentin's estimation by her conduct with Georgina and Ruth. Without quite knowing the reason for his change of attitude towards her, she was nevertheless pleased to be treated as a contemporary, rather than a tiresome schoolgirl.

In answer to a query, Quentin said, "Don't build too much upon it, Chloris, but if Matt has shown exemplary conduct throughout his service, things may go easier for him, even to the extent of a remission of his sentence."

She turned shining eyes to his. "You mean he might be released when they dock?"

"It has been known but we must wait and see."

In her joy, she flung her arms round Quentin's neck and hugged him. His hands gripped her waist for a moment, then he put her away gently.

"Still the same impulsive Chloris," he said, with a hint of his old manner, but the gray eyes were smiling. "What would Matt say if he saw you do that?"

"I've grown so fond of you, Quentin, I wouldn't care."

The smile was still there but it had twisted slightly. "Shameless!" he said with a touch of mockery. "And both of us committed to matrimony. Why didn't you grow up sooner?"

"What difference would that have made?"

He smiled at her puzzled look. "Probably none at all. Sudden impulses have a nasty habit of rebounding on us at times but your action in deciding so quickly was perhaps the right one for you, and in keeping with your nature."

"I don't regret marrying Matt."

"I don't think you do either but people change—or are changed by their experiences. He will come back a different man. You must allow for that."

"Yes," she said slowly. "I keep thinking of him as he was in prison but he is sure to be a little changed." She looked up confidently into Quentin's face. "But he will still be Matt."

"I have no doubt of that at all," he replied

dryly. "But the difference will be that now he has a wife. He will do well to remember it."

"That sounds remarkably like a threat."

"Not a threat, my dear, just a hope that Matt will consider his new responsibility seriously and keep away from the sort of friends who put him where he is today."

Chloris reflected guiltily on her own connection with the smugglers. Quentin made it sound so serious and of course he was right. She should never have joined Sefton. What justification could she offer for her own conduct if Matt sought them out again? Beyond Matt's return, she had not considered the future. What would he want? Surely not to carry on in the same way? That would be a continuation of the risk of capture, too dangerous to be contemplated a second time.

"What are you thinking, Chloris?"

Her head came up sharply. Quentin was watching her with a unfathomable look in his eyes. She hoped no guilt showed on her face. Quentin had an uncanny habit at times of reading one's mind.

"I—I was just wondering what Matt will do when he comes home. They won't want him in the shipping firm now."

"Yes, that has me worried too, but chiefly on your account. No money and no job is not the best way to begin a marriage. You must use your influence to encourage him in a new start."

"My influence! Matt never cared what I thought!" It's true, she realized with sudden clarity. All her life Matt had only to say "come" and she came. He had laughed at her fears for him and gone ahead in his own way. When had he ever listened to her?

"If he loves you," said Quentin, "and he must

to have made you his wife, then he will be influenced by your desires."

Yes, I'm his wife, she thought, but does he love me? Why did she so suddenly doubt it? Because he had not actually said the words? The atmosphere at their last meeting had hardly been conducive to tender words and yet—he could have whispered those three important ones. She gave herself a mental shake. Falling into morbid sentimentality was ridiculous. He must love her or why make such a plea for the marriage to be performed so urgently?

"Is Georgina in?" she asked, in an effort to quell the strangely hollow feeling that had risen in her.

"Yes, she is, but surrounded by dressmakers and hat designers, submerged in rolls of silk and sinking under the weight of those things without which no lady of fashion could even contemplate marriage."

He looked suddenly tired and the lines beside his mouth deepened as his lips compressed into a straight line.

"Do you object to all this preparation?"

"Not at all. Georgina may have as many new outfits as she chooses. As for the groom, he may travel to Tibet and not be missed, it appears." He shook his head in amazement. "And this is to be a quiet country wedding! I give thanks that Hanover Square was not chosen as the scene of all this turmoil."

Chloris laughed. "Well, you must hold yourself to blame. If you will propose to a young lady of fashion, you must expect her to equip herself in the proper manner."

"Did I do that?"

The question took her by surprise and she stared at him. "Don't you remember? You called her 'dearest' and offered eternal devotion.''

"So I did. She looked so small and frail—like a damaged kitten. My heart went out to her." His voice was soft, almost as if speaking to himself. His gaze rose over her head and he stared into space.

And you were overwhelmed by tenderness, Chloris thought, and in that unguarded moment offered her the very thing she had been sent to Dorset to obtain. No wonder Mrs. Davenport was creating no problems. She saw clearly that Quentin was no Society youth to be bent to her will, but a man more used to having others do as he required.

Choosing her words carefully, Chloris said, "Georgina is so pretty and charming, she has already become a great favorite in the neighborhood. A more gracious hostess for Field House would be hard to find."

His eyes came down to hers. "She is all of those things. A sweet, gentle girl who treats me as if I were a lord of the Universe." He smiled ruefully. "It's very flattering to the ego but something to which I am not accustomed."

"You'll get used to it. What more could a husband want than to be reminded of his importance so constantly?"

The dark shadow lifted from his face and he grinned. "I should be thankful she hasn't a tongue like yours, young Chloris. I hope Matt will teach you a proper respect for husbands."

"He may try," she commented lightly, glad to have dispelled Quentin's pre-marriage doubts. "But he will not find me as biddable as Georgina."

"I'm sure of that and I begin to pity the poor man already." His smile held such charm that it warmed her heart and they strolled back across the lawn. "Did you want to see Georgina?"

"Not if she is engaged with her trousseau. Some other time, perhaps. And Quentin—don't be impatient with her. She has been brought up to consider this sort of thing as part and parcel of the betrothal rites. Don't make her unhappy by criticizing it all."

He raised her hand ot his lips in farewell. "I won't. I promise."

She rode home, silently comparing her own wedding with the one being prepared for Georgina. A hurried hole-in-the-corner affair without a single friend in attendance and a groom dragged away within minutes could hardly be compared with a church ceremony and a magnificent reception at Field House. But the comparison was unfair. Matt could do not better under the circumstances. They were just as married as Georgina and Quentin would be in the summer.

The third of April came swiftly, too swiftly for Chloris's peace of mind. Each time she galloped home past the Martello Tower she looked at the moon and remembered her promise to Sefton with increasing dismay. The last time, she vowed, the very last time. If the run was good they should have accumulated sufficient money to give Matt a good start. They might even go away. However hard life became, he must not be tempted to join up with the smugglers again.

The house was quiet when Chloris slipped away that night. From the back of her wardrobe she had dragged out the boy's clothes and donned them with a shiver of excitement and a little fear. Once outside the house she glanced up at the sliver of silver moon, masked at times by gently rolling clouds. With her hands pushed deep into the jacket pockets and the boy's cap dragged down to her eyebrows, she hurried from the garden and

set out for the cliffs. She strode along with
swinging step, such as a boy might use, she hoped
praying that she encounter no-one of he
acquaintance. But the story of the ghost lady ha
done a thorough job for the cliffs were deserted
Even the naval ship was in darkness. Since th
night of the Heron's capture there had been n
further alarms in the village and patrols ha
become spasmodic.

She passed the Martello Tower, movin
silently, and went on to where the cliffs swept int
broken curves creating small coves until sh
reached the place where Croker had stared up a
her. There had been a fall of rock sometime in th
past and the descent was steep but provide
footholds if taken carefully. She managed to reac
sea level without disturbing anything more than
few pebbles, then paused and stared about her
There was no sound but the shush of water as i
swept over and withdrew from the stony beach
With her arms hugging her shoulders, she sat on
rock and waited.

It was with relief akin to meeting an old frien
that she spied Sefton coming stiff-legged toward
her. Thank heavens it wasn't Croker. He was s
big and rough-looking, she might have turned an
run had he been the first to arrive.

Sefton greeted her quietly, then nodded for he
to follow. From where she had been sitting, ther
was no sign of a cave-mouth but farther along an
a few yards higher was a narrow opening
concealed from the sea by a large bush, clingin
with incredible tenacity to the side of a deep clef
Sefton held back the bush and she entered
roomy cavern. At the far end a flight of roughly
hacked steps disappeared upwards into th
gloomy likeness of a great chimney.

"The Tower's up there," he said with a jerk o

the head. "Crocker's there too." He indicated a pile of barrels and boxes at the foot of the steps. "These have to go tonight to make room for a new delivery. Croker and a couple of men will drag them up by rope, attached down here by you and me. The stronger fellows will be carrying the new stuff up from the beach. All right with you—lad?"

Chloris nodded, avoiding the knowing gaze and wishing this night was over. A slight sound from above brought her head round. A man stood in the narrow stepped chimney leading to the Tower. It was not Croker but she kept her head lowered. She must remember to keep to the shadows during the night in case Croker should look down. He might recognize her as the boy cousin of Matt's but he must not connect her with the rider on the cliff.

Settling her cap firmly down over her eyebrows, she followed Sefton's instructions and began the task of attaching ropes to the casks and boxes. The chimney was too narrow to allow two men to carry up the contraband and her job was to guide the roped boxes and prevent them becoming jammed between the rock walls as they were dragged upwards. It was not an easy task as the steeply rising tunnel was only only roughly hewn but it could be managed with care. Behind her she heard the first of the freetraders depositing the new load but she kept her eyes fixed on the job in hand.

The piles of contraband about her grew less as the night progressed. Sefton gasped and groaned beside her and Chloris herself felt the strain on her shoulders. Perspiration and rock dust smeared her heated face, yet she dare not remove the heavy serge jacket that disguised her figure, although a fleeting glimpse behind showed that some of the men had stripped to the waist.

Sefton grinned as she wiped the back of her hand across her brow. She smiled back, relieved to see that very few barrels remained to be taken up. Perhaps another half-an-hour and she would be free.

The last barrel was on its way up the steps. It must have been weariness that made the roping so hard. Her fingers were numb and sore from the rough fibres and the binding was not as tight as it should have been. Half way up the barrel sagged and spun. The jerk it received turned it about and it jammed between the walls. There was a curse from above and Chloris sprang up the steps to steady the barrel and try to right it.

"Slacken the rope!" she gasped hoarsely.

The barrel came down with a rush, almost flinging her down the steps, but she managed to cling, winded, to the rock she had fallen against. Her cap tipped back, exposing her face.

"Fool of a boy!" growled a voice, terrifyingly close.

Involuntarily, her gaze flew upwards and she beheld Croker, tall and black-bearded, staring furiously at her. She dragged her cap forward, thankful not to have lost it altogether. Her hair was still securely confined inside. Turning the barrel and retying the rope, she was conscious of Croker's face only inches away. Head downbent, she waited for him to draw the barrel up. He did not move. She retreated down the steps.

"Wait!" he called. "Come here, lad. Where have I seen you before?"

She stayed where she was, her heart beating fast, annoyed that her fumbling with the last roping had brought her face to face with Croker. "On the beach," she growled, dusting down her jacket with a fierce concentration.

"Those green eyes," he muttered. "A boy with

green eyes. Where else have I seen you?"

She shrugged and to her horror saw his boots descending the steps. She turned, her gaze searching for Sefton as she fell back another step, but Sefton was talking to a man at the cave-mouth.

"Damn you, boy, look at me! Don't keep moving away." He lunged forward and grabbed her, the hard fingers digging into her shoulder. In sudden panic she struck his arm aside but in doing so her head came up and she was staring into Croker's puzzled face. Her wrists were caught in one large hand, the other moved to drag off her cap. She struggled, suddenly furious.

"Let go of me!" she panted. "The barrel's ready. Take it up and leave me be. Go and do the job you're paid for."

"Insolent pup! I'll break your neck if I've a mind to it. Nobody talks to Croker that way. Now, let's see what you look like without that great cap."

A voice like a muted scream echoed round the cave. "Dragoons!"

"Where?" he called.

"Across the cliffs. They'll be here in five minutes. They must have spotted the boat pulling away."

Croker's hand dropped from Chloris. "I'll stop them. Throw me that rope."

All was confusion in the cave as Croker caught the coil of rope and leapt back up the steps. Sefton hurried to the cave-mouth to warn the others. There was an exodus of flying figures. Chloris rubbed her wrists, thankful for the interruption that had saved her from discovery. How did Croker intend to stop a body of horsemen? she wondered. Looking over her shoulder she saw the cave clearing miraculously. Safer, perhaps, to make her own way out of the Martello Tower. She ran lightly up the steps, pushing her way between stacked barrels. She was also very curious to see how Croker intended to carry out his threat.

Cautiously she edged her way out of the Tower. She could hear the thundering hoofbeats as the soldiers galloped round the curve of the bay, intent on reaching the spot above the landing place that must have been spotted by a sea patrol. They had to pass the Tower first. Where was Croker? She bent low and ran to a rock, her eyes searching for him in the pale moonlight. A dark, moving shadow caught her attention. Crouching lower, she watched as he bent, then straightened to run across the grass to a further point. He disappeared from her view.

Hoofbeats came closer, the riders, some half-dozen, were upon them swiftly, horses going at full stretch. As she glimpsed the gold-fogged tunics and the short cloaks, she was aware that Croker had suddenly risen, then her view was blocked by the leading horse.

As if a knee-high brick wall had materalized in front of it, the horse struck solidly and cartwheeled, screaming in terror, its rider hurtling over its head to land crushingly on the grass. Too late to halt, every horse was caught in the same way, some obstruction felling them into a tangled heap of groaning, screaming men and horses. Chloris dropped her head in sick horror, realizing what Croker had done. A trip rope, stretched in their path, had brought down every horse. She was trembling with shock at his callous way of dealing with the dragoons.

A rattle of shot brought her head up. A dragoon, on his knees, fired at the fleeting figure of Croker. Savagely she hoped his aim had been good but there was no sound or cry. She rose to her feet with the idea of going to aid the soldier. A wild, wavering shot in her direction brought the awareness that an injured man might consider her motives less than helpful. She dared not approach them but she could send help. Slowly, she crawled away, out of range. To her intense relief, a party of coastguards, alerted by the shots, passed her, ~~making teir way with more caution towards the~~ making their way with more caution towards the scene of carnage. There was nothing now for her to do but go home.

sick and shaking, her mind full of the scene she had just witnessed. Croker was completely evil, a heartless murderer. Could many of the dragoons have survived that massacre? Only one had risen while she was there but his aim had been unsteady. Croker had escaped.

If anything was needed to convince her of the folly of her actions, it was this. She never wanted to see Croker or Sefton again. The sound of screaming men and horses was something that would stay with her for a long time.

Her hands, tightly clasped, dropped suddenly to her lap. A trip rope? How strange that Neil Kernick had implied something of the sort in connection with her mother's death. A pulse began to hammer in her temples and the sick horror of suspicion flooded her body in a wave of choking heat.

Croker had grabbed the rope instantly and leapt up the steps without a moment's hesitation. He knew what he was going to do! He must have done the same trick before. Was it remotely possible that on the night Estelle Blair died, he mistook the two riders galloping on the cliffs for dragoons and fixed the trip rope before realizing his error? There had been a run that night. Sefton had said so.

Had the man with her turned back earlier? Or

had he evaded the trap, leaving her mother to crash over the rope? Was Croker the murderer of Estelle Blair or had there been collusion between Croker and the mystery man, the one driving her mother in the right direction, the other waiting to spring the trap?

And Croker had been terrified enough to shoot at her the night she impersonated her mother. It would need more than a ghost story to frighten him. It would need the ghost!

21

Chloris woke the next morning stiff and tired after restless night. She groaned as Molly, in a cheerful mood, clattered a cup and saucer on the bedside table and flung wide the curtains.

"A lovely day, Miss Chloris," she said, standing with arms folded over her ample bosom. "You'd never imagine, seeing that lovely calm view from your window, the uproar in Gilminster this morning."

Chloris eyed her maid blankly. "What do you mean, Molly? What uproar?"

It only needed that encouragement for Molly to launch into a graphic account of what she had learned from the cook who lived out.

"It seems there was a battle royal last night between the military and the smugglers. I don't know how many dead but several soldiers according to cook, and the cliffs fair littered with horses. The coastguards joined in and chased off the smugglers. Some were caught though a few escaped by boat."

Chloris sat up, ignoring the pain that seared through her shoulders. "Do you know who was caught? Any names, I mean?"

Molly sniffed. "How would I know that, miss
Villains all, I've no doubt, but the coastguard i
cock-a-hoop about one of them. Very important h
must be, cook says. Somebody they've bee
wanting long enough, she heard."

Let it be Croker, prayed Choris fervently. Fo
what he did last night he deserves to be hanged
Even without proof of his involvement in he
mother's death, he was guilty of the murder o
several dragoons.

"And Mr. Justice called early to court," wen
on Molly. "Goodness knows when he'll be back."

Chloris rested her elbow on the pillow an
sipped her tea reflectively. She'd give a lot to knov
if Croker was to appear before him this morning
If she hurried there might be a chance of seein;
the prisoners brought to court from the priso
where they were customarily lodged for the night

The morning was well advanced as she rod
into the village and dismounted near the court
house. Two constables and numerous revenu
officers stood on guard at the doors of th
building, showing stern faces to the crowdec
market street. If Croker had indeed been
captured, their attitudes indicated a deter
mination to allow no chance of escape a second
time.

Chloris positioned herself behind a group o
local shopkeepers, still in their aprons and
working clothes. A few minutes' leave from thei
duties to gather information would provide then
with a topic of conversation with which to regal
their customers throughout the day.

She was only just in time. The growing sound
of heavy, horse-drawn cart had the crowd buzzing
with anticipation. A black-painted, closed vehicl
drew up beside the steps. Necks were craned a

the guards moved to open the double doors at the rear. A number of men, strangers to Chloris, were helped out, each man manacled at the wrist to another. The crowd surged forward, eager for a look at the prize capture. Chloris found herself swept forward amongst the onlookers.

It was unfortunate that a shopkeeper, recognizing her, edged her politely to the front of the group when Croker dropped from the van. There were no high shoulders to mask her and she found herself almost face to face with him. His gaze swept the crowd contemptuously, then abruptly swung back in her direction. Wedged tightly, she was unable to do more than look away and make herself as small as possible.

With a sudden movement that flung his guards aside, Croker was reaching for her, his eyes wild. "You!" he roared. "Green-eyed witch! What are you—human or demon? I'll kill you and be rid, once and for all!" He hurled himself forward. The crowd scattered, screaming and pushing to avoid him. Freed from the press, Chloris ducked, evading his gasping fingers, and fell into the solid arms of the butcher. The guards, recovering from their rough treatment, drew batons and flung themselves on Croker. He went down, roaring, in a flurry of blows. Chloris found herself lifted bodily by those same solid arms and deposited without ceremony in a shop doorway.

The butcher looked shaken. "That was a close call, miss. If ever I saw a madman, that was one. Whatever made him go for you like that?" To her relief he went on without giving her a chance to speak. "A dangerous brute, all right. Not local, praise be for that. Some sort of foreigner, I don't doubt, maybe from Cornwall way." He stared down with sudden intentness. "You didn't know him, did you, miss?"

Chloris shook her head. "I understand his name is Croker but apart from that, I know nothing of his past." That was true enough, she thought.

After thanking the butcher for his quick action, she turned to where Bessie was tethered. Any idea she had of entering the courthouse was dismissed instantly. There was no point in risking another outburst from Croker. He might still be uncertain as to the identity of the boy in the cave but Chloris he had linked with the ghost lady on the cliffs in that illuminating moment when she was in full glare of the lightning. Her distinctive green eyes had been enough to trigger off the explosion.

She untied Bessie's reins, still engrossed in her thoughts. The voice startled her.

"Good morning, Chloris." Across Bessie's flanks she met the penetrating gaze of the tall, fair-haired man. Although his face was expressionless, she felt her color rise guiltily.

"Oh, good morning, Quentin. What a—a nice surprise to see you," she returned, uneasily aware of her slightly ruffled appearance.

"Is it? You don't look too sure about it."

"Have you—have you been here long?"

"Long enough," he said crisply, "to catch the excitement."

"Oh." She could think of nothing else to say.

He moved round Bessie and, taking the reins in one hand and Chloris firmly by the elbow in the other, he began to walk her along the street and out of the village.

"A strange scene," he remarked on a musing note. "If one had a suspicious mind, one might imagine all sorts of things leading up to that."

"And you have a suspicious mind?"

"Of course. Haven't you noticed?"

She glanced up at him. It was a mistake. His eyes were as cold as marble. He can't know anything, she thought wildly, and yet the impression he gave was of knowing everything. She shrugged and said casually, "They say he's mad. That big, bearded smuggler, I mean."

"Do they? I don't think so. I'd say he's bearing a grudge against somebody—and that somebody had better be careful."

"Really? But he's in custody now."

"Let us hope they can continue to hold him."

In spite of herself, Chloris shivered.

"Feeling the chill, Chloris?" Quentin asked with a hint of sarcasm in his voice.

She chose to ignore what was obviously a double-edged question and replied calmly, "Of course not. Why should I? The weather is quite mild."

"Well, you know best," he said on a kinder note. "And far be it from me to tell you what to do but I think you should have an early night. You're looking tired." He raised a sardonic eyebrow. "Too many nocturnal rambles, I'd say."

Guilt made her tone sharper than she intended. "Well, thank you! When I need your advice I'll ask for it."

"There are times when I wish you would!" he said harshly.

"I can take care of myself. I am not a fool!"

"Neither am I, Chloris, and there are limits to my patience."

"I haven't asked you to concern yourself in my affairs," she flung at him hotly. "What I do is my own business, not yours. Perhaps," she added cruelly, "you are not so much concerned with me as with the reputation of my parents—or should I say—my mother's? But it's a little too late for that!" She stared up defiantly, her green eyes blazing, then caught her breath.

His face held a stricken look but it was gone in a moment. His jaw hardened and the anger flared in his eyes. "What I'd give to put you over my knee," he gritted. "You're spoiled, reckless and as stubborn as any mule."

Suddenly, all the anger drained out of Chloris. Why had she let her tongue run so wild? She stopped walking and turned towards him. "Quentin, forgive me. That was a terrible thing for me to say. I know you were very fond of my mother. She was reckless too but she was good. I must be such a disappointment to everyone, especially to my father and—it seems—to you, too."

She must have been more tired than she thought for the tears pricked her eyelids and she bit her lip to keep from crying. Turning her head away so that Quentin should not see her tears, she laid her forehead on Bessie's soft neck and fought for control.

Like a father embracing an errant child with a kind of loving exasperation, Quentin's arms encircled her, turning her into his shoulder. There was such comfort in the feel of his beating heart beneath her cheek that she clung to him weakly.

"Dear, foolish, Chloris," he murmured into her hair. "What am I to do with you?"

"Leave me to my fate," she said in a muffled voice. "It's all I deserve."

He laughed softly. "Don't tempt me."

She raised her face to his and was strangely moved by the tender expression. "Why do you bother with me, Quentin? I'm an ungrateful, hot-tempered idiot. I shall probably come to a bad end like a character in a novel. You'd far better stop trying to reform me."

"I don't want to reform you, only to save you from your own actions."

"It's a waste of time."

"I don't see it that way. I know you're involved somehow with the smugglers. I can't say I approve but I don't want to see you sent to prison."

"Prison?" She stared up at him.

His mouth twisted. "They do send women to prison, you know. Hadn't you thought of that?"

She shook her head. "No. It was just a game. I was bored and lonely but I've finished with it all now."

"Truly?"

"On my honor."

"And have they finished with you?"

She thought of Croker and a tremor ran through her. "I see no reason for them to bother with me again. I'm not important."

"Perhaps not to them but you are to—to us. Take my advice and keep Bessie stabled tonight and every night until these committal proceedings are over."

"I will." She looked up at him mistily. "You really are good, Quentin. I don't know why I always fly out at you so."

He grinned. "I'm too righteous. You told me that yourself."

"That must be it," she said, smiling. "If you were not always right and I was not always wrong, I dare say we'd deal better together. Perhaps I should model myself on Georgina. She is everything that I am not."

"And nothing that you are. You're entirely different."

"Luckily for you. I'd make a poor sort of squire's wife, always in the briars, and you'd get sick of beating sense into me. But you'll never have that trouble with Georgina." She drew back from his arms. "I hope she realizes how lucky she is."

For a long moment his gaze rested on her, his expression quite unreadable. She found herself looking at him with new eyes. The tanned skin and strong planes of his face beneath thick fair hair, curving to the fair chin and mobile mouth, seemed suddenly a face she was unacquainted with, the face of a stranger. No longer the older, more serious-minded and slightly disapproving Quentin of her younger years, but a man combining strength with tenderness, patience with passion, and one who would do what he thought right, whatever the cost to himself.

Unaccountably, the tears pricked her eyelids again and she felt a wild compulsion to fling herself into his arms, to seek comfort and shelter, to feel his heart beat against hers and to lay her cheek against that smooth brown one. Just lack of sleep, she thought, dizzily. It made one feel low and dispirited. One was apt to become emotional out of sheer weariness. She drew a deep breath and smiled.

"Goodbye, Quentin. Thank you for being so understanding."

He helped her mount Bessie and she rode home, determined to take his advice and keep close to home, at least until Croker was taken to Dorchester prison to await the Assizes. He would not be kept long in Gilminster, she was sure.

During the afternoon she rested and by the time her father arrived home, she was recovered from her low spirits. Mr. Justice Blair sank into his cushioned armchair and ran a hand tiredly down his face.

"I don't like these cases of contraband-running, my dear," he said. "But of those brought before me today, I was happy to see that none of our vllagers was included. It is most distressing to sentence one of the local people."

"Have they all been sent to Dorchester?"

He nodded. "All had previous convictions, I'm afraid. There was a particularly violent man amongst them and we thought it best that he travel alone in a different conveyance. He seemed unable to accept the thought of capture and raved on about being betrayed to the military by some woman. A very unbalanced sort of man. He had to be manacled hand and foot."

Even without Croker's capture, Chloris knew that she could never have gone on with the smugglers, not after last night. She had been so sickened by the violence, her heart had revolted at the idea of assisting them further. Quentin had brought the notion of her own danger into the forefront of her mind, a thing she had blithely ignored in the excitement. The stupidity of her behavior lay exposed before her and she burned with shame. Let there be no more unhappiness to bring on her father and those who held her in regard.

The future was more important now. With Quentin's help—her thoughts stopped abruptly. Quentin? She must not rely on Quentin anymore. He belonged to Georgina. The wedding would ensure that. It was Matt—her husband, her love—to whom she must look for help. Gay, reckless Matt. Of course she loved him—she always did. There was no question about that. How could she doubt what had always been true?

She frowned, trying to recapture her last picture of Matt as they said goodbye in prison. Furious with her father, he had left her with stiff formality, his face hard and angry. Not even a look of tenderness, she recalled. But he had been as

shocked as she was by their abrupt parting. That
was then excusable in the circumstances. When he
came home, there would be time for tenderness.
He had never previously shown her any, she admitted in honesty, but Matt was never the gentle
lover, always the exciting adventurer. She had not
even known he loved her until the marriage had
been arranged. Why hadn't he waited? as Quentin
said. Why did they have to rush into such a
scrambling hole-in-the-corner ceremony? She
would never understand the reason for that.

A thunderous knocking on the front door
brought both Chloris and Mr. Blair from their
separate reveries into the present. Mr. Blair
frowned and glanced at the clock. "Are you
expecting anyone?"

"No, Father." She rose and went through to
the hall, her heart thudding unaccountably. No
casual visitor would attack the door with such
ferocity. Over her shoulder she was relieved to see
her father close behind.

"Mr. Justice!" called a voice she at once
recognized as the police sergeant's. Her heart
steadied and she opened the door.

He had obviously flung on his clothes hap-
hazardly for his uniform was only half-buttoned
and his helmet pushed back from his turkey-red
face. He wiped his brow quickly with an enormous
spotted handkerchief and came to attention,
breathing heavily.

"What is it, Sergeant?" asked Mr. Blair.

" 'Twas not our fault, your honor, for we
turned 'em over right and tight to those revenuers
from Dorchester, sent special to get 'em."

"What are you talking about?"

"The second prison van, sir, never got near
Dorchester."

"The one in which the man, Croker, was taken?"

"That's right, your honor. The first one unloaded the felons at Dorchester prison and set off back. On the way they came across the other van in a ditch, shaft-horse gone too. A bit of searching and they found four revenue men. Been knocked about something cruel, they had. No sign of the prisoner, sir."

Mr. Blair looked bewildered. "But the man was manacled, hand and foot! Are you telling me he overpowered four men and made his escape in that condition?"

"Seems, sir," said the Sergeant, staring woodenly at the door post, "they unshackled his legs so he could climb into the van."

"But his hands?"

"They do say he caught one officer round the throat with the chain and swore to choke him unless they unlocked the manacles. They must have thought they could handle him, even so he be free of the chain." He looked down his nose. "The revenuers don't get our training, sir."

"Have you alerted everyone—the soldiers and the coastguards?"

"Yes, sir. And I sent a runner to Sir Lionel to borrow some horses."

"Thank you for letting me know. I'd better come at once to the station."

"I'm here to escort you, sir. There are two of my men outside with a gig."

"Escort me? For what reason should I need an escort?"

"Well, sir." The Sergeant looked acutely uncomfortable. "The revenuers—those in a condition to tell us anything—say Croker threatened to 'do you in' for what you said in court.''

"It was no less than the truth," said Mr. Blair sharply. "The man is an evil character and previously involved in crimes of violence. He deserves to hang."

"I agree, sir," returned the Sergeant hurriedly. "A black-hearted murderer he is and hang he will, but it don't mean he likes to be told by a beak he'll get his neck stretched—er, by a Justice, I mean, sir—even in legal words."

A tiny smile twitched at the corner of Mr. Blair's mouth as he looked at the profusely perspiring officer.

"Very well, Sergeant. If you think I need protection I will accept your escort." He turned to Chloris. "Don't wait up for me, my dear. I'll take my latchkey. I've no idea how long I will be."

"All right, Father." She helped him into his coat and stood at the door as he accompanied the Sergeant towards the gig drawn up at the gate. She watched until they were out of sight, then closed the door.

So, Croker was loose again. It was not a comfortable thought but if his vengeance was now transferred to the magistrate who had sent him to await the Assizes on a capital charge, she felt her father would be safer at the police station than here. But if Croker had any sense, he would not waste time on staying in the neighborhood. By dawn he could be miles away. She returned to the sitting room and poured herself another cup of coffee.

It must have been an hour later when she first heard the noises. Sitting erect, she listened, without any sense of alarm. It was probably the wind or the stabled horses or some tiny creature caught by an owl.

And then the sound of a foot on gravel sent the

blood pounding to her head. This was a human sound! There was someone outside. Could the Sergeant have left a man on guard? Why should he? The guard had been for her father, the man against whom Croker had uttered his wild threats.

For a long time there was no other sound and gradually she relaxed, prepared to admit that her imagination was over-active tonight. Even so, no harm would be done by checking the catches on the windows.

The sitting room and hall were secure, as was the dining room and her father's study. She wondered, with a flutter of her heart, if the back door had been locked when Molly went to bed. But it was Molly's night off! She would not be back until tomorrow. There was no-one but herself in the house.

She lifted the oil lamp from the carved table in the hall and moved with determination into the kitchen. It was no use flinching the task and flying for her bedroom. What key there once was had long been mislaid.

The kitchen door opened silently to her hand. The glow from the lamp spread to every corner. It was empty. Realizing her hand was trembling, she set the lamp on the table and approached the back door, her gaze on the polished brass knob. She was halfway across the kitchen when the knob turned, fractionally at first, then more fully. Immoderate horror welled up sickeningly in her throat. There was someone on the other side, cautiously testing the lock. The large key beneath the knob—had it been turned? The key was miles away, her feet would not obey her, and then it was too late! The door was opening, the well-oiled lock making no more than a tiny click.

She backed away until the table caught her hips. Her eyes stared, wide and green as a deep sea pool. Run, her body screamed, but the glinting knob trapped her mind into stillness as it revolved full circle and a wedge of darkness crept in.

As on the steps of the cave below the Martello Tower, the first thing she saw was a boot—a sea-boot! A grimy hand gripped the door. It opened wider to reveal a dusty shoulder of rough blue serge. A moment's pause, then a man stepped fully into the kitchen. For a second he was not aware of her, this bearded, hard-eyed man, then his eyes slid round to rest on her.

Surprise, incredulity, then savage triumph lit his face. "You!" he breathed gustily and the stench of rum reached her. "I made 'em tell me at the cottage back there, where the Justice lived. I didn't know as how I'd be lucky enough to find you here too. Where is he?"

Chloris dredged up all the courage she possessed, caught the leaping flicker of fear and damped it down ruthlessly. She stared with cold disdain at Croker. "You're too late. He has gone."

"I saw a gig in the road but no matter, he'll be back." His gaze swept over her. "I suppose you're his daughter. You've got the same high and mighty look. No charity for poor fellows like me, trying to make a living. You're all the same, you nobs. Hang 'em, put 'em away, send 'em to the hulks, that's all you think of. What chance have we got against people like you?"

Chloris forced herself to speak, realizing that his emotional outburst was rising to a dangerous level. "As much chance as anyone born," she said clearly. "No-one put you into a life of crime. You chose it of your own free will. You can't excuse your actions by blaming others for your misfortunes. You're not a child."

He grinned alarmingly, showing blackened teeth. "But I can still get back at that Justice through you. If I can't break his body, I'll break his heart. With your sort that hurts more." He stepped forward and Chloris retreated round the table.

If she could get him away from the door, there might be a chance to escape. Keep his attention on her and his mind busy, she thought desperately, as fear clutched her throat. "You've already broken his heart," she gasped. "You killed his wife. Don't you remember?"

He stared at her across the table from narrowed eyes. Had it been a mistake to say that, she wondered? But then, her position could not be made worse whatever she said and if it cleared up the mystery of her mother's death, she need no longer be suspicious of anyone else. The irony of the thought struck her. If Croker was intent on her murder, would it matter one way or the other if she learned the truth?

"What do you mean—killed his wife?" he demanded.

"Such a small incident to you, I suppose," she flashed back at him, sarcastically, with the idea of goading him into confession. "Hardly worth the remembering of how you used your trip-rope on a lone woman riding the cliffs last year. Not as satisfying as bringing down a whole body of dragoons, I dare say, but that woman was Mrs. Blair, wife of Mr. Justice, not to mention my mother. Can you deny it?"

" 'Twere a mistake, that. I heard a galloping horse coming straight for the Martello—thought it was the military. It was done before I realized it was only a woman. She went down and lay still—I was sure she was dead, along with the horse—but I saw her again the night of the storm. I was confused."

"And fired at her—just to be friendly, I

suppose?"

"I thought she'd 'come again' like they said in the village. There was a green light and her eyes were like emeralds staring down at me. I had to fire to drive her away." He shook himself like a dog shedding water. "But she was dead all along. It was you. I knew it outside the courthouse." His eyes narrowed in suspicion. "But how did you know abut the trip-rope?"

"I saw you."

"You can't have. There was nobody else there. I should have seen another rider."

"I wasn't riding. I followed you and watched you fix the rope. You were so efficient I knew you'd done it before. Perhaps many times. It wouldn't surprise me."

"Where were you then? How did you come to be in that spot? No-one was about when I left the—the . . ."

Chloris smiled thinly. "The Martello Tower?"

"How do you know of that?" he demanded hoarsely. "Nobody knew but—" he broke off, his brow corrugated with thought, then he stared hard and she knew he was remembering. "The boy! I knew I'd seen him before—the boy with green eyes." He uttered an oath under his breath. "Damn my bones—it was you again. What are you—some kind of witch? A ghost and a boy and now the daughter of a Justice." His lips drew back in a snarl. "If I kill you now I'll be rid of all three and you're the only witness to what I did."

"Aren't you forgetting the dragoons?"

"They never saw me. They can't prove it was me. I was arrested later because of my record. A bit of trouble down Weymouth way when a fellow died. But this job they're not going to fix on me. Only you know about it and you're going to have an accident."

His gaze slid round the kitchen, then returned rest on the lamp. One sly upward glance from nder his heavy brows and Chloris knew what he d in mind. She gripped the edge of the table as a ave of horror drew the blood from her heart.

"They used to burn witches, didn't they?" He ave a satisfied chuckle. "A fitting end to one at's been haunting me."

His big hands met round the brass base of the mp. He's going to enjoy this, thought Chloris, credulously, and knew she had but one chance ft. She took a deep steadying breath. He raised e heavy lamp, watching it rise until it was over s head. She moved then, while his eyes were llowing the lamp.

He caught the sudden movement and swung und, the lamp still held high. His arms went ack as if to throw it as she ran. It had never emed so far across the flagged stone floor before d her breath caught raggedly as she stumbled er her skirt. Her hand reached despairingly wards the knob. There had been no sound to arn her but the door, of its own accord it seemed her startled eyes, flew wide and crashed into e dresser. The china cups tinkled and shook on eir hooks and then she was looking up into the hite set face of Quentin. The pistol in his hand as rock steady and pointed straight at Croker.

The impetus of her wild dash hurled her into s arms and he caught her against his shoulder ith his left arm. The gun still pointed at Croker.

"Lower the lamp slowly and replaced it on the ble," ordered Quentin in a voice Chloris had ever heard him use before. "Very slowly and ith extreme care—if you value your life."

"I could still throw it and start a fire," lustered Croker.

"Certainly you could, but escape would be

difficult with a bullet in each of your knees. As yo
see, I carry a second pistol in my belt."

The lamp came down onto the table with
little thump. Chloris felt Quentin relax a fractio
but he still gripped her to him and she was conte
to stand within the circle of his arm, her chee
pressed against the fabric of his jacket. H
strength was returning, she could have release
herself and stood unaided, but the comfort of h
arm was too great and she remained where sh
was.

Only when she heard the thud of hoove
approaching with great rapidity, did she raise he
head. Without looking at her, Quentin said, "I le
orders for our grooms and stable lads to follow m
with all speed. As soon as we received th
Sergeant's message, I knew Croker would com
here." One brief glance he spared her. "I think yo
knew it too but thank God I arrived in time."

The horses were all round the house now, an
attracted by the lamp-lit kitchen, heavy step
thudded up to the open door. They wer
surrounded by a surprising number of men an
boys, all employees of the Field family, clothe
tossed on anyhow in their eagerness to attend M
Quentin.

Following their master's order to secur
Croker, they bound him with ropes. Croker stoo
quiescent, realizing he had no chance against thi
milling crowd, but his eyes were full of hatred a
he glared at Chloris.

"Take him away," said Quentin, curtly.

The men were only too happy to obey an
pulled Croker across the kitchen. As he passed th
man with the gun, he dragged back on the rope
and stared fully into Quentin's face. Fierce deligh
lit his countenance.

"I knew I'd seen you before but I couldn

place you 'til now." His glance slid to Chloris, his teeth baring in a satisfied smile. "You ask this fine young gentleman about the dead lady, miss. I reckon he knows more about her than I do. Ask him why he was chasing her along the cliffs that night. Ask him what happened and why she was going full stretch as if all the devils in hell were after her. You ask him that, miss!"

22

t was very quiet in the kitchen after they had
one, the Field House men escorting Croker
riumphantly to Gilminster prison. Chloris found
erself sitting on a hard wooden chair, staring
nto the ashes of the kitchen grate, her mental
owers temporarily suspended. Quentin sat on the
orner of the kitchen table. The glow from the
amp left half his face in shadow, but the half
lluminated showed a great weariness, not only of
ody but of mind, to judge from his attitude.

Neither had spoken since Croker's outburst.
Quentin had released her, then slowly and with
reat deliberation turned to place the pistol on
he table before leaning tiredly against its edge.

Was it never to be ended? thought Chloris, her
nind stirring from its lethargy. The suspicion and
he doubt? It would have been so simple to hold
Croker alone responsible for her mother's death.
She turned slowly towards Quentin.

"Is it true?"

He raised his head. The gray eyes were so
lark and shadowed, she felt he was hardly seeing
er. "Yes, it's true."

Subconsciously she had hoped for a denial but

the words shattered that hope and cut into her s
sharply that she cried out in anguish. "But why
Why were you there? Why were you chasing m
mother?"

"There is nothing I can tell you."

"For God's sake, Quentin, you must. You ow
me that!"

He shook his head. "I'm sorry, but you mus
believe I had nothing to do with her death. I don
know what happened after I left her."

"She ran into Croker's trip-rope, just as th
dragoons did."

"He admitted that?"

"Yes, but that doesn't explain your part.
know she dined at Field House that night. A fare
well party for Lord Chalmers, I believe, but wha
happened aferwards?"

Again he shook his head. "Let it be, Chloris
Her death was a terrible accident. Leave her i
peace."

"If you hadn't been chasing her she migh
have seen the rope in time," she said accusingly
"You were heard to call her name. Did yo
quarrel? Were you angry with her? Did she—wer
you—?" She stopped abruptly, recalling som
phrase of Molly's, so long ago it seemed
Disappointed in love, poor man. Her eyes widened
"You were in love with her, weren't you?"

"Perhaps. At least, I thought so bu
infatuation is a similar emotion."

"Did she reject you? Was that why you wer
so angry?"

"No, Chloris," he said harshly. "There is n
simple explanation to give you. Why rake ove
dead ashes? I can tell you nothing without hurtin
you more and that I refuse to do, indeed I cannot.

She rose to her feet, bewildered and shakin
with sudden fury. "You cannot or will not?"

"Does it matter?" He gestured wearily. "It alters nothing in the end. Your mother is dead."

"And you drove her to it! By refusing to explain I can only suppose you meant her harm, even though Croker was the actual instrument of her death; a convenient instrument for you it must have seemed at the time."

"That is not true, Chloris. Why should I wish to harm her?"

"Perhaps she changed her mind and refused to elope with you. I know she had a packed bag with her that night. I found it later. My father must have known too. No-one but he could have put it back in the wardrobe." Her breath caught on a sob. "Poor Father. He loved her enough to protect her, even after she was dead."

Quentin was on his feet, staring at her. "Oh, God, yes! I prayed he would never realize the significance but it seems he did. No wonder he turned in on himself and refused all invitations."

Chloris laughed, a hard tight sound. "Why should he torture himself by going to Field House and meeting the man who betrayed him? You must think he had little pride." She turned her back on him and stared unseeingly at the grate. "I should be obliged if you would leave now. We have nothing more to say to one another."

Without a word, Quentin lifted the pistol from the table and strode to the door. She heard it closing and then the sound of hooves fading in the distance.

For a moment she stood rigid, then turned blindly towards the inner door, traversing the corridor and climbing the stairs, dragging herself to the bedroom to collapse on the bed as if she were an old woman. Dry-eyed she lay staring at the ceiling, drained of all emotion but despair. Quentin, whom she had trusted, a man she had been on the brink of loving, had been her mother's lover! Infatuated perhaps with a beautiful older woman, dazzled by her charm and gaiety, but nevertheless he was a factor contributing to her death. How much of a factor she could not tell—he had not answered her questions honestly. Some mystery was still hidden, some incident he refused to talk about, perhaps some fact incriminating to himself.

She turned her face into the pillow. What had she expected? An admission of murder? But Croker had set the trip-rope. Had Quentin seen it and let her mother ride on? Just one more murder added to Croker's record and no-one the wiser, while Quentin, son of the respected Sir Lionel, escapes scot-free without a stain on his character? The candle guttered in its socket and went out.

The next thing Chloris knew was the sunlight glinting on her dressing table mirror. She was still dressed, even to her slippers, and the early dawn was cold. Climbing stiffly from the bed, she removed her clothes and slipped into her nightgown. She wondered vaguely if her father was home, then the bed received her warmly and she fell asleep again.

Years later it seemed, she opened her eyes and saw Molly tiptoeing towards her, round-eyed and anxious. Letting out a gusty sigh that rocked the cup and saucer dangerously, Molly came closer.

"Your tea, miss," she said in the hushed voice one uses to an invalid. "Up and down I've been all morning but you sleeping like the dead. Mr. Justice said not to wake you."

"Thank you, Molly." She took the tea and sipped it gratefully. "What time is it?"

"Near midday, miss."

"Good heavens, I must have slept for hours."

"And not surprising after what you've been

394

through." She shuddered, theatrically. "We could all have been murdered in our beds and known nothing of it."

Chloris smiled. "Well, you weren't here and I wasn't in bed. How do you know what happened?"

"It's all over the village how that villain, Croker, was captured. And in our kitchen, too! Lucky for you, Mr. Quentin thought he might head this way after threatening Mr. Justice."

"Yes," agreed Chloris. But not so lucky for Quentin, she thought. Ill-luck indeed, to run into the only man to have seen and recognized him that night on the cliffs. But there was nothing she could do about it now except cut Quentin completely out of her life.

Later that morning she talked with her father. Shocked as he was by the events of the night, he had only praise for Quentin. Chloris gritted her teeth and agreed. Why burden her father by dragging up the past again?

During the afternoon, wheels were heard rumbling up the drive.

"It's the carriage from Field House," announced Molly, peering down from the window.

Anger swept through Chloris. How dare he come after last night!

" 'Tis Miss Georgina," said Molly.

Unwilling as she was to see anyone connected with Quentin, Chloris knew she could not refuse to see Georgina without good reason. "Very well, Molly, I'll go down."

They met in the hall. Georgina looked enchanting in a gown of pale blue and a matching hat, adorned with dyed ostrich feathers. She carried a figured silk parasol of the same shade of blue and her chestnut hair fell in a profusion of curls to her shoulders.

"Come in, Georgina. How good of you to call."

To the maid she said, "We'll take tea in the sunroom, please."

She led Georgina through to a glass-walled room overlooking the garden, where rattan furniture was grouped in a sunny corner.

"So lovely to see you looking just the same," said Georgina, giving her a quick hug. "I should have been prostrate for days after such an experience but you're so brave. Quentin says . . ."

"Please, Georgina," interrupted Chloris. "Let's not talk about it."

"Of course not. Quentin said I shouldn't and I won't. I just wanted you to know that I feel for you."

"Thank you." Chloris searched her mind for a safe topic of conversation but could think of nothing unconnected with Field House.

Georgina saved her the trouble. "Do you remember," she asked, "months ago, when I first came to Dorset, we talked about—about poetry?"

"About the poet, I think, rather than the poetry," commented Chloris with a smile.

"Well, yes, perhaps that was it," Georgina giggled and gave Chloris a dazzling smile.

"Don't tell me you've heard from him again?"

"Not from him, no, but of him."

"Has he become famous then, with his book of verse?"

"Not exactly. I had a letter from a cousin of mine telling me that he has become rich all of a sudden and everyone is talking about it. It seems he really had an old bachelor uncle who went to Canada before Robert was born and made a fortune out of stocks and shares. It is a sort of gambling, isn't it, although not on the tables?"

"I suppose it is but the gentlemen on the Stock Exchange would not put it exactly like that. They consider themselves the height of respectability."

"That makes it all the better for Robert. He is now very rich and his fortune was respectably earned."

"So now," Chloris said with a trace of cynicism, "he is quite eligible and received in all the best circles."

"Exactly. Isn't it strange the way things work out? You once said to me that he might win a fortune at the tables or find he has a long-lost relative."

"Did I?" asked Chloris in surprise.

"I remember quite clearly and although his money did not come in the usual way of gambling, it all turned out as you predicted. I am so pleased for him. I hope he will be very happy. If only—" she paused, catching back the words.

"Yes?"

"Nothing. Nothing of any consequence."

"If only it had happened sooner," Chloris said softly. "Is that what you were thinking, Georgina?"

"A little sadness perhaps, for he was my first love, but no childish regrets. It makes not a scrap of difference now. Everything is arranged and Quentin has been so good to me that I could not bear to hurt him or Sir Lionel by the merest hint of repining. Truly, it will be all right, Chloris. I really am extremely fond of Quentin and he will make a good husband. When I think of some of the so-called eligible men presented to me in London, it makes me glad to be engaged to a nice man like Quentin."

Chloris turned her gaze to the window, trying to keep her expression calm. A nice man like Quentin, indeed! A man who had coveted another man's wife and hidden the fact. A man who professed ignorance as to the manner of her death. He had not denied involvement but had refused explanation. Quentin Field was the one person in the world she had no wish to discuss and certainly not with Georgina. How could he have been so base? They had come very close, dangerously close, and remembering that look of pain over Georgina's bed, the almost reluctant proposal of marriage had made her wonder if, had she been free herself—? Then that kiss which had thrown her off balance. She bit her lip, unaware of Georgina's intent gaze. Oh, yes, she admitted bitterly. She could have loved him. Thank God she had learned the truth from Croker.

Georgina rose, startling her. "Dear Chloris, you are not quite yourself yet. Forgive me for calling so soon. I should have allowed you time to recover from the shock of that dreadful happening. I really came to say goodbye. Quentin is driving me to London, so that I may complete my trousseau. I shall, of course, stay with Mama and he will come for me later, in time for the wedding in June."

23

At the end of May, the ship from the West Indies was sighted, standing off Portsmouth. The news raced along the coast reaching Gilminster and Chloris one hot clearing morning.

Mr. Justice Blair returned from Dorchester that evening with more news for Chloris. It had been decided at a meeting with the ship's officers and the civil authorities that Matthew Trevelyan should have the remaining months of his sentence remitted. During a storm off Jamaica, he had shown great gallantry in rescuing the first officer from drowning after being washed overboard. Leaping from the side with a rope attached to his waist, Matt had brought the injured man back to the ship. His modest disclaimer of heroism had so impressed the captain that he recommended Matt to be released, subject to the court's agreement.

Chloris and Mr. Blair faced each other over the dining room table. For a moment Chloris felt nothing at all, no stirring of the blood, no surging delight, but the memory of Matt and all that he once meant to her—still meant, she corrected herself—gradually warmed her and she regarded her father with a steady gaze.

"That's wonderful. Will he come home immediately?"

"He should be here in a few days, pending the formalities of discharge." Mr. Blair looked intently at her. "If it is still your intention to make a life with Matthew, then I will accept him into this house willingly and treat him him as a son-in-law. Will you arrange with the servants to have him move into your bedroom, my dear, or shall we give him another room until he has become more accustomed to his freedom?"

"I think," said Chloris slowly, wondering at her hesitation, but grasping the alternative gratefully, "that a different room might be better until we become accustomed to each other."

"Very wise, my dear. After so long apart, there will be adjustments to make, strangenesses to overcome. I will do all I can to make his homecoming happy for you."

"Thank you, Father. You are very kind."

"Because I love you, my dear, and want only your happiness."

Quentin Field heard the news on his return from London. He was dining in Weymouth with his friend, Jim Hunter and his wife. As the senior Customs Officer, and because he knew of Quentin's association with the Trevelyan family, Jim recounted the court's decision to release Matt.

"A brave act," he said. "And well deserving a remission of sentence."

"And well in keeping with Matt's character," Quentin said with a grin. "I wonder if life at sea has chastened him. I certainly hope so." He stared thoughtfully into his wine, his mind going back to the last time he had seen Chloris. That curt dismissal still hurt but there had been no simple explanation he could offer, not yet anyway. And now, with Matt's return, it would be too late. Too late for any of them to achieve true happiness.

He was roused by his host's remark, as they sat over wine in the dining room. "Sorry, Jim. What was that?"

"I was saying that we found a body this morning, wedged tight in a small cave east of Weymouth." He grimaced. "Well, not so much a body as the remains of one, more like a skeleton. From the belt and bits of rag that survived, we would guess he was some kind of seaman."

"Washed overboard, do you think?"

Jim Hunter's strong dark face held a grim look. "It appeared so at first sight, but the post-mortem revealed death by violence. There was a bullet embedded in the base of his skull."

"Good God! Shot and thrown overboard?"

Jim shrugged. "Shot, anyway. Whether on board or on land, we don't know. He could have been shot where he stood, on that patch of shingle, and then dragged into the cave which is usually covered at high tide."

"How did it come to light?"

"The passage of time and the pull of water released the body."

"Has he been identified?"

Jim shook his head. "Not on the missing persons list but we do have a name. He wore a medallion on a chain. Whoever shot him missed that." He rose and opened a desk drawer. "We've cleaned it up and as far as I can make out, his name was Robbins. Ever heard of a Robbins?"

"Afraid not," said Quentin. "I don't know of a Robbins in Gilminster."

Jim sighed. "A pity."

"Well, perhaps someone will claim him when you make it public."

Jim resumed his seat. "I mean to hold back on

that for the present until we've dug a little further into who was operating in this neighborhood about twelve months ago. The surgeon believes the corpse to be all of a year old. I'd be obliged if you'd treat this talk as confidential, Quentin."

"Yes, of course, but after so long you'll be lucky to find your murderer."

"Maybe, but there are one or two people we've a mind to question on a merchantman lying in Portsmouth. A couple of ratings joined her when she left for the Far East last year. Mighty keen to volunteer they were, and not an ounce of seamanship in them. I find that a trifle suspicious."

"You're a suspicious character yourself, Jim," Quentin said, laughing. "Must be that training you had in the London docks."

Jim laughed too. "Well, informers have their uses, especially if they're afraid their own necks stand in danger of being stretched. I've arranged for these two to be brought overnight from Portsmouth. They'll be questioned in the morning."

As Quentin was taking his leave, Jim Hunter asked, "Are you in a hurry to leave Weymouth tomorrow?"

"No, not until afternoon. I have business at the office of our shipping agent."

"Come and lunch with us, then. If anything develops from our interview, I'd like you to carry the information to Mr. Justice Blair, if you would be so kind."

"Of course, though I hope we're not housing your murderer in Gilminster. We've had enough trouble this past year."

The next day was spent anticipating Matt's arrival. Chloris helped to turn out the room next to hers and by dinnertime she was ready waiting, in a fresh silk dress, her hair brushed and tied with ribbon. Mr. Blair placed a tray and decanter on the small table by his chair.

"A welcoming glass," he said, smiling. "A toast to the returned member of the family."

They heard the hoofbeats coming up the drive. The day was dying, the last fiery threads of gold skimmed the far hills to companion the sun in its decline below the horizon. Chloris turned and faced the door. Her father stood by the window watching her. With a fast beating heart, Chloris waited as the doorbell rang and was answered.

Then Matt was standing in the doorway, his eyes glinting, his teeth showing in a triumphant smile. They stared at each other for a long moment, then he was across the floor in two strides, swinging her into his arms.

"I've waited a long time for this but now I'm here to claim what's mine." His lips came down and he kissed her hard, passionately, again and again.

"Matt, please!" Chloris struggled to release himself, her cheeks burning. "Father is here, waiting to pour you a homecoming drink."

"Very well. Let us get the civilities out of the way," said Matt, dropping his hands. "Good evening, sir. What are you offering me?" He flung himself into a chair and Chloris sank breathlessly onto the couch with time to study her husband.

He seemed taller and broader than she remembered. Tanned to a deep brown, his dark hair still fell across his forehead and the light in his eyes was as reckless as ever. The seaman's clothes he wore did not detract from his looks; he had always been handsome, but gave an air of rough vitality.

Mr. Blair poured out three glasses of wine and

handed one to Matt, who eyed it contemptuously.

"You've no rum, I suppose?"

"I'm afraid not," replied Mr. Blair with a smile. "It is not a drink I care for."

"One acquires a taste for something stronger in the Navy," said Matt. "We'll lay some in, in the future."

"Certainly, if you wish it." Mr. Blair's voice was non-committal. Only Chloris who knew him so well detected a slight stiffening in his bearing. Easy, Matt, she begged silently. This is still my father's house.

Matt stretched out comfortably and looked over at Chloris. "Has it seemed a long wait for me, sweetheart?"

"Yes, Matt. Even nine months seemed an eternity."

"I knew you'd be waiting, however long it took. My faithful Chloris, now my faithful wife. It might have been longer without your father's good offices but I knew he would do his best for his son-in-law—for your sake."

"And your own bravery earned you a remission."

"Oh, that," he shrugged. "A calculated risk but it paid off."

"How do you mean? It was a courageous act."

'I was in two minds about risking my own life but the captain was on deck so I decided to chance it."

"I don't quite understand you."

Mr. Blair spoke in a dry tone. "What Matthew means, Chloris, is that his rescue of the first officer was stage-managed for the captain's benefit. Had there been no-one of authority to bear witness, I imagine the man would have been left to drown."

"I don't believe it! You wouldn't have done that, would you, Matt?"

He grinned. "I never cared overmuch for the first officer."

Chloris stared at him, aghast. Was it true, as Quentin had said, that Matt cared for no-one but himself? She must not think this way. She was his wife, for better or for worse. The slight lack of manners she glimpsed was due entirely to the hard life endured over the past months. Now that he was home, he would become again the man she remembered.

"Well, that life is over for you now. We must look to the future. Have you any plans?"

Matt looked at Mr. Blair. "Not yet, but I am sure Mr. Justice will be happy to help us—until I decide on something suitable. Isn't that so, sir?"

Some kind of communication passed between the two men, some unspoken challenge that puzzled Chloris. The smile on Matt's face was answered by a smile of a different kind on the face of the older man.

"Let it be clearly understood, Matthew, that the past is over—quite over. It will do no good to speak of it again. The best thing for you to do now is make a new arrangement for your future."

"Which will include Chloris."

"I am well aware of that and have made my plans accordingly. Chloris will remain under my roof until such time as I deem fit. Several local employers have shown interest in you, having known your family well, so there should be no difficulty there in finding a position that will support you."

Matt stiffled a yawn. "Thank you, sir, but I am in no hurry to tie myself to a new arrangement." He grinned. "I appreciated the old one."

"I'm sure you did but the term of it was not indefinite."

Listening to this interchange, Chloris had the feeling that each man was conveying something to the other behind the spoken word. What arrangement, if not the obvious one, were they speaking of? Of course Matt must find an occupation but her father had no need to speak of it so soon. Matt was independent, he would not accept charity for long, but newly back from sea he must have time to adjust.

She sipped her wine and watched Matt renew his glass several times. There was something wrong—she felt it. After the first breathless greeting, Matt had hardly glanced in her direction. She sensed an antagonism between the two men.

A log cracked in the grate and the clock above chimed. It was ten o'clock. No-one seemed in a hurry to go to bed. Her thoughts wandered. Was this cold empty feeling only to be expected after the first excitement was over? For so long she had dreamed of Matt being home. What had gone wrong? Had they acted on impulse as Quentin had suggested? To the devil with Quentin, she thought savagely. Was she always to be recalling things he had said? The revelations of the night of Croker's capture had revealed Quentin as he really was. A liar and a cheat, a man prepared to elope with another man's wife. The sooner she put him completely out of her mind the better.

A hammering on the front door brought them all upright. Mr. Blair rose and crossed the room, passing into the hall. He closed the door behind him.

"Expecting anyone for the homecoming, Chloris?" Matt asked.

She shook her head. "Not by my invitation."

"Good. I want you all to myself tonight. We'll

406

go up as soon as your father returns."

It was the casual way he spoke, not exactly as an ardent and impatient lover, that caused Chloris to speak her mind suddenly. "Matt, I know we're married but tell me why we had to marry in prison so hurriedly. Why couldn't we have waited until now?"

"Didn't you want to marry me?"

"That's not the point. Why did you insist on it before you went away?"

"I told you then. I wanted you to be waiting here for me when I returned."

"And that's all you told me, Matt. You didn't even say you loved me."

"Could there have been any other reason?"

"I don't know but a girl is surely entitled to be told, just once on her wedding night."

Matt's eyes crinkled with amusement and he spread his hands. "You must admit we had little time that night to exchange more than marriage vows."

"Yes, I do, but now we have plenty."

"And now you want me to say it?"

Chloris felt herself color under his bantering tone but she kept her gaze on him steadily and said nothing.

"Let's talk of it later," he said. "Or perhaps," he grinned, "there'll be no need to talk."

"Very well," she returned calmly. "We'll talk of it another time. We have put you in the room next to mine. It used to be my mother's room."

For a moment he was silent. "Your mother's room? Not yours?"

"No, not mine. Father felt you needed time to adjust to life ashore, time to realize you are a free man again."

"The devil he did!" Matt's face darkened. "How dare he interfere in my affairs!"

"After almost a year apart, Matt, we meet rather like strangers. We both need time. I agreed with him."

"What's the old boy got in mind? I wonder. Does he think to rob me of my reward after nine months in a stinking man-of-war? A bargain's a bargain, even with a devious-minded—" he broke off suddenly as the sound of voices reached them. "I'll be damned if that doesn't sound like another one with a devious mind."

He moved catlike across the room and silently opened the door an inch.

"Matt!" said Chloris, shocked by his action.

"Quiet!" he hissed back.

The voices were clearer. Men's voices—and one sounded like—her heart jerked, then slowed as she clasped her hands tightly—like Quentin. There was the click of a door closing and Matt was back in his chair as Mr. Blair re-entered the room.

"Who was that, sir?" asked Matt, turning up an innocent face.

"Quentin Field." Mr. Blair was smiling and this time the smile reached his eyes. "With some rather strange news from Weymouth. It seems a body was washed out of a cave two days ago."

"Nothing unusual about that, sir. Probably drowned, poor fellow."

"Not drowned, Matt, but shot in the head. He has not been identified as someone reported missing."

Matt stood up and stretched, stifling a yawn. "Well, that is more serious, sir, but he was probably some kind of villain. Do they know who shot him?"

"It is to be hoped they soon will. According to Quentin, the authorities are questioning a man just returned from a long voyage on an East Indiaman. He was thought to have been in the vicinity at the time but shipped out to avoid arrest on some other charge. If he, himself, is not the villain, he will certainly make the most strenuous efforts to recall the happening in his own interests. A description and certainly a sketch of the murderer should be circulated by tomorrow."

"Well, I hope they catch him, sir."

"So do I, Matthew. I should be very happy to have him appear before me."

Chloris rose too. "Is that all Quentin Field came for? How inconsiderate! Couldn't this unpleasant story have waited until morning instead of interrupting our evening?"

"It could, my dear, but Quentin thought I should know of it tonight."

"Then I'll bid you both goodnight. I feel rather tired."

"Goodnight, my dear. Another drink, Matt?"

"No, thank you, sir. I feel like a breath of fresh air. Come with me, Chloris? Just a stroll in the garden before you go to bed."

"Chloris is tired, Matthew. Let her go."

"I'm merely asking my wife to take a stroll, sir. It's still quite warm." His face wore a stubborn expression as he met Mr. Blair's eyes.

"I would rather Chloris retires as she wishes," stated Mr. Blair firmly.

"She will be quite safe with me in the garden," Matt retorted with a little heat. "You surely don't expect your murderer to be hiding in the bushes, do you, sir?" He laughed derisively and took Chloris's arm. "He very likely took a sea voyage as well and will not be back. He would be pretty stupid to come back to the same place."

Mr. Blair spoke musingly. "Yes, strange how they often do. It's as if they're drawn back by some overpowering fascination to the scene of the crime. Or perhaps it's a monumental conceit in their nature that convinces them they won't be caught. But this time there will be no escape. By tomorrow, everyone will know his face."

Chloris felt the pressure of Matt's hand on her arm and decided to accept his invitation. She was too tired to face an argument. "I'd enjoy a stroll in the garden," she said. "We won't be long, Father, just a few minutes in the fresh air." She looked appealingly at him and he smiled.

"Very well, my dear, but don't overtire yourself."

The garden held the scent of honeysuckle, fragrant and sweet. Chloris breathed in deeply, letting the peaceful scene steal restfully into her mind. With Matt's arm about her shoulders, they strolled backwards and forwards, Matt glancing at the lighted window of the house each time they passed.

He laughed softly. "I don't believe your father will go to bed until you're back inside. Doesn't he trust me?"

Chloris looked up into the face so close to her own. "Of course he does. It will take him a little time to accept the fact that we're married now. It has been just the two of us since Mother died. Be patient, Matt."

"I've been patient for nine months," he said with a hint of anger in his voice. "But now I'm free and even your father has no right to question every move I make concerning you or my future prospects. He made it perfectly plain that I may expect no help from him."

"He's only doing what he thinks is best."

"I make my own decisions in my own way. I still have contacts. I don't need your father."

"Oh, no, Matt!" she said in distress. "Not Sefton. You wouldn't go back—"

"Do you see me clerking for a pittance? Being

given a job out of pity? Oh, no! I have better things in mind. Come on."

"Where, Matt?"

Without noticing it, she found they had walked as far as the stable. Still gripping her arm, Matt opened the door and pushed her inside. He led out her father's horse from the stall and in a few minutes had a bridle and saddle in place.

"Matt! What are you doing?"

"We're going for a ride. Get up."

"No. I want to go back to the house. We said we wouldn't be long."

"You said that, I didn't. Do as I tell you."

"But Matt—" She found herself flung up in front of the saddle, then Matt was behind, gripping her round the waist. He kicked in his heels and the horse sprang forward through the open doorway and down the drive, hooves thudding on the hard earth.

Chloris twisted her head and in the last moment before the night closed in saw light suddenly stream from the front door. The wind of their passage struck cold through the thin silk of her dress. She shivered. "Where—where are we going, Matt?" she gasped as the motion of the flying horse jarred her.

"To my own house where I should have taken you straightaway."

"But it has been closed for nearly a year."

"Then we'll open it."

A closed carriage loomed up before them. Matt swung the mare aside and the carriage swerved and shuddered to a halt. Chloris had a swift glimpse of two occupants, then they were past and turning off towards the Trevelyan house.

It had a forlorn and deserted air, with unclipped creepers half-masking the door and untended grass thick underfoot. Matt tied the reins of the horse to a fencepost, then lifted Chloris down. He took her cold hand and urged her to the front door, producing a key from his jacket pocket.

"I really can't see the necessity for this, Matt. The house is quite unprepared for visitors. Why can you not accept Father's hospitality? It was kindly meant."

"As long as I do as he suggests, he'll tolerate my presence for your sake. Well, I've had enough of being told what to do. This is my house and this is where we'll stay. If your father wants you back he'll have to come begging and then it will be on my terms."

Chloris stared incredulously into his bitter face as he bent to light a lamp. "I don't understand you at all, Matt. You speak as if I were an object to be bartered over. Why should my father come begging?"

He looked at her with something like contempt curling the corners of his mouth. "He will—make no mistake. The last thing he wanted was for us to marry but he had no alternative when I put it to him. I knew I could rely on you to agree."

"I don't know what you are talking about."

He pulled her into his arms and laughed. "Never mind. Tomorrow it won't matter." He began to kiss her and it was nothing like she had dreamed. There was a fierce, hurtful quality in his kisses, a strange lack of tenderness, and his hands moved over her body in a way that made her gasp. She tried to push him away but her struggles seemed to inflame him into rougher treatment and she found herself borne down onto a dust-sheeted couch by the fireplace. His body pinned her there as one hand grasped the neck of her silk dress. The frabric ripped and her shoulder was bare.

412

From the depths of her being a sudden revulsion rose and swept through her. Anger joined as she fought to avoid his searching fingers. "No, Matt, no!" she gasped furiously. "I can't!"

He raised his eyes to hers. "You're my wife. You cannot deny me." He caught her wrists, forcing them upwards. She winced in pain.

"Matt, you're hurting me."

"I'm just a rough seaman," he mocked. "Your father made me one so why should you complain? If you want finesse, you should have married someone like Quentin."

"I wish I had!" she retorted, stung into an unwise remark. "He would treat his wife with more consideration."

Matt's face darkened and the palm of his hand struck her across her cheek, knocking her head into the rough-sheeted horsehair. Tears of shock sprang to her eyes.

"How—how dare you? Do you take me for some tavern wench?"

"I'd get more joy from one of them," he said. He rose and pulled her roughly to her feet. "But I'm damned if I'll let your father win. He'll not be so high and mighty when you're no longer his sweet young daughter." He dragged her towards the staircase, smiling grimly at her struggles. "If madam would rather have a bed with sheets, then a bed she shall have, though the sheets may be damp, but let us, by all means, observe the ceremonial rites which well-brought-up young ladies set so much store on."

Neither of them had heard the sound of wheels approaching but the slam of a carriage door halted Matt in his tracks. He released Chloris and sprang towards a walnut bureau by the hearth, pulling out a drawer. A gun was in his hand. He checked it swiftly.

"Still loaded, thanks be," he muttered and swung the barrel in line with the door.

Chloris shrank back against the newel post, staring at the pistol with horror.

"Matt, you must be mad! Are you seriously considering using that on my father? For heaven's sake, why? What has he done to you?"

"I've spent nine, hard, backbreaking months thinking about your father," he said harshly. "He agreed to our marriage for your sake, then had me dragged away the minute the ceremony was over. Now that I'm back, I am still forbidden my wife and flatly refused the help I expected as his son-in-law." He flung her a savage look. "What use is a dowerless wife to me?"

"It's true then—you never loved me but used me for your own ends. I was a fool not to have realized."

They both started at the sudden clangor of the door knocker.

"Open the door for his honor, Mr. Justice Blair," ordered Matt, levelling the pistol.

Chloris crossed the room slowly. She must warn her father of the pistol, warn him to stay away, even if the price was for her to spend the night here with Matt. Her mind shied away from the thought, but what else could she do?

"And don't try to warn him, Chloris," Matt said, reading her thoughts. "Or I may just fire before you get the door open."

She threw him a look of hatred, then turned the heavy key, pulling open the door. The figure on the doorstep was not the one she expected. For a moment Chloris stared, then as he stepped forward the flickering lamplight revealed a tall, red-haired man with a determined chin and a set expression.

Matt looked at him blankly. "What the devil do you want, Kernick?"

The man's eyes moved coldly over Matt, then dropped to the pistol in his hand.

"We were in the carriage you passed so recklessly. We were on our way to see Mr. Blair and his daughter but changed our direction and followed you here."

"Why? And who is 'we'?"

Neil turned and drew forward the girl who had been standing in the shadows. His arm remained protectively round her shoulders. She was pale but her face held as determined a look as Neil's.

"Ruth!" exclaimed Matt. "What on earth are you doing here?"

"Put away the pistol, Matt," she said quietly. "There are a few matters to clear up and a few things Chloris should know."

Matt sat on the arm of the chair and laid the pistol on the table within reach. "A little late in the day for revelations, isn't it?"

Neil's lips tightened at the sneer on Matt's face and the tone of his voice.

"Not too late," Ruth replied. "This is the time for honesty, then Chloris need not suffer as I did. After our talk we will take her home."

"I don't think so," said Matt. "Her place is with me."

"That is for her to decide."

"Chloris is my wife."

"Only because it was the price of your silence in court." She turned to Chloris. "Matt threatened to reveal your part in the smuggling if your father would not agree to the marriage. Sefton and others were prepared to testify—at a price—that you were with them on the beach. The short sentence that puzzled everyone was another condition. Your father betrayed his principles for your sake, Chloris, and Matt knew the bargain would be kept if you were tied to him by marriage."

"How did you know we were married?" asked Chloris, bewildered.

Ruth smiled. "I heard Quentin come to the same conclusion on the Field House terrace that night last summer. I was walking in the garden and couldn't help but overhear. I moved away soon afterwards to High Ridge farm."

"But why were you going to my father's house tonight, so late?"

Ruth glanced at Neil Kernick. He smiled encouragingly and nodded.

"I heard Matt was there and thought to settle things immediately before any harm was done. I also wanted to tell your father that I shall never forget his kindness to me but now that Neil and I are to be married, he may discontinue the allowance he gave me for my son—my son and Matt's."

"Matt's son?" asked Chloris faintly.

"I was foolish, I know, but Matt was very persuasive. I've regretted it bitterly and I'm sorry if I've hurt you."

How strange, thought Chloris, I feel nothing—no anger or hurt—no jealousy, just a sick emptiness. She raised her eyes to Ruth. "How do you know what happened at the trial? How do you know these things you're telling me?"

"It was when Quentin came to my cottage one day and found me unwell. I had to confide in someone and Quentin was the best person. Neither of us could understand why Matt had married you when I expected his child, but Quentin thought he must have had some very strong personal reason." Her gaze flicked over

Matt contemptuously. "Matt never loved anyone but himself—he merely made use of people. Quentin took me to see Mr. Blair, who was so shocked to hear of Matt's treatment of me, that he told us how the marriage came about."

"I seem to have been the only one left in ignorance," said Chloris with a touch of bitterness.

"Would you have believed any of us if we had told you?"

"No, I suppose I wouldn't have at the time."

"That's what we thought. When I heard that Matt was being released earlier than expected, I came to tell you the truth about me. Now that you know everything, you can make your own choice."

"Chloris made her choice when she married me," interrupted Matt. "We're legally married and there's nothing you nor anyone else can do about it."

Chloris turned on him furiously. "Do you think I would have married you if I'd known all this? How you blackmailed my father and deserted Ruth and your own child? All this deceit for the sake of, perhaps, another year in the Royal Navy?"

"Call it insurance, rather," said a new voice behind Ruth. Quentin stepped soft-footed into the room. "You were Matt's insurance, Chloris. He pleaded guilty because he needed a quick conviction, with no prolonged investigation into his past. He was wanted on a far more serious charge than mere smuggling and he knew it. Had he been charged with it last year, not even marriage to you would have saved him but we had no proof then, so he was lucky to get away with a short sentence. This time, Matt, there will be no-one to blackmail, not at the Dorchester Assizes."

Matt became very still. His eyes glittered as they rested on Quentin. "Am I supposed to know what you are talking about?"

"You should. Mr. Blair told you of the near-skeleton found in Wymouth. He told you too, I believe, that a description and sketch of the murderer would be circulated tomorrow."

"He did mention something of the sort."

"Is that why you brought Chloris here? To hurt Mr. Blair as much as possible while you still had the chance?"

Matt shrugged. "Really, Quentin, you are talking wild rubbish. None of it makes any sense to me." He peered over Quentin's shoulder. "Ah, Sefton, come in. A friend at last. I never expected so many people to call, it's almost an embarrassment on a man's first night home, his wedding night, too."

Sefton sidled in, his bemused gaze passing over the five people assembled.

"Heard you were back, Mr. Matt, then I saw the light in your old home. Thought I'd give you a word of welcome. I'll not intrude any further."

"Don't go, Sefton," said Matt. "You might as well hear this wild story Quentin Field is concocting."

"I already did," said Sefton, apologetically. "I was in the doorway, wondering whether to come in or not." He looked at Quentin. "A bit hard to identify, surely, sir, after so long?"

"There was a witness to the murder, Sefton."

Matt came to his feet. "I've had enough of this. I suggest you all get out and leave us alone."

To Chloris's surprise, Quentin nodded. "Perhaps you're right." He looked at Neil. "Take Ruth back to the carriage, Neil, and go home."

Neil met Quentin's steady gaze and nodded as

if he read a message there. He ushered Ruth from the room.

"Get out, Field. You won't take Chloris." Matt said in a savage tone.

"Then I won't go," Quentin replied calmly.

In the silence of the room they heard the carriage move away.

"Sefton," said Matt. "Hold this pistol on Mr. Field. I know there's a rope somewhere in the kitchen. If he won't go of his own accord, then he can spend a night in the stables."

Sefton took the pistol and covered Quentin. "Sorry, sir. I don't believe in violence myself but if Mr. Matt's in trouble, I've got to help."

"I wonder," said Quentin, raising an eyebrow, "if you'd be interested in looking at something that was found on the body. You were in Wymouth last year on a matter of business, weren't you?"

"Aye, sir, but I know nothing of any murder."

"Let me show you the sketch I have in my pocket."

Matt had paused in the kitchen doorway. He frowned. "Mr. Blair said it was coming tomorrow."

Quentin's smile was unpleasant. "I know. I told him to say that, so that any action you took would be tonight. I waited in the garden, knowing that you must make a move." He opened his jacket slowly to show Sefton he was not armed and removed a slip of paper. He unfolded it and handed it to Sefton. "That is the artist's impression of the murderer from the witness's description. I think you know him."

Sefton stiffened, staring into Quentin's face suspiciously. "Why, that's—"

"Indeed," Quentin interrupted smoothly. "And here is something found on the body. Does it mean anything to you?"

Sefton reached out a hand slowly towards the medallion and a grayish pallor crept over his skin. "Aye, I know it."

"He was shot in the back of the head, Sefton. Cold-blooded murder."

Sefton went even paler. "You're sure, sir? No doubt about it?"

"None at all, according to the witness's statement under oath."

Matt was beside Sefton. "Let me see those."

Sefton handed them over silently, his eyes fixed on Matt's face. "Is it true, Mr. Matt? Did you kill Robbins?"

Matt shrugged. "He threatened to inform on us if he didn't get more money. I had to, don't you see? I did it to protect us all. He was a danger to us."

"You told me he got tired of the game so you paid him off and he left."

"I couldn't chance him talking. He would have betrayed us. I had to kill him, Sefton, surely you see that?"

"I wish you hadn't, Mr. Matt. Robbins was my brother—leastways my half-brother. I was fond of him." The pistol in his hand changed direction. Now it was pointed at Matt, who stared down in disbelief at the barrel.

"Don't be a fool, Sefton! What does it matter now? It was over twelve months ago. Forget it, Sefton. He wasn't worth it."

"He was to me, yet you shot him down like a dog. You knew he was my kin but you didn't give me the chance to talk some sense into him. Like Miss Ruth said, you use everybody for your own purpose, then throw them aside. But no more, Mr Matt, never again!"

Chloris saw Sefton's eyes suffuse with anger

The pistol rose, held steady. Matt flung out his arms in protest, turned in an effort to escape, then the heavy bullet took him in the chest. The impact hurled him backwards to crash over a small table. He fell into the empty hearth and the fire irons shook and rattled about him.

24

The noise stilled and there was no sound from anyone, just a horrifying cessation of all movement. Chloris, on the verge of collapse, could not tear her gaze from that lifeless form sprawled grotesquely in the hearth. Matt, so heroic in childhood, so daring and vibrant, was the illusion. Matt, the callous murderer, the liar and cheat, was the reality.

Through the mist that clouded her thoughts, she caught Quentin's words, low and urgent. "Get out, Sefton, quickly. There's a merchantman due out of Weymouth on the tide. I don't want to see you hang for this."

It was even quieter after Sefton's departure, then Chloris felt arms guiding her to a chair. She sat dumbly, hearing the sound of a cupboard being opened. A glass was thrust into her hand, strong fingers closing hers about it.

"Drink it quickly," Quentin ordered and she obeyed, gasping as the spirit took the breath from her. "I'll take you home now."

He swung her into his arms, his shoulders masking the view of the body on the floor, and strode from the cottage. Once more she was perched on a saddle with strong arms holding her steady. But this time she was too tired and drained of emotion to make any comment on the way home. She lay against Quentin in a state of mindless apathy. He was silent too, his eyes never leaving the road ahead.

Mr. Blair had the front door open as they came in sight of the house. His taut face relaxed as he saw Chloris but his gaze went questioningly to Quentin and neither man spoke. Mr. Blair nodded to Molly waiting in the hall and she gathered Chloris to her and led her upstairs without a word.

"She's all right, sir," said Quentin. "Just badly shocked."

Both men watched as Chloris stumbled up the stairs, guided by Molly, then Mr. Blair touched Quentin's arm. "Come into my study, Quentin. You look as if you need a drink," he said gently.

"Matt's dead, sir. Sefton shot him." Quentin drew in a deep ragged breath. "It seems that Robbins was his half-brother."

"Oh, my God! Where is Sefton now?"

"I let him go."

Mr. Blair nodded. "Perhaps it's as well for Chloris's sake. It would have been a hanging matter otherwise for Matthew. She will be spared the horror of all that now."

For two days Chloris kept to her bedroom, her sleep constantly broken by recurring nightmares of horror. She would wake gasping, seeing again and again Matt's body hurtle across the room, the crash of fire irons ringing in her head. During the day she sat silently by the window, staring without interest across the fields leading to the coast. She could not grieve for Matt or her lost marriage, there was no emotion left but shame that she had been duped so easily. In spite of all the warnings she had gone ahead like a foolish, headstrong child, opposition making her all the more determined to have her own way.

On the third morning, the air was warm under a blazing sun. The scent of flowers drifted in at her window, tempting her to walk in the garden. The house was silent, Mr. Blair having gone to Dorchester. She knew it concerned Matt but she had not wanted to know of it. It was all in the past and best forgotten.

As she strolled across the lawn, she envisaged the future stretching bleakly and endlessly in front of her. What was there left but a quiet existence in her father's house? Well, it was better than she deserved.

She turned to walk back and stopped abruptly as she saw the tall figure approaching her across the lawn. The sunlight glinted on the fair hair and the gray eyes in the unsmiling face were fixed on her. Her heart leapt but she remained rigidly unmoving. He halted in front of her. She expected a polite inquiry after her health and was framing a cool reply but when he spoke his voice was cold and without interest.

"Do you feel well enough to come to Field House?"

Her eyes widened and the old animosity flared. "What should I want at Field House? Leave me alone. I have no wish to see you again, ever."

"I am not inviting you to a social function," he returned harshly. "I understand your feelings towards me but I cannot avoid this meeting, however much we both wish it."

"But why do you want me to go to Field House?"

"There is someone there who wishes to talk to you, about your mother."

Chloris caught her breath. "My mother?"

"I can tell you nothing more. It would be to your advantage to accept."

"Very well."

"I have the carriage here."

They crossed the lawn and he handed her into the carriage. Chloris was full of questions but one look at Quentin's forbidding expression and she quelled them. Neither spoke on the short journey. When they entered the sitting room at Field House it was empty.

"Probably in the garden," said Quentin. "Take a seat and I will send him in."

"Will you—will you come back?" she asked nervously.

"No. There is no need for me to be present. You will recognize him." He went through the french windows and disappeared, leaving her alone with her apprehensions.

A few moments later a tall man, blue-eyed and fair-haired, stepped through from the terrace. He looked as nervous as she felt, Chloris thought in surprise.

"Miss Blair, forgive me for not calling on you. I am too ashamed and guilt-ridden to risk meeting your father."

She rose. "Lord Chalmers, isn't it? I understand you have something to tell me."

He nodded and the color rose under his fair skin. "May we sit down?"

"Of course."

He sat on a straight-backed chair, his elbows resting on his knees, his gaze on the carpet. He took a deep breath. "You are under the impression, I believe, Miss Blair, that Quentin was your mother's lover and in some way connected with her death?"

When she made no reply he glanced up, then resumed his study of the carpet.

"On the contrary, Miss Blair, he was not. I was that person."

He looked so miserable that Chloris was almost sorry for him. "Would you care to tell me about it?"

"It would be a relief," he said simply. "It all began when I visited Quentin that Spring. Your mother was quite often at Field House. She was so beautiful and charming that both Quentin and I formed a deep attachment to her but I went beyond the bounds of that. I fell in love with Estelle and tried to persuade her to elope with me. She laughed at first, then on my last afternoon here, before I went abroad, she agreed, saying she would send me a note of the time to meet her. I received the note, telling me to wait on the cliffs near Field House at ten o'clock. We had dinner here with Sir Lionel and she left. She'd packed a small bag, it was on her saddle. That was in case she decided not to return home first. I waited for over an hour at that spot but she never came so I collected my bags and rode on to Weymouth where I was to embark. What I didn't know was that Quentin had taken in the note and altered the time from midnight to ten o'clock."

"Why should he do that?"

"To protect your mother from acting on impulse and regretting it later. He knew her nature far better than I. He met her himself at midnight and told her of his action. She admitted that it had been an impulsive whim and she had no intention of eloping but even so she was angry with Quentin for interfering and rode away furiously. He followed her but she was too quick for him. He called her name several times, then gave up and went home. My ship had sailed by that time so he decided she would just go home too."

"I see. Thank you for telling me. You were not

truly lovers in the real sense, then?"

He shook his head. "No. Estelle was too fine a person to be unfaithful. I made the mistake of taking a flirtation seriously. She would have told me that herself if we had met, I know. Later, Quentin wrote to me in Italy and gave me news of the tragic accident. I was truly sorry. He told no-one of the events that night, in order to protect both your mother and me. So you see, Miss Blair, I am the one to blame. Quentin would not tell you the truth without my agreement. I thought it only right that I should tell you the whole, myself."

"Thank you for your honesty, Lord Chalmers. I really cannot blame you for falling in love with my mother. She was very beautiful."

"I shall never forget her, or you for being so understanding." He rose. "Goodbye, Miss Blair. I leave immediately for London."

"Goodbye, Lord Chalmers."

Chloris remained in the empty room for a long time. So now she knew the truth, the truth Quentin had tried to keep from her, even to the extent of remaining silent in the face of her accusations. It only remained for her father to be gently informed that his beloved Estelle had not been on the point of leaving him.

She wondered if Quentin would come back to the house now that Lord Chalmers had gone but as the time lengthened, she realized that the next move was up to her. She could take the carriage home—without seeing him—but did she really want to do that? Would an apology be sufficient to erase all the hateful things she had said to him. She took a deep breath and tried to control her emotions. There was no alternative but to see him out. Remembering the coldness of his expression on their journey here, her heart quailed. But it had to be faced.

Crossing the room, she stepped out onto the terrace and glanced about her. No-one was in sight. The lawn stretched away to a small copse through which a stream ran. Perhaps he was down there, waiting for the sound of the carriage taking her home before he returned to the house.

She had reached the shelter of the trees before she saw movement. Approaching quietly, she came upon him standing by the water's edge, skimming pebbles across the stream's surface. The sight of that tall figure, the brooding face under breeze-ruffled hair, stabbed at her heart and sent her pulses racing. If only she had not been such a fool over Matt! If only—but it was too late. In a few short weeks he would be married to Georgina. The thought bit sharply like a sudden knife wound. She had to get away—Dorchester—even London. Seeing them together in their happiness was something she could not endure.

Quentin swung round suddenly as if sensing a presence. She had no time to school her expression, her heart was in her eyes. Without being aware of it, her feet moved, flying over the grass. His arms opened and she flung herself into them, clinging fiercely to him and blinking back the tears.

"I'm sorry, Quentin. Can you ever forgive me for all the dreadful things I've accused you of? I ought to be horsewhipped."

"At the tail of a cart? I could arrange that if you'd really like it."

She glanced up and smiled shakily. "It would be less that I deserve. I'm sorry for hurling myself at you like this. I—I only come to apologize."

"I like the way you do it, Chloris. Much more fun than a dignified apology. Perhaps I can think of some more things that you need to apologize for."

"I know you are trying to make it easier for me and I am grateful," she said, drawing back and smoothing down her skirts with nervous fingers.

"Is it only gratitude you feel for me, Chloris?"

She looked up into his suddenly serious face and the blood rushed to her heart then receded, leaving her pale. "I have no right," she whispered, "to feel anything else." Her green eyes were wide and dark as she stared at him, unable to hide the desperate longing that swept over her.

His arms drew her back gently and he kissed the top of her head. "I've always loved you, Chloris, ever since you were a child, but it was always Matt with you. Can you put him out of your mind and marry me?"

"Easily," she said in wonder, then looked up, horrified. "What are we doing, Quentin? You are engaged to Georgina!"

"Not any more."

"What do you mean? Where is she?"

"Still in London shopping for her trousseau, but not for my benefit. She is going to marry the man she loves."

"Robert Courtney?"

"The same. You know I drove her to London a week ago?"

"Yes. She came to say goodbye."

"I stayed overnight in town and in the morning took Georgina walking in St. James Park. We came upon her Robert unexpectedly and the poor child burst into tears. We all retreated hastily into the shrubbery and talked things over. Georgina had suspected for a long time, she said, that I was not truly in love with her but with you and, rich or poor, she could not forget her poet. The upshot was that, armored with our convictions, we presented a bold front to Mrs. Davenport, outflanking her on all sides. Since

Courtney is now a reasonably wealthy man, dear Mama did not prove too difficult," he finished dryly.

"Dear Georgina. I'm so happy for her. She deserves her happiness now."

"After being engaged to me, do you mean?"

"Well," Chloris said, teasingly, her heart as light as thistledown. "You are not everyone's choice. She was a little afraid of you."

"Good God! Was she really? I can't imagine why. Did she think I would turn into a wife-beater?"

Chloris linked her hands behind his head and regarded him, questioningly, her head tilted to one side. "I don't know. Will you?"

He laughed and kissed her soundly. "I'm sure there'll be times when I'm sorely tempted but if I can depend on you to throw yourself into my arms like you did just now, then we shall no doubt make our peace without coming to blows."

His arms tightened about her, his gray eyes no longer hard but warm and glowing. Whatever she intended to say in reply was lost as his lips came down on hers, lost forever, as her heart to this man.

Make the Most of Your Leisure Time
with
LEISURE BOOKS

Please send me the following titles:

Quantity	Book Number	Price
_____	_____	_____
_____	_____	_____
_____	_____	_____
_____	_____	_____
_____	_____	_____

If out of stock on any of the above titles, please send me the alternate title(s) listed below:

_____	_____	_____
_____	_____	_____
_____	_____	_____
_____	_____	_____

Postage & Handling _____

Total Enclosed $_____

☐ Please send me a free catalog.

NAME _____
(please print)

ADDRESS _____

CITY _____ STATE _____ ZIP_____

Please include $1.00 shipping and handling for the first book ordered and 25¢ for each book thereafter in the same order. All orders are shipped within approximately 4 weeks via postal service book rate. PAYMENT MUST ACCOMPANY ALL ORDERS.*

*Canadian orders must be paid in US dollars payable through a New York banking facility.

Mail coupon to: **Dorchester Publishing Co., Inc.**
6 East 39 Street, Suite 900
New York, NY 10016
Att: ORDER DEPT.